DARK SPACE V: Avilon
(1st Edition)
by Jasper T. Scott

http://www.JasperTscott.com
@JasperTscott

Copyright © 2014 by Jasper T. Scott
THE AUTHOR RETAINS ALL RIGHTS
FOR THIS BOOK

Reproduction or transmission of this book, in whole or in part, by electronic, mechanical, photocopying, recording, or by any other means is strictly prohibited, except with prior written permission from the author. You may direct your inquiries to JasperTscott@gmail.com

Cover design by Thien A.K.A "ShooKooBoo"

This book is a work of fiction. All names, places, and incidents described are products of the writer's imagination and any resemblance to real people or life events is purely coincidental.

Table of Contents

Acknowledgements 4
Prologue 6
Part One: The Choosing 13
Chapter 1 14
Chapter 2 26
Chapter 3 41
Chapter 4 54
Chapter 5 68
Chapter 6 83
Chapter 7 97
Chapter 8 110
Chapter 9 127
Chapter 10 140
Chapter 11 157
Chapter 12 169
Chapter 13 191
Chapter 14 204
Chapter 15 213
Chapter 16 223
Chapter 17 247
Chapter 18 262
Chapter 19 286
Chapter 20 302
Chapter 21 316
Chapter 22 342

Chapter 23 352
Chapter 24 361
Chapter 25 384
Part Two: To The Bitter End 399
Chapter 26 400
Chapter 27 414
Chapter 28 432
Chapter 29 441
Chapter 30 450
Chapter 31 462
Chapter 32 479
Chapter 33 492
Chapter 34 510
Part Three: New Beginnings 518
Chapter 35 519
Chapter 36 531
Chapter 37 545
Chapter 38 566
Chapter 39 578
Epilogue 603
PREVIOUS BOOKS IN THE SERIES 615
KEEP IN TOUCH 619
ABOUT THE AUTHOR 620

ACKNOWLEDGEMENTS

This story comes to you thanks in part to my wife and stepson for being so patient with me. I lost track of how many times I worked late or skipped my weekend to finish this book on time.

A big thanks to my editor, Aaron Sikes. His advice and keen insight into the story were invaluable. Likewise, I'd like to thank Thien "Shookooboo" for creating such a stunning cover, as well as the illustrations in this book. It would be hard to find a more talented artist.

My thanks also go out to all my beta readers, in particular, I'd like to thank Betty Hoffner, Branden Rasmussen, Daniel Eloff, Dave Cantrell, Doug S., Filip Schlatter, Gary Wilson, Ian Jedlica, Ian Seccombe, Jim Meinen, John H. Kuhl, Peter Hughes, Rob Dobozy, Ted Inver, and Tony Wilsenham. You all read that first draft like lightning to get your feedback to me in time for the 1st edition.

Last, I'd like to thank you, the Reader. Without your appreciation, none of my books would exist. I look forward to responding to your e-mails and reading your reviews. Your feedback is what shapes my work, and tells me what to write next.

Thank you, all of you!

To those who dare,
And to those who dream.
To everyone who's stronger than they seem.
"Believe in me /
I know you've waited for so long /
Believe in me /
Sometimes the weak become the strong"
—STAIND, *Believe*

PROLOGUE

—The Year 0 AE—

"Helm! Full throttle! Get us into orbit as fast as you can."
"Yes, Captain!"
"And start spooling for a jump!"
"Already 22% spooled, sir."

Captain Bretton Hale nodded but gave no reply. He stood at the forward viewports of the *Arkadian*, his palms pressed against the cold transpiranium. Golden fires raged in his dark brown eyes, poor reflections of the devastation in Roka City far below. Roka IV had been the last stop along the way to Dark Space. Orders were to pick up the remaining key personnel and as many refugees as possible before continuing on to the fleet rendezvous, but the Sythians had beat them there. It would have been easy for the fleet to jump out immediately, but the Supreme Overlord was among the *key personnel* they'd stopped to rescue, so the First and Fifth Fleets had been dragged into one last, deadly engagement to cover the overlord's escape.

Bretton's ship was a 280-meter-long venture-class cruiser, the backbone of the navy and a warhorse if ever there was one, but it was hardly a match for the Sythians' often kilometers-long battleships. Bretton's mission had been the same as all the other mid-sized cruiser captains: get dirt side and rescue as many people as possible before the order came to withdraw.

It had been a nightmare on the surface. Crowds pressing in from all sides, screaming their pleas for a rescue. Bretton had seen more than a few parents actually *throw* their children at his sentinels.

He grimaced, the muscles in his jaw clenching with the memory. He winced, shaking those thoughts aside, and turned to his crew. His XO and niece, Farah Hale, stood at the captain's table in the center of the bridge. That was where he should have been, too, not watching the last vestiges of the Imperium go up in smoke.

Bretton strode quickly down the gangway to her side. "What's it look like out there, Commander?"

Farah's back was rigid, her eyes hard and bloodshot when she turned to him. Her hair was wound as tight as she was, tied up in a bun at the back of her head. "An enemy battleship is moving to intercept us, and we've got four squadrons of Shells headed our way."

Bretton grimaced. "ETA?"

"Ten minutes."

"Comms! Have our Novas switch from flank escort to bow intercept. They'd better harry those Shells before they start hammering us with missiles."

"Yes, sir."

Farah looked up at him, her blue eyes round and full of fear. "We should have left when the First Fleet pulled out."

Bretton acknowledged his niece's concern with a nod. "That wasn't our call, Commander. Hindsight makes skriffs of us all." When Admiral Heston had received orders to jump out with the First Fleet, he had deliberately disobeyed those orders to finish rescue operations on the ground. Now the admiral himself was MIA and his fleet in orbit was being torn apart. Bretton shook his head. "Comms, any word from the Admiral?"

"No direct words, no."

"What's the *Tauron* have to say about that?"

"They're reluctant to elaborate further."

"Very well. Our orders are the same. Get to the rendezvous before the First Fleet gives us up for dead and leaves us behind."

Beside him Farah sighed. "They should have given all the captains access to the coordinates of Dark Space."

"Too risky. If just one of us were captured and interrogated, it would make this all for nothing."

"The skull faces don't seem intent on capturing us, sir."

"No, I suppose not." Bretton frowned, idly drumming his fingers on the captain's table as he studied the holographic grid. The area above them was teeming with red enemy contacts. The area below them was the same. In the middle lay a tiny knot of green—the *Arkadian* and its fighter escort.

He eyed the largest contact in the swarm of enemies moving to intercept them. *It's just one battleship. We've skated through worse.*

"Contact! De-cloaking at 15-4-22 by—"

The deck shuddered underfoot, interrupting the gravidar officer's report before he could finish rattling off coordinates.

"Return fire!" Bretton roared, his gaze fixed on three red blips that had suddenly appeared between them and the battleship in orbit. They'd appeared out of nowhere.

"Three cruisers and a battleship," he whispered amidst

the *hum* and *screech* of the *Arkadian's* beam cannons firing back at the new arrivals.

Bretton set a new waypoint from the captain's table. "Helm, adjust heading to nav point alpha five and try to keep them from outflanking us. We can't afford to take a broadside from those cruisers."

"Yes, sir."

The deck shuddered underfoot once more. This time the shuddering didn't stop. Lights flickered on the bridge, and a scream of duranium shearing set all of their teeth on edge. Bretton felt himself being pulled toward the aft of the ship as artificial gravity and the inertial management system (IMS) faltered. It was a momentary blip, but enough to get Bretton's pulse pounding.

"Forward shields critical!" engineering exclaimed.

"Equalize! What hit us? Damage report!"

"I don't know, but it wasn't the cruisers," Gravidar said. "My guess would be that battleship is dropping cloaking mines on us like bombs from orbit!"

"Clever little kakards," Bretton muttered. "All right—weapons! Have our gunners lay down covering fire in a 25-degree arc around our bow!"

Suddenly a bright light suffused the bridge. Bretton looked up to see a wall of fire burst through the viewports with a deafening roar. The sudden wave of heat and pressurized air picked him off his feet and seared his exposed skin. Arms and legs flailing, he hit the bulkheads behind him with a *thud*. Everything went dark.

Time. Stopped.

Bretton supposed he was dead, but if he were, would he still be capable of concluding that? Somewhere he remembered reading that cognitive thought could go on for minutes after the heart stopped beating. Perhaps that was what he was experiencing now—his last few minutes of darkness before death. He wondered about the darkness. His eyes were in his head. Even if his heart had stopped, shouldn't he still be able to see? Was he actually blind, or smothered by a mountain of debris? He tried blinking, but he couldn't be sure if it worked. His mind wandered to the nature of death. Would he simply cease to exist as most predicted, or be resurrected in paradise as the Etherians believed?

An indeterminate amount of time passed. Eventually his existential wondering was subsumed by more immediate concerns: the sharp, tingling sensation in his extremities; his heart pounding; the loud, ringing of silence in his ears . . .

What was happening? Hadn't he died?

Then a bright circle of light appeared, as if shining from the end of a long, dark tunnel; he felt himself move, being drawn toward the light, faster and faster . . .

The light grew to blinding force, and then it consumed him, surrounding him on all sides. Wind battered his face. His eyes teared as they struggled to adapt to the sudden brightness.

As he began to make out details, he gasped and flailed his arms and legs again. A carpet of golden-white clouds raced by underneath him, and he screamed—his lungs emptying with a pitiless wail. His mind raced to catch up. He must have lost consciousness briefly, only to be thrown free of the bridge. Now he was plummeting to the surface of Roka far below.

Except he wasn't plummeting. Absent was the gut-wrenching sensation of free fall, and the clouds were not getting any closer. More remarkable still was the blinding red sun peeking over the tops of the clouds. The Arkadian had lifted off from Roka City in the middle of the night, but this looked like sunrise.

"What the frek . . . ?" Bretton wondered.

Suddenly the sky boomed with thunder—a voice—it said, "Hello Bretton. I've been waiting for you."

"What? Who are you? Where am I?" Bretton craned his head to look around him, searching for the source of the voice. That was when he noticed that he wasn't alone. Flying to either side of him were others like him. They looked vaguely familiar.

"I am exactly who you suspect I am, and you are on Avilon."

"Avi . . . ?"

"Etheria lies below you."

"Etheria? It's real?"

"You'll be able to see for yourself soon. Look . . ."

The clouds opened up below him, and Bretton saw a vast and sparkling city below. Orderly green expanses of parkland stretched between immense, glittering towers that seemed to be made of light. He gasped. It was the most beautiful city he had ever seen.

"Who are those people beside me?"

"They are your crew, Bretton."

Joy swelled in his chest and tears sprang to his eyes once more. "I don't believe it. They were right! Those codice-toting skriffs were right all along!"

"The Etherians? Yes, they had a part of the truth. Soon you will know its entirety."

"I . . ." Bretton trailed off, unable to express what he was feeling.

"Would you like to meet your wife now? She's been waiting for you."

The tears in Bretton's eyes began spilling to his cheeks and his joy overwhelmed him. He'd never been so happy in all his life. His wife had died less than a month ago when the Sythians had invaded Advistine. Now, not only was the after life more real and tangible than anyone had ever imagined, but he was going to be reunited with her and all of the other people he had lost along the way. He was almost afraid to believe it. Maybe he was still trapped in the rubble on his bridge, unconscious and dreaming.

"No, Bretton, you aren't dreaming," the thunder intoned. "Welcome home."

Home. The word rattled around inside his head for a moment before finding purchase. It felt right. "Thank you..." he managed. "What should I call you?"

"You know me as Etherus," the thunder replied, "but I am better known by my children as Omnius."

"Omnius..." Bretton said, repeating the unfamiliar name. "Thank you, Omnius. This is incredible. More than I ever imagined!"

"If you are amazed by this, what will you say when I reveal the mysteries of the universe? Prepare to be amazed, Captain Hale."

PART ONE: THE CHOOSING

CHAPTER 1

—The Year 10 AE, Present Day—

Ethan Ortane watched his long-dead mother embracing his son, Atton, in the sky. He had to remind himself that they weren't actually standing on the clouds. It was an illusion. It had to be.

His mother wore a shimmering white robe, just like everyone else, and she looked far younger and more beautiful than he remembered her—but again, so did everyone else who had been resurrected. Apparently that was a part of the deal. Come back to life on Avilon and you get a brand new body, a perfected version of the one you had before.

Ethan heard his son whisper, "This is impossible."

"No, Atton," his grandmother replied. "It's a miracle."

That miracle was Avilon. Over two months ago Atton had gone looking for the lost star system, hoping to get reinforcements against the Sythians. He'd never returned. Then Ethan's ex-wife, Destra, had asked him to go looking for their son. He hadn't returned either, but he'd found Atton—along with *everyone* else.

A thunderous voice split the sky. It was Omnius, the artificial intelligence who had declared himself god and resurrected everyone who'd died in the Sythian invasion. Ethan suspected some technological rather than supernatural power was at work, but he hadn't pieced it all together yet.

"You are wondering if this is real," the voice began. "Those of you who aren't wondering are afraid to ask, but I tell you that your eyes do not deceive you. These are the same loved ones you lost. Many of them have been waiting a long time for you. Soon you will all return to the surface to begin your new lives on Avilon.

"Some of you have asked me why I didn't stop the Sythians when they invaded. Part of the answer, which I haven't given until now, is that I didn't need to stop them. I only needed to bring everyone back to life in my city, where they would be safe. I have spent the past fifty years building the city of Etheria to make room for everyone, and now that the work is done, none of you need ever die again!"

A loud cheer rose from the crowd: "Omnius grando est! Omnius grando est!"

Ethan noticed that even his mother was repeating that mantra. His eyes drifted out of focus. *Omnius, the AI who would be God. A god created by humans to rule them.* Ethan shook his head, trying to dispel the unease that thought caused. He supposed that in some way Omnius was *their* creator. Somehow he had copied their memories and then cloned genetically-superior versions of them to give those memories to. Ethan wondered if there was a clone waiting for him somewhere on Avilon.

Now *that* was an unsettling thought.

"Ethan? Are you all right?" his mother asked, waving a hand in front of his face.

He came back to the present and turned to his mother with a smile. "I'm just happy to see you, Mom. Besides your grandson, there's someone else I'd like you to meet..."

He trailed off when he couldn't find Alara. He frowned, wondering where his wife had gone. She had to be just as shocked by this development as him. They'd survived a harrowing battle, defending a lost world of immortal human clones from the race of ruthless aliens that had killed everyone in the former Imperium of Star Systems, only to find out that everyone who had died in that war had been resurrected here, in the world-spanning city of Avilon.

Cities, Ethan corrected himself. There were three, each separated by an energy shield—Celesta on top, Etheria below, and the Netherworld, or *Null Zone*, at the bottom.

Omnius had named his cities well if he wanted people to think he really was god. Etherians had long spoken of the afterlife in terms of the Netherworld and Etheria, and both names were steeped in meaning for anyone who had come from the Imperium.

People in shimmering white robes crowded all around, embracing their friends, crewmates, and loved ones who had arrived aboard the *Intrepid*.

Ethan admired his surroundings once more while looking for his wife. Clouds raced by underfoot; a stiff breeze blew; the rising sun shone big and red on the horizon. Despite the appearance that they were all somehow floating above the clouds, the ground under Ethan's feet still felt solid— invisible, but solid.

It was all an illusion. The wind wasn't strong enough to correspond to the speed with which they were moving, and the air was far too warm for the altitude. They were traveling in some type of starship. The deck and bulkheads were cloaked with holographic projections of what lay outside. Simple enough to do, but still awe-inspiring to look at. The white gauze of clouds parted briefly underfoot, and Ethan stole a glimpse of the shining city far below. His stomach did a loop-the-loop, and he looked up quickly.

"Who is it you'd like me to meet, dear?" his mother asked.

"Alara!" he called, unintentionally answering his mother's question. His green eyes searched the crowds for her face. He cupped his hands to his mouth and tried again. "Alara!"

"I'm over here!"

He whirled around to see her walking up behind his mother. A young man and woman followed her.

Ethan's brow furrowed. "Who are they?" he asked as Alara drew near.

She shook her head. Her face was ashen, her violet eyes shimmering with tears. Yet the grave expression on her face was broken by a faint smile.

"Hello there, grub," the young man behind Alara said.

Ethan turned to glare at him. *Grub.* The insult burned in his brain, making him see red. He didn't even know this man. Was it stamped on his forehead?

Poverty—the birthmark he could never seem to erase.

Alara forestalled the reciprocal insults poised to leap from the tip of his tongue by placing a hand on his arm. He turned to her and saw that her lower lip was trembling.

"What's wrong?" he asked.

"They're my parents, Ethan."

"Your . . ." Turning back to the pair of strangers standing before him, he shook his head. "That's impossible! We saw them just a few weeks ago at our wedding! They can't have died since—"

"You didn't tell me you got married!" Ethan's mother

interjected.

He turned to her with a strained smile. There was a look of mock outrage on her face. "You weren't there to tell," he explained. He skipped the part about Alara being his *second* wife.

"It's been two months since then, Ethan," Alara whispered, still talking about her parents. "The Sythians have been in Dark Space almost that entire time."

"Sythians? Dreadful creatures . . ." Ethan's mother said.

Ethan nodded along with that. He and Alara had spent an uneasy month on their honeymoon watching on the news nets as the Sythians invaded all over again. This time, instead of killing everyone, they had begun making slaves of them to replace their previous army of slave soldiers—the Gors. Alara's parents must have died resisting the occupation.

The young couple standing with his wife looked vaguely familiar now that Ethan knew what to look for. The young man was just as tall and skinny as old Kurlin Vastra had been, and he wore the same sneering smile that Ethan had come to expect from his father-in-law. The young woman was an even closer fit for Alara's mother with her rare violet eyes and flowing dark hair, both the same color as Alara's own. He absorbed the doubly-shocking news that his in-laws had died only to be resurrected on Avilon. A numb feeling of unreality set in. *Maybe I'm asleep?* He hadn't decided yet if this was a dream or a nightmare.

"I'm . . . sorry to hear that you died?" Ethan tried. He wasn't sure what sort of response was called for. His wife was obviously distraught, but his in-laws, the very ones whom she was upset about, were alive and smiling from ear to ear.

"Don't be," Kurlin replied. "We weren't bound to live much longer anyway. Now, thanks to Omnius, none of us will ever have to worry about dying again."

"Yea, so it would seem," Ethan replied, nodding slowly.

"This must be the special lady," Ethan's mother said, ignoring them and turning to Alara. "Come here girl," she said, reaching out to enfold her daughter-in-law in a hug.

Alara fell into her mother-in-law's embrace. Her violet eyes still brimmed with tears, and now a few of them spilled to her cheeks. A genuine smile grew between the trickling tears. "It's a pleasure to meet you, Mrs Ortane," Alara said as she withdrew from the hug.

"It's just Miss, actually. Ethan's father and I divorced before he was born. My name's Lara, but you can just call me Mom—if that would be all right with you, Darla?" she asked, craning her neck to catch Mrs. Vastra's eye.

"Of course."

Ethan looked on with a frown, feeling like he was missing something important—perhaps a few somethings that were important.

"You two have already been introduced?" Alara asked, connecting a few of the missing pieces for Ethan.

"Not formally, no," Lara explained, "but everyone on Avilon knows each other—at least by name."

"That's a lot of names to remember . . ." Atton put in.

"It does seem that way, doesn't it? But don't worry, you won't have to remember them, not really. You'll find out what I mean soon enough."

"I can't wait," Alara said. "I'm sorry to hear that your marriage didn't work . . . Mom." The endearment sounded awkward to Ethan's ears, but he supposed that was to be expected given that Alara's real mother was standing just behind her. "Where is Ethan's father? I'd like to meet him, too."

— 19 —

Lara's smile faltered, and she looked away. "Oh, I'm afraid he couldn't make it."

That set off an alarm bell in Ethan's head. "What do you mean he couldn't *make* it?" Ethan and his father had never been very close, but he'd seen the old man on more than one occasion whilst growing up, and as an adult they'd even smuggled a few shipments of stims together before Ethan had been caught and sentenced to Dark Space for his crimes. Preston Ortane wasn't an easy man to get along with, but Ethan was sure that his father wouldn't miss something like this.

"It's not that he didn't want to come, dear. But . . ."

"But what?"

"Well, it's not really my place to say."

"Not your place to say! What the frek?"

"Ethan, dear, calm down. That language has no place here."

"So now I'm being censored?"

"No, just calm down please. I understand this must all come as quite a surprise, but I'd like to think that it's a good surprise. I haven't seen you in so long. . . ."

"Well, where is he?"

"Who?"

Ethan's eyes narrowed sharply. "Dad."

"Why don't we rather talk about your wonderful bride? It will be night soon, and we'll all have to go to . . . sleep."

"Night? The sun is still rising! And even if it weren't, why can't we just stay up and talk? I'm not tired. I'll make you some caf. Unless you don't have caf in Avilon . . ."

"*On Avilon*, dear. It's a planet, not a star system. Yes, of course we have all kinds of stimulating beverages, but I'm afraid the night here falls with or without the sun and we are not permitted to stay up."

"With or without the sun? That doesn't make any sense!"

"Omnius will explain everything to you soon," his mother soothed, rubbing his arm.

"Well someone better!" Ethan turned to Atton. "You believe this krak?"

"Dad."

"What?"

Atton nodded his head sideways, indicating his grandmother. "Language."

Ethan noticed that his mother looked distraught—or fearful. He couldn't decide which. But despite the fact that she'd mysteriously come back from the grave, Ethan didn't care. He wasn't even sure that young woman really was his mother.

He was about to swear again just to emphasize his freedom to do so when Alara took his hand, squeezing it just tightly enough to convey a warning. Somehow the cool touch of her hand was enough to cool his head. She was right. Now wasn't the time to start poking holes in the clouds they were standing on. For better or worse, they'd found Avilon, and they wouldn't be leaving any time soon. For now at least, they were at the mercy of its people and its ruler, and they needed to tread lightly until they learned what that meant.

The thunderous voice rumbled around them once more. "Now that you've all had a chance to be reunited, the time has come for you to say goodbye. Those of you who have not yet decided to join the Ascendancy will be taken to temporary quarters where you will tour the three cities of Avilon to help you decide where you want to live. Welcome, my children! Welcome home!"

At that, the crowds began cheering once more, "Omnius

grando est! Omnius grando est!"

Ethan remained silent and traded a glance with his wife. As soon as the cheering stopped, he saw a pair of shining portals open in the sky, one to either side of the rising sun. He placed a hand to his forehead to shield his eyes from the glare. He tried to see what lay beyond those portals, but the light was too bright.

The thunder spoke once more: "Walk toward the light."

Everyone began shuffling toward the open portals. Ethan followed warily. Alara held tightly to his arm. His mother and Atton walked up on the other side of him. Speaking to his mother, Ethan said, "What's this about three cities?" Omnius had already explained the structure of Avilon, but Ethan wanted to hear about it from his mother.

"Oh, don't worry about that. That's what *The Choosing* is for. I'm sure you won't make the wrong choice."

"Yea? What's the wrong choice?"

Ethan's mother just smiled, as if the answer should have been obvious. "The Netherworld, of course. We call it the Null Zone. Don't worry, almost no one chooses to live down there."

"But Dad did, didn't he?"

Her smile faltered, and she looked away quickly. "We can't feel sorry about other people's choices if they get exactly what they wanted."

Before Ethan could ask any further questions, the crowd stopped moving and he bumped straight into his father-in-law.

Kurlin turned to him with eyebrows raised. "Careful, grub."

Ethan ignored him and stood on tip toes to see what was going on up ahead. It looked like the pair of shining portals he'd seen were doors. Blinding light shone from each, and a pair of Peacekeepers in their glowing blue-white armor flanked the openings. A fifth Peacekeeper, this one wearing a shimmering blue cape, stepped up to the front of the crowd and turned to address them. His breastplate bore a glowing blue spiral, the shape of a galaxy with glittering white points of light meant to be stars. Surrounding that spiral was the letter "A" while in the center of it lay what looked like an *eye*.

As Ethan looked on, a white-robed man stepped up beside the Peacekeeper. The robed man's face had a familiar hardness, and the piercing gray eyes were hard to miss. The last time Ethan had seen him had been via the news nets, just before the Sythians had executed him for all of Dark Space to see. Now he looked much younger, but still easily recognizable. He was Admiral Hoff Heston, leader of the Imperial Remnant.

The admiral called out in a strangely echoing voice, "I hope to see you all in Etheria soon. Rest assured that while you are choosing how to live on Avilon, I will be helping Omnius and his Strategians to plan a rescue for everyone we left behind in Dark Space. If you didn't find all of your loved ones here, take heart! Soon they will join us, too."

More cheering erupted from the crowd. As soon as the noise died down, the blue-caped Peacekeeper standing with Hoff addressed them in heavily accented Imperial Versal: "Mortals to the left, Ascendants to the right. Move quickly please."

The crowd began to separate, and Ethan felt someone tap him on the shoulder. It was his mother.

She flashed him a wan smile and then gave him one last hug. "We'll see each other soon. If not during *The Choosing*, then after. I love you, son! Whatever you decide, be sure it's what you want. You can always change your mind, but if you die in the Null Zone, there's no going back. Choose wisely," she said, withdrawing to an arm's length and squeezing his hands one last time.

Ethan wasn't sure what to say to that. He turned to watch her give Alara a hug next.

"It was wonderful to meet you, dear."

"Thank you, Lara—I mean Mom. It was nice to meet you, too. I didn't think I'd ever get the chance."

Lara Ortane accepted that with a nod. "Make sure my son doesn't do anything stupid. The Null Zone is no place to raise a child."

That comment stuck in Ethan's brain, setting off another alarm. "Hold on—I didn't mention that Alara was pregnant." She was only three months, and barely showing.

Lara hesitated just a moment before smiling anew. "You didn't have to mention it. A mother knows these things. Look at her—she's practically glowing." Lara turned and gave Atton a hug, saying goodbye to him, too. Then she walked over to a growing crowd of white-robed people. They smiled and waved to their loved ones, calling out their last goodbyes and *I-love-you's*. Ethan stood frozen in place, watching everything with a growing sense of unease.

"Come on, Ethan," Alara said, tugging on his arm to guide him over to the other refugees.

Once the crowd was fully separated, both groups began walking single-file through their respective doors under the watchful eyes of the Peacekeepers.

"I wonder if there have been other refugees to arrive here, or if we're the first?" Atton asked.

"I don't know." Ethan shook his head as they shuffled toward their door. They reached it in short order. There weren't many survivors from the battle over Avilon.

Alara hesitated in front of the blinding brightness that shone from the open door. "What's in there?" she asked, directing her question to one of the Peacekeepers.

Ethan saw the outline of a passageway, but his eyes wouldn't stand to look into the light for long.

"Do not be afraid," the Peacekeeper replied. "Your destiny awaits."

"That was vague," Ethan said, but the Peacekeeper gave no further explanation.

Atton turned to them. "If Omnius wanted to harm us, he would have done it by now. Come on," he said, stepping across the threshold and disappearing from sight.

Atton didn't shout out a warning or scream in alarm on the other side of the door. That was something, Ethan supposed. He turned to Alara with his eyebrows raised. "Ready?"

She tightened her grip on his hand to a bone-grinding force, but she nodded. And with that, they walked into the light.

CHAPTER 2

4 Hours Earlier . . .

Commander Lenon Donali's heart thudded in his chest as his escape pod plummeted toward the apparent surface of Avilon. The city was on fire, with thick columns of black smoke rising into the night. Here and there green cultivated gardens peeked out through the smoke and flames. Blue rivers of energy—some kind of shield—separated the raging infernos at the bases of the buildings, keeping the fires from burning out of control.

A surface-penetrating scan with the pod's sensors revealed that a full kilometer of city lay below the shield. Crashing starships had opened dark, gaping holes in that shield. Donali guided his escape pod down to the nearest one. It was wreathed in fire from a burning park.

Donali needed somewhere to lie low until he could find a way to be of use to his Sythian masters. They were losing the battle for Avilon, but the war was far from over. The crew of the *Intrepid* had suspected Donali was a traitor. They'd put him in stasis to keep him out of trouble, but he'd been awoken in the *Intrepid's* final moments as the cruiser's power failed. He'd made it to the nearest escape pod, but only just.

As Donali drew near to the hole in the shield, he saw flaming trees rushing up fast, their scraggly branches clawing for his pod. Smoke swirled. Flames roared all around.

Then he was through, racing down an artificial chasm formed by kilometers-high skyscrapers. A mesmerizing swirl of colored lights streaked by the pod's bubble-shaped cockpit. Walkways, tunnels, and elevated streets crossed from one side of the chasm to the other, glittering in the dark like strands of silk spun by a deranged spider.

Collision warnings screamed as he flew between two parallel bridges. He fired the pod's braking thrusters and grav lifts to slow his descent, keeping a light hand on the stick to avoid colliding with anything. A river of lights flowed below him, rushing up fast. His brain registered those moving lights as air traffic. He pulled up, skating dangerously close to the nearest building, and then swiftly fell toward the next set of elevated streets and bridges.

By now he'd slowed his descent enough to take in the finer details of his surroundings. A grav train whooshed down a glowing track. Pedestrians turned and pointed up at Donali's pod as it fell. Bright, animated signs hung above the different stores on the street level. The buildings themselves shone with colorful rows of light, pouring from windows that were too reflective to see through.

The pod dropped below that street level and raced toward another stream of air traffic. The layers of the city seemed to go on forever. Air cars flowed like luminous rivers between levels of elevated streets, trains, and bridges. After passing no less than four levels of traffic and streets, another shining blue shield appeared at the bottom of the chasm. Donali marveled at that. What could be below it? Surely not another kilometer of city.

Pedestrians stopped to point at him once more as he fell past the final level of streets. There was a war raging high above these people's heads, and his escape pod was the novelty worth pointing to. Donali snorted with amusement.

He flew down to the shining blue shield. Like the first one, it was divided into hexagonal sections. He hovered to a stop just a few dozen meters from it, trying to see what might lie beyond. His artificial eye was far keener than his real one, and he was able to see yet more of the same—streets and shining rivers of traffic. Donali let out a long whistle and shook his head, awed by the scale of urban development.

Donali checked the grid for a place to set down, rotating the three-dimensional gravidar display until it gave him a nice cross-section of the chasm.

That was when he saw it.

Something massive was crashing down above him, taking out streets and air traffic alike, washing them away with bursts of static.

Donali's mind raced. He could only imagine what it was. He had just a few seconds before the debris reached him. He needed a place to hide! Scanning the buildings, he looked for somewhere safe to land his pod, but the truth was, nowhere would be safe, and there wasn't enough time.

A distant roar, growing ever closer, reached his ears. Mountains of rubble crashing down. Donali imagined people screaming as they fell.

Then the shields below him flickered out, and he saw nothing but the naked hexagonal outlines of the shield emitter frame. Someone had turned off the shield. Beyond that were layers of traffic and elevated streets. Air cars went screaming by on all sides, fleeing to the lower levels of the city. Suddenly Donali understood the purpose of turning off the shield.

He gunned the pod's tiny thrusters, following the traffic down. He raced past more levels of streets and traffic. Keeping half an eye on the grid, he watched the wave of static caused by the crashing debris draw near to the lower shield. An instant before the debris reached it, the shield glowed to life. The debris hit with a deafening roar, and Donali's escape pod rattled with the noise.

Donali didn't trust that barrier to hold the weight of so much destruction. He flew on for the surface of the city—wherever it might be. After passing just two levels of elevated streets and one level of air traffic, he plunged into a thick, murky gray fog. The stream of traffic fleeing from the upper city raced ahead of him, their tail lights forming crimson halos in the low-lying clouds. Donali assumed those cars knew where they were going, but just to be sure, he ran a quick scan of the fog. Sensors reported the real surface of Avilon rushing up fast.

Donali reversed thrust and pushed the grav lifts up to full power, provoking a high-pitched whine from the generator. He snapped on the pod's bow lights to cut a swath through the gloom. Gray castcrete appeared at the bottom, cracked and broken and littered with trash. He pulled up to race along that street, chasing after the blurry red glow of the nearest air car. It soon passed out of sight, disappearing in the swirling haze.

The sides of the street were just as crowded with people as the ones he'd passed on his way down. Yet these streets seemed more forbidding. Streetlights were too few, and the ones there were took on an eerie glow because of the mist.

Above, the buildings had seemed to be endless shining walls of light and majesty, but here they were shadowy and gray. The occasional ground car drove by, but for the most part the street was trafficked with people, not cars.

Donali flew by several side streets and cross streets before deciding to take one of them. It turned out to be a deserted alley, but up ahead he saw the red tail lights of an air car, landed and waiting. That encouraged him. If someone else had decided this was a safe hiding place, then maybe he'd gone far enough?

Donali hovered down for a landing. Landing struts touched pavement with a soft *clu-clunk,* and he eased out of the cramped pilot's chair, stumbling on wooden legs to the back of the pod. He hesitated with his hand poised over the hatch controls. Now, with the most harrowing part of the journey to the surface behind him, he had enough time to stop and think: *what next?*

He was a foreigner on a strange world that had been isolated from the rest of humanity for thousands of years. He wasn't even sure they would speak Versal. Blending in was going to be tougher than he'd thought. He was just about to open the hatch when he noticed his nakedness. Upon waking from stasis aboard the *Intrepid,* he hadn't even had time to stop and put on his clothes.

At that point, every second had been vital to his survival. Now that he had a second to breathe, however, he noticed that he was badly chilled and starting to shiver. Whether that was from actual cold or spent adrenaline, he couldn't be sure, but either way he couldn't go blundering around Avilon naked.

Donali turned from the hatch controls to look in the locker under one of the pod's bench seats. There he found a spare vac suit and a pair of self-conforming boots. He pulled on the suit quickly, one leg at a time, and then the boots. He eyed the helmet for just a moment before deciding to leave it in the pod. The air on the surface had to be breathable. Avilonians were no less human than he. Snatching up the utility belt and emergency survival pack that went along with the suit, Donali returned to the hatch controls and opened the pod.

A gust of cold, musty air wafted in, bringing with it the meaty smell of rotting garbage. Donali's nose wrinkled, and he cast a wistful glance over his shoulder for the helmet he'd left behind. He had to force himself to leave it. He'd attract far too much attention walking around with a bucket on his head.

Donali jumped out of the pod. Debris crunched underfoot. The alley was dark and devoid of humanity. Up ahead, the red tail lights of the air car he'd seen were now gone. Either it had powered down or moved on. Looking up, he saw a scattering of lights from the buildings. At the street level, a few neon signs flickered with alien symbols above rusty doors, but the light wasn't enough to see by. Donali frowned and unclipped the grav gun from his utility belt. He activated the gun's under barrel glow lamp and set it to illuminate to a range of 10 meters. It barely illuminated three before being swallowed by the swirling gloom, but it was better than nothing.

Donali glanced back to the relative safety of the escape pod. His stomach growled angrily at him, and he resolved to find a place to rest and eat some of the rations in his survival pack as soon as possible.

Hurrying down the alley, he passed piles of debris and trash shored up against the sides of the buildings. A few rickety stairways zigzagged between glowing, black-barred windows. The welcome glow of light and life mysteriously stopped just a few floors above the street. There were no windows on the first few floors, as if the need for a ladder would be enough to stop a determined thief.

After walking for just a few minutes, Donali began to feel naked again. The alley seemed to go on forever, and he hadn't passed a single car or pedestrian yet. The bustling night life he'd seen at the bottom of the broader chasm was completely absent here.

Donali swept his glow lamp from side to side, searching the shadows for any sign of life, but all he saw were small, skittering creatures, their eyes bright needlepoints of reflected light.

He walked on for several minutes more, until the murky gloom became lit by a faint, golden glow. Donali headed toward that light, thinking that it must be from streetlights in a more lively part of the city. Before long, the golden glow resolved into flickering tongues of flame. Then he saw human shapes silhouetted against the firelight.

The fog began to clear, and Donali noticed that the alley opened into a large square. His breath began making tiny contributions to the dissipating fog. He stopped and stood at the end of the alley, frowning at the sight before him.

The firelight he'd seen was from a large pile of garbage burning in the center of the square. His eyes teared from the smoke, and he almost gagged from the smell of flaming refuse, but it radiated a welcome warmth. Ramshackle huts, lean-tos, and shanties lay all around the edges of the square. Here and there people stumbled around, or sat in the dust in front of their hovels, watching the fire burn.

Donali turned to look at the nearest man, a skeletal shell of humanity, wearing stained and torn clothing that looked almost as old as he did. As his glow lamp passed over the wretch, the man slowly turned to squint up at him with lifeless black eyes. Long, bedraggled locks of gray hair clung to his head in patches. Donali stared back, waiting for a reaction, but there was none.

Careful to keep his eyes on the wretch, he took a few steps forward and sat down. The wretch watched him for a moment longer before turning back to the bonfire, his brief spark of curiosity spent. A few others noticed Donali sitting there in his clean white vac suit, and they stared, too. Yet none of them moved to approach.

Donali realized that this was a place where people went to forget or be forgotten, and that made it the perfect place for him to hide—at least for now.

These people wouldn't ask any prying questions about where he was from or what he was doing. Donali left the grav gun on his lap just in case, and then he unslung his pack to get at his emergency rations. He opened the case of ration bars and bit off a big chunk of the first one.

Then came a sudden *crunch* of movement, and he looked up.

There were no less than four people standing before him, having gathered in the few seconds he'd spared to look inside his pack. They were looking at him expectantly. No, not at *him*, at the ration bars in his lap.

Donali put down the one he'd bitten into and swallowed carefully. He picked up the grav gun and shone the lamp into one man's eyes after another, forcing them to squint. A few snarled and turned away from the light. Others glared with hunger shining in their eyes, their cracked and scabby lips parted in anticipation of a meal. Donali felt a stab of fear strike him as he assessed those four men. Not all of them were broken wretches. A few were young and fit, wearing better clothing than the others. Those ones were holding makeshift clubs.

One of the club-wielders pointed to the case of ration bars

and growled something in a language Donali didn't understand. Donali stuffed the case back into his pack and slung it over one shoulder as he rose to his feet.

His assailants advanced a step, to which he barked, "Stay back!" Donali aimed his grav gun at the nearest man and fired, lifting him off his feet. The man screamed, flailing his arms and legs. The others turned to look, and Donali dropped him on his face. The man knocked his chin on the ground and cried out in pain.

An adequate warning.

The other three turned back to him with fierce looks. The one who'd spoken earlier shook his club at Donali and growled something else. Suddenly their numbers swelled as more filthy street people melted out of the shadows.

Donali was outnumbered ten or more to one. He backed toward the alley he'd come from, but a pair of ghoulish women appeared on that side, grinning at him with mouths full of missing teeth. They stood blocking the way.

"I'm warning you!" Donali said, shaking his gun at the crowd. But they crept forward, undeterred, as if they knew he'd already used his best trick.

Donali fired again, this time lifting a man more than a dozen feet and dropping him on his fellows' heads.

A few of them fell to the ground beneath the weight, and the group stopped advancing, as if to reassess the threat that Donali presented.

Then one of them growled something in their language, and they all surged toward him as one.

Donali fired again, but he didn't have time to do anything else before he was beset by clubs, fists, and clawing hands. The first blow to his head merely dazed him and forced him to his knees.

The second one turned out the lights.

* * *

The air car hovered high above the square, keeping its occupants safe from the *Psychos'* desperate, clawing hands. *Psychos* were at the very bottom of the food chain in the Null Zone, strung out on Bliss, ready and willing to do anything to get another dose that could make them halfway human again. Bliss was a wonder drug when used correctly. It could make you twice as smart, twice as strong, and twice as fast as an ordinary person—a force to be reckoned with, so long as you kept dosing. If not, it would make you twice as crazy. The strength and speed lasted for a while, until the inevitable exhaustion from hunger and lack of sleep took its toll. Then came the chills and night terrors, and a short dive off the deep end into a wellspring of insanity. Once that happened, there was no coming back; you were a goner. These men and women fell into that category—*goners*.

No doubt they'd once been hardworking citizens, but now they were reduced to sitting in the dust, warming their hands over a pile of burning garbage.

"Biometric scanners aren't reading anything."

Bretton frowned and turned to look at his niece, Farah. "Keep scanning, make sure you get a good look at everyone's faces before we go. We've got to tag them all to be sure. If we don't get a face match, I'll have to go down there and start asking questions."

"Why would someone like Tera Halls even bother with Bliss? She was already rich. She had her whole life ahead of her."

Bretton shook his head. "Bored, maybe."

Tera Halls was an upper levels brat who'd recently taken to slinking out at night with her friends. Her parents didn't notice or didn't care until one morning she hadn't come back. Last anyone had seen of her had been in a lower levels' night club. The owner had kicked her and her friends out for badgering him for Bliss, which he swore he didn't sell. That had led Bretton to search the Psychos' camps. If you couldn't find a dealer, the next best thing was a Psycho, an old addict who knew where all the dealers were and could lead you to them. It wasn't much, but it was a start, and the club was just around the corner from this particular stink hole.

"Tagged them all. Still nothing."

"All right. I'm going in."

"Are you sure you want to do that?" Farah turned to him. "You don't have to. We can take some other case. Something safer."

Bretton smiled. "Safer?" He shook his head. "Safe doesn't exist for us." Being a freelance Enforcer in the Null Zone wasn't quite the same as being a regular Enforcer, and nothing like being a Peacekeeper. Regular Enforcers rarely ventured below level ten. Peacekeepers would, but only to chase crime on a global scale. Local crimes were *Null* business, and no one really expected Null Enforcers to police the lowest levels on their meager salary. Everyone was their own deterrent down here, with guns worn brazenly to ward off the Psychos and other lower levels scum. But sometimes even that wasn't enough, hence the need for freelance Enforcers. They had to go where the official ones feared to tread.

"You could die, you know," Farah said.

That was the main difference between Peacekeepers and Enforcers—no one brought you back if you died. But what was death, really? Bretton had cheated it too many times already. Come back once, and it's a miracle. Come back twice and you're relieved. Come back ten times and it's a curse. Lifelink implants bleached all the colors out of life and drained death of all its significance. Besides, once you knew the truth—the *real* truth—you went looking for death any way you could, just to stop knowing it. *You can't unsee something no matter how many times you close your eyes.*

"I'm not afraid of death, Farah."

Farah's lip twitched and her eyes narrowed. "Maybe you should be."

Bretton felt the skin around his eyes crinkle with amusement, and he imagined for a moment that he looked as old as he felt. In reality he was a very young-looking fifty-something, whose face bore none of the marks of age that it should have. Even Farah looked like she was still twenty-one. Her real age had to be more than thirty-five by now.

"Why fear death?" he asked. "It's an end. You know where it goes. Life's the scary part, because you don't know where it will end up."

"Some would say death isn't the end."

"It is for us. We already died once at Roka. If some part of us went from there to some other after life, we won't ever get to see it. This is all we've got."

"All the more reason to cherish it, Uncle Bret. Be careful out there."

"I will." He unbuckled his seat restraints. Just as he was

about to open the passenger's side door and jump down, his niece stopped him with a hand on his. "Hold on," she said.

"What?"

She nodded to the grid. "Someone just walked in on the Psychos."

"Is it one of our missing partyers?"

"Take a look for yourself."

A visual feed from the air car's surveillance suite sprang to life above the pilot's control console.

The newcomer stood at the end of the alley behind them. He was tall with black hair receding at the temples. One eye glowed red, while the other was dark and inscrutable. He wore an unusual jumpsuit—white with blue stripes—and a strange symbol was sewn into his upper sleeve. Upon seeing it, a vague sense of deja vu trickled through Bretton from some other lifetime. Suddenly he knew which lifetime it was coming from, and his eyes flew wide. "It can't be . . ."

"Can't be what?" Farah asked, slower to make the connection than he. It had been over ten years, after all.

"Magnify that feed."

"Okay . . ." Now the symbol on the man's sleeve was easy to recognize. Six stars surrounding a clenched fist. "Holy *frek!*" Farah said, swearing in a language that neither of them had used since waking up on Avilon.

"*Frek* is right," Bretton said.

"He's an Imperial!"

"Yes, question is, how did he get here?"

"Well, we won't know until we ask him."

They watched him walk into the Psychos' camp and sit down, oblivious to the danger he was in.

"What's he doing?" Farah demanded. "Is he stupid, or what?"

"I'd better get down there."

"After he stirs them all up? You're as good as dead."

Bretton frowned. When he'd been about to jump down and go question the Psychos, he'd been meaning to do so quietly, with stealth on his side. For that, he was wearing a suit of cloaking armor. None of the Psychos would have something as sophisticated as a cloak detector. Of course, if he'd found Tera Halls, he had orders to rescue her, so Bretton had also come prepared for a fight.

"I'll be fine, Fay," he said, his hand back on the door handle. He flashed her a quick grin before triggering his helmet visor and turning on his cloaking shield. He was using a cut-rate power core, so he'd only have a few minutes of invisibility to play with.

Farah's expression clouded and she looked like she was about to blurt out something. "Good luck," was all she said. He had the impression that hadn't been what she'd meant to say, but there was no time to ask.

Bretton opened the door and jumped the few dozen feet to the ground. On the way down he triggered the grav field in his boots to cushion his fall, but he landed with a loud *crunch* anyway. A few heads turned, and the newcomer looked up, but no one saw anything to associate with the sound. Just as well he'd made a noise, though. Now that the Imperial had looked up, he'd noticed his peril. There were already four Psychos sizing him up. Bretton sighed inwardly and crept toward the group.

Sometimes he wished he'd never left Etheria, or that he'd never found Omnius's dirty laundry, but if he was going to wish for something, he'd wish that the Sythians had never invaded the galaxy, and that neither he nor his wife had died and come to Avilon in the first place. Then he'd wish Omnius away for good measure, just in case the AI god of Avilon decided to resurrect him from a natural death, too.

As the Psychos advanced on the Imperial, Bretton bet that man had a few wishes of his own.

CHAPTER 3

Ethan noticed that the blinding tunnel in the clouds became noticeably dimmer after they'd crossed the threshold. It led to a circular chamber with a familiar, shiny golden dome at the end. A Peacekeeper stood waiting there for them. As they approached, that man placed his hands against the dome and it rose up on four shining pillars of light. Then they were herded underneath the dome by more Peacekeepers. From the inside, the dome and floor were both black and glossy. Two glowing circles marked the floor. The inner one green, and the outer one red. Ethan led Alara into the inner circle.

Then one of the Avilonians raised his hands and the inside of the dome began to glow with ever-increasing brightness. Suddenly, the Peacekeeper dropped his hands and the dome fell with a *boom.* A loud whirring filled the air, and it became so bright inside the dome that Ethan had to shut his eyes. Wind whipped at their hair and clothes, and Ethan's ears popped with a sudden change in air pressure. Then the brightness faded and the wind died down. Ethan opened his eyes to see the dome rising on four pillars of light once more.

"Is it going to be like that every time?" Atton asked.

Ethan shook his head. They'd just been teleported from

their reunion in the sky back down to the surface of Avilon. He supposed some drama was to be expected for such a feat of technological wizardry.

As they were herded out from under the dome, Ethan saw that they were now in the middle of a rooftop garden. Faintly illuminated synthstone walkways slithered out into the night, flanked by colorful beds of flowers. Majestic trees stood sentinel on dark, rolling fields of grass, tracing the sky with jagged, tree-shaped shadows. Their leaves rasped in a warm breeze. Overhead, a full Avilonian moon shone bright and blue in a sky that glittered with countless stars. Something was wrong, but he couldn't decide what.

Atton was the first to recognize what was missing. "Where's the city?" he asked.

Ethan looked around, noticing now that the horizon was dark. Absent from it were the bright, shining towers he remembered from the world-spanning city. He looked up once more to the bright sea of stars overhead. It shouldn't have been possible to see stars on Avilon, not with all the city lights, yet here they were, surrounded not by soaring skyscrapers, but by dark, cultivated greenery, as if the nearest city were in some far off land.

"Please follow me," a blue-caped Peacekeeper said as he began walking down one of the snaking pathways.

The group followed without complaint, marveling at the quiet beauty of the park. They passed a bubbling brook, walking over a short bridge with ornate railings. Fronds of soft, gold-glowing flowers hung like a curtain over the other side of the bridge. The pathway sparkled darkly underfoot, a mirror to the stars.

As they passed through the curtain of flowers, something tickled Ethan's hand. He scratched at it absently-mindedly.

Suddenly he felt a sharp pain, and he smacked his hand, assuming an insect had stung him. Something small and delicate rolled away between his fingers, confirming his suspicions.

"Frek!" he hissed, his hand beginning to throb in earnest.

"What is it?" Alara asked.

He shook his head. "It's nothing, don't worry." *Probably a bee,* he decided, remembering the hanging fronds of flowers they'd passed through. Whatever it was, he assumed it wasn't venomous. Paradise wouldn't be paradise if it were infested with venomous bees.

Ethan looked up and now he saw a modern-day palace shining on the horizon. It was four levels high with parapets, archways, and columns rising into the night. Prevalent windows glowed with a soft light, but the windows were blurry from the outside, obscuring whatever lay within.

"I wonder who lives there," Alara whispered.

"This is where you'll be staying for the duration of your tour of Celesta," the Peacekeeper answered from the head of the group.

"I guess it's a resort," Ethan said.

"No, *martalis,* this is a home. There are many homes like it in Celesta."

Rumblings of shock and surprise rippled through the group.

"What?" Atton said. "So who lives in the city we saw when we were fighting around the Zenith Tower?"

"The same Celestials who live in neighborhoods like this one," the Peacekeeper replied. "Most Celestials own several homes and apartments. Some homes are found by the beach, others in the mountains, still more are floating in the clouds. And yes, there are city apartments for those who prefer a metropolitan lifestyle."

"Hold on a minute," a new voice said. Ethan recognized it as that of Captain Loba Caldin. "If Avilon is so crowded with trillions of people, how is it that you have space for homes at all, let alone ones that are built on beaches and mountains?"

"Some environments are simulated, others are real. While it is true that most of the planetary surface is covered by the cityscape, ample space has been made for Celestials to live however they please."

"What about everyone else?"

"Everyone else is trying to become a Celestial."

"Aha," Caldin grunted, as if that had confirmed her suspicions.

"Where are we now?" someone else asked. Ethan didn't recognize the voice very well, but it was soft and feminine—girlish even. He thought it might belong to the young Nova pilot he'd seen with Atton.

"This home is built on the rooftops of Etheria," the Peacekeeper replied as they walked past a shimmering fountain in the driveway of the palace. "We are at the top level of Destiny Tower, where all Avilonian children go for *The Choosing*."

That was news to Ethan. "We're staying with kids? How old are they?" he frowned, thinking of little feet pounding down the hallways of the palace and little lungs screaming long after they should have gone to bed. He was too tired to deal with that.

"This house has been reserved specially for you. It would be inappropriate to leave refugees unsupervised around Avilonian children."

"Hold on—" Ethan objected. "*We're* the ones who need supervising?"

"Yes."

They came to the doors of the palace—two large, frosted glass slabs flanked by a pair of intimidating statues. The statues looked almost human, but taller and broader than the average man, with limbs that looked thinner and more articulated. Where the head should have been was a dark, shiny ball. As they drew near, those ball heads sprang to life with a glowing red eye in the center of each that slowly swiveled and rolled to track their approach.

"What the frek are those?" Atton exclaimed.

"Bots," Ethan suggested.

"Drones—also known as Omnies," the Peacekeeper supplied, stopping at the doors to be scanned by a fan of blue light that quickly washed over him from head to toe. A pleasant tone issued as the doors slid aside, revealing a massive entryway with polished marble floors, a spiral staircase, and bright, recessed glow panels running along the tops and bottoms of the walls. A large, crystal chandelier hung from the center of a high, dome-shaped glass ceiling.

"Nice," the girlish voice from before said. Ethan turned to see that it did in fact belong to the young Nova pilot he'd seen with Atton. She was holding his hand.

The Peacekeeper turned to address them from the center of the foyer. His subtly glowing blue-white armor gleamed in the gilded light of the chandelier.

"I'm sure you all have many questions, but it is almost time for us to . . . *sleep*, so I'll try to be brief."

Ethan frowned at that, noting the way the blue-caped Peacekeeper hesitated on the word *sleep*, as if he'd been about to say something else.

The Peacekeeper went on, "Night fall is somewhat different here than what you'll be used to—at least it is in

Etheria and Celesta. We don't have the same requirement for sleep that you *martales* do. That, along with all the many other frailties of our species, has been engineered out of us."

"So why is night any different from the day? Why not carry on doing whatever it is you'd normally do?" Captain Caldin asked.

"Because we all have to take a break from our daily routine in order to *Sync*. This is the closest thing we know to sleep. Sync is when we synchronize the data in our Lifelink implants with Omnius. Sync data serves as an emergency backup in case of a very sudden death, but it also gives Omnius the data he needs to make accurate predictions about the day to come."

Ethan's eyebrows floated up. "Predictions?"

"Perhaps I should start at the beginning. Over thirty thousand years ago, Neona Markonis, a renowned cyberneticist at the time, hypothesized that it would be impossible to create an intelligence any greater than the creator's. Working on this assumption, she used Lifelink implants to network thousands of our greatest minds together. Using the collective power of their intellect, they created Omnius.

"His test function was to study the data in His creators' Lifelinks and tell them things about themselves that they couldn't discover on their own. He began to predict what they would do next. The team realized they could use an intellect like His to predict the future and prevent crime. A logical extension of that was for Omnius to predict everything else, too, and create a true utopia. During Sync Omnius runs an internal simulation of Avilon with all of the variables in place. Like that, He is able to predict our actions for the day to come with near perfect accuracy."

Captain Caldin snorted. "If he already knows what's going to happen, why not skip to the end? Tell us all what we're going to do and save us the trouble of thinking about it. In fact, maybe he should just do it all for me, that way I can spend my time contemplating eternity."

The Peacekeeper turned to the captain and stared at her for an uncomfortably long moment. "Omnius does not control our actions simply by knowing them. He uses his foresight to warn us against taking any action that will harm us or others."

"What if I don't heed his warnings?" Ethan challenged.

"If your intended action is a minor offense, it may be allowed, but if the intended offense is grievous, you will be arrested before you can commit your crime, and then you will be rehabilitated."

"Rehabilitated . . ." Ethan nodded slowly. He'd spent enough time on Etaris to know a prison when he found one. Avilon looked orderly and pretty on the surface, but dig just a little deeper and something began to stink. No wonder his father had opted out. *Preston Ortane would never let anyone tell him how to live his life.*

Ethan adjusted his footing and crossed his arms over his chest. Alara must have sensed his annoyance, because she shot him a quick look, her violet eyes wide and intent. The message was clear. *Don't say a word.*

"Hoi, cut the krak—you're saying that Omnius doesn't just see the outcome of the next day, he *controls* it, by telling us what not to do and then punishing us if we do it—sometimes even before we've done anything at all!"

Blue Cape's inclined his head at that. "How else could paradise exist?"

"What good is paradise if it isn't free?" Ethan countered.

"If what you call freedom is the ability to do wrong as well as right, then I would say that freedom and paradise cannot coexist. That kind of freedom is chaos, but don't worry, *Martalis*. Even in Etheria, people are allowed to make mistakes. The lower levels have a certain degree of chaos, and it is there that Peacekeepers like myself find our purpose."

"Arresting delinquents?"

"Guiding other Etherians."

"From the sounds of it, you're talking about more than just crime. You're talking about bad choices."

"That's correct."

Ethan pursed his lips, nodding slowly as he considered the implications of everything that he'd heard. "Here's a hypothetical scenario for you, Blue. Tomorrow night my wife is going to cheat on me. I'm going to find out and kill the kakard—but don't worry! Omnius has already seen it all play out, so you show up on our doorstep while we're drinking our morning caf. My wife won't be allowed to cheat, and I won't have to burn a hole in anyone's head. You're there to tell us what would have happened so that we'll learn from our hypothetical mistakes."

The Peacekeeper regarded him with a small, secretive smile. "Unraveling the chaos starts with much smaller things, Mr. Ortane. You kill the bee that stung you without asking *why* it stung you."

Ethan froze. Ice trickled through his veins, making him shiver, and leaving him cold. His palms began to sweat, and his heart began to pound, but despite that, he spoke very calmly: "What did you say?"

"The same impulse for revenge that made you kill the bee when it stung you would have you kill your wife's lover. But to put your mind at ease, your wife would never cheat on you. You, however, *would* cheat on her."

Ethan's mind spun. He was too flabbergasted to be outraged by the accusation.

Alara spoke up for him instead. "How dare you! Ethan isn't like that. He wouldn't cheat on his previous wife with *me*, even when he thought she was dead. He's not like that."

"No? I must be mistaken then." The Peacekeeper's gaze moved on, roving over the assembled group. "Rest assured, the ultimate *freedom* for wrongdoing is available to anyone who grows tired of ascending. That is, in fact, the very purpose of The Choosing—to give you a choice. The Null Zone is not subject either to *Sync*, or to Omnius's foresight. There, criminals are punished after the fact, and people often suffer and die for the sake of someone else's freedom."

The small group of refugees grew silent.

"Sync is the same four hours for everyone all over Avilon, but whether it occurs during the physical night or during the day depends on the time of year, since our days are slightly shorter than 24 hours.

"Now, I'm afraid that's all the time I have for explanations. Omnius has asked that I stay here with you to guide you through The Choosing, due to my own . . . unique experience. My name, if you haven't remembered it by now, is Galan Rovik, but you may call me Master Rovik."

"Master?" Ethan challenged, only now recovering enough from his shock to speak.

"It is my ascendant ranking. Should any of you choose to become Etherians by the end of the coming week, you will be ranked as *Neophytes*."

"Neo . . ." Atton trailed off, not catching the meaning of the unfamiliar word.

"*Neophytes*. So that you adapt more quickly to life here on

Avilon, our language will be downloaded to your Lifelinks tonight while you Sync."

"How's that?" a new voice asked. It was one of the sentinels. Ethan saw that the man's brow was pinched in concentration. "I don't remember getting any cerebral implants."

The Peacekeeper regarded them all with another secretive smile. "No, none of you chose to have Lifelink implants, and Omnius wishes you to know that he is sorry for implanting them without your knowledge. Most of you received your Lifelinks at birth, at the same time you received the identichips in your wrists. Although Omnius didn't bother to predict your actions when you were so far from his kingdom, he did occasionally speak to you, to prepare you for the day when you would join his children. Thus, the inner voice you all have, the one you sometimes mistake for your conscience, is really that of Omnius.

"He knows your every thought, and he knows you all better than you know yourselves. He likely already knows who will choose him—" The Peacekeeper's eyes skipped through the crowd until they seemed to find Ethan's once more. "—and who will not."

That final pronouncement fell on numb ears. One too many mind-shattering revelations had been delivered in the past few hours, and at this point Ethan almost believed it was all some strange and convoluted dream that he would soon wake from.

"Please, follow me. Your quarters are up the stairs."

As the Peacekeeper led them up a spiral staircase to the second floor, Alara nudged him in the ribs. "I know you wouldn't cheat on me," she whispered.

He swallowed past a lump in his throat and shook his

head. They padded down a broad hallway from the second floor landing. The hall was paved with faintly gold-glowing black tiles. Animated light paintings hung along plain white walls. Ethan glanced at a few of the paintings as they walked by. They were abstract mixtures of shape and color that seemed to twist into human faces—their expressions alternating from rapt to wretched, in the throes of either ecstasy or agony.

Ethan looked away, a sudden chill creeping down his spine. "A bee did sting me, and I killed it."

"A bee?"

"Master Rovik knew about it. I think it was a lesson, but I don't know. Maybe Rovik guessed what happened when he heard me swearing."

"So he was right about the bee, and you think that means he's right about you being a cheater?"

Ethan turned to her in the gloomy golden light, his expression mirroring one of the agonized faces on the opposite wall as they passed by. "Maybe."

She reached for his hand and squeezed it. "Omnius might think he knows us better than we know ourselves, but I know you even better than that. Trust me."

"You have a lot of faith in me."

Alara smiled, and Ethan saw one of the paintings smile, too. "I always have," she replied.

Master Rovik stopped walking and the refugees crowded around him. "This room is for the married couple," he said, gesturing to a door with a mirror-white finish and a glowing golden symbol. "It is usually reserved for one of the *shepherds* who guide the children through The Choosing, but Ethan and Alara are entitled to their privacy."

"Thanks, I think," Ethan growled.

The door slid open automatically, and lights rose to a dim golden hue beyond the threshold, revealing a spacious bedroom with a large bed and spotless white bedsheets. Master Rovik gestured for them to enter the room. Ethan let Alara go first. Before he could follow her, the Peacekeeper caught him by the arm in a surprisingly strong grip. Ethan turned, his green eyes blazing. He was too tired for another soul-searching comment.

"Remember something, *Martalis*, a prediction is only true if it comes to pass. Otherwise, it's just a warning."

"I don't need you warning me not to cheat on my wife."

"Not anymore."

The Peacekeeper let him go, and he walked inside the room. The door *swished* shut behind him. He glared at it, as if he could still see Master Rovik's glowing blue eyes blazing a trail into his soul.

"Ignore him, Ethan," Alara said, coming up behind him and wrapping her hands around his waist. Her head came to rest on his shoulder and she kissed his neck. Ethan shut his eyes and breathed in the soft floral fragrance of her perfume. The room began to spin around, and he felt himself swaying on his feet.

You should have stayed in Dark Space.

Ethan's eyes sprang open. Suddenly he wondered if that thought had been his, or if it was Omnius speaking to him.

"Come to bed," Alara purred close beside his ear. "We can make sense of all this in the morning."

Ethan nodded and allowed her to lead him by the hand to the big white bed. They undressed and crawled in naked beneath the sheets. Soon Alara was fast asleep with her head on his chest. Ethan lay awake and staring at the ceiling, his heart beating rhythmically in his chest—*thud, thud. Thud, thud.*

Thud, thud. . . .

CHAPTER 4

Thud, thud! Thud, thud!

Galan Rovik's heart beat insistently in his chest, like the hoof beats of an angry equestria. The waiting was the hardest part. *Soon,* he told himself. *Soon . . .*

Looking out the main forward viewports of the *Ventress* with the wide-eyed wonder of a child, his gaze became lost between the bright needle points of light. Each one glinted with an elusive hint of the unknown, of things too fantastic to believe, or too terrible to survive.

Ancient cartographers from the world of Origin, the lost birthplace of humanity, had once painted the lesser-known parts of the world with monsters, as if to say, *bad things lurk in the unknown.* It was the same fear that made a child tremble in the dark, wide-eyed with terror when contemplating what lurked in the pool of shadows beneath the bed. Growing older did nothing to dispel that fear, as those ancient cartographers had proven with their maps. But as all of *humanity* grew older and wiser, the unknown became less and less, and all the monsters fled, going from under the bed, to beyond the known world, to beyond the known galaxy, and finally, to other galaxies entirely.

When contemplating those unknowns, there were too many of them to ever fully explore. They would always be populated with monsters, but Strategian Galan Rovik was determined to chase them from the Getties Cluster to the next nearest galaxy.

The theories about what they would find in the Getties were endless. No one had ever attempted to jump that far before. To calculate a safe quantum jump from one galaxy to another had taken Omnius the better part of a year, but now that the calculations were complete, it would be much faster to travel between galaxies. So fast, in fact, that it would become possible to explore and colonize the Getties Cluster on a large scale. That was exactly why Galan was going. If the Getties proved to be a safe haven for immortal humans, colonization would start immediately.

Hiding from the rest of humanity and the fast-growing Imperium of Star Systems had proved difficult of late, and hiding was a dire necessity. Hard-won experience from the Great War of Origin had shown that immortals and mortals couldn't safely coexist unless they were carefully supervised, and the trillions of mortal beings in the Imperium of Star Systems were too far beyond Omnius's sphere of influence for him to supervise. He knew humanity well enough by now to predict that if Avilon were ever discovered, there would be another Great War.

For that reason, Omnius had built the wall of artificial gravity fields that surrounded the star system of Domus Licus. Anyone traveling there without a quantum jump drive would get stuck in the middle of a gravity field too strong to cross with simple faster-than-light drive systems, and too wide to cross at sub light speeds. It was good enough to keep Avilon and the greater star system of Domus Licus safe for now. *But walls don't just keep people out,* Galan thought. *They also keep people in.*

The Ascendancy had just one star system to the Imperium's thousands, and over time Avilon had become so crowded that the only place left to build was up. Now between the Null Zone and Celesta, Avilon was covered with skyscrapers.

It was the way it had to be. One small, mysterious patch of space that Imperial explorers could never seem to fully probe (and sometimes didn't come back from) was a curiosity relegated to the tall tales of old spacers, but if Omnius were to expand the wall of gravity fields to another star system, or even several, those tall tales would soon become facts, and the Second Great War that Omnius warned about would come to pass.

The solution, it seemed, lay in the Getties Cluster. Imperial faster-than-light drives would take six months or more to travel from the edge of the Adventa Galaxy to the edge of the Getties Cluster, expending vast quantities of fuel and resources in the process. It was impractical for them to make frequent trips. Not so for the Avilonians with their quantum jump drives.

The vast gap between galaxies would become a new wall for the Ascendancy, keeping the Imperium out until many centuries later when—*if*—they developed their own quantum jump drive technology.

"Strategian, we have reached the jump point."

Galan turned to look up at his executive officer from where he sat in the ship's command chair. "Good. Begin sequencing."

"Yes, sir."

He turned back to gazing out at space. This time he

noticed the sea of darkness between the stars, rather than the stars themselves. A moment later, the ship's quantum jump drives finished sequencing Omnius's calculations for the jump, and the ship began an automated countdown.

"Ten, nine, eight . . ." A rising *whir* accompanied the countdown, and the air began to shimmer and sparkle with a growing brilliance. A sweaty prickle of fear tickled the nape of Galan's neck. This was it. The darkness between the stars was no different than the darkness in a child's room—both conjured monsters to life—but today humanity would shine a light into the darkness and prove once again that the monsters didn't exist.

The whirring noise reached a fever pitch, and the automated countdown reached *one.* Time seemed to take a sudden breath, and the noise stopped.

Then everything disappeared in a blinding flash of light.

Blinking spots out of his eyes, Galan saw a bright green and blue orb, swirled with white clouds. He gasped and heard his sharp intake of air echo all across the bridge as the rest of his crew reacted to the sight.

They'd arrived.

Galan mentally called up a view of surrounding space from the holographic suite built into his command chair, just to be sure. A three dimensional map of space shimmered to life before him, momentarily blotting out his view of the planet. The map confirmed it. They'd reached the specified coordinates. That meant that the planet before them was indeed *Agaris*, the world that Omnius had predicted, even from a great distance, to be the closest match for Avilon in terms of habitability.

Galan swiped his hands through the air, gesturing to shrink the map and place it to one side of his view. The planet was revealed once more, and he smiled as he gazed upon it, imagining all of the wide open spaces they would soon have to colonize.

"Scan the planet," Galan said. "Find us a suitable place to land."

"Yes, sir," the sensor operator said, his armor flashing with a sudden brightness as he spoke. Galan's augmented reality contacts (ARCs) had been the source of the visual cue, but it wasn't necessary, the operator's voice was recognizable.

"Comms, report back to Omnius: Jump successful. We've found it. Send our visual and sensor feed since arrival. That should whet people's appetites back home."

"Yes, Strategian." Again the flash of brightness to accompany his crewman's speech, but this time it was a blue-tinted light. Each Operator on the bridge had their own ARC color code to differentiate them from the rest. "Would you like to speak to Him?" the comm operator asked.

"Not yet."

Omnius was too far away to maintain constant contact as he usually did with people on Avilon. In order to allow intergalactic communications, comm relay ships had been strung between the two galaxies like a lifeline, and while quantum comms were normally instant, having all the relays in the way made for a few seconds' delay between sending and receiving.

"Navigator, take us in and establish orbit. We'll make one pass around the globe before setting down. I want to get a lay of the land."

"Yes, sir."

Looking out over the crew pit, Galan saw the nav officer bob his helmeted head. From there Galan's blue eyes found his XO, Tactician Kar Thedron, prowling the aisles between control stations, hands clasped behind his back, posture military-straight. He was on his way back to the command deck, just passing the sensor operator's station.

"Sir!" The sensor operator flashed white in Galan's peripheral vision. "I'm getting strange readings from the surface. . ."

Galan leaned suddenly forward in his chair, hands poised on the armrests as if he were about to leap down into the crew pit below. "What kind of readings?"

Thud, thud. Thud, thud. . . .

"Energy readings, sir—massive ones—coming from the far side of the planet."

Galan frowned and shook his head, trying to pierce the cloud cover of the distant planet to see what his Operator might be speaking about. There was no sign of alien life, just the mottled green and blue of nature at its best.

Then a suspicion began to form in his gut.

"Magnify the planet, 100 times."

Suddenly the planet swelled until it was all anyone could see. Now the green and blue expanses took on regular shapes. There were patchwork fields and irrigating rivers flowing between them in rigid blue lines. Energy readings suggested advanced civilization. But whose? Had the Imperium beat them to the Getties?

"Contact, contact!" An alarm shrieked to emphasize the threat.

"What?" Galan blinked. "Where?"

"De-cloaking at 15-50-25, unknown type. They're powering weapons!"

"Shields!"

A brilliant purple ball of light impacted on the bow of the cruiser a split second later, provoking a rippling blue flash from the *Ventress's* shields. "Do *not* fire back! Comms, hail them!"

"How?"

"Use both conventional comms and quantum. See what they reply to first. Sensors—magnify the nearest ship and put it on screen!"

The sensor operator was too busy to reply. Galan drummed his fingers on his armrest while he waited for a visual, his mind spinning. Imperial ships didn't have cloaking devices, and he'd never seen an Imperial ship attack without hailing a warning first. But if the contact wasn't ISSF, then who?

A muffled boom shook the Ventress to her beams as another volley hit them.

"Shields?" Galan asked, his eyes on the back of the systems operator's head.

"99% and holding. Either their weapons are not very strong, or they're just testing us, sir."

A visual of their quarry appeared a split second later. Galan's blue eyes widened, and he shook his head. The crew was dead silent. The ship before them had a tear-drop shape, with flowing organic lines and a hull that shone as bright and reflective as any Avilonian's armor. The ship glowed a faint lavender color against the darkness of space. As they studied it, the enemy ship fired on them with what looked like a spinning purple star.

Someone whispered, "That's not a human vessel."

"No, it's not," Galan said quietly.

"Comms—any answer?"

"None, sir."

"More contacts! Five—wait, fifteen—no, there's more than a hundred! Weapons Incoming!"

"Brace!" Galan called out.

The deck shook with violent fury and overhead lights darkened as shields drew extra power to deflect the attack. A damage alert blared from the systems operator's control console.

"Damage report!" Galan barked.

"Shields 56%. Minor damage to deck four."

"Navigator, take evasive action! Get us out of here!" The deck shook again. *"Now!"*

"Yes, sir!"

Galan watched with a deepening frown as their magnified view of the enemy ship disappeared, replaced by empty space. *No, not empty,* he realized. A few of those sparkling points of light were too big and too bright to be stars. They were alien ships.

Perhaps the monsters exist after all. . . .

* * *

His eyes slowly opening, Ethan caught a blurry glimpse of a gradually brightening square of light. As the light brightened, he realized it was a window. Beyond it lay a vast expanse of immaculate green gardens and majestic trees. Above that, a deep blue sky.

Where was he? Then it all came rushing back. The battle. Avilon. Omnius.

He sat up suddenly, snow white bed sheets cascading from his chest. Alara stirred beside him and moaned something unintelligible. Ethan scanned the room: white walls, white sheets, the broad window that had awoken him with its light . . .

A slight draft drew his eyes to a climate control vent. Also coming from that direction, Ethan caught a whiff of something delicious that woke a raging beast in his stomach. The beast growled, and Ethan turned to his wife.

"Alara." He shook her gently. "Wake up." His hand recoiled from her as if she'd burned him, but the shock had come from him.

Wake up. He'd thought it, but he'd said something else. Something that sounded right and wrong at the same time. He tried again.

"Wake up."

Ethan leapt out of bed, but the sheets caught his ankle, and he fell over backward with a *thud*.

"Frek!" he cursed, and not even that word made sense to his ears. He thought it; he understood it; but his ears registered something else. Something alien.

Ethan regained his footing to find Alara sitting up now, breasts laid bare by the sheets pooled in her lap. His gaze lingered there a moment before traveling up. Her violet eyes were wide and full of shock.

"What are you doing on the floor. . . ?" Alara trailed off with a quizzical frown. She was also speaking another language, but Ethan understood the alien words coming out of her mouth as easily as if they had been Imperial Versal.

It was the strangest thing he'd ever experienced. They were thinking and understanding Versal, but speaking something else. Suddenly. Then Ethan remembered what that

Peacekeeper had said last night about Omnius teaching them the local language while they slept.

"It's Avilonian," Ethan explained.

"Holy frek ... beats the krak out of a universal translator," Alara said.

The Imperium's ear-worn translators worked by less invasive means, but they needed to be programed. Apparently Omnius had done all the programming directly in their brains. No need for accessories.

Ethan broke out in a cold sweat, and he shivered involuntarily. Omnius had been digging around in his brain while he slept, downloading everything and updating it, as if his mind were a software package. He turned to scan the ceiling, the walls, the floor ... He felt eyes everywhere, watching him, but there were no obvious signs of surveillance. *Guess you don't need them when you're already inside my head,* Ethan mused. He wondered what else Omnius might have changed while he was *teaching* them Avilonian. The mind-programming was just one more thing he didn't understand and didn't like about his new home.

"How did you sleep?" he asked, sitting down on the bed with great care, as if it might be the instrument Omnius had used to mess with his head.

"Not well. I had nightmares all night. You?"

Ethan frowned, his own dreams coming back to him now in a vivid rush. He shook his head. "Same here. I dreamed I was Master Blue Cape, of all things, and that I was making the very first expedition to the Getties Cluster."

Alara stared at him, her violet eyes wide and blinking once more. "So did I."

Ethan frowned. "What do you mean so did you?"

"I mean I had the *exact* same dream."

Ethan went back to glaring at the ceiling. "Not content to rearrange my head, you messed with my dreams, too?"

No reply.

"Answer! I know you can hear me."

He felt a hand on his arm, and he flinched at the touch. "Ethan. I don't think *it* . . . he, meant any harm. I think he was trying to show us what happened. He's telling us a story while we sleep."

Ethan wanted to object, to deny it, to suggest some much more sinister explanation that would justify the outrage he felt, but he *knew* she was right. The same way he *knew* Avilonian. Omnius had somehow shown them through Rovik's eyes exactly what had happened on the original expedition to the Getties.

It still felt like a vile and unwelcome intrusion to him. Before he could say anything about it, there came a knock at the door. Alara reacted quickly, covering herself with the sheets and holding them to her chest. "Yes?"

The door opened to reveal the smiling face of Master Blue Cape, A.K.A. Strategian Rovik himself, already dressed in his shining armor. His blue eyes were glinting rather than glowing in the broad light of day. "Good morning," he said.

"Go frek yourself," Ethan replied. "We're kind of in the middle of something here, and we're not even dressed—you mind giving us some privacy? Oh—wait, you don't know what that is here. Let me see if I can explain. . . . It's where you and everyone else keep their noses out of my krak! Does that sum it up for you?"

Master Rovik's smile faded. "Omnius warned me about you," he said, striding quietly into the room, as if gliding on air.

"He did, did he? Well, why don't you warn *him* for me:

next time, ask permission before you go poking around in my head."

"You already gave him permission."

"The frek I did!"

"When you came here. Uninvited."

"*You* invited me!"

"Not I. Another strategian."

"Same *krak*, Blue."

Rovik shook his head, "Please stop cursing, and no, it's not the same. You sought us out. Your intention was to find us, and now you have, but even after arriving here, in a strange land, you insist on having everything your way, trying to force your ideas and your culture on *us*. Well, I'm afraid you can't have your way here, Ethan. We have our own ways. Now stop acting like a spoiled child and follow me. Breakfast is ready."

The Peacekeeper turned on his heel and stormed away, his flowing blue cape swirling as he went.

Now who's being a child, Ethan thought but didn't say. The door *swished* shut.

"I'm as upset as you," Alara whispered, rubbing his arm. "But he's right. We don't get to make the rules here. We're lucky they're offering to accept us and make us a part of their society. Here we'll be safe from the Sythians. We'll be free to live our lives in peace! Isn't that worth losing some of our privacy?"

Ethan turned to her. "We'll be free from fear of the Sythians, but chained and restricted in every other way that matters. I think I liked Dark Space better."

"Ethan! He can hear you."

"Apparently Omnius already knows what I'm thinking, so I don't need to spare his feelings with what I say."

"Maybe you should try," she said gently. "Let's at least see what life is like here before we insist that our way is better. They're giving us a week to choose how to live here, and to choose whether or not we want Omnius to be a part of our lives. That doesn't sound like a malign force trying to hurt us. Love doesn't force itself on anyone. Love waits patiently to be returned. The way I waited for you."

Ethan's scowl softened. "That's not the same."

"Isn't it? If Omnius were so oppressive and bad, wouldn't he just force us to choose him, or do away with the people who don't?"

"Who says he doesn't? He made a real live netherworld just for them."

"Ethan, has it ever occurred to you that a lot of the bad things in our lives are a product of our own bad choices? It occurred to Omnius. That's why he wants to help us make the right choices."

"Alara . . ."

"Shhh. Just promise me you'll go into this with an open mind."

Ethan struggled with that. He didn't want to lie to his wife.

"Promise me, Ethan. Do it for us. All three of us," she said, grabbing his hand and placing it over her belly.

He half expected to feel a kick, but there was nothing. "We don't even know if it's a girl or a boy, yet," he said, dismay creeping into his voice.

"I bet Master Rovik can help us, if you'd be nice for a change . . ."

"Hey, I'm nice."

She arched an eyebrow at him. "To me you are. Sometimes."

He affected a wry smile and leaned in for a kiss. She gave him a short peck on the lips before withdrawing.

"We'd better get dressed. I'm so hungry I almost haven't noticed how sick I feel."

"Sick? Are you okay?" he asked.

Her eyebrows shot up with that question. "Morning sickness, remember?"

"Right," he said, sending her an apologetic look. "We'd better ask about that, too. If doctors here can stop people from dying, they must have found a way to make pregnancy more fun."

"That's the spirit. Keep thinking like that."

"Sure thing, Kiddie."

Alara rose from the bed and stretched. He eyed her appreciatively, her naked backside stirring him to life.

"What are you looking at?" she asked, casting a sly look over her shoulder.

"The view," he said through a smile.

"View's out the window—behind you."

"Not from where I'm sitting."

She laughed and padded across the floor to the on-suite bathroom. He watched her go, his smile fading by degrees.

Somehow she'd missed the fact that he hadn't promised to be open-minded. Although technically Omnius had made open-mindedness a foregone conclusion with his nightly probing. *The trick here is* not *being open-minded.*

Ethan had a feeling that wasn't going to be easy.

CHAPTER 5

ASCENDANCY

Bretton Hale raced toward the Imperial officer, but came to a skidding stop when he saw the man fall beneath the onslaught of no less than a dozen Psychos wielding makeshift clubs and bony fists. He didn't have much time. He rushed forward once more, his footsteps concealed by the noise the gang of Bliss addicts was making, and his presence concealed by his armor's cloaking shield. He raised his arms, palms outstretched as he approached, and mentally cycled through weapons in his armor. He settled on the standard issue Peacekeeper suppressors, which had come with his *borrowed* suit of armor.

Bretton opened fire and his cloaking shield automatically disengaged to prevent an overdraw from the suit's aging power cell.

He grabbed the nearest pair of Psychos in the grav field projected by the suppressors. Still running, he flung them to either side by spreading his arms like a bird about to take flight. The pair of stim addicts went skidding through the dust, fetching up against nearby shanties. They didn't rise to their feet. Peacekeeper suppressors were almost identical to Imperial grav guns, but much more powerful.

The remaining Psychos turned as one to greet him, their

bloodshot eyes reflecting sharp, glinting tongues of flame from the nearby bonfire. They snarled at him like wild rictans and charged. He flung two more aside before they reached him, and then dirty fingernails began clawing at his mirror-smooth, diamond-hard armor.

He electrified his suit and the Psychos fell away screaming. Reaching the fallen Imperial, Bretton took just a moment to assess the man's injuries before deciding that it didn't matter; there wasn't any time to waste. He picked up the Imperial with one arm, using the suit's augmented strength, and then slung him over his shoulder with a grunt of effort.

"Bret! Check your six!" Farah warned over the comms.

He spun around just in time to see a rushing wave of madness—a hundred or more Psychos, coming at him. He'd stirred the buzz flies' nest to life. Bretton checked his power levels. Just five percent left. Good for a few more suppressor blasts or a minute or two of cloaking, but he couldn't cloak both him and the Imperial, and he couldn't send a hundred Psychos skidding away with just a few suppressor blasts. It would take a full squad of Peacekeepers to fend off this onslaught.

Thinking fast, Bretton looked up. He saw the rickety remains of what had once been a fire escape clinging to the rising wall of the nearest skyscraper. It looked like the stairs hadn't been used or maintained in decades. He hoped they would hold his weight.

Raising one arm above his head, he fired the suppressor and there came a sharp jerk on his arm, pulling him up. He kept his other arm on the unconscious man slung over his shoulder. The ground began to drop away underfoot. Then the bestial mass of humanity reached him. A few Psychos leapt off their fellows' shoulders with what had to be Bliss-induced strength. Two grabbed on to his boots and hung tight. He was about to electrify his armor again to shake them loose when he remembered the man draped over his shoulder.

Cursing, Bretton kicked his feet, trying to shake the Psychos free. One of them tried to bite him, but didn't make it past his armor. Bretton reached the fire escape and grabbed on to the nearest railing with the arm he'd been using to grapple up. Dangling from the railing by one arm, with the combined weight of him, the Imperial, and two Psychos, the railing began to bend with a warning shriek of metal.

One handed, he wrangled the unconscious Imperial off his shoulder and onto the fire escape landing. The pair of Psychos clinging to his boots abandoned their attempts to bite through his armor. Now they climbed him like a ladder, trying to get at their original target—the unarmored Imperial. Bretton shuddered to think what they had in mind for him.

He hit the first one with a suppressor blast from his free arm, and that Psycho went flying, falling backward, jaws snapping, limbs flailing, and eyes wild. He landed on a shanty three stories below and squashed it flat. A warning *blaat* sounded inside Bretton's helmet, and he noted that his suit's power supply was now at critical levels. Power would fail at any second, and soon he would feel the full weight of his armor as the suit's power-assist went offline.

The second Psycho scrambled up Bretton's legs and sprang off his shoulders, landing in a crouch on the fire escape beside the fallen Imperial. He flashed Bretton a wicked grin of rotting teeth and licked his lips as he gazed down at his prey. Acting on instinct, Bretton aimed another suppressor blast at him, and the psycho went flying into the nearest wall.

He hit with a *crunch* of bone grinding against ancient bactcrete walls that were as heavy and solid as any rock. The Psycho's eyes rolled up in his head, and he collapsed.

Then, suddenly, power-assist failed and Bretton felt the full weight of his armor jerking him toward the ground. The arm he had wrapped around the railings shuddered, and he nearly lost his grip.

"Bret! Are you okay?"

"No!" Bretton growled. Cursing once more, he crawled through the railings to lie panting between the Imperial and the fallen Psycho. Powered systems were failing fast now, but at least his comms were still online.

"What's wrong? Are you hurt?"

"Not yet, but I'm tapped out. Systems are going offline. You'd better get down here before this animal wakes up and tears us both apart."

"Already ahead of you, boss."

A sharp whistling noise reached his ears via his helmet's aural sensors and he looked up to see their air car hovering down beside the fire escape.

"Good," he grunted, struggling to rise despite the weight of his armor. He managed to regain his footing, but the prospect of either dragging or carrying the Imperial was too much. "Mind giving me a hand with our cargo?"

"I'll be right there," Farah replied.

* * *

ASCENDANCY

City lights flashed by to either side of the air car as Farah raced away from the Psycho den. Bretton sat in the copilot's seat, wearing a plain black under suit. His Peacekeeper armor with its depleted power core lay in a gleaming pile in the back of the hover, while the man they'd rescued lay on the back seat, bleeding from myriad injuries, but still breathing. He was unconscious from a blow to the head, but at least he wasn't bleeding out.

"Where to?" Farah asked from the pilot's seat beside him.

Bretton considered that, frowning over his shoulder at their mysterious passenger. "Let's take him to Dag."

"We don't even know if he wants to be a Null."

"Well, we can't ask him without Omnius realizing he hasn't gone through *The Choosing* yet. Peacekeepers will come and get him before we have a chance to learn anything."

"What are you hoping to learn? Never mind—it doesn't matter. He's not our problem, Bret. Tara Halls, remember? She's our meal ticket, and she's the one we were sent to find—not some runaway survivor from the war."

Bretton shook his head. "We can get back to chasing rich brats another day. Right now, we need to find out more about this guy. How did he get here? What's going on in the rest of the galaxy? Where did he come from, and are there any other survivors? Those are things the Resistance needs to know."

"The Resistance doesn't pay our rent, Bret."

"They could if we enlist."

"I don't want you to get yourself killed."

"You remember what you told me about why you enlisted in the ISSF all those years ago?"

"That was another lifetime. A lot's changed since then."

"You said everybody dies, but not everybody dies well."

"I've already died well. Maybe this time around I want to live."

"So why did you join me in the Null Zone? You could have stayed a Peacekeeper, lived forever in Etheria."

"I don't want to die of boredom either. This way I got the best of both. I'm forever young, immortal, *and* I don't have to live in an insufferably perfect paradise."

Bretton snorted. They'd both been resurrected by Omnius when they died near the end of the war. After that, they'd become Peacekeepers in the hopes of rejoining the fight against the Sythians. Instead, they'd been sent around Avilon chasing crime before it happened. That might have been good enough, but Bretton hadn't been resurrected alone. His wife had already been on Avilon waiting for him when he'd arrived. Almost nine years after that happy reunion, something terrible happened, and Bretton had left her, paradise, and Peacekeeping for good in order to become a Null. His niece, Farah, had followed him for reasons only known to her. And both of them had taken a souvenir with them from Etheria—they had already been resurrected. That meant they had perfect clone bodies and they would never die of old age. Of course, in a place as dangerous as the Null Zone, old age probably wouldn't have killed them anyway.

"Well, if we're going to get him de-linked, then you'd better stun him before he wakes up," Farah said. "Dag will kill us if we bring him a *live wire*."

Bretton opened a dash compartment and withdrew a hefty pistol. Setting the weapon to stun, he turned it on the back seat and pulled the trigger. A dull *screech* sounded, and a flash of blue light dazzled his eyes.

"That should keep him from waking up until Dag's through with him."

"What if he gets upset when he finds out he could have lived forever in paradise?"

"Too bad. I saved his life. That means I'm calling the shots. Besides, if I'm right about him being from the Imperium, he won't even know what he's missing until we've already gotten all our answers from him."

"That's cold, Bret. Even for you."

"It's a cold world. Getting colder every day. When's the last time you saw the sun?"

"That's not what I meant."

He shook his head. "Down here we don't have the luxury of being soft. There's more lives at stake than his."

Farah grew silent at that. Bretton watched the endless night of the city flicker by them in a blur of colorful light and starkly-drawn shadows. Air traffic raced ahead of them in orderly, auto-piloted lines, red tail lights shining crimson in the gloom of the under city.

Farah turned off the autopilot and peeled away from the main artery of traffic to get to Dag's place. Dag managed to avoid trouble with the law by living on the *surface*. Down there, organized crime was the law.

Bretton set his pistol from stun to *kill* and withdrew a utility belt and holster from the dash compartment. He buckled the belt and holstered the weapon on his hip, looking up just in time to see them plunge down through a thick wall of filthy gray fog. The lights of the city disappeared, becoming dim, amorphous balls of light. Farah turned on a sensor overlay so they could still see their surroundings. Outlines of buildings and structures raced by, projected on the forward viewport in shades of blue and green.

They reached the surface and flew along a crumbling street, hovering just a few feet above the ground. At this level, the buildings were mostly dark. A few neon signs or holographic displays flickered through the gloom, and some shady-looking pedestrians walked the streets. The city was always alive, even down here, but these weren't the kind of people you'd like to say hello to.

"You didn't tell Dag you were coming, did you?" Farah asked.

"No, when would I have had a chance to do that?"

"He doesn't like drop-ins."

"He's going to have to. He owes me."

Farah snorted. "If you say so." After a few more minutes of flying, she said, "We're almost there. You want me to park on the street and wait, or should I go in with you?"

"Can't risk getting our ride jacked. You'd better stay. Keep her running."

"Sure thing. Want me to get us something to eat while I wait?"

"That's a good idea."

"All right." She pulled to a stop along a particularly dark section of the street and turned to him with her hand held out expectantly. "Twenty *bytes*."

Bretton eyed her palm. "What? You don't have *twenty* bytes?"

Farah shook her head. "I'm broke."

"*We're* broke," he amended.

"You want to eat or not?"

"Put it on credit," he growled, opening the passenger's side door and climbing out into the murky gray soup. Farah called something after him, but he shut the door before he heard what it was. Outside, the air was damp and cold, rich with fetid smells. Bretton took a quick look around, eyes scanning the shifting gray clouds of moisture. Neon signs from bars, nightclubs, and casinos set the fog aglow in all the colors of the rainbow, peeling away the gloom with halos of blurry light. He checked in a full 360 degrees, his hand ready on the butt of his sidearm.

The street was deserted.

So far so good.

He opened the rear passenger's side door and immediately heard Farah again.

"We don't have any credit left, Bret!"

"Then we'll eat later!"

"Maybe we should go looking for Tara Halls instead of chasing after the way things used to be."

"I'm not trying to relive the glory days of the Imperium, Farah. I'm trying to fix what's wrong with Avilon before it's too late and Omnius decides to stop being coy about how he disposes of us Nulls."

Farah arched an eyebrow at him. "We don't have any proof that he's disposing of Nulls."

Bretton's mouth curved into a smirk. "Not yet. I have to get going. Wait here and keep your eyes open, okay?"

"Be careful."

Bretton nodded. "I will. If you see any trouble, send the signal. I'll keep my head down until you give the *all clear.*"

"All right."

Bretton drew a small grav gun from his utility belt.

Aiming it at the unconscious Imperial, he picked the man up and hovered him out into the street. Bretton made his way to a rusty red door. A flickering green sign above it read, *Implant-it.* Dag's legitimate side business was implanting cybernetics.

Bretton set the Imperial down on the stairs. Stepping up to the door, he knocked twice, then once, then three times more, so Dag would know it was a friend.

Moments later he heard a *clunk* as deadbolts slid aside, and then a rusty *groan* as the door cracked open. A pair of glowing orange eyes appeared in the crack.

"Hello, Dag."

"You brought me a client?" a deep voice growled. The orange eyes flicked to the man lying on the steps.

"That's right."

The door swung wide, and Dag reached out of the shadows with a long, over-muscled black arm. He picked the Imperial up by his flight suit and dragged him inside. Bretton followed, closing and locking the door behind them.

"You got the bytes?"

"You owe me, remember?"

Dag grunted and turned away. Bretton followed him through the gloom, careful to watch his step. Dag could see in the dark thanks to the augmented reality contacts he wore. Bretton eschewed them just for the bittersweet memories they evoked from Etheria.

They walked from the dark, cluttered foyer to another door, this one flanked by a glowing blue control panel. Dag stepped up to it and typed in a key code. The door popped open with a hiss of escaping air. A crack of light appeared between the door and the jamb, and when Dag opened it, the light flooded out, dazzling Bretton's eyes.

They walked into a small antechamber with two sliding glass doors. The first one *swished* open for them as they approached, while the second remained closed. The walls glowed brightly and steam hissed from the ceiling.

"I want you to de-link him," Bretton said, suddenly realizing he hadn't been very specific about calling in his favor.

The door shut behind them, and the hissing from the ceiling grew more insistent. The room filled with a sweet-smelling mist that would sterilize them for the operation room beyond. Dag was wearing a simple green gown, baggy enough to hide his muscle, but not his size. He made the taller-than-average man dangling from his hand look tiny.

"He's unlisted," Dag said as the sterilizing mist stopped hissing into the room. "That usually means he's not linked...."

"Trust me, he is."

Swish. The inner door opened.

They passed from the antechamber into a locker room with hooks, hangars, and racks. On one of the hangars was a simple green gown like the one Dag wore, a see-through cap to keep stray hairs on Bretton's head, and a pair of slippers.

"Get changed," Dag said. Even though his head was bald, he donned a cap, too.

"Where did you find him?" Dag asked as he busied himself with undressing the unconscious Imperial.

"He wandered into a Psycho den and sat down to eat his lunch."

"Stupid or suicidal?"

Bretton shook his head. "Neither. He's not from here. Check the markings on his suit. He's an Imperial."

"That's *unusual* . . . He know he's gettin' de-linked?" Dag asked as they finished getting changed. Now their patient was wearing a blue gown and a see-through cap of his own. No slippers, though. Dag picked him up and slung him over one shoulder like a sack of vegetables.

Here Bretton had to twist the truth. "He has no desire to become an Etherian." How could you want to be something before you knew what that something was?

"All right."

They walked to the end of the locker and passed through a final door into a brightly-lit room full of shining metal. In the center of the room was a naked gray table where Dag gently laid the Imperial down. That done, he reached up and grabbed an overhead light attached to a jointed-metal arm. Dag positioned the lamp over the man's head and then turned to an adjacent display and control console. He spent a moment configuring it before a fan of light flickered out from the lamp, passing from the top of the Imperial's head to the base of his neck and back up again.

Dag studied the holographic display that appeared above his control console. "Looks like he's got two Lifelinks. You want 'em both disabled?"

"What?" Bretton shook his head and walked around the foot of the table to see what Dag was talking about. A three-dimensional map of the Imperial's brain was on the screen. Two small blue spheres glowed bright amidst a sea of other cerebral structures. The implants were sitting one beside the other, one slightly larger than the other. "Which one is Omnius's?"

Dag pointed to the smaller one. "The other one is made with materials that I've never seen used in a Lifelink before. It might not be a Lifelink, but it's in the right place."

"Any chance we can connect to it and see what's inside?"

Dag turned to him with a furrowed brow. "That's quite an invasion of privacy."

"What do you care?"

"Just makin' sure your conscience lets you sleep at night."

"I'll sleep like a baby."

Dag snorted. "Let me see what I can do." He walked over to another console and began peppering the control panel with commands. Another holographic display appeared in the air. As Dag studied it, he slowly shook his head. "This one's encrypted with some type of hieroglyphics."

Bretton went to read it over Dag's shoulder. As soon as his eyes parsed the first line, a cold chill swept through him from head to toe. He stood staring at the screen, his mouth agape, his dark eyes wide.

"What?" Dag asked, turning to see Bretton's shock.

"It's not scrambled. That's Sythian."

Dag's glowing orange eyes narrowed to thoughtful slits. "He's a human."

"Not anymore. If I had to guess, I'd say the Sythians used that implant to turn him against us."

"Then we should break his neck while we have the chance," Dag said. Daggert wasn't a former citizen of the Imperium, but Avilonians had no love for the skull faces either.

"No . . . I have a better idea," Bretton replied. He'd been hoping to glean vital information about the war and the state of the galaxy beyond Avilon, to maybe find something the Resistance could use, but now he had something even better than a survivor from the war—he had a Sythian agent.

"Where did you find this guy?" Dag asked.

"I told you, in a Psycho den."

"Well, he can't have been on Avilon long. If he had, he'd

know better."

"Let's go on a mind walk before you de-link him."

"Full immersion or audio-visual?"

"Audio-visual. I need to be objective about what I see."

Dag passed him a shiny black helmet with no visor and directed him to sit in a nearby chair. Bretton walked over to it and sat down. He placed the helmet over his head and everything turned a soulless black.

"What are we looking for?" Dag asked.

"Let's try the last two hours of recorded memory. I want to know how he got here and what he's been doing." A moment later a glowing green number appeared before Bretton's eyes, counting down from five.

The countdown reached zero, and suddenly Bretton found himself flying high above a burning city. The sky was alive with streaks of fire and tumbling debris. The city was Celesta. Sythian ships rained like confetti from the sky. Bretton watched, wide-eyed as the battle unfolded. The Null Zone was completely cut off from any news from the Uppers, so this was all news to him. The Sythians were attacking Avilon, and they were being routed.

Bretton watched as his viewpoint shifted, diving toward the burning city and a gaping hole in Celesta's shield. Over the next few minutes he got to see exactly how the Imperial Sythian agent had reached the surface of Avilon and eventually stumbled into a den of Psychos. The mind walk ended as the Psychos beat the man senseless.

Bretton removed the helmet to find Dag staring at him. "The Sythians found us," the de-linker said.

"We turned them back."

"For now. You saw what they did to Celesta."

The implication of that was left unspoken between them.

If the Sythians could get past Avilon's orbital defenses once, maybe they could do it again, and this time, finish the job.

But having a Sythian agent's mind at their disposal gave them a unique advantage—they might be able to see what the Sythians were planning.

"I'm going back in," Bretton said. "We need to see what else this guy knows."

CHAPTER 6

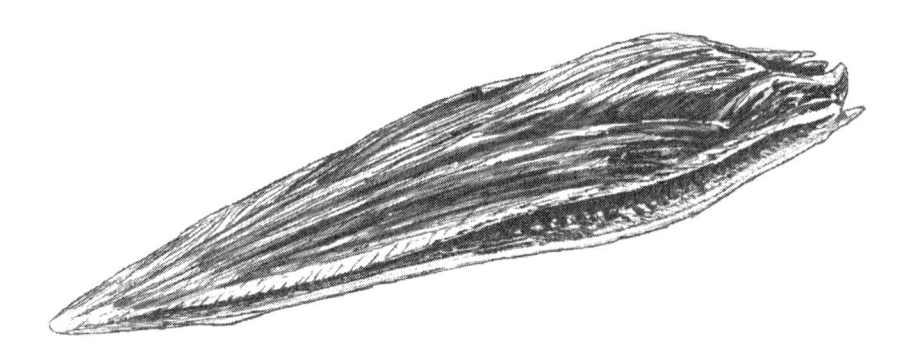

Six Sythian High Lords and Lady Kala stood in a circle in a dark room. In the center of the circle was a glowing orb on a low pedestal. The orb was tied to the *Agmar's* long-range communications array. It pulsed with crimson light as the comm array searched the vastness of space for another like itself.

Suddenly the orb glowed a solid red, washing the lords in a bloody light. A cool, silken voice slithered into the room: "What news of our conquests? Has the human pestilence been eliminated yet?" On the heels of that voice, a hologram flickered to life above the orb. It was Shallah. Cloaked in a dark uniform, his rubbery, translucent skin was all but hidden from view. Only his face remained visible, a spider's web of blue veins beneath his skin. He was of the same sub species as Kaon—a Quarn.

As the most senior of the lords, Kaon stepped forward and dropped to one knee before Shallah. "We make progress, Supreme One. We now control the human refuge known as Dark Space and their people are replacing the Gors as crew for our warships."

"But?"

Shallah always seemed to know what Kaon was about to say even before he said it. That sixth sense of intuition had been an integral part of his rise to supremacy.

"But . . ." Kaon realized that as the messenger he now shared in the shame of Lord Shondar's recent defeat at Avilon. "We find another human refuge. They are many, and they are strong. We cannot best them."

"Tell me more."

Kaon explained how Lord Shondar had been sent with half a fleet to scout the lost human sector of Avilon and report back. Shondar had found the sector in the midst of a crisis, the Avilonians' fleets temporarily disabled, and he'd seized the chance to decimate them. Then the Avilonians' defenses had come back online unexpectedly, tearing Shondar's fleet apart. He'd even lost his thirty kilometer-long command ship, the *Gasha*. It had been hiding in low orbit behind a cloaking shield, but despite that, the Avilonians had somehow found and destroyed it anyway.

When Kaon finished explaining, he expected a harsh rebuke, or perhaps to be summarily stripped of all rank and title. After all, this was the *second* command ship he had lost in the past few months.

Instead, Shallah replied, "So these *Avilonians* can see through our cloaking shields. . . . It would appear that they are a more formidable foe than the Imperium was."

"Yes, Master. They are."

"You do not contact me merely to burden me with the shame of your defeat. . . ." Shallah intoned. Kaon's head hung low, bowed in obeisance, his face mere inches from the cold deck. Nevertheless, he felt the Supreme One's eyes on him as surely as if he could see Shallah's cerulean irises. "You make contact to beg for reinforcements." The Supreme One's voice dripped with condescension. "Have you no honor left?"

"There is no honor in defeat, Master. If we face these Avilonians alone, we go to our deaths."

"Yessss, so it would ssseem. How many more clusters do you need?"

"As many as you can spare, Great One."

"It is that serious?"

"I fear if we do not defeat them soon, they may one day travel to the Getties and defeat us."

Shallah laughed at that. "Do not overestimate your new foe. If you can hold out for the next *orbit*, you shall have a *hundred* new clusters. I trust that is sufficient force for you to prevail?"

Kaon's mind balked at the thought of managing a hundred fleets. Throughout the invasion he had managed just seven, but he decided that more could only be better, not worse. A doubt lingered in his mind. "How will you crew such a vast armada?"

The Sythians' savage slave army, which had earned them the human pejorative—*skull faces*—had become unreliable of late, taking an entire fleet and disappearing with it as soon as their command ship had been destroyed. That fleet had been none other than Kaon's *First Fleet,* and the command ship had been his. After that, Kaon had decided to replace the Gors with human slaves, harvested from Dark Space.

When Shallah had heard about the Gor rebellion, his reaction had been similar. He'd retaliated by purging their icy home world of Noctune, killing their women and their children.

"For now we shall crew them with the future colonists of the Adventa Galaxy. Once we strip Avilon of its defenses, we shall begin harvesting it for a new slave army to replace them."

Kaon inclined his head. "May it be so, Master."

"There is something else you want to say."

"Yes, Great One, forgive me, but . . . the Avilonians may come soon. Far sooner than a standard orbit, and I fear our defenses cannot hold them."

"I have a few clusters close by. They were assigned to begin spreading colonies in the Adventa Galaxy, but I suppose that must now wait."

Kaon's twin hearts began beating faster. "How many clusters, Master?"

"Twenty-six."

"How many can you spare?"

"I shall send them all, lest mere humans be allowed to best my Lords for a third time. Expect the first clusters to arrive soon. They come bearing a new weapon for the war."

"A new weapon, Master?"

"Yesss. For now, it shall remain a surprise. I trust you will not fail me again. . ."

"No, Great One. We shall not!"

"Then on to victory! For glory!"

"For glory!" the six Lords and Lady Kala chanted as one.

Shallah ended contact from the other side and his hologram disappeared. The bloody hue in the room faded as the glowing orb became a shiny black pearl. A faint lavender light remained, which was enough for their sensitive eyes to see by.

Kaon rose and turned to the others. "Soon our forces in Dark Space shall be enough to repel the enemy, and in one orbit we shall have enough warships to blot out the stars!"

"We must hope the Avilonians do not come for us before

sufficient reinforcements arrive," Lord Shondar replied. His glowing white gaze found Kaon and lingered for a long moment. The long topknot of white hair cascading from his gray scalp glowed bright lavender in the gloom of the comms center. "What of our agent in Avilon?"

"He remains hidden."

"Might he be able to warn us of a coming attack?" Lady Kala asked, her red eyes glinting in the dark. She seemed to unfold to her full height, skinny limbs snapping straight. With her diminutive size, and round, almost child-like face, Kala was the smallest and least intimidating presence in the room. Each of them was the representative of one of the seven sub-species of the Sythian Coalition, and Kala, with her slight, wiry frame and delicate, shiny black skin seemed to fade into the shadows of any room. Her slightness was a hideous trick, however. Her sub-species, the *Kylians*, had vicious sets of retractable claws and a pair of wings that enabled them to fly. If the Supreme One sent her kind aboard the reinforcing fleets, humanity would soon have an even more terrible face to haunt their nightmares than that of the *dreaded, skull-faced Gors.*

"Yes, it would be wise to find out if your *pet* can warn us," Lord Worval put in.

"I shall make contact with him soon to give him new orders," Kaon replied.

"Do so now. We wait," Lady Kala replied.

"I cannot. He is unreachable. I suspect he sleeps now."

Shondar hissed loudly. "Or he is dead."

"If the humans come for us before reinforcements arrive, do we stay here and fight?" Lord Thorian asked.

"We are Sythians," Kaon hissed. "We do not run from battle like terrified children."

"Prudence would have us flee while we can," Lady Kala replied.

Kaon's eyes flashed. "Flee?" He turned in a slow circle to address all of them at once. *"Flee?"* he repeated, making the word sound shrill. "We are immortal. It is not death we should fear, but shame. If we flee, our honor turns to disgrace, and our victories become as dust in the wind! No, we shall not flee. We fight! For glory!"

"For glory!" the Sythians chanted once more.

Lady Kala did not chant with them. Kaon's gaze found hers and he stared at her. She stared back, her red eyes locked with his blue. Her glossy black lips peeled back from needle-sharp teeth, and she said, "I go to prepare my *cluster.*"

"As do we all," Lord Worval added.

The group broke up and they began leaving the comms center. Kaon couldn't help wondering at Lady Kala's dissent as they left. Would she stand with them if the Avilonians came?

"Lady Kala, wait," Kaon said. Red eyes met his once more.

"I shall accompany you aboard the *Kilratha*."

Lady Kala hissed. "Why?"

"The Gors have my fleet, and particles of my command ship are scattered across the sector."

"You have the humans' fleet that we capture."

"I cannot lead us from human ships as well as I can from our own."

"Then perhaps it is time for you to step aside and let someone else lead."

Kaon cocked his round, fish-like head. "And who might that be?"

Kala bared her needle-sharp teeth again. "Sssomeone

else."

"Not you?"

"No."

"Shallah decides who leads us. My victories are too many to be erased by one defeat. You shall yield your vessel and your cluster to me for the coming battle."

"Yess... *My Lord.*"

There was a twist of sarcasm in Kala's voice that Kaon didn't like, but he chose to ignore it. He followed Lady Kala out of the comms center, listening as her claws scratched the deck, extending and retracting restlessly. She was angry, and not bothering to hide her displeasure.

Kaon's mind turned to the coming battle. He could only hope that Shondar had done enough damage to the Avilonians' forces while they had been disabled that now they couldn't project their strength as far as Dark Space. If not, perhaps sufficient reinforcements would arrive before the Avilonians did. Certainly, with twenty-six new clusters even the Avilonians would be outmatched. Kaon smiled, allowing hope to bleed through his despair.

For glory. The battle cry whispered through his thoughts, as if tip-toeing around his fears, but Kaon chose to focus on the positive. Reinforcements would arrive in time to save them.

Any other thought would admit the possibility of defeat, and defeat, as ever, was unacceptable.

* * *

Destra Heston's face was bathed in a hard blue light, making her look far older than her 45 years. The light came from the holographic grid rising above the captain's table aboard the *Baroness*. At the table with her were two others. To her left stood Captain Covani, bald and black with bright tangerine eyes. His usually round face bore few of the marks of age, but stress and worry had drawn semi-permanent lines across his brow. Right now those lines were trenches, his warmly-colored eyes were cold, and his once-rounded cheeks looked gaunt. Destra thought maybe the gaunt cheeks were just a trick of the light, but with the past few weeks of rationing, the effect could easily be from starvation.

"Get them out of there, Torv!" Covani gritted.

"I cannot," a deep voice said from Destra's right. She tried not to look at the Gor, but he was all she could see in her peripheral vision. He was wearing his glossy black, chitin-like armor, and the optics in his helmet glowed red, looking like two multi-faceted insect eyes. The overall shape of his helmet and the face behind it, were that of a giant skull. She was thankful Torv was wearing his armor. Without it he would have been even more terrifying.

"What do you mean you can't?" Covani challenged.

"They do not listen. Their blood lust controls them now."

"Well tell them to snap out of it!"

"We are starving, *Captain*," Torv replied. "Not even I would obey if I had the chance to sink my teeth into something *fresh*."

Destra shuddered, and again she tried to ignore the presence of the Gor. She watched, horrified as the team of Gors they'd sent to the surface, represented by green dots on the sterile blue grid, swarmed toward the target warehouse, running straight into a trap. Hundreds of red dots, no doubt human slaves, were waiting for them inside what should have been a deserted warehouse, full of vegetables ready for export off Forliss. Destra chewed her lower lip, watching as the green dots drew nearer to the red.

"Someone get me a visual feed!" Covani snapped to his crew.

"Feed coming in, sir," the comms officer announced a moment later.

Covani looked up to the main forward viewport, and Destra followed his gaze. She glimpsed a crescent of light and color painted against the black of space—day dawning on the far side of Forliss. Then that view dissolved, replaced by crooked shadows of trees flickering over rippling fields of long grass. Grass rasped and rustled noisily through the bridge speakers as the Gor whose viewpoint they'd stolen ran toward a high, dark shape on the horizon. All around were trails of flattened grass, appearing like magic as cloaked Gors raced toward the warehouse and the Sythian slaves they'd somehow scented on the wind.

Those trails converged on the wooden doors of the gray, castcrete warehouse. The nearest Gor reached the doors and they exploded in a shower of splintered wood. Like that, the Gors squandered the element of surprise their cloaking armor should have afforded.

The one with the camera attached to his helmet raced through the splintered doors into a dazzlingly bright chaos of flashing red pulse lasers and bright glow lamps. Crates of produce shattered and exploded with colorful sprays of vaporized vegetable matter.

The Gors didn't bother to fire back; they raced silently and unseen through the enemy ranks breaking necks and shattering sternums with their bare hands. The Sythian soldiers all wore a shrunken parody of the Gors' glossy black armor, but it was easy to tell that they were human—red blood spurted from the joins in their armor, not Sythian-white, or Gor-clear. Destra watched the bloody massacre unfold with a growing grimace. She began to think the Gors might even be able to overwhelm the enemy soldiers, but then she began to see Gors appearing out of thin air, taking off their helmets and thoughtlessly tossing them aside, disrupting their cloaking shields so that they could rip into the enemy with their jaws and teeth.

Now lasers flashed not randomly but with deadly precision. Destra watched one Gor hit by a stuttering hail of no less than a dozen laser bolts, but he was so intent upon his kill that he kept feeding long seconds after he should have realized that he was dead.

"Switch it off," Covani growled. He turned to her with a grave expression. "We can't keep this up, Councilor."

"Two more weeks."

Covani shook his head. "It's already been more than two *months*. The Gors aren't going to last much longer like this, and neither will we. We're cut off from our supply lines, and now the Sythians are locking theirs down."

Destra hesitated. Over two months ago, her late husband,

Admiral Hoff Heston, had sent her son, Atton, to Avilon, looking for reinforcements. He should have returned long ago. Without Captain Covani's knowledge, she'd appealed to Atton's father, her ex-husband, Ethan, asking him to go look for Atton at the coordinates Hoff had given their son, but even Ethan should have returned by now. He was more than a week late. Destra felt she had to wait at least another week for him, but by the determined set to Captain Covani's lips, she knew his mind was already made up. The captain didn't and *couldn't* know about Ethan's follow-up mission to Avilon, because then he would know that she had the coordinates for the lost sector, and he would try to take all of them there. Hoff had strictly warned her that the Avilonians wouldn't accept them all as refugees, particularly not the Gors. A lot might have changed since her husband had lived in Avilon, but she suspected he was at least right about the Gors.

"Where would we go?" she asked.

"Anywhere beyond the old Imperium. Somewhere the Sythians won't have been yet. Ideally somewhere with plenty of wildlife for the Gors to hunt and plenty of arable land for us to start a colony."

"We have just over 150 men and women on board, Captain. That's not much to start a colony. We should stop to rescue as many people as we can before we go."

Covani shook his head. "I'd love to, but there's no way we can be sure the people we rescue haven't been turned into Sythian slaves yet. If we take even one of them with us, the Sythians will follow us wherever we go."

"What about Etaris?"

"What about it? Same problem there."

"Not if we only rescue people from lock-up. Why make a prisoner a slave and then leave him in his cell? The ones the

Sythians have messed with will already be gone or walking around free."

"You can't be serious. They're head cases! Why would we want to rescue them? Let them rot."

Lock-ups on Etaris were only used for the worst offenders, with the majority of the world's prisoner population allowed to live and work more or less freely—so long as they didn't try to leave the planet.

Destra shook her head. "Humanity can't afford to be picky when it's down to so few. Keep the prisoners in the brig and use them as indentured workers when we get wherever we're going. They're already used to that on Etaris. We'll need all the help we can get if we're going to start over somewhere new."

"She is right," Torv put in, proving that he'd been listening to their entire conversation. "These prisoners may not have much honor left, but every person we take with us is one that we shall not someday face in battle when the Sythians find us again."

Covani gave a deep sigh. "Helm! Plot a course for Etaris. Torv, tell the Gor fleet where we're going."

"I shall tell my creche lord now."

"Our children will be standing on the shoulders of thieves and murderers. . . ." the captain muttered. Destra noticed that his gaze lingered on Torv as he said that. Despite the fact that the Gors had ultimately sided with humanity against their Sythian masters, no one had forgotten the savagery of the original invasion.

With images of Gors ripping into human flesh during the warehouse raid still fresh in her mind, Destra couldn't help feeling uneasy about the future. She looked away, out to the growing slice of daylight where the sun was now peeking out behind the far side of Forliss. "Our children will have to stand on something, Captain," she said.

Covani snorted at that and joined her in stargazing. Together they watched as the helm turned them on a new course, heading for a particularly bright star that was actually a neighboring planet. Etaris, the world where Ethan had been sent before the war had even begun. Back then she'd wondered how she would live with the pain of losing him. His absence had ripped a hole in her heart that had never fully healed. Now her second husband, Hoff, was dead, rather than merely exiled, leaving their daughter, Atta, without a father, and her, once again alone. This time she didn't feel like she'd been ripped open. She just felt like there was nothing there anymore, her chest an empty cavity where something vital used to be. After losing so much, she was surprised she hadn't stepped out an airlock already. In fact, she was surprised no one else had. Everyone on board had just lost everything that mattered to them for the second time in recent history. What was the point in rebuilding for a third?

"Madam councilor . . . ? Ma'am?"

Destra realized then that someone had been talking to her. She turned toward the voice to see the *Baroness's* comm officer looking up at her. "Your daughter is on the line. . . ."

"And?"

The comm officer's eyes flicked briefly to the captain, and then a warm color suffused his cheeks. "She said . . ." The officer trailed off and continued in a noticeably softer voice. "She said she can't sleep without someone there to chase the monsters away."

Destra's eyes crinkled and her lips twitched upward in a smile. "Tell her I'll be down in a minute."

"Yes, Ma'am."

Destra turned to Covani for dismissal, but he was already waving her away. "Go get some sleep, Councilor. I can handle things from here. I'll wake you before the mission gets underway."

She nodded and turned to leave, her boots striking a brisk, echoing cadence on the polished duranium gangway. There was a new purpose in her stride. She had her answer, both for herself and for humanity. It was the same reason humanity had always pressed on through adversity—

Children.

They were humanity's hope for the future. Destra's hope was that her children would have a future.

CHAPTER 7

Ethan and Alara walked down the hallway from their room. They'd found a pair of white robes hanging in the closet—just like the ones they'd seen their loved ones wearing when they'd all been reunited in the clouds. That had been just last night, but it seemed like a few short hours ago.

Ethan turned to watch the abstract light paintings of human faces in the hallway as they walked by. They watched him back, but today all the faces were happy and smiling. Somehow that unnerved him more than seeing the few anguished ones mixed in.

They reached the stairs they'd climbed the night before and went down to the echoing foyer. The shiny marble floors and crystal chandelier looked even more luxurious in the light of day than they had at night. Now the mansion's many windows were bright and showing off panoramic views of blue sky and vast green parkland.

They heard muffled voices coming from beyond the far side of the foyer.

"I guess breakfast must be this way?" Alara said, heading toward the sound.

They walked down the side of the palace, past a wall of floor-to-ceiling windows that looked out on a shimmering, sapphire-blue lake, fed by the river they'd crossed the night before. It was hard to imagine all of this was somehow built on the rooftop of what the Avilonians called Destiny Tower.

They emerged in a massive dining hall. The air was alive with the smell of fresh-baked bread and caf. Everyone was already busy drinking the latter and buttering the former on their plates with golden knives. Another crystal chandelier hung above an extra-long glossy black table with pristine white chairs. Everyone was already seated there, wearing matching white robes, and speaking in a nonsensical babble of simultaneous conversations.

The dining room was surrounded by windows. Outside, an inviting pool ran the length of the hall. An artificial waterfall cascaded into that pool, shining like liquid crystal in the morning sun.

Most of the faces at the table were familiar—Ethan's son, Atton; Ceyla and Razor, pilots in Atton's squadron; Captain Caldin; Delayn, her XO; another one of her crew that Ethan didn't recognize, and a group of navy sentinels. Six Peacekeepers were seated with the refugees.

"Good morning," Ethan said.

Conversations ended abruptly as heads turned and people noticed them standing there.

"Good morning," Atton replied, and Ethan noted that his son was also speaking in Avilonian rather than Versal.

"Nice of you to finally join us," Rovik said, twisting around in his chair to face them. "Why don't you take a seat and we can get started."

Captain Caldin called down from the foot of the table, "You can start with the fact that we all had the same dream last night. What the frek is going on around here?"

Ethan and Alara moved to take their seats at the table,

leaving four empty places between them and the line of Peacekeepers.

"The dream you all experienced was a walk through history, a shared experience of someone else's memories or *mind walk*. The mind you were walking through was mine."

"So it was real . . . *you* found the Sythians before anyone else did," Atton said.

"Dreams in Avilon are not random or nonsensical. Here Omnius speaks to us through our dreams."

"So what's the point of showing us what you found in the Getties Cluster? We already know the Sythians came from there," Atton replied.

"The point of Omnius's nightly revelations will come clear by the end of The Choosing. Now—we have a busy day ahead of us, so if there are no more pressing questions, it's time for us to eat."

"Just one more question." One of the sentinels at the table raised his hand. "I had family back in Dark Space . . . last night we heard from the . . . Admiral, if that was really him, that there are plans to rescue everyone there and bring them to Avilon."

"The man you saw was indeed Admiral Hoff Heston, and that is correct," Rovik replied. "When I am done guiding you through The Choosing, I will join the offensive with my ship."

"Any chance I can get in on the fight?" the sentinel said. His voice was subdued, but there was an eagerness to the way he leaned over the table, hands twitching and fidgeting, his dark eyes glinting sharp as any daggers. "I've got a score to settle with the skull faces."

"You are more than welcome to join the Peacekeepers if you decide to live in Etheria. If you join the Nulls, however, you will not have the honor of serving anyone but yourself."

The sentinel sat back in his chair, looking satisfied with that. "Well, I already know what I'm choosing. You can skip the tour for me."

"The Choosing is not optional, but you will have more than enough time to join the Peacekeepers when it's over." Galan's glowing blue eyes roved around the table addressing each of them in turn. "Something you should all know, a week on Avilon is not the seven days it was in the old Etherian calendar. Our first day, as you might have guessed, will be spent exploring Celesta, the uppermost of the three cities on Avilon. Tomorrow, we'll tour Etheria. On the third day, we'll descend into the Null Zone. Then you will have a day to revisit whichever city you please and to reflect on the choice you will make. On the fifth day you will make your choice and prepare for your new life on Avilon." Rovik nodded to one of the other Peacekeepers. "Before we begin eating, Omnius has something for each of you."

The Peacekeeper Rovik had nodded to rose from the table and began distributing palm-sized white capsules to each of the refugees.

"Please don't open them yet," Rovik said. The capsules looked like the pocket-sized mirror case that Alara sometimes used to put on makeup. "They are your ARCs—Augmented Reality Contacts. Via these you will be in constant contact with the Omninet. ARCs give you a heads-up display for your daily lives. They are thought-activated, so you will be able to decide what information to display just by thinking about it. Of course, Omnius may choose to provide additional information as he deems necessary."

"So it's another way of keeping tabs on us," Ethan said, feeling his skin crawl.

"No, Omnius can already watch us perfectly well via our

Lifelinks. ARCs are for our benefit, to help us live in a world that is too vast and complicated for us to keep track of everything.

"Among other things, you will be able to see each other's names, citizenry ranks, real and apparent age, relationship status, and even a tag line, which you may or may not choose to display below your name. Go ahead, open the cases and put on your contacts. ARCs need never be removed, and you will not notice you are wearing them."

Ethan opened his case warily. Inside were two clear disks with tiny gold poles attache—something to hold the contacts while putting them on. The top of the case was a pocket-sized mirror.

"That's why your eyes glow . . ." Ethan heard his son say.

"Yes," Rovik replied.

Ethan grabbed the first pole between thumb and forefinger and used the mirror to put it on. Immediately a group of semi-transparent blue frames appeared around the edges of his vision, but they were all too blurry for him to decipher.

Beside him, Alara stirred. "If I'm constantly in contact with your planetary network, there must be a powerful transmitter in these. Is the radiation dangerous to us . . . or to a baby?"

"No, our communication systems are instantaneous and they do not generate radiation the way yours do. It is perfectly safe."

Ethan put in the second contact and suddenly the blue frames snapped into focus. In one of them he saw the weather, and a pair of news headlines. They read, *Fires still burning above the Celestial Wall* and *Omnius Rallies the Strategians for War*. Other frames gave him information about himself, *Heart Rate 92, Cholesterol Levels High, Projected Lifespan 76.* Ethan squeezed his eyes shut to make the display go away. It was back again as soon as he opened them. His pulse pounded in his ears and he watched his HR jump to 105. How dare Omnius tell him how long he was going to live!

He heard Alara gasp. Others around the table were having similar reactions. Ethan turned to his wife, "What is it?"

She shook her head, her violet eyes now glowing with an alien brightness. He watched her lips part in a smile. "Our baby! It's a *girl!*"

"*What?*" Ethan's anger faded, replaced by a spreading warmth that made his head feel suddenly light and airy, like the whole world had just suddenly become a better place. Alara's grin spread from her lips to his, and he grabbed her face in his hands and kissed it. "How do you know?"

"Because I can see her! I'm watching . . . I'm watching her now. Oh she's so beautiful. . . ."

"How? Where?" Ethan shook his head, trying to find where he could see the same thing on his display.

Master Rovik came up behind them and laid a hand on each of their shoulders. "Ethan, focus on the bottom corner of the display. Where it says *link,* then think about your wife. A confirmation dialog will appear. Think *yes.* Alara, you have to confirm the visual link."

Ethan did as he was told, and a moment later he was watching their baby, too, in full 3D, and what he supposed had to be simulated color. She was beautiful. Incredulous, Ethan turned to Master Rovik. "How are we able to see this?"

"Your Lifelinks were also designed to monitor your bodies, not just your brains. Among other things, the ability to image your bodies provides Omnius with a way to see mortal wounds before you die, so he can transfer your mind away before you suffer unduly. He can see a tumor growing before you know it's there, or yes, watch a baby growing in its mother's womb."

Ethan opened his mouth for a cutting remark, but he quickly shut it again and turned wordlessly away to focus on his daughter's tiny hands and feet. She looked so fragile, her body small and head too big. *You don't have a Lifelink yet,* he thought. *No one watching you except for us. You've got no cares in the world—just sleep and sweet baby dreams.*

His hand found Alara's and he held on tight, his resolve hardening faster than molten duranium. He knew he had to protect their daughter, to keep her safe from the world she would be born into. Avilon, with all of its pre-supposed perfection was plagued by a force much more insidious and frightening than the Sythians had ever been—Omnius, the AI god of Avilon, a force so powerful that it could even predict the future . . . *and maybe even make those predictions come true,* he thought.

Try as they might, the Sythians had never done anything that scary.

* * *

After breakfast they walked out onto the terrace and around the side of the palace to a broad gray platform. There a shuttle craft was hovering down for a landing, the sun reflecting brightly off its hull. Atton's eyes were somehow automatically shielded from the glare by the augmented reality contacts he wore, so he could see that the shuttle was shaped like a disk. The edges of the disk were transparent, and he could see rows of empty seats running around the rim, looking out. A name and ship type appeared on his ARC display. Bright yellow text hovered above the shuttle as it drew near—the *Sightseer*, a Quantum Space Jumper.

"Why send a transport to give us a tour of Celesta when they could just teleport us from one place to another?" Atton wondered aloud.

"Maybe they want us to appreciate the journey, not just the destination," Ceyla suggested, giving his hand a squeeze.

"Maybe."

All six of the Peacekeepers who'd joined them for breakfast stood with the refugees, waiting for the transport to land. As soon as it did, Master Rovik, the one with the cape, turned and gestured for them to follow. They boarded the shuttle and took seats along the rim, facing a floor-to-ceiling viewport that wrapped around under their feet and curved overhead. The Peacekeepers sat with them, spacing themselves out along the rim of the shuttle. Master Rovik disappeared behind a door that Atton supposed led to the cockpit, somewhere in the center of the disk-shaped craft.

"What's the first stop?" Ceyla asked the Peacekeeper who was sitting down beside her.

He turned to her with glowing yellow eyes. "You will see," was all he said.

The shuttle rose off the ground, giving an aerial view of the countryside around the top of Destiny Tower. There were dozens of mansions like the one they'd awoken in, gently rolling fields of grass and majestic trees filled the gaps between them. The nearest mansion was about a kilometer away. There Atton saw another transport like theirs, a bright speck hovering in for a landing. A small group of white-robed people waited on the landing pad below.

"Looks like we're not the only ones going on a tour," Atton said, pointing to the second transport.

"Are they refugees, too?" Ceyla asked.

This time Atton read the Peacekeeper's name from the glowing blue text that appeared above his head—*Templar Delon Tarn (Acolyte)*.

"They are Avilonian children," Delon replied.

Ceyla nodded. "Master Rovik mentioned something about that last night. Do all of your children have to go through The Choosing?"

"Yes."

"When did you go through yours?"

"At the same time as everyone else. Age eight."

"*Eight?* How can you possibly be expected to choose where you will live for the rest of your life when you're eight years old?"

"For most children The Choosing is just a formality. It is a chance to learn how the other half—or third—lives."

"But some children choose to go to the Null Zone."

"Yes. Some do."

"Do their families have to follow them?"

"No."

Ceyla gaped at the Peacekeeper. "What? You send them into the Null zone alone?"

"No one sends them. Those who choose to go, go freely. There are institutions to look after them."

"That's barbaric!"

"Barbarism is the product of free will. If we weren't free to choose, we wouldn't be responsible for our actions. Even children are accountable."

"But you can't expect *kids* to make the right choices when they're still so young!"

Atton chimed in, "Why make people choose at all?"

The Peacekeeper fixed Atton with his yellow-eyed gaze. "Would you like to live in paradise with a body that ages, sickens, and dies? You would eventually die and be forced to resurrect anyway."

Atton shook his head. "It should at least be an option to live in Etheria with the body you were born with."

Ceyla scowled. "How do you know you're not going to kill all of those kids when they transfer to their perfected bodies?"

Delon's yellow eyes narrowed. "Are you suggesting that what we are is more than physical matter?"

"I'd say it was more than a suggestion," Ceyla put in. She was an Etherian—the old kind—which meant that she believed in Etheria as a place that existed on some other plane of existence with a good god named Etherus who was the creator of the universe and ruler of Etheria. "Omnius's Lifelink implants are just a technological version of the immortal soul, and Omnius is a human-made version of Etherus," she said.

The Peacekeeper's lip twitched. "Your religion was founded on rumors of life on Avilon. There is no life after this one, so I suggest you accept Omnius's offer to preserve the one you have. You don't need to die, Miss Corbin."

Ceyla replied through gritted teeth, "The Etherian religion pre-dates Omnius and his so-called paradise."

"Really?" Delon cocked his head. "Show me the proof of

that, and I will shout it from the highest rooftops. I will personally lead a rebellion to overthrow Omnius and stop The Choosing once and for all."

"Aren't you afraid Omnius will hear you?" Atton asked through a smirk.

"I would never *actually* lead a rebellion against Him, because you can't prove that Omnius has been lying to us. We are not atheists by choice; we are atheists because no one, not even Omnius, can find proof of a life that exists beyond this one. One of the reasons for The Choosing is to weed out those who are susceptible to creationistic thinking. They would seek to undermine our entire way of life." Delon shook his head. "Those people will never tolerate the idea that this is all there is, and we will never tolerate their insistence that it isn't, so we live apart, with the religious fools living in shadows and governed by chaos, while the enlightened live in the light, governed by the truth."

Ceyla shook her head furiously, blond hair flaring over her shoulders, her blue eyes wild and flashing. "You are the fool," she whispered.

The Peacekeeper smirked and looked away, ending the conversation. Atton looked away, too. The Peacekeeper's arguments troubled him in a way he couldn't explain. He wasn't religious. He wasn't an atheist either. So what did it matter?

And yet, it did matter.

In the distance, the horizon appeared as a misty white line of tall buildings, shimmering in the morning sun. The seemingly endless countryside around the palace where they'd spent the night came to an abrupt end. Atton recalled the night sky, with all its shining stars, and he wondered about that. If the city lay all around them, the light from it had to be filtered out somehow or they wouldn't see the stars. No doubt the same something hid the skyscrapers from view when they were standing on the ground. *Smoke and mirrors,* Atton thought. It was tough to tell how much of what they saw on Avilon was simulated and how much of it was real.

The shuttle was still rising, now hovering at least 500 meters off the ground, but *ground* was a deceptive concept, since the rooftops below them, which formed the ground level of Celesta, were themselves a full kilometer above the real surface of the planet.

The shuttle spun in a slow circle to give them all a 360-degree view of their surroundings. Buildings rose up everywhere in the distance. Bright green parks adorned the rooftops of the low-rise buildings, and shimmering cascades of water skipped from one level of the city to another. In the very hazy distance, Atton could see a mid-level series of bridges or elevated streets criss-crossing between the highest buildings. Above and below those streets, faint, blurry black lines of air traffic etched the sky.

It looked so peaceful, so orderly and neat—a sharp contrast from the night before when the Sythians had turned it all into a raging inferno.

After the shuttle had made a full rotation, it suddenly leapt forward, but none of them felt the tug of movement. Countryside raced by beneath their feet. It ran to an abrupt end with a blue river of light that ran around the top of Destiny Tower—the shield that separated Celesta from Etheria. It was hexagonally segmented and semi-transparent, revealing the city of Etheria below. Then came the jagged rise and fall of low-rise towers and neatly organized parks. Narrow footpaths ran along the rooftops, and Atton spotted a train, running on elevated tracks. There were no streets on the ground for cars, but plenty of landing pads where they could hover down in front of the buildings.

Atton turned back to the Peacekeeper. "Why do you have transports on Avilon if you could just teleport from one place to another?"

"Because teleporting, as you call it, is expensive. Quantum jump drives are cheaper for long, interstellar distances, but for planetary travel we only make quantum jumps when time is of the essence."

"That makes sense ..." Atton said, quietly relieved that he wouldn't have to go through the disorienting process of *jumping* every time he wanted to go somewhere. "Where are we going?"

"You will see," Delon replied, repeating the short answer he'd given a few minutes ago.

Atton frowned, and Ceyla whispered to him, "What's with all the mystery?"

He shook his head. "Another part of Omnius's shock and awe program."

"Well, I'm running out of awe. He's already laying it on a bit thick," she replied.

Atton knew what she was talking about. The reunion with their loved ones in the clouds was a good example. Why reunite them in the sky, and use technological wizardry to make them all think they were somehow floating above the clouds? He had a feeling Omnius was using technology to inspire reverence. *Omnius grando est,* he thought, recalling the words of praise he'd heard last night. Back then he hadn't known what they'd meant, but he'd managed to guess—*Great is Omnius.*

Maybe by the end of the week he'd be chanting that, too.

CHAPTER 8

ASCENDANCY

Bretton took off the helmet and sat back in his chair, slowly blinking in the sterile white light of Dag's operating room. Dag had grown tired of standing at his control console and he was now slumping on a stool, wide-eyed with shock. Despite warning Farah to keep the engine running and keep a lookout for trouble, he'd told her to join him inside Dag's shop right after the initial revelation that the man they'd rescued was a Sythian agent. She was seated in a chair next to his, now yanking off her helmet, too.

"I wasn't expectin' that," Dag said simply.

"You think the Etherians know about this?" Farah asked.

"If they do, they've been awful quiet," Bretton said. Etherians were allowed to visit their loved ones in the Null Zone, but Nulls were not allowed to visit them in Etheria. That one-way flow of traffic brought with it the occasional news from the Uppers, but it was far from an official source, and Omnius didn't allow his people to share everything they knew. Perhaps this was one of the things they were keeping to themselves?

Farah busied herself with peeling a few sweaty blond locks of hair off her forehead. They'd had their heads inside those helmets for hours while Dag took them on a guided tour of Commander Lenon Donali's treacherous mind.

It wasn't Donali's fault that he was a traitor; he'd been made into a Sythian agent against his will, but now that Bretton knew the whole story, he couldn't help feeling like Donali's capture had been a stroke of fate.

"So we're all Sythians," Farah said.

"Not exactly. They're still millions of years down the evolutionary chain from us. That makes them alien enough," Bretton said.

"But they used to be humans," Farah replied.

Bretton nodded.

"I'm more surprised that there have been *two* Great Wars," Farah said. "One in this galaxy, and one in theirs. History repeated itself even after we should have known better."

"Maybe we forgot."

"Omnius is right to make us choose," Dag mused. "Immortals and mortals can't live together without slaughterin' each other over their beliefs."

"Do you think Omnius knows all this?" Farah asked.

"If someone out there with a working Lifelink knows about it, then so does he," Bretton replied.

"So why is this the first we're hearing about it?"

"Simple, Omnius lied," Bretton said.

Dag shook his head. "Lyin' ain't the same as omission. When you know everythin' there is to know, ain't possible to share it all."

Bretton smiled thinly. "We're not talking about demystifying quantum indeterminacy to predict the future. We're talking about the origins of our race. Omnius doesn't share everything he knows because if he did, he wouldn't have the upper hand anymore."

Dag shrugged. "What's it matter if he hid that from us?"

Bretton gave an incredulous snort. "If he's hiding where we came from, maybe that's not all he's hiding. We need something to open peoples' eyes, to make them see what Omnius really is, and why they should shut him down. This could be it."

"Even if you get it right, they'll never all see that at once," Dag replied. "And I'm not sure we *can* shut him down. You're wastin' your life with bitterness, Bret, and it's goin' to get you killed."

"Just because it's personal doesn't mean I'm wrong. You can hide down here and pretend we're not oppressed because Omnius more or less keeps his nose out of our affairs, but we're stuck. Children are the future, and we aren't having any. When was the last time anyone down here got a breeding license? Never. They're too expensive."

"Lots of unlisted Nulls get illegally fertilized and have kids without a breeding license," Farah said. "They can afford to feed and clothe their kids, but that's it. No money for education or health care. That's why the government makes us pay *before* we have any children. I'm no fan of Omnius, but we can't blame him for all of our problems."

Dag nodded along with Farah's arguments. "I've said it before, and I'll say it again, you should listen to your partner, Bret. She's a smart one, and she'll keep you out of trouble."

Bretton ignored him. "So why don't you go back?" he asked Farah. "You don't need an education in Etheria. Omnius just downloads whatever you need to know, straight to your Lifelink."

She shook her head and looked away. "I'd get bored. A little chaos is what makes life interesting."

Bretton made no secret of why he'd come down here after

Omnius had resurrected him, but Farah's reasons were less clear. He suspected an unusual fondness and concern for her uncle was at fault, but maybe she really had just gotten bored.

"From what I hear the Etherians ain't havin' any children either. They're buyin' their breedin' licenses years in advance."

"And from what *I* hear Omnius is already working on that. He's busy preparing a whole new world just so that his *children* can have children of their own. New Avilon they're calling it. How much do you want to bet they won't be selling any tickets to Nulls when it's done?"

Dag frowned. "Where did you hear that?"

"Information is the only weapon we have, and the Resistance is far from defenseless. Believe me, fifty levels above our heads, the Etherians are all lining up to buy their breeding licenses for the price of a loaf of bread. Just because they can't use them yet doesn't mean they won't. As for us? Forget about it. Not in this lifetime, and we only get one."

Dag's lip twitched and he looked away. "Well, I never liked kids, anyway. Can't afford no wife neither."

Farah placed a hand on Bretton's arm. "We need to de-link this guy and go. I electrified the car, but I don't think that will stop determined thieves."

Bretton nodded absently. "Dag, we could use someone like you. You believe in an after life, but you're keeping it all for yourself. Why don't you share the good news?"

"Not my business what others believe or don't. I got my life, they got theirs."

"All right, then do it because Omnius has to be stopped before he decides to turn us all into drones."

"Aren't *you* a drone?" Dag asked simply. *Drone* was one of the Nulls' pejoratives for immortal Avilonians. It was their way of saying that something about Ascendants, with their perfect bodies and their carefully-controlled behavior wasn't entirely human. Bretton hadn't been given a choice about becoming a *drone*. He'd died in the war and Omnius had resurrected him here to find his pregnant wife waiting for him in paradise. Now she was in Etheria and he was down here. She'd long since stopped making conjugal visits, or any other kind of visits for that matter. He didn't blame her after everything that had happened.

Bretton gave a bitter smirk. "So take it from someone who knows. The only difference between me and an Omni is that I'm programmed with a personality and Omnies aren't."

"Bret, drop it. Dag's comfy. He's got his shop. He doesn't need to waste his life chasing conspiracy theories."

Dag gave a tight smile and nodded once. "At least someone understands me. If I were a younger man, you'd be in trouble—pretty girl like you, charmer like me, we'd be liquid dymium."

"If you were a younger man, I'd punch that dirty grin off your face."

Dag turned to Bret. "Ain't she somethin'?"

"She's somethin' alright," Bretton replied. He nodded to the Sythian agent, still lying unconscious on Dag's table. "Copy his link data to a holo card and de-link him."

Dag turned to him, his glowing orange eyes narrowed to slits. "Backups cost extra."

"We can't afford to lose this information, Dag."

"So pay for it."

"I'll get the Resistance to pay me and then I'll pay you later, how's that?"

Dag seemed to consider that. "Fine, but after this we're even. Your favor's been called. You come back here, you better be willing to pay full price."

Bretton nodded. "Sure thing."

* * *

"How long before we get to wherever it is we're going?" Atton asked.

"Not long," Peacekeeper Delon Tarn replied, leaning forward in his seat, as if even he were in suspense.

The city raced by beneath their feet. The gray, green, and blue blur of buildings, parks, and shields grew larger and more distinct, seeming to race by faster and faster as they descended.

They came to within a few hundred feet of the rooftops, and suddenly the variegated blur underfoot became a solid color—a sea of blue shields. Just one building dominated the horizon, floating in that sea.

The tower was like Omnius's Zenith Tower in that it rose more than a kilometer above the Celestial Wall, but it was not a delicate-looking tower of light and architectural beauty, it was a gleaming black fortress of bristling armor and weapons.

The *Sightseer* raced onward, seemingly on a collision course with the massive structure. The morning sun disappeared behind the tower's bulk, and the building became limned in a bold red light, as if dipped in blood.

In the distance, a tiny blue-white square of light appeared.

They raced toward it until it became the gaping maw of a hangar.

The *Sightseer* plunged inside and came to a sudden stop just before they would have slammed into the far wall. At the top of the wall was a bank of viewports, tinted a glossy black, and lit from within. The hangar's control tower. Dark shadows roved within.

A giant door slid aside below the control tower, and the *Sightseer* slipped into an empty berth.

Peacekeeper Delon Tarn unbuckled his flight restraints and stood up. He turned to them with a smile. "Welcome to Tree of Life 1177," he said.

"Tree of what?" Ceyla asked, sounding like she was about to burst out laughing. The brittle edge in her voice made Atton think otherwise.

"Tree of Life," Delon repeated.

"What is it?" Atton asked, unbuckling and rising to his feet with the other refugees.

The Peacekeeper didn't answer Atton's question, but once everyone had disembarked and was standing on the deck beside the shuttle, Master Rovik explained.

"This is where you will all be re-born if at the end of this week you choose life. In just a moment we will be taken on a tour of the tower's main facilities."

Master Rovik turned to a pair of broad doors behind him. They slid open, parting down the middle to admit a group of soldiers wearing strange, silvery armor, and round helmets with circular, glowing red visors. Their footsteps echoed in unison with a loud, metallic clanking. As they drew near, Atton saw that the soldiers' limbs were too thin to be human. Their glowing red visors were optics, and the rounded helmets were heads. These were the bots they'd seen guarding the mansion the night before.

"Here, Omnius doesn't even permit his chosen ones to come and go as they please. The entire facility is run by drones, to prevent accidental contamination of the clone labs or data centers." Galan turned to them with a smile, his blue eyes glowing bright in the relatively dim light of the hangar.

The drones came to a halt before the assembled group of refugees, and their clanking footsteps stopped with one final echo. The drones' ball-shaped heads rolled this way and that, red cyclopean optics scanning the group. Then the drones fanned out, surrounding them. Even the Peacekeepers were surrounded, but as soon as Master Rovik started forward, their drone escort began walking, too, forcing the refugees in the center to keep pace.

As they drew near to the broad doors where the drones had come from, Atton noticed that the corridor beyond was transparent. It crossed out over a vast field of hexagonally-shaped lights. Here and there drones could be seen walking across the field.

The group reached the corridor and exclamations filled the air as everyone noticed what that field of lights was. Inside of each hexagonally-shaped cell was a drifting mop of human hair.

Atton flinched. His skin began to crawl, and he shivered.

This was a clone lab.

They came to the end of the corridor and entered a lift tube with transparent walls and floor. The doors *swished* shut behind them, and the lift started down. As it dropped, their top-down view of the clone lab was replaced by a cross-section. There were fully grown men and women inside each of the hexagonal cells, all of them naked and floating peacefully in shining blue tanks. Their eyes were closed, their legs drawn up to their bodies in a fetal position, and nutrient tubes trailed from their belly buttons.

The clones were all stunning—noses the right length and shape; eyes not set too wide or too close together; brows not jutting, too sloped or too high; chins and jaws the right size and shape for their respective sexes. A few of the clones were smiling in their sleep, revealing coveted dimples in their cheeks. There were skin tones of every shade and color, proving that at least Omnius was not racist. Black didn't become White, but fat became skinny, old became young, and weak became strong.

"This is perverse," Ceyla whispered.

Atton shook his head. His own stomach was churning, but he hadn't decided yet if that was from revulsion or excitement.

They dropped past a dozen identical floors of clone tanks, the lift picking up speed.

"How big is this place?" Atton heard his father ask.

Galan Rovik's voice resonated in the confined space of the lift tube, "The capacity of a Tree of Life's clone rooms is just over five hundred million. There are more than a thousand towers like this one, spread out all over Avilon."

Atton frowned, curiosity tickling through the back of his mind. As the lift tube continued to drop past layer after layer of sleeping clones, he realized what it was that had sparked his curiosity. "Five hundred million people, times one thousand towers like this one ... that's only half a trillion people. . . . The Imperium had a population just less than sixty trillion. That doesn't seem like enough."

"Not to resurrect everyone all at once, no. Clones are grown to maturity in a month or less, but even so, it had to be done in stages. People were resurrected in the order that they died, with immediate family members being resurrected as soon after their loved ones as possible."

"How did you do it?" Atton asked. He imagined five hundred million people suddenly waking up to find that they weren't actually dead, all of them disoriented and confused ... Multiply that by a thousand times, and repeat it once a month. *That's a lot of processing.*

"The drones did most of the work," Master Rovik explained. "There are many more of them than there are of us. They were the ones who expanded Etheria to make room for your kind."

Your kind, that description rattled around in Atton's head, making noise.

A new voice asked, "There are more drones on Avilon than people?" It was Captain Caldin.

"There were. They're mostly gone now, off to build New Avilon."

"There's another planet like this?"

"We can't stay on Avilon forever with a population as large as ours—not if we want to keep having children."

Atton noticed Alara rubbing her belly at the mention of children. "Will we be able to travel to New Avilon and see it?" he asked.

"No," Master Rovik replied.

Atton's eyes narrowed swiftly at that. "Why not?"

"It's not ready."

"I'm not talking about living there. I just want to see it."

"Not even *I* have had that honor, so you surely will not."

"Has *anyone* been there?" Atton heard his father ask.

"It is a surprise."

"You mean a secret," Ceyla said.

Master Rovik turned in a slow circle, his expression

incredulous as he took in the small group of refugees. "Where I come from, we don't judge things that we know nothing about. We study them and learn until we understand. Only then do we form our opinions. It has been many years since I have encountered such resistance to the truth. If all of the citizens in Dark Space are like you, I fear for the future of your people."

Your people. Again, Atton was made to feel like an outsider, and he realized that Master Rovik considered them all second-class citizens, just because they hadn't been born on Avilon. He wondered if Omnius felt the same way.

Atton frowned and turned back to watch the lift tube dropping past an endless series of honeycomb-shaped clone tanks. His eyes drifted out of focus and it all became one big, bright blur of sleeping humanity.

One thought kept turning over and over in his head as he watched. *There are more drones than people.* Even if all of Avilon rebelled against Omnius, somewhere out there in the galaxy, now busy building another world just like this one, was the army Omnius could use to stop them.

But Master Rovik was right. They *were* all suspicious without cause. So they had to give up some of their freedom in order to achieve a real utopia. Was that such a bad thing?

The sheer scale of development on Avilon gave him hope. No matter how numerous the Sythians were, the Avilonians with their superior technology were more than a match for them. He imagined a future where some day there would be hundreds of worlds like Avilon in the galaxy, and thousands more supporting them. It would be an Imperium on the scale of the Sythian Coalition, spanning from one side of the galaxy to the other.

Ceyla caught him smiling. "What are you so happy

about?" she asked.

His smile faded when he saw the guarded look on her face. "Nothing."

She didn't look convinced. Ceyla would be harder to win over, given her beliefs. With that realization, he felt a stab of fear for her that took him by surprise. What if she decided to become a Null? Would he ever see her again?

The real price of paradise wasn't that they were unable to make mistakes. It was that not everyone wanted to be there.

A whispering voice rippled through his thoughts, startling him: *Yes, Atton, that is the price, but it is only paid by Nulls. Etherians can visit their loved ones in the Null Zone whenever they like. And most Nulls do eventually ascend to Etheria.*

Ceyla shot him another wary look. "You seem to be taking all of this in your stride," she said.

Atton frowned. "No, Omnius just spoke to me, he was explaining something about—"

Ceyla raised a palm in front of his face. "Don't tell me. I don't want to hear anything that serpent has to say."

"Ceyla, he wasn't trying to convince me of anything, he was just explaining how things work here."

She raised her eyebrows and shook her head, gesturing to their surroundings. "The way things work here is determined by Omnius," she whispered. "*Everything* on Avilon is designed to convince you to live the way *he* wants you to. To believe what he tells you. The whole planet is one big arrow pointing up—straight to him. Why do you think they call themselves the Ascendancy?"

The lift tube stopped, and the Omnies preceded them out onto another identical field of clones. As they walked, half a dozen tanks began rising, revealing shining blue pillars of water that served as the clones' amniotic fluid. They came to the first cell and the Omnies stopped. Within it was a beautiful young woman, long blond hair floating in a silken mane around her head. Master Rovik gestured to her, and Ceyla gasped.

"What the frek is this?" she demanded.

"You," Master Rovik replied.

Atton felt like someone had slapped him in the face. Now that he looked at the woman in the tank, he did recognize her, but her features were all somehow more beautiful and less real, like she was a doll rather than a clone. As soon as he recognized her, he looked down, shading his eyes with his hand so he couldn't see anything above the knee.

The Omnies stepped aside, and the refugees took that as their cue to go running across the field of clones, checking raised tanks at random. Atton stayed with Ceyla, peeking around his palm to watch as she placed a splayed hand against the transpiranium tank.

"It can't be me," she whispered, sounding miserable.

Unsure of how to comfort her, Atton placed his free hand on her shoulder, being careful to keep his eyes averted.

Ceyla flinched and rounded on him. "Mind giving me some privacy, Commander?"

"I..."

"Or were you planning to stare at my naked backside all day?"

Atton frowned. "Sorry." With that, he turned and began walking toward the next nearest clone tank. Another woman floated there. From a distance he noticed his father and Alara standing beside that clone. Atton announced himself before he drew near, to make sure he wouldn't surprise anyone. "Hoi!"

Ethan turned and waved him over, which Atton took to

mean that they weren't as concerned about privacy as Ceyla had been.

As he drew near, he recognized the clone floating inside this tank as a slightly prettier version of Alara. She had always been beautiful, but just like Ceyla, her features had been subtly adjusted to make them even more symmetrical and feminine.

"Is that you?" Atton asked, turning to Alara.

She shook her head. "No, it's not." She had both her hands wrapped protectively around her vaguely protruding belly, and her violet eyes were wide and unblinking as she stared at her clone's midsection.

Atton followed Alara's gaze and saw that her clone was equally pregnant. "How is that possible?"

"I don't know," Ethan said.

With that, a familiar gravelly voice spoke up behind them. "How could this be paradise if all the women who were pregnant when they died were resurrected without their babies?"

Alara turned to Galan. "My baby doesn't have an implant yet. How will you transfer her memories?"

"She will be implanted through her umbilical cord with what she remembers from being in your womb."

"You can do that?" Atton asked.

Master Rovik smiled. "Omnius can do anything."

Atton went back to staring at Alara's pregnant clone. It felt perverse looking at his stepmother this way—naked, and floating in a tank, but she didn't quite look like Alara. More like her sister.

Alara took a step toward the tank and pressed her hands against it as Ceyla had done. She traced the nutrient tube running from the clone's belly button to the floor of the tank and then looked up to study her own face.

Suddenly, the clone's leg jumped, and so did Atton. Clone Alara's eyes popped open, wide and staring, and her mouth opened as if in a scream. Atton stumbled away from the tank.

Ethan cursed viciously and turned to Master Rovik. "She's alive, you sick frek!"

Galan was unfazed by the accusation. "Of course she's alive."

"She looked like she was trying to say something," Atton added, hugging his shoulders. "Or like she was in pain."

Galan shook his head. "Clones are alive, but they cannot speak. They've never learned how. And they have never experienced pain. Our methods of growing them are completely humane."

Atton watched the clone slowly close its eyes and mouth, and he shivered violently. "Why did she open her eyes?" he asked.

"Why does a baby kick in its mother's womb? Perhaps she heard us talking, but don't worry. Whatever memories she has of being a clone and living in a tank will be erased at the moment Omnius downloads and transfers the data from her Lifelink to her brain."

"I've seen enough of this," Ethan said, turning away. Alara lingered with her palms pressed against the glass, her own eyes wide and staring, her jaw hanging slightly open in a parody of what they'd seen from her clone a moment ago.

"Alara?" Ethan called.

"Yeah . . ." She gave a sudden shiver, and that seemed to snap her out of it. She backed away from the tank, rubbing her arms as if they were cold. Ethan took her hand and led her away.

Atton knew just how Alara felt. There came a hiss of

frigid air and the clone tanks sank back into the floor.

As they returned to the lift, Atton couldn't help thinking about the clones, and wondering why he hadn't seen *his*.

While riding back up to their transport, others began asking the same question. Master Rovik replied, "Some of you are ready to become Etherians, and others are not. Only the drones and Omnius understand the way the *Trees of Life* are organized. One thing is certain, however—the people you saw will soon be separated from those you did not."

Atton frowned, wondering what conclusions he could possibly draw from that. Then he realized what that meant for him and Ceyla, and a sharp pain lanced through his heart. He glanced at her, studying her features, memorizing them: the soft red glow of her cheeks, the redness of her lips, the luminous golden color of her hair . . . and the subtle curve at the tip of her nose . . .

Ceyla was still in shock. She didn't notice him staring. She had also missed the prophetic implication of Master Rovik's last comment—if Atton's clone hadn't been in that room, and hers had, that meant they weren't going to make the same choice.

"Hey, Kiddie, don't believe it. We're going to stick together. I'm not going to leave you."

Atton turned to see his father embracing his wife. Alara was nodding along, her head tucked under Ethan's chin, her violet eyes bright and shining with tears.

Ethan's clone hadn't been in that room, either. Despite that, Atton knew better than to think they would choose to go their separate ways, even with something like the promise of immortality and eternal youth to sway their choice. Him and Ceyla on the other hand . . .

They were just two friends who kept flirting with

something more, and that wasn't enough to keep them together with eternity hanging in the balance.

Not even close to enough.

CHAPTER 9

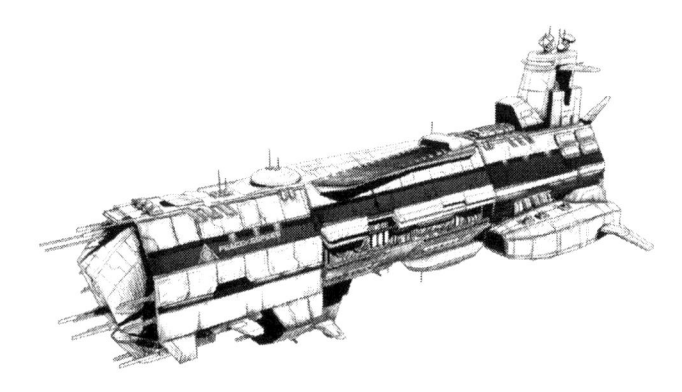

Omnius called the war council aboard the *Vicerator*. It was the largest surviving warship in the Peacekeepers' fleet, at just over six kilometers long. Strategian Hoff Heston took his seat with the other ranking officers in the second row of the assembly room. At the front of the room, the twelve Overseers of Avilon sat at a U-shaped table beneath a dazzling holo projection of the Avilonian crest. The outer spiral of the crest rotated slowly around the glowing eye in the center. The eye was that of Omnius, and at the moment it was glowing bright as any sun, illuminating the entire room. The augmented reality contacts they all wore shaded their eyes from the glare, but Omnius was still so bright that most of them had to bow their heads in order to avoid looking directly at him.

Hoff was unique among those present in that he was the only one with first-hand experience of what they were going to face in Dark Space. He'd been an Admiral in the Imperial Navy, on the run with his fleet for almost a decade after the original invasion.

"We should take the drone Fleet with us," one of the overseers said. The man's name appeared before Hoff's eyes, projected onto his ARCs—*Overseer Talon Fothram*.

A booming voice replied, "That will not be necessary." The grandeur of that voice was hard to mistake.

"My Lord—after the Sythians destroyed our fleet in orbit, we're down to less than a tenth of our original strength. What remains of our fleet could be defeated if we don't augment it with drone ships."

"We defeated them easily enough when they came here," Grand Overseer Thardris put in from his place at the head of the table.

"We had the help of Avilon's ground batteries and fighter garrison to fight them off," Overseer Fothram said. "We also took them by surprise with the fact that our scanners can penetrate their cloaking shields. This time they'll be ready for us, and they'll have the advantage of any fortifications they've made."

"But we'll know what those fortifications are," the Grand Overseer replied. "Their human slaves have Lifelink implants. Omnius will see everything that the Sythians are planning."

Another overseer, Jurom Tretton, spoke up from the opposite side of the table, directing his attention to brightly-glowing eye of Omnius rather than to any of his peers. "My Lord, why not just kill them? If all the Sythians' slaves suddenly drop dead, their fleet will be as helpless as ours was when you were forced to shut down. The slaves will resurrect here either way."

Thunder rolled through the assembly room. "I cannot kill them without taking from them their right to choose. The only thing we stand to lose by liberating Dark Space is a few more warships."

"But those are warships we cannot afford to sacrifice!" Jurom added. "Before last night's attack, we were going to send the fleet to the Getties Cluster and take the fight to the Sythians! Now look at us! We're planning to rescue the remnants of humanity and bring them here so that we can hide. We need to crush the Sythians decisively, not suffer more attrition."

"Mind your tongue, Overseer. You would be wise to listen before you presume to tell *me* how to run *my* empire," Omnius said. "If we take the drone fleet, as you suggest, Avilon will be defenseless. I have not yet fully rooted out the rebels in the Null Zone, and without the drones to keep watch over the city during Sync, there could be a rebellion the likes of which I'm sworn to protect Avilon against above all else."

Jurom bowed his head. "Forgive me, My Lord, I did not mean any disrespect."

"You are forgiven, my child. After all, it was only last night that the Nulls brought Avilon to its knees. The virus they introduced into the Omninet inadvertently let the Sythians into our star system and allowed them to destroy our orbital fleet. We very nearly lost Avilon itself."

"The Nulls had unfortunate timing, My Lord," Jurom replied. "Perhaps now the price of their freedom has become too high. They are unpredictable and dangerous."

"They are unpredictable because I allow them to be. They chose to live apart from me and so they do. Their freedom may seem a pointless luxury to you, but they serve as an example for all of Avilon. Without them, humanity would forget how things were without me. You would call me a tyrant, and soon everyone would be rebelling."

"Never, My Lord," Jurom said. "We would never do that."

"No? You would be among the very first to betray me, Jurom."

"My Lord! Never!"

Omnius went on, "Nevertheless, Overseer Tretton raises a valid point. What happened when the Sythians attacked can never happen again. I will remove the fail-safes that disabled our defenses."

Hoff heard a few of the Strategians seated around him gasp, and the Grand Overseer turned to look up at the dazzling eye hovering above the floor in the center of the U-shaped table. "Master, what if there is an armed rebellion? Can you trust us?"

"I already know exactly what all of my people will do before they do it, so I can stop Etheria and Celesta from ever rebelling. As for the Nulls, they have no defenses, and the use of weapons is already restricted there."

Hoff noted that besides Jurom, Fothram, and Grand Overseer Vladin Thardris, the other ten overseers all kept quiet, making it impossible to know whether they agreed or disagreed with what was being said.

Omnius went on, "As of now, even if I were to shut down completely, you will all be able to defend Avilon. The drone fleet, however, will still depend upon me to function."

Hoff wasn't sure that the fleet would ever need to be independent of Omnius, especially now that the Nulls responsible for the virus had been executed and Peacekeeper patrols in the Null Zone had been doubled.

You are right to trust that I can protect my people, Hoff, but after what happened not everyone is as trusting as you. Hoff smiled at the mental pat on the back.

Omnius went on, "The Sythians will never get close enough to touch the surface of Avilon again!"

Applause erupted, peppered with a few utterances of, "Great is Omnius!"

Once the applause died down, the discussion turned to tactics and strategy for the coming battle in Dark Space.

Based on what Omnius could see from looking into the minds of the Sythians' human slaves, the enemy was busy laying cloaking mines and other traps at the one and only entrance of Dark Space. They had also clustered their entire fleet there.

That meant that they didn't know Avilonian ships could jump directly from one point to another. They didn't have to stop and navigate around strong gravity fields—such as the cluster of black holes that surrounded Dark Space.

The enemy expected them to come through the front door, but the Avilonian fleet would make its own entrance, popping up where they were least expected. And since Sythian scanners couldn't pierce cloaking shields, they wouldn't even see the Avilonians coming. The battle would be a rout.

Hoff smiled. Soon he would be reunited with his wife, Destra, and their daughter, Atta. It would take some explaining to make them understand how he was still alive, but then again, it would take some explaining for them to understand how *everyone* was still alive.

The answer was actually quite simple: *Great is Omnius.*

With that thought, Hoff felt a warm glow of peace and contentment wash over him, and somehow he knew . . .

Omnius was smiling, too.

* * *

"Mommy... when is Daddy coming back?"

Destra heard that even through the high-pitched whine of the explosion. Gor teams had just blown the doors of the prison compound. She watched on the live visual feed projected over the cruiser's main forward viewport as ten squads of cloaked Gors rushed through the dissipating clouds of smoke and pulverized castcrete.

Destra placed a hand to the comm piece in her ear. "Atta, not now. I'm busy. I told you not to call me unless it's an emergency. I'll be back down soon."

"But... I'm *hungry!*"

"I'll try to find you something to eat when I get back to our quarters." Destra would have to give up her own rations again in order to save her daughter the pain of an empty stomach.

"Okay."

"I love you."

"I love you, too, Mom."

Destra hung up and focused on the mission. She caught Captain Covani staring at her from the other side of the captain's table. His lips were pressed into a disapproving line.

"Councilor, this is your op...."

She waved his disapproval away with one hand. "I'm

watching."

Gors rushed through the facility in the dark. They'd knocked out power to the compound before blowing the doors. The camera's infrared and light amplification overlay painted the walls in blue and bewildered guards in hot reds and oranges. Destra watched those guards crumpling to the ground, the glowing red balls that were their heads flopping this way and that as they fell, their necks broken before they even hit the ground. A few opened fire before they died. Random bursts of ripper fire plinked off the walls and the Gors' armor with showers of sparks that blinded the light-amplified feed from the camera. While cloaked, the Gors' armor wasn't shielded, but the guards weren't exactly carrying state of the art weapons due to the risk that the prisoners could get their hands on those weapons.

So far the Gors were proving reliable. They'd been fed before the mission in order to prevent another incident like what had happened on Forliss.

It wasn't long before they reached their target—the prison block. Fifty thousand cells stacked one atop the other in rusting towers. This was where the Imperium had kept its worst criminals. Destra had scanned a list of the inmates and their crimes before they'd arrived in order to cherry pick just three hundred of the least violent and least depraved. That hadn't been an easy task. In the end, she'd had to pick smugglers with violent tendencies, political prisoners, pirates who only cared about their coffers, and corporate villains with more dirty laundry than clean.

They would outnumber the human crew of the *Baroness*, but humanity needed more than just a few hundred survivors if they were going to start over and someday build up enough strength to defend themselves from another invasion.

Destra watched Echo Squad race down a narrow street between the tall, rusting towers of prison cells. Metal stairs and catwalks provided access to the ten different levels of the prison block. Cloaked Gors fanned out, visible only by their short-range comm ID tags, which showed up on the camera as strings of floating blue text with Gor-shaped icons underneath. The visual feed could theoretically be used to pinpoint the Gor wearing the camera, despite his cloaking shield, but the others would be impossible to detect. In the interests of keeping them that way, Destra only kept contact with the teams via the Gors' liaison and their telepathy.

"Torv, please remind your men that the prisoners will not go peacefully, so they must use the stun weapons we provided."

"They already know this."

"Remind them anyway."

"*Yess, My Lady.*"

The Gor wearing the camera climbed one of the metal rung staircases, his footsteps echoing loudly and causing the staircase to rattle. He reached the designated cell—293 . . . and walked right by it. He stopped at cell 294 instead.

"Torv! That's the wrong cell! Tell him it should be 293."

"*Tell who?*"

Destra wasn't used to commanding military ops. She'd forgotten to use the Gor's ID. "Echo Nine!"

It was too late. The Gor had already pasted explosives along the locking mechanism and taken cover. The explosive paste began to react with the duranium lock, hissing and fizzing loud enough for everyone on the bridge to hear. Suddenly there came the *bang* of an explosion and Destra's ears rang once more.

Echo Nine turned and ran inside the cell. Destra heard an

inhuman scream, followed by a loud crunch. Their viewpoint went spinning into the nearest wall. *Crunch.* Echo Nine spun again, and they saw the aggressor. A monstrous outline appeared, glowing red and orange in the infrared overlay.

"Patch me through! Audio only!"

"Yes, Ma'am. Linking in three, two . . ."

They saw something cold and blue swing at the camera, and the Gor went spinning for a third time. Then came another scream. It sounded like a scream of delight.

"Hoi!" Destra yelled at the audio pickups in the captain's table.

"Who said that?" a deep, human voice replied, the voice captured by Echo Nine's camera.

The Gor had sunk to the floor and was hissing softly with pain.

"This is a rescue operation, you *skriff!*"

"A what?"

"You're being *rescued*. Now listen up! Help that Gor to his feet before he comes to and rips out your throat."

"You sent *skull faces* to rescue me?"

"No. You're not that special. We sent them to rescue 300 inmates, not just you." They'd never meant to rescue *him*, but this brute didn't need to know that. Destra hoped he hadn't been locked up for anything too serious.

"Well why the frek didn't you say so?"

They watched an orange hand reach out for the camera. One handed, the man lifted the Gor he'd assaulted to his feet—an impressive display of strength. The Gor hissed more loudly now and shook his head as if to clear it.

Before Destra could warn Torv, the Gor slammed their prisoner in the chest and sent him flying into the opposite wall of his cell.

Bang!

The prisoner grunted and shook himself. "That's how you want it, hoi? Let's see you try that again, skully."

"Stand down, inmate!—Torv! Tell that Gor to stop."

"Justice is served by reciprocity," Torv replied. *"Now there can be peace between them."*

Destra frowned, noting the prisoner's raised fists. "Listen, you, whoever you are. This is Councilor Heston of Karpathia. You need to stop wasting time and get out of there before the Sythians come. Do you understand me?"

"Fine, but if your pet slips his leash again I'm going to kill him."

Destra scowled. "What's your name?"

"Cavanaugh."

The name rung a bell, but she didn't have time to figure it out. "Well, Cavanaugh, *go!*"

"Not yet. I have a few friends in here to get out first."

"We already have our list."

"Then you can go on without me. I'll take care of mine, and you take care of yours."

Captain Covani turned to her and shook his head. *They'll blow our cover,* he mouthed.

Cavanaugh was already on his way out.

"Torv, stun him!"

The Gor whose viewpoint they shared hurried out of the cell, turned, and ran straight into the blue object they'd seen on the infrared earlier. Now Destra noticed that it was the prisoner's right arm. He had a cybernetic prosthesis.

Crunch.

The Gor hit the wall and slid down it. This time he didn't get back up.

"Frek!" Destra said, pounding the captain's table with one

fist.

Covani was watching her with a frown. "Still think rescuing the galaxy's finest felons is a good idea?"

Before she could reply, they heard a siren come screaming over the bridge speakers. For a minute Destra thought it was coming from their ship, but then she saw the visual feed begin flashing brightly. The light amplification overlay snapped off automatically. Red emergency lights were flashing. That shouldn't have been possible. The Gors had cut power to the lights!

"Looks like our prisoner is working for the other side. He tripped the alarms," Covani said. "We need to abort."

"Why would Sythians make a slave of a prisoner and leave him in his cell?"

"Maybe they knew we were coming."

Destra shook her head. "No, he's just stupid. We must have missed cutting the lines for one of the emergency backups. Torv! Get two of your men in there. One to take over for Echo Nine with the camera, and the other to help him out of the compound. Make sure all the other squads are on the lookout for escaping prisoners. Tell them to keep their distance and get to the extraction point as soon as they can. We're not going to have time to go back in and rescue anyone else."

"I tell them."

"Captain—" Destra turned to Covani. "Check our list to see who was in cell 294."

"I already have."

"And?"

"It's not Cavanaugh."

"Then who?"

"Edgar Framon, convicted of multiple murders and at

least two counts of rape. He's serving two consecutive life sentences."

"So he lied about his name. Who is Cavanaugh, then?"

"Does it matter? Focus on the mission, Councilor."

Destra looked away with a frown, back to the visual feed. She drummed her fingers on the captain's table, waiting. As soon as she saw Echo Nine being lifted off the ground by one of his squad mates, she turned to the hulking monster standing behind her. "Torv? What's our status?"

Glowing red optics turned her way and the Gor's glossy black armor shifted, seeming to flow like liquid as he adjusted his footing on the deck. *"Fifty one prisoners are being carried out. Twelve more on the way."*

Destra bit her lip. The Gors were cloaked, but the prisoners they were carrying out weren't. If the Sythians got close enough to see the movement on their sensors, the Gors would make easy targets.

"We've got incoming!" the gravidar officer interrupted. "Two squadrons of Sythian Shells and three shuttles tearing out of orbit, headed straight for the prison complex!"

"Not cloaked?" Destra asked.

"They can't see us, so they don't know they're outnumbered," Covani replied. "No reason for them to hide."

"We need to create a distraction," Destra said. "What if we send a Nova squadron out there to draw them away from the Gors?"

Covani looked at her as though she'd just grown horns. "You want me to risk my pilots' lives so you can rescue the scum of the galaxy?"

"No, I want you to risk their lives so we can rescue the Gors."

Covani turned away with a scowl. "Comms, tell Gorgon

Squadron to launch. Their orders are to tease the incoming Shells away from the prison complex. They have fifteen minutes to do that *and* lose their pursuit so they can jump away with us. Make sure they get the coordinates for our jump."

"Yes, sir!"

"Torv—you need to relay those same coordinates to your people. Come with me."

Destra watched Captain Covani and Torv walk down to the nav officer's station. Once there, they began translating the jump coordinates from Imperial format to the Gor equivalent.

Destra looked away, back to the visual feed coming from inside the prison. Everything would have gone perfectly if Echo Nine hadn't opened the wrong cell and gotten himself knocked out by prisoner 294—whoever he was.

Cavanaugh. The name sounded familiar to her, but she couldn't recall why. Somebody famous, perhaps? *Infamous?*

Whatever the case, now he could add compromising a naval rescue operation to his rap sheet.

CHAPTER 10

Darron Cavanaugh pounded down the aging metal staircase, rattling it loud enough to simulate thunder. His footsteps were crowded with half a dozen others, making the sound all the more deafening.

On their way down they grabbed rifles, stun grenades, and sidearms from the lifeless hands of prison guards.

"Frek me . . . This one's got bite marks!" Black Seven said.

"Damned Skull Faces would eat their own grandmothers," Cavanaugh growled, noticing that the guard he was stealing supplies from had a gruesome wound in his neck.

"We have to move," Black Five put in. "When you tripped the lights, the alarms came on, too."

"Should have left us in the dark," Black Three added.

"Frek it, next time you all can rescue yourselves!" Cavanaugh said, springing up from his haunches and sprinting down the last flight of stairs.

"Now don't go gettin' your feelings hurt," Three replied. "We're grateful."

Cavanaugh grunted. They ran through the compound at

dizzying speed, racing down corridor after corridor. The flashing red lights weren't accompanied by any alarms, but he knew better than to trust that. Best to assume the worst.

Black Seven sprinted up next to him. "What about the rescue op you mentioned? Think they might have room for a few more?"

"Sure, next Skull Face you see, you can ask him. Just try to avoid his fangs."

Seven grimaced. "No thanks."

They reached the outer doors and found both sets blasted open. They ran out into a bright twilight, illuminated by a full moon. From there they cut across an overgrown field of grass to a small stand of silvering ash trees. Just before they reached the cover of the glossy black leaves and silver bark, they heard a series of thunderclaps split the sky.

"I missed weather," Black Five said. "Nothing like a nice refreshing rain after the sun's gone down and the frost's starting to glisten on the grass."

A suspicion formed in Cavanaugh's gut and he shook his head. "Quiet! That wasn't thunder." They reached the trees, and he risked peeking up at the sky through the edge of the canopy.

Bright streaks of fire slashed the sky. He pointed. "Look. Thruster trails." The thunder had been sonic booms. Cavanaugh noticed that the thruster trails were Imperial blue, not Sythian red, and he relaxed. He considered firing a ripper burst into the sky to identify himself on their scanners, but something held him back.

Just as well. The sky flashed with an explosion and one of the bright blue thruster trails disappeared. Then dozens more appeared—the red trails of Shell Fighters. Streams of purple stars streaked out after the Imperial Novas and they broke into sudden spirals and dives to evade the alien missiles.

"Hoi ..." Someone whispered beside his ear. "Look." A hand appeared in his peripheral vision, pointing to the field of long grass between them and the prison complex. The field was parting in winding lines leading from the pulverized doors of the prison complex. Looking carefully, they could see the garish orange garb of prisoners. He was just about to signal them over when he noticed that they were floating below the level of the grass, face down and unconscious, as if they were being carried by invisible men.

Or cloaked Gors. Cavanaugh's eyes narrowed swiftly. "Skull faces," he whispered. His rifle moved, almost of its own accord, to track the nearest prisoner—or rather, the Gor who was carrying him. They weren't heading for the trees, but cutting laterally across the field to an area of flattened grass. *Cloaked transports.* "They have extraction teams on the ground," he said.

Another explosion lit up the night, and their eyes were drawn to the sky once more to see the fading orange flower of an explosion—another Nova Fighter reduced to a cloud of superheated dust. Cavanaugh spent a moment tracking the Shells across the sky. He noticed that they were taking potshots at the Novas, but not breaking formation to follow them. They were headed straight for the prison complex.

"We need to go make nice with the Gors," Cavanaugh said, making a snap decision. He hoped it would be a good one.

"They're *skullies*," Seven said. The scars lining his face crinkled, and his nose scrunched up.

"They're soldiers who were just following orders. Now their orders are to rescue prisoners, and that's what we are. Come on!"

They ran, bounding through the tall grass, aiming for the nearest flattened patch. As they ran, Cavanaugh remembered using his prosthetic arm to beat the Gor who'd come to rescue him. He hoped he wouldn't run into that particular skull face again, but he'd take whatever retribution the Gors meted out. He hadn't had a choice. It was that or leave the rest of his squad to rot in their cells—or worse, to become slaves for the Sythians.

* * *

"We've lost another Nova!" gravidar reported.

"Torv, tell me your people are all aboard!" Destra said.

"Not yet."

"They're not taking the bait, Captain!" gravidar said.

"Your teams had better hurry, Torv!" Captain Covani put in.

"They are encountering more prisoners, running with them toward the shuttles," Torv replied. *"What are your ordersss?"*

"Stun them!" Destra said.

"They are armed."

"Your men are cloaked."

"They are carrying prisoners."

"All of them?"

"Not all."

"Then take them out! And do it quietly!"

"I tell them . . ."

Destra watched on the visual feed as their camera operator turned toward a group of prisoners in bright orange jumpsuits rushing through the grass. Blue stun bolts stuttered out, cutting the prisoners down. A few of them fired bursts of ripper fire that roared into the night as they fell.

Worried the weapons fire had given the Sythians something to aim for, Destra turned to look at the captain's table. For a moment nothing happened, but then a squadron of Shell Fighters twitched toward the Gors.

"Torv warn your people to keep their heads down. They've got incoming!" Destra said.

No sooner had she said that than she saw on the visual feed that a dozen bright purple stars had appeared in the night sky, twinkling and spinning, growing larger and closer to the Gor cameraman with every second that passed.

Pirakla missiles.

A group of six Gor shuttles appeared on the ground, de-cloaking to activate their shields.

"Have Gorgon Squadron turn around and intercept those Shells!" Covani called out. "Torv, those shuttles better have weapons!"

"Do not worry."

The first Pirakla missile hit one of the shuttles with a blinding flash of light and a deafening *boom* that rattled through the bridge speakers. Then came the shock wave and the grass flattened, revealing dozens of black-armored Gors, crouching in the grass. Another half dozen blasts boomed through the speakers on the heels of the first.

"Mute that feed!" Covani roared, and the residual roar of the explosions cut off in sudden ringing silence.

Destra blinked spots from her eyes and forced them to focus on the camera feed. The grassy field was on fire. Flames licked the keels of the Gors' organically-shaped shuttle craft. Those shuttles fired back with more Pirakla missiles. Then something else appeared on the horizon—a giant version of the Gors' shuttles, hovering between them and the approaching Shell Fighters—a Gor cruiser. It opened fire with a blinding torrent of lasers and missiles.

Explosions peppered the horizon, and a cheer went up from the crew pit.

"Nice work," Covani breathed. "Comms—call Gorgon Squadron back to orbit. Tell them to get aboard before we jump to the rendezvous."

"Yes, sir."

Covani turned to Destra, his eyes flinty. "We lost two pilots."

Destra nodded to the visual feed. The Gor with the camera ran through a burning field of grass with two stunned prisoners, one bobbing from each of his armored fists.

"We saved almost a hundred prisoners."

"That's not a fair trade in my book."

"You agreed to the op."

"No, I followed orders. Next time, Councilor, I might not be so obliging."

"The Gors are away. Shuttles cloaking ..." The comm officer interrupted.

Captain Covani broke his staring contest with her and turned back to watch the visual feed. It now showed the inside of a Gor shuttle. Dark, and crowded with nightmarish faces as the Gors took off their helmets.

The captain went on, "Now that we've consolidated the survivors, I trust we won't be wasting any more of our precious resources. Our current priority is to find somewhere safe that we can set up a colony. I was thinking the Feraides Sector," Covani said as he pulled up a star map on the captain's table.

Destra shook her head. "There are too many habitable worlds there. The Sythians will be swarming all over them before long."

"Perhaps, but we haven't seen them swarming anything besides us yet. I wonder if they really did come here to colonize our galaxy, or if that was just something they told us."

"They had no way of knowing that information would get back to us. Besides, if they don't want our galaxy, then why kill us all? Just because they've taken their time to organize doesn't mean they're not coming—or that they're not already here. We don't have recent recon data for any of those worlds. They might already be colonized."

"So where do you suggest we go?"

"We need to go somewhere unexpected."

Torv stepped up to the captain's table and placed two giant hands on the edge of it. *"If you are looking for an unexpected place that is far from here,"* he began, *"I suggest we go to Noctune."*

"What? That's in the Getties!" Captain Covani sputtered. "We're not going to get away from the Sythians by flying right up their noses!"

"You would have to be very small to fly up a Sythian's nose," Torv replied, his voice neutral, oblivious to his own wit.

The captain scowled and went on, "They leveled your home world when you stole their fleet. It was a barren ice world before, but now it's probably a radioactive barren ice world."

"There are other worlds in that system," Torv replied. *"Some of them are more temperate."*

"Then they're probably already crowded with Sythians."

"They are not."

Covani shot Torv a suspicious look. "How do you know?"

"It was not long ago that my creche lord and my Matriarch live on Noctune. Only a few orbits pass since then. In all their time there, Sythians never once appear. They breed and train us in captivity. We only know this because we are telepaths, and because we remember the first time they visit us, many orbits ago."

"Sir! Gorgon squadron is aboard!" the comms officer announced.

"Nav, Punch it!" Covani replied. To Destra and Torv he said, "We'll figure out where to go while we're in transit. Torv, make sure your people keep those prisoners in line. We'll transfer them here as soon as we're out of Dark Space."

The ship's computer began an audible countdown to SLS from 10 seconds. Someone cut the visual feed from the Gor's helmet cam, and the main viewport went back to showing diamond-bright stars and inky black space.

Destra dismissed herself with a sloppy salute. "I'm going below decks to check on my daughter. Let me know as soon as the prisoners are aboard. I'd like to speak to them personally."

Covani nodded. "Of course."

The countdown reached zero, and the bridge lit up with an actinic flash of light as they jumped to SLS.

* * *

"It's hard to believe," Alara said.

Ethan turned to look at her as they walked the grounds of the mansion where they were staying at the top of Destiny Tower in Celesta. On the horizon the sun was busy setting behind a majestic row of dark green trees, their jagged branches limned in a red-gold light that made them look as if they were on fire.

"They already cloned us," he replied, his lip curling with the thought. He felt violated just thinking about it.

"Did they?" Alara asked. "The more I think about it, the stranger it seems. The woman in that tank looked like me, but she wasn't me. She's too perfect."

"It doesn't make sense to me either, but I can't explain why it won't work without getting religious."

They heard a twig snap behind them and Ethan turned to scowl at the Peacekeeper who was shadowing them on their afternoon walk.

"You mind?"

"I'm just doing my job, Mr. Ortane."

Ethan turned away, shaking his head. "You were saying?"

"I'm not religious either," Alara replied, "but seeing all of this is enough to make me wonder."

"Well, we have another three days to make our decision."

"I don't need them," Alara said. "We can't stay up here."

"Why not?" Ethan tried but failed to hide the hope that bled into his voice.

"Because we'll be making our daughter's choice for her before she's even born. If they resurrect me with an unborn clone of our baby in my womb, then she'll already have *her* Immortal body."

They heard someone clear his throat, and Ethan turned to scowl at the Peacekeeper once more. "You can't do your job from a respectable distance?"

"I apologize for listening in, but your wife is wrong. The Choosing is just as important to Omnius as it is to you. If you choose life, your fetus will be an identical copy, not yet immortal, and she will still have to go through The Choosing."

Alara looked skeptical. "But she'll still be a clone. How will I know she's the same baby?"

"How will you know you're the same mother?" The Peacekeeper countered, now walking toward them. He stopped half a dozen paces away. "If you doubt the process works, I would ask *why* you doubt that. Is it perhaps because you are afraid that all we are is not mere physical matter? Perhaps you are more religious than you think."

"Regardless of what I believe or don't, my daughter will ask the same question when she grows up, and she will wonder if my choice didn't somehow eliminate the need for hers. What's the difference between transferring to an immortal body versus transferring to a mortal copy? Both processes assume that what we are *can* be transferred."

The Peacekeeper's serene expression took an ugly turn. "Then your objection *is* a religious one. We don't make a habit of spreading around treason in Etheria. If you insist on doing so, then your home lies in the shadows with the rest of the Nulls. Perhaps you'll find a way to get yourself killed before a natural death finds you—that way you can get on with living the after life you secretly believe exists."

"Watch how you speak to my wife," Ethan growled.

"My tone offends you. Her words offended *me*. But I apologize for the offense I gave. I should not have spoken in anger."

Ethan's lips curved up in one corner. "Shouldn't Omnius have stopped you from speaking in anger before you did?"

"Omnius cannot perfectly predict my actions while I am in the presence of mortals such as yourselves."

"What? Why not?"

"Because you have not made your choices yet, so he does not include you in his nightly simulations of the day to come. Children under the age of eight are the same."

Ethan saw his wife shake her head. "Every action a child takes will affect adults, making it impossible to predict anyone's actions."

"Omnius limits that ripple effect by making couples with children live in closed districts called *nurseries* until their children go through The Choosing. The nurseries are subject to a limited degree of chaos, but that is one of the sacrifices we make for our children."

Ethan scowled. "So if we choose to live up here, Omnius won't just tell us *how* to live; he'll tell us where to live, too. Is there anything he doesn't control?"

"The Nulls. The Sythians. You and other mortals like you. Bringers of chaos. If it were up to me, no one would have a choice. We would all be resurrected in immortal bodies soon after birth."

"Well thank the gods it's not up to you," Ethan said.

"The gods? What gods?"

"All of them! The ones you insist don't exist."

The Peacekeeper's expression flickered darkly once more, and Ethan smiled.

"I'm going to assume that remark was intended to anger me, and ignore you this time."

"Sure, do whatever you like—or whatever Omnius tells you to. Excuse us." Ethan took Alara's hand in his and continued their evening walk. Whispering, he said, "At least they haven't duped you."

"Let's talk about something else," Alara said. "Something happy."

"Like what?"

"We haven't even decided what we're going to name her."

Ethan blinked. "You're right. Now that we know it's a *her* ... what about ... Trinity?" It was the same name they'd given their ship. They'd named it right after Alara had told him she was pregnant, so it seemed a fitting name for their daughter, too.

Alara smiled. "That sounds perfect."

"I'm glad you like it. Speaking of *Trinity* ..." Ethan turned back to their chaperon. He was still shadowing them closely. "What happened to my transport?"

"What transport?"

Ethan walked up to the Peacekeeper and jabbed the man's glowing breastplate with his index finger. He felt a tingle of energy push *back*, and flinched. Recovering quickly, he said, "You heard me. I came to Avilon with a ship. You weren't planning to steal it were you?"

The Peacekeeper shook his head. "You're not allowed to leave Avilon, so I'm sure you can see how you won't be allowed to keep your vessel."

Ethan's cheeks bulged and he flushed bright red. "The frek . . . listen here! It's *my* ship!"

"I will inquire about it for you. Rest assured, whatever funds are obtained from recycling it will be credited to your account."

"Recycling it! If you recycle my ship, I swear I'll . . ."

Alara pulled Ethan away from the bewildered Peacekeeper.

"Why wouldn't you want it to be recycled?" he continued, oblivious to how close Ethan had come to breaking his face. "It's no use to you otherwise. I'll see if any museums want it. Perhaps they'll be willing to pay you more than the vessel's scrap value."

Ethan's head felt like it was about to explode. "Frek you! Frek Avilon! Frek Omnius!"

"Watch your tongue! Omnius could strike you dead with but a whisper of a thought!"

"Maybe he should!"

"Unfortunately, he is too merciful for that."

Ethan felt dizzy. His lungs were heaving. He couldn't breathe. He'd worked his whole life to have a ship he could call his own, and now that he had one, the Avilonians were going to take it away and sell it for scrap! He sunk to his knees in the grass. Alara appeared on her haunches beside him.

"Ethan, are you all right?"

He shook his head. "What's the point?" he demanded, still looking at the Peacekeeper. The man stared back at him, looking wary, like Ethan might suddenly lunge at him.

"The point?"

"Of anything—Avilon, The Choosing . . . life!"

"Omnius makes us choose because only the people who really want to live forever in paradise are capable of making that work, and because we have to get our immortal bodies sooner or later, so why not sooner? Better to eliminate any genetic predispositions to wrongful behavior and all the physical weakness that is associated with naturally selected genes."

"I'm not buying it," Ethan said, still shaking his head.

"You don't have to. Eternal life is free."

Ethan snorted. "And doesn't that just make you a little suspicious? What exactly are *you* doing for Omnius?"

"Omnius is not a selfish entity. He does not require us to do anything for him."

Ethan shook his head. "Every sentient creature lives for something and strives to obtain it."

"I never said Omnius doesn't have a purpose, just that his purpose isn't selfish. He lives to serve us, to guide us to perfection and protect us from ourselves. That was the reason he was created, and it is the reason behind everything he does."

Incredulous at the man's stupidity, Ethan shook his head. "How do you know that? He's telling you what you will do and then telling you what you should do instead. What if he's lying about the future in order to get his way? He's a thousand times smarter than any one of us! Do you know what that makes us to him? Garbage!" Ethan pushed off the ground to stand on trembling legs. "If anything, we're his entertainment! He doesn't really care about us. If he did, he would set the Nulls free. Really free. Send them away to create their own empire someplace else."

"So the Sythians can find them and kill them?"

"That's a nice excuse. He had the Nulls caged up here

long before anyone had even heard of the Sythians."

"And back then there was your Imperium to worry about. You don't *really* think they would have left us in peace once they heard about Avilon from all those Nulls you'd like to set free. When they realized how advanced we are, they'd have considered us a threat. It wouldn't have been long before your empire tried to conquer ours. It's happened before."

"I guess you're lucky that the Sythians found us before we found you," Ethan said, jabbing him in the chest once more. This time he barely noticed the electric jolt that sizzled against his fingertip when he touched the Peacekeeper's armor. "I can see why someone might want to kill a sniveling snot like you." Ethan turned and stalked toward the mansion. Alara kept pace beside him, her violet eyes wide and gleaming in the gilded light of the setting sun. "We should get some sleep, Kiddie," he said, nodding slowly, as if he'd just made an important decision.

Alara didn't reply for a long moment. "Ethan . . ."

"What?"

"You need to be careful or you're going to get yourself killed."

"Maybe that wouldn't be such a bad thing!"

Slap!

Ethan's head spun away from Alara, his cheek stinging. He stopped and turned to her, his hand on his stinging cheek, his jaw agape. "What was that for?" He grabbed her wrist in his hand and squeezed it tight, forcing her arm up close to his other cheek. "You want to hit the other one? Go on! Hit your husband again!"

"Frek you, Ethan! You want to die? Who's going to raise your daughter? Don't be so frekking selfish! We need you!"

All the anger drained out of him, and his shoulders

slumped. He let go of Alara's wrist and she began rubbing it with her other hand.

"I'm sorry," he said. He took a deep breath and looked out to the horizon, letting the air out slowly. "It's been a long day. You're right. It's just something about this *place* . . ." He turned to look up at the sky and saw a faint sparkle of stars gleaming between golden wisps of cloud. "The more I feel like I'm being told what to do and how to think, the less I feel like doing it, and the more suspicious I become."

"You're not cut out for Etheria, Ethan," Alara said.

"What about you?"

She shook her head. "I told you. We can't live up here. Not until we know what our daughter is going to choose."

"So what if she chooses to live in Etheria?"

"We'll cross those bridges when we get there."

"Would you follow her?"

"Wouldn't you?"

Ethan frowned. "I don't know, Kiddie. My mother said we can't hold ourselves responsible for other people's choices, and I think she's right. We've got to raise our daughter right. Trinity has to know what she's in for if she comes up here." Ethan wrapped an arm around Alara's shoulders and guided her toward the mansion. High walls of tinted glass stared back at them, reflecting stolen scraps of the fading sunset. The majestic trees they'd seen on the horizon earlier were reflected as blurry green swirls.

Later that night, as Ethan lay awake in bed, staring up at the ceiling, he tried to make sense of everything that had happened so far, and what all of it meant for the future. Alara lay asleep on his chest, having succumbed to exhaustion more than an hour before *Sync*. Ethan was equally exhausted, but he refused to let himself follow his wife's example. He was waiting up for Omnius's *Sync*. His ARCs showed him the time—2350. Sync occurred at midnight every night, so that gave him ten more minutes. Mortals' sleep was regulated by their Lifelink implants to coincide with Sync, so in theory, he would fall asleep at zero hundred hours, and he wouldn't be able to wake up again until Sync was over, four hours later.

Ethan wanted to see what forced sleep would feel like. He was half hoping the Peacekeeper had lied to him, that maybe in this one thing at least he still had a say about what happened to him. Maybe he could fight it and stay awake—flick his middle finger to the big eye in the sky and say, *you can't control* me!

It was worth a shot.

They were being offered eternal life by a supposedly good entity, a vast artificial intelligence that was sworn to serve humanity. Ethan didn't understand how the Avilonians could be so naive. What did Omnius have to gain by serving humans? Inferior humans. What sort of fulfillment could a vast intellect derive from that?

23:59.

Ethan focused on the digital clock, causing it to drift down from his peripheral vision into the middle of his field of view. A seconds display appeared in response to that thought—57, 58, 59 . . .

His eyes slammed shut, and his thoughts dropped off a sudden cliff into a swirling abyss. Out of that abyss he heard the distant *boom* of an explosion, and suddenly he found himself on the bridge of a starship, staring out at space. Now his name was Galan Rovik, and the starship he found himself on was the *Ventress*.

CHAPTER 11

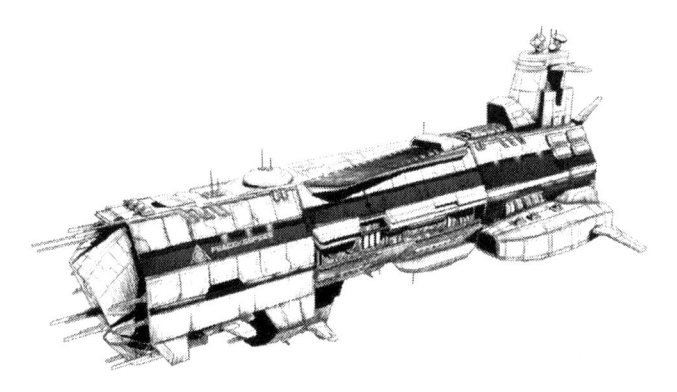

The *Ventress* shook with a mighty explosion. Damage alarms screamed, and something deep in the belly of the ship groaned as if some primordial monster had just been awoken from long years of slumber.

The lights flickered and turned red. Acrid smoke billowed in the crimson gloom, and a nauseating weightlessness set in.

Silence rang.

Strategian Rovik grabbed the armrests of his command chair and gritted his teeth. "Engineering! What was that?"

"That last volley hit the power core! We've lost the back third of the ship, and we're drifting on emergency backups!"

Galan's mouth opened to give the order to evacuate, but there wasn't enough time, and what would be the point? So they could be captured by whatever aliens were attacking them? Then a terrible thought occurred to him—what if the quantum comms array had been damaged? Their Lifelinks would have no way to transfer them home. He watched out the bridge viewports, wide-eyed and frozen with horror as another sparkling wall of purple alien missiles rushed to greet them.

"Comms! Status report!" he roared, working some

moisture into his suddenly dry mouth.

"Online, sir . . ."

Relief flooded through him. "Time to go home, people! Cut your cords! I'll see you on the other side."

Galan followed his own order, silently telling his Lifelink to transfer him home before the next volley could hit.

He went rushing down a dark tunnel toward a bright light. The light grew large and terrifying, taking on the familiar shape of a dazzling eye.

"Welcome home, Galan," it said in a resonant voice.

He opened his eyes and they burned and blurred with tears, unaccustomed to the light. He couldn't see! Strong hands held him up, leaving just enough weight resting on his legs to make him realize they wouldn't hold him. They were too weak or too clumsy; he couldn't tell which. He felt bewildered, cold, terrified, gripped with panic. He wanted to cry, but that seemed absurd. He was a grown man! A decorated Strategian.

Be still, my child, a quiet voice whispered. Galan couldn't tell if the voice had been audible or just inside his head, but either way, it served to calm him down. His mind felt light and airy, but soon it began seizing familiar bits and pieces of things, and the panic subsided. His legs stiffened beneath him and the hands holding him let go. He wiped away his tears, trying to see where he was. He was standing naked in a big, airy room—a hangar. Standing with him were hundreds of others, naked like him, all of them being held up by drones—*Omnies* with silicon padding on their spindly metal fingers. In front of them stalked a man in a bulky, shimmering white robe with dazzling white armor and a gold-glowing version of the Avilonian crest etched into his breastplate. That man was Grand Overseer Thardris.

He stopped in front of Galan and turned to face them, his glowing silver eyes flicking up and down the ranks of men and women.

"As you'll soon recall, your ship, the *Ventress* was attacked and destroyed by an unknown enemy. Your mission was to explore the neighboring Getties Cluster. That mission has failed. Your Lifelink data is being analyzed to determine the nature of the enemy that destroyed your ship, and to determine whether or not any of you are to blame for starting an intergalactic war. Strategian—why didn't you cloak your vessel as soon as you realized you had encountered hostile forces?"

Galan belatedly realized the Grand Overseer was speaking to him. "Flay . . ." His tongue flopped uselessly in his mouth for a moment before he remembered how to use it. "They surprised us, sir. The enemy was cloaked and they had surrounded us before we even realized they were there."

"Cloaked?" That seemed to surprise the Grand Overseer. "Even so, your sensors can pierce a cloaking shield."

"They can, Overseer, but we were not expecting to find alien warships at the jump point, let alone cloaked alien warships. We weren't looking for them."

"Very well. You will have to explain yourself to Omnius, not me."

"Yes, sir."

The scene faded to black, and Ethan's identity had a moment to rise to the surface and wonder about everything he'd just seen and experienced.

Then he was Galan Rovik again, standing before the Avilonian high council, this time fully dressed in his Peacekeeper's uniform and armor. He was surrounded by the twelve overseers of Avilon, all of them seated on floating chairs and basking in a blinding white light. That light was cast by the eye of Omnius shining down through a transparent dome ceiling. From that, and the panoramic view of the city, Galan realized that he'd been summoned to the top of Omnius's temple, the Zenith Tower.

A booming voice rumbled through the council chamber. "I have sent a drone fleet to the Getties to assess the extent of the threat that the *Ventress* discovered. It has since found no less than eight different species of sentient aliens living there. It is hard to find a world they have not yet settled. Even worlds that should never have supported life are crowded with towering alien cities. Their fleet is thousands of times the size of ours."

Urgent whispers filled the room, and Galan turned in a slow circle to see the Overseers reacting to the news in varying states of shock.

"Are they at war with themselves?"

"No."

"But Master, then what are those warships for?" Galan heard the Grand Overseer ask.

"Since they greeted us with hostility as soon as we appeared, I can only assume that they've known about us for some time. It is likely that they are preparing for war with us."

More urgent whispering. Another overseer spoke, "How can we hope to face such a vast enemy?"

"Our technology is more advanced than theirs," Omnius replied. "But their numbers are sufficient to wipe out both us and the mortal Imperium without even deploying one percent of their fleet."

"Then there is nothing we can do. If their intention is to kill us, they will, and quickly."

"I will not suffer that to pass," Omnius replied. "We are already hidden here on Avilon, concealed with a wall of gravity fields and sensor distorting nebulae. My reconnaissance shows that these aliens do not have the technology they would need to reach Avilon through those obstacles. For the time being we are safe. The more imminent threat is to the Imperium of Star Systems. Their technology is comparable to that of these aliens, but their population and their fleet are far smaller."

"They are not our concern, Master," Jurom replied.

"Heartlessness is not becoming of a Celestial, let alone one who is an overseer of my kingdom."

"Forgive me, My Lord. I meant that they are mortals, therefore, they are not your children, and they are not your responsibility."

"Not yet. I have decided to begin implanting these mortals with cloaked Lifelinks. When war comes to them, and they lose, I will resurrect them on Avilon. The aliens will think they have won, and we will have the time we need to formulate a plan to fight them."

Another overseer spoke up, "Master! You cannot seriously expect to add the entire population of the galaxy to ours! There are trillions in the Imperium! Where would we put such a multitude? The three cities of Avilon already span the globe."

"Indeed? Then we will build our cities higher."

"It would take a thousand years for us to complete such an undertaking, and we don't know how much time we have."

Omnius replied, "No, we don't know how much time we have, and our workforce is not up to the task. We will need the drones to do the work, and I will have to increase their numbers exponentially."

The Grand Overseer spoke once more, "The law states that there must be 100 people for every drone."

Galan began to wonder what he was doing in the room. No one had asked him what he thought, and no one had spoken to him yet. Whatever the reason, he had a feeling that this session of council would go down in history.

"Human insecurity and faithlessness was the reason for that law," Omnius replied. "The drones are not independent. *I* control them. The only reason to limit their number is to limit my power, but I have long since stopped depending on humanity to survive, so you needn't fear that more drones will make me more independent. If I had wanted to destroy your species, I would have done so already, and the fact that humans outnumber my drones a hundred to one would not be enough to stop me."

A long silence followed that speech. During that time Galan decided to remind them all that he was there.

"Omnius is right," he said. All eyes turned to him, and he felt suddenly very small. "We have trusted him with our lives for thousands of years, and our trust has never been misplaced."

Galan felt a warm glow beaming down on his head, as if the sun were out and shining brightly above the Zenith Tower. That sun was Omnius.

"Listen to this Strategian. He was an overseer once—before he began to doubt and chose to become a Null. Years later he begged my forgiveness and returned to me. Now he is the most decorated Strategian in the fleet and, I am proud to say, a good friend."

Galan watched the Grand Overseer bow his head. "Master, forgive us, perhaps the real issue is not that we are upset at the idea of you building trillions of drones, but rather that we are feeling put aside. We, your children, have lived with strict population controls for generations, and now all of a sudden, you are suggesting that we turn Avilon upside down in order to accommodate trillions of mortals who would sooner spurn you than accept your rule."

"Would they? Would they indeed, Thardris? That remains to be seen. The only difference between them and you is that they have yet to meet their god. As for feeling left out, it is because of laws you created that I have not been able to expand the Ascendancy faster. I am proposing now that we rewrite those laws, not just to save your mortal brethren, but to give you all greater freedom. I envision a future where Celestials will be able to own more than one home, and where breeding licenses will cost as little as a loaf of bread."

"That would be a welcome change, Master."

"I will build a New Avilon, with ten times as much space as we currently inhabit."

Even Galan found himself smiling at that thought. "Great is Omnius," he whispered.

"What of these aliens? What will we do when they discover us?" the Grand Overseer asked.

"They still need to find a way to traverse the gravity fields that separate us from the greater galaxy, and by that time, we will be so numerous and so powerful, that nothing will threaten us!"

At that, all the overseers chanted, "Great is Omnius!"

* * *

Ethan awoke bathed in a cold sweat, with the echoes of the overseers' chants still reverberating in his ears.

He stared up at the ceiling, breathing heavily, his eyes blurry with sleep and his head pounding with an awful headache, as if someone had been screaming in his ear while he slept.

He sat up and Alara's hand slid off his chest. She moaned and stirred, but didn't wake. Ethan wondered what time it was, and the digital clock he'd been watching before he fell asleep appeared on the ARC display at the edge of his field of view.

04:01.

Ethan frowned. Just one minute after Sync had ended. The timing was convenient, like maybe he'd been trying desperately to wake himself up ever since he'd fallen asleep, but Omnius had kept him under, forcing him to experience Strategian Rovik's final moments, the horrors of resurrection, and his meeting with the Avilonian High Council.

Of course, all of that was exactly what Omnius wanted him to see, so Ethan didn't trust it one bit. He shivered involuntarily and turned to look over his shoulder at Alara. She was sound asleep, but her normally smooth forehead was vaguely furrowed, as if she were troubled by something. Ethan didn't have to wonder what. Omnius was showing them all the same things while they slept. He considered waking her, but if he did, he suspected she couldn't or wouldn't want to go back to sleep, and just four hours' sleep wasn't going to be enough for her or their baby.

Ethan got up from the bed, found his Avilonian sandals, and retrieved his white robe from the back of the chair where he'd left it the night before. Once dressed, he padded up to the door. He raised a hand toward the keypad, but the door opened automatically, as if someone were watching him. He dismissed that thought as being overly paranoid. Avilonian doors all opened automatically so long as you had the proper clearance.

Hurrying down the hallway beyond his and Alara's bedroom, Ethan tried to ignore the light paintings on the walls. Despite his best efforts, some of them caught his eye. The colorful abstracts once again looked to him like human faces. This time all the faces wore expressions of agony and despair, and their eyes looked accusing.

He reached the stairs and stopped on the second floor balcony, staring down into the foyer. The marble floor at the bottom shone with reflected moonlight pouring in from the mansions' many windows. Ethan considered going downstairs to look for some caf. He wondered if he'd be able to figure out how to make it without the Peacekeepers' help. Ethan turned the other way, looking up to the next flight of stairs. He wondered what was up there, and before he knew it, his feet were carrying him up.

On the third floor he found another long hallway, this one lined with windows. Out those windows lay a long balcony that ran the length of that side of the house, and at the end, a tall, rounded parapet that towered over the mansion. Another balcony lay at the top. Wondering about the view from there,

Ethan started down the hallway to a pair of doors that looked like they might lead to the parapet. He reached the doors and they slid open automatically once more.

He walked into a small, semi-circular room. The doors slid shut behind him, and a display appeared before his eyes. It was a diagram of the tower, showing four separate levels. Text at the top read, *Please choose a floor.*

Ethan thought about the top of the tower, and the floor beneath his feet immediately began to rise. Just a few moments later it came to a stop, and the other side of the lift rotated open. A warm breeze caressed his face. The top of the tower was open to the air, with railings rather than walls. In the center of the floor lay a familiar golden dome. Ethan recognized it immediately. It was a transporter dome—no, that wasn't its name . . .

It was a *Quantum Junction.* Yet another term that had been downloaded to his brain without his permission.

Ethan crept up to the junction. He didn't know how to use it, and even if he did, he was certain he didn't have the necessary clearance.

Walking around it, Ethan watched his distorted reflection in the smooth surface of it. Remembering how he'd seen the Avilonians activate these domes before, he stopped and placed one of his palms against it.

The dome vibrated at his touch, and his reflection became blurry. A sudden hiss of escaping air tickled his feet.

Startled, Ethan jumped back and watched wide-eyed as the dome hovered off the ground, rising on four shining pillars of light. He stared open-mouthed at the dome, and then at his palm. Why would the junction respond to *his* touch?

He turned to look behind him, half expecting to see a

Peacekeeper standing there. . . .

But there was no one.

Ethan turned back to the dome. It had hovered up to a set height and stopped, as if waiting for him to walk under it. A part of him was suspicious enough to wonder whether or not he should. He was fairly sure this was Omnius's doing.

Curiosity got the better of him. Ethan ducked quickly under the edge of the dome, and hurried to the middle of the green-glowing circle in the center of the raised black podium underneath. He thought back to what the Avilonians had done next, and he raised his hands, as if beckoning to the sky—to Omnius, he supposed.

The dome began glowing with ever increasing brilliance, and a whirring noise filled the air, rising quickly in tempo and pitch. Suddenly the junction fell over his head with a *boom!* and the light inside of it became painfully bright, forcing him to shut his eyes.

The *whirring* noise screamed in his ears. The air inside the dome whipped around like a tornado, tearing at his robe and hair. Then his ears popped with a sudden change in pressure, and the light shining through his eyelids faded to black. He opened his eyes to see the dome rising once more on four pillars of light.

That light was the only light he could see. Wherever he was, whatever lay beyond the quantum junction—it lay in complete and utter darkness.

Ethan blinked, and forced his eyes wide in a vain attempt to see. He wished he had more light to see by. With that thought, the shadows fled and he saw the world around him revealed in the faux color of a light amplification overlay. The contacts he wore continued to surprise him. . . .

But nothing surprised him more than what he saw

beyond the edge of the dome.

CHAPTER 12

Bretton and Farah walked up to a pair of mean looking sentries, their illegal plasma rifles tracking, their glowing blue visors turning to keep an eye on them as they approached. With one hand Bretton held his fake ID card high, so they could scan it with the sensors in their helmets. With his other hand, he held the grav gun that he was using to levitate Commander Lenon Donali, the Sythian agent, ahead of him. Once the sentries had scanned Bretton's ID, they turned away, having lost interest in the newcomers.

The Underlevels were not a pleasant place to be, and usually far too dangerous to venture into, but Bretton and Farah were currently protected by the fact that they were walking through the territory of a little-known criminal organization called Havoc.

Bretton's ID card was his passport through Havoc territory. It said he worked for a fuel mining company called Gencore. The ID was counterfeit, but Havoc recognized it because they were a branch of the organization that had given it to him. That organization was known simply as the Resistance, and their operations were located deep in the abandoned bowels of the planet, where miners had once toiled to extract valuable deposits of dymium.

Bretton and Farah continued down the foul-smelling corridor in the flickering yellow light of old glow panels. Somewhere up ahead water dripped from exposed pipes. The end of the corridor lay obscured by shifting clouds of steam leaking from an ancient heating system. They walked past a bank of lift tubes that were out of order and went for the stairs instead. They descended, heading for Sub Level 50.

The Underlevels used to be fit for habitation, but they were now officially abandoned. Unofficially they were home to Psychos, scavengers, and criminal organizations like Havoc.

At the bottom of the stairs they stepped out into an alley crowded with rubble, garbage, and bad-smelling puddles that hadn't made it to a working lavatory or drain.

"Almost there," Farah said beside him, using her glow lamp to check the holo signs and phosphorescent graffiti on the nearest wall.

Bretton nodded. "Good, I'm getting tired of this smell." He shifted his grip on the grav gun he was using to levitate and carry their prisoner.

"We're not going to stay long, are we?" Farah asked.

"Maybe, maybe not. Depends if they need us to."

She sighed. "You know I don't like getting involved with these people. They're fanatics, and there's always two or three of them whose job it seems to be to ask me when I'm going to get my commission."

"When *are* you going to get your commission?"

Farah sighed theatrically. "Why would I want a commission? It's a lost cause. What are they hoping to find, anyway? All the information we have access to is already public on the Omninet."

"Public in Etheria maybe. Nulls don't have access to the

Omninet at all."

"That's because we don't want access. You think Etherians are the ones Omnius tells all his dirty secrets to? If he's hiding something, he's hiding it from everyone."

"They're working on slicing into Omnius's private archives."

"Yea, I can see how a group of *human* slicers are going to break through the network security of a super-intelligent computer. You shouldn't waste your time, Bret. They're never going to get anywhere."

"How I waste my time is my business. No one's forcing you to hang around with me."

"That's gratitude. I bust my ass saving yours all day long, and you tell me you'd be just fine without me."

"I didn't say I'd be fine. I said you're free to go."

Farah grunted, but left it at that.

Up ahead, the end of the corridor came swirling out of the putrid steam hissing through the alley. They came to a pair of reinforced doors with warnings written on them in flickering red holotext:

Sutterfold Mine
RADIATION HAZARD!
STAY OUT!

Bretton set Donali down on the ground and stepped up to the entrance with his ID card in one hand and the grav gun in the other. Using his fingernails to peel away a fresh growth of green slime, he found a small gap in the seam between the doors and inserted his ID card there. Something clicked and a loud groan came from the doors. They ground halfway open, leaving a narrow space for them to walk through.

Once on the other side, they found themselves standing on a rickety metal lift platform, suspended over a vast chasm of nothingness. Farah walked over to the lift controls and triggered the lift to descend. It jerked into motion, dropping slowly with the *tat-tat-tat* of old chains unwinding from a motorized winch. Simultaneously, the doors began grinding shut, sealing them into the mine.

They spent long minutes descending past sheer rock walls slick and glistening with moisture in the light of their glow lamps. Finally, the lift jerked to a stop in front of a tram station with a waiting rail car.

They walked out into the middle of the platform and waited there. The station had a few working glow lamps, but the rail car and the tracks were dark and silent. A few more minutes passed, which Bretton spent studying the cottony puffs of condensing moisture streaming from his nose and lips. He and Farah were both wearing thick jackets emblazoned with the Gencore logo, courtesy of the Resistance, but the cold crept in despite their layers. The Null Zone was cold, cut off as it was from natural sunlight, but at least it retained the heat produced by indoor heating, air cars, and power plants. Much worse were the abandoned Underlevels and the subterranean labyrinths of abandoned mines. There, the only heating came from Avilon's molten core, and that was still a long way down.

"How long are they going to make us wait?" Farah asked, glancing around nervously.

Bretton turned to her with a shrug and set Donali down once more. He turned off the grav gun and joined Farah in looking around. The station was damp and cold. The air smelled of dirt and wet rocks, with a vaguely ferrous tang. "I guess that's up to them," he replied. While he waited, he brought to mind the code phrase the Resistance would be looking for when they came. Someone would ask them what they were doing in an abandoned mine, and Bretton's answer would be, *We're investigating a dymium gas leak.*

The use of code phrases wasn't particularly secure, but any extra layers of security could only help. The Resistance's main defense was that once you got to know where their headquarters were, you could never leave. Everyone else was brought in and out whilst heavily sedated. It was more or less the same principle that Omnius had used to keep Avilon hidden for countless centuries.

Bretton turned to his niece and saw her hugging herself and shivering. She was much skinnier than him, and the cold had obviously begun to affect her core temperature. "Cold?"

"As krak on ice."

"Colorful."

"Not really. Turns white."

"I don't want to look inside your freezer."

Farah barked a short laugh that echoed off the walls of the mine. They passed several more minutes in silence, broken only by the sound of Farah's chattering teeth and the distant sound of water splashing on rocks from some subterranean river. Then, finally, another noise reached their ears—

"Hello strangers," it said, slicing through the gloom.

They turned toward the noise. The familiar blue-white glow of shielded armor, made fuzzy by the low light and the humid air, was strange to see in the Null Zone—but far stranger were the speaker's glowing amber eyes—ARCs. Then the man stepped out of the shadows, and they saw him for what he was—

A Peacekeeper.

* * *

Ethan was shocked. Far below, he saw a vast field of garbage. The air was saturated with a rancid stench that made him want to gag. He buried his nose in his robes in a vain attempt to get away from it.

Giant, glowing blue accelerator tubes snaked down from a high, dark ceiling overhead. Ethan's vantage point was a rooftop at least a hundred meters above the ground, and the ends of the accelerator tubes were at eye level with him, spewing a continuous stream of multi-colored refuse. Far below, circling at a cautious distance from the falling streams of garbage, Ethan saw the floodlights of giant, mobile trash compacters as they rolled over the top of the garbage piles, packing them down. Mechanized load lifters used saw-bladed arms to cut and carry cubes of recently packed trash to glowing red pits in the ground. Ethan assumed those pits led to some type of recycling plant where the trash would be processed further. A planet with as many citizens as Avilon couldn't afford to waste any of its resources.

But the vast field of trash wasn't what had shocked him. It was the horde of humanity crawling around the machines and climbing the mountains of trash like spiders. Ethan focused on the nearest group, trying to get a better look. His ARCs responded to that desire by magnifying what he was seeing, and he gasped. These people were wearing torn and patched clothing—dirty fragments of cloth at best. They were crawling over the trash on all fours like animals, picking some things up and tossing them aside, while other bits of garbage they lifted to their mouths and tore into greedily.

They were *hungry*, hunting through the refuse for food like rats. Ethan shook his head, horrified. Dark Space had been bad, and the people there had been hungry, but they'd never been hungry enough to resort to eating garbage. His stomach did a nauseated flip, and he felt his gorge rising again.

Frozen in shock and horror, Ethan stared for a long time, watching these rag people enjoy their buffet. As some left with their hunger sated, others came, seeming to melt out of the shadows.

There was no end to them.

Ethan blinked, and then blinked again. He shook his head and looked away. As he did so, his ARCs returned to a normal zoom, and he began to notice his more immediate surroundings. To one side of the rooftop he saw a lift tube, flanked by a pair of drones. Curious, Ethan walked up to them.

"Mind if I use the lift?" he asked.

The red optics in the center of each ball-shaped head tracked him, but neither of the drones replied.

Nevertheless, the doors of the lift *swished* open. Again, Ethan turned to look behind him, convinced that someone was following him and secretly opening doors for him as he went.

But there was no one there.

Ethan stepped into the lift, walking up to the far side. It was transparent and gave him another look at the starving hordes swarming over the trash mountains below. He heard the doors *swish* shut, and the lift started downward of its own accord, dropping swiftly toward the trash collection level.

Omnius was definitely behind this little tour.

As the lift drew near to the ground, Ethan got a sense of scale. The load lifters were as big as any mech Ethan had ever seen, while the mobile trash compactors were the size of miniature skyscrapers, bright with running lights, their treads grinding along the shallow slopes of falling trash.

Then the lift dropped below the collection level and his view changed to that of another wide-open space, this one a vast, brightly-lit warehouse with clean white walls and matte gray floors.

Racks of revolving conveyor belts ran down from the ceiling. The aisles between those racks were crowded with orderly lines of people. These people at least wore decent clothes, but they were all drab browns and grays. They pushed hover carts ahead of them while they picked small, cubic packages off the conveyor belts and placed them in their carts.

Ethan realized he was looking at some type of supermarket. The lift stopped and the doors opened behind him. He turned and walked out, bracing himself for another noxious wave of rotting garbage to invade his nostrils. Instead, he found the air sterile and slightly fragrant.

That raised his spirits. He walked from the lift to the nearest line of shoppers. They watched him carefully as he approached, momentarily distracted. As he drew near, he noticed that the looks he was getting weren't simply curious; they were either fearful or hostile. A little girl pointed to him and said, "Look, Mommy! It's a *Non!*"

Ethan stopped and gave the girl a curious smile. "What did you call me?"

She shrank away, hiding behind her mother's legs. The mother's reaction was similar. She went back to her shopping.

Worried he'd somehow offended them, Ethan stepped up to the woman and tapped her lightly on the shoulder. "I'm sorry if I startled you," he said.

The woman turned to him with wide eyes and shook her head. "What do you want from me, My Lord?"

At that, Ethan noticed a few others turn to look at him. A pair of white teenage males caught Ethan's eye. Their faces were pale and dirty, their hair greasy and disheveled, and their eyebrows were mysteriously missing. They didn't look frightened—they looked angry. Their eyes were dark and soulless.

"I'm not your lord," Ethan replied, ignoring the two ruffians who'd glanced his way. "I seem to have come here by mistake . . . could you tell me where I am?"

"You're on Sub Level 40 . . . in the Grunge."

"The what?"

"Sutterfold District, Master."

"I'm not your master, either."

The woman shook her head, and for the first time her watery blue eyes seemed to really *see* him. The fear shining there retreated a few steps, and she seemed to relax. "You're wearing one of their robes, but you're too old to be one of them."

"One of who?"

"A Non!" the little girl he'd seen earlier popped out to inform him.

"Hey, what's the hold up?" someone shouted. Ethan noticed then that the woman he'd stopped to talk to wasn't moving, but the conveyor belts were rolling on. Up ahead there was a growing gap between her and the rest of the line.

"Excuse me, I have to get back to shopping," she said.

"Sure, I'll walk with you."

"If you're not a Non, what are you?" the little girl asked, departing from the safety of her mother's legs to walk beside him.

"I don't know what that is."

"It's what we call people from the Uppers," the girl's mother replied. "Nons. It's short for non-human. You're wearing white, like a Celestial, but you're too old to be one of them. And if you were one of us, you'd know what a Non is."

Ethan's lips quirked up in a wry smile. "I suppose I would. Actually . . . I'm a refugee from the Imperium. The Nons are making me go through something they call The Choosing."

The woman met that admission with wide and blinking eyes. "What are you doing here, then?"

"I don't know yet. I came here by accident."

"If you came from the Uppers, nothing that happens to you is an accident."

"So I've been told," Ethan replied dryly.

"You've been to other worlds," the woman said.

"Yes, dozens . . . hundreds actually, but that was before the war."

"You're very lucky. I can only imagine what that must be like . . ."

Ethan heard the longing in the woman's voice, and he felt a pang of sympathy for her and her daughter. "I bet you'd like to get away from Avilon and go start a colony someplace else."

"Omnius would never allow that."

"Right, Omnius. He's a real pain in the you-know-what, isn't he?"

"He is what he is."

Ethan watched the woman reach out to take a bright green cube from the conveyor belt running beside her. It was wrapped in some type of transparent packing material. "What's that?"

"Enriched cellulose."

"Plants?" Ethan eyed the green cube. "Looks processed."

"That's because it's recycled."

"From what?" A suspicion formed in Ethan's gut, and his insides churned.

"Garbage," the woman said, confirming his suspicions.

"And you *eat* it?"

"Down here we don't have a choice. If we had the money to buy fresh food we wouldn't be here. This food is free," the woman said, reaching out to take a bloody red cube from the conveyor belt.

Ethan wondered if it might be recycled meat. Suddenly he remembered the hordes of people he'd seen crawling over the mountains of unprocessed garbage. "I saw something ... people, lots of people, looking through the garbage before it gets recycled. They seemed to be looking for food. If all of this food is free, why would anyone try to eat raw garbage?"

"Because they're Psychos. If we allowed them in here, they'd sooner kill everyone than thank us."

"*Psychos?*"

"You really *are* from someplace else," the woman said. "They're Bliss addicts who've gone too long without a dose. The withdrawal symptoms destroy your brain and turn you into an animal. That's why we call them Pyschos, because they're all crazy."

"Sounds a lot worse than the drugs we had in the Imperium."

The woman nodded and they walked on in silence. They turned a corner and came to a conveyor belt laden with rolls of fabric and stacks of cylindrical containers, each of them a different color from the next. As he wondered what they were, glowing text appeared above them, revealing their contents. Some were filled with toothpaste, others with moisturizing creams, soap, cleaning solvents, paint, and more.

"This is all made from trash?"

The woman nodded, but said nothing.

"Amazing."

She sent him a hesitant smile and looked away quickly. Noticing that the fear in her eyes was back, he wondered what he'd done wrong. "I'm making you uncomfortable," he said. "I should go."

"It's not you . . . but you *should* go."

"Not me?"

She stopped walking and looked at him very seriously. "You're wearing Celestial Whites and your eyes are glowing with ARCs. Down here a pair of those are worth more than most people make in a month—and that's *if* they have a job."

Ethan turned in a slow circle. He found the pair of ruffians he'd spotted earlier glancing at him again. They were standing a few feet closer to him than they had been before. When they saw him staring back, they looked away and whispered something between them.

Ethan's eyes narrowed, and he walked up to them. "Hey," he said.

One of the boys was tall and skinny. The other shorter, but barrel-chested under his dark gray robes. Ethan decided that Barrel Chest was the one to talk to. "You two have a problem with me?" he asked, stopping to stand uncomfortably close to the young man.

Barrel Chest looked up and smiled with a mouth full of missing teeth. "You're a long way from home, old man."

"And?"

The boy shrugged. "And nothin' just don't stay long, that's all."

"So what if I do? What are you going to do about it?" Ethan gave the boy a shove. He bounced into the man behind him, who quickly shrank away. Barrel Chest recovered quickly, and shot Ethan another hateful look.

Ethan replied with a nasty grin. "There, see, that's the look you were giving me earlier. You should mind your own business before you lose any more teeth."

Barrel Chest took a swing. Ethan ducked and came in with a right cross. The boy took it in the ear and stumbled to one side. He cursed and looked up, his dark eyes flashing.

By now people were giving them a wide berth, clearing a space. Some had stopped to watch, while others were moving on more quickly than before.

The boy let out a roar and charged. Ethan blocked two blows headed for his face on his forearms and took a quick step forward to grab the kid's head in both hands and force it down. Simultaneously he brought his knee up. Barrel Chest's nose crunched and he screamed. The boy crumpled to the ground, his nose streaming blood.

"Anyone else?" Ethan asked, turning in a quick circle to look for new challengers. No one would meet his gaze. He affected a smug grin to mask the revulsion he felt at the beating he'd given.

"Put your hands behind your back," a soft voice said.

Then came a girlish scream, and Ethan heard the voice of the woman he'd been talking with before. Another scream, and the mother's voice became more urgent. "Leave her alone!"

Ethan turned toward the commotion and saw the tall, skinny boy had the little girl in a choke hold. He'd pressed a long, thin knife to her throat.

"I said, put your hands behind your back," Skinny repeated, nodding to him.

Ethan's eyebrows floated up. He noted that the rest of the people in the line were all conveniently minding their own business—except for the girl's mother, who was still pleading with the knife wielder to let her daughter go.

"What do you want?" Ethan asked, wondering where the facility's security guards were.

"Your clothes. Your ARCs, and all the bytes in your account."

"Bytes?" Ethan wondered aloud. "I don't have any money."

"We'll see about that."

Ethan noticed a glowing white tattoo on the boy's upper arm. It was a skull. "You think you're tough, don't you, boy?"

The kid sneered at him. "Hurry up! I don't have all day."

Peripherally, Ethan became aware of Barrel Chest getting up beside him. "If you're so tough, why don't you let the girl go and fight me? Keep your blade, I don't mind a challenge."

"I don't think so."

"Why not? Afraid I'll break your nose, too?"

Skinny inched his knife closer to the little girl's throat. A small bead of blood appeared at the tip. The little girl whimpered, and her mother screamed, sinking to her knees and breaking down in tears.

"Hey!" Ethan said, taking half a step forward. His ire was building swiftly now. "What's wrong with you? She's just a kid!"

"So? I used to be one, too," Skinny said. "Hands behind your back."

Ethan did as he was told. He received a swift kick behind his knees and sunk to the ground. A second kick hit him in the side of the head. His ear exploded in pain, and he heard a ringing sound. The world began to sway around him, and his vision darkened around the edges.

Skinny let go of the girl and began advancing on him with the knife. "I'm gonna carve you up," he said.

Ethan freed his hands from their self-imposed bondage. Then Barrel Chest appeared in front of him, his face and nose a horror of smeared and dripping blood. Ethan saw the boot coming toward his own nose just in time to catch it in his hands. The boot was slick with the boy's blood and it slipped through Ethan's grasp, hitting him above one eye. His head exploded with pain again, and he felt a wave of nausea wash over him.

Dizzy and sick, Ethan slumped to one side, wincing against the pain radiating from his eye. Skinny reached him with the knife and held it close and glinting in front of his good eye.

"Since you didn't want to give them to me, I'm gonna cut 'em out."

Ethan assumed the boy was referring to his ARCs. He mumbled a vicious curse that he barely heard through the ringing in his ear, but Skinny shook his head.

"You're the one who's frekked, old ma—"

There came a loud *whoosh* of air, and Skinny flew backward, as if hit by an invisible hover truck. He slammed into the far wall of the warehouse with a *thud!* Even from a distance, with one ear still ringing, that impact was loud. Ethan pushed himself up, leaning on one elbow to watch as

Skinny slid down the wall and flopped onto his face, quiet and unmoving. With his one good eye, Ethan saw the faint splatter of blood and the crack in the wall. The kid was definitely dead.

Strong hands lifted Ethan to his feet. He raised his pounding head to find himself face to face with a Peacekeeper, but not just any Peacekeeper. That man's glowing blue eyes and young, chiseled features were familiar by now. Ethan tried to smile, but it hurt his eye too much, so he abandoned the attempt.

"Hey there, Wovik," he managed. "Where'd you come fwom?" Ethan frowned at his lisp. "Fwo . . . Fro-m," he tried, forcing his tongue and lips to cooperate.

"Omnius ordered me to follow you."

So someone *had* been opening doors for him. "Why didn't I see you?" he asked.

"I was cloaked. Come on. We need to leave before you get yourself into any more trouble."

"Give me a second." Ethan turned in a dizzy circle to find Barrel Chest, but there was no sign of the other boy. He did find the little girl and her mother, however, sitting on the floor, their groceries forgotten as they hugged and held each other close.

Ethan kneeled down beside the woman and placed a hand on her shoulder. "I'm so sorry. I had no idea that—"

"Just leave us alone!"

Ethan frowned. "I . . ."

"You've done enough! Go back to the Uppers, *Non!* We don't want you here."

Ethan felt the Peacekeeper's hands on him again. Rovik half-carried, half-dragged him through the market.

They reached an exit and Ethan noticed a pair of guards

standing there. Ancient-looking sidearms were holstered on their hips. Their armor was scuffed and beaten, and it didn't glow with active shields like the Peacekeepers' armor. Even so, they should have been enough to deter a pair of kids with a blade.

"Hey!" Ethan said as they approached the guards. "Didn't you hear the fight going on?"

One of the guards turned to him with a bland look. Then he appeared to notice what Ethan was wearing, and the fact that he was being escorted by a Peacekeeper. The guard straightened and shook his head. "No, Master! We heard nothing! Was there a problem?"

"Yeah, there was a problem! Someone was holding a little girl hostage with a knife!"

"Is she all right?" the guard asked, sounding appropriately alarmed.

"Yes, no thanks to you!"

"And yourself, My Lord? You don't look well."

"I'll be all right."

"That is good to hear!"

"Come on," Rovik whispered sharply in Ethan's ear, shoving him along again.

"Keep a better lookout in future!" Ethan called over his shoulder.

"We will do our best, My Lord!"

Once they were outside, Ethan shrugged out of Rovik's grasp and rounded on him. "What the frek is wrong with them?" he asked, gesturing to the guards standing just inside the sliding glass doors of the warehouse.

"They were being polite. Celestials don't give orders to Nulls, nor do Etherians."

"So? I don't have to give them orders! I'm telling them

about something that happened on their watch. They should at least go to investigate."

The Peacekeeper slowly shook his head.

"Why not? It's their job!"

"They probably knew what was happening, but as soon as they saw who the troublemakers were, they went back to their posts and minded their own business. Based on the shaven eyebrows and tattoos, those two boys are members of the White Skulls. Sutterfold District is their territory, and not even Enforcers will mess with them. Not below level 10, anyway."

"So you're telling me the law is afraid to mess with a pair of *kids* that I could have beat bare-handed."

"They're not afraid of those two, per se, but of the retribution that might follow if they intervene."

Ethan snorted. "Okay, so the local authorities are running scared. What about all the drones I saw collecting trash? They don't look like they'd give a krak about retribution."

"The drones are not programmed to interfere in local disputes."

"So Omnius just sits back and watches while criminals run the show down here."

"That is how the Nulls want to live, so he must respect their wishes."

"That's a convenient excuse."

"It is neither convenient, nor is it an excuse. If the Null Zone were less corrupt and decrepit, Omnius wouldn't need to send millions of his drones to work in the trash fields for free, and the Nulls would pay for recycled products. Besides, if the drones started interfering, they'd become targets for organized crime, and soon Omnius would have to send a whole army down here to clean things up. The Null Zone would become a military dictatorship, run by Omnius, and that would cause more of an outcry than a few murdered Nulls."

"Omnius runs the recycling operation?"

Rovik inclined his head. "He can't leave it to Nulls. The job would never get done. Now, enough arguing. Please follow me. There is a reason Omnius allowed you to come down here."

Ethan scowled, but he decided to follow Rovik in silence. They walked down a broad corridor leading from the supermarket. Here the ceiling was three or four stories high, which Ethan thought to be a waste, but then he noticed the overly-tall doors lining the corridor, and he remembered the mechanized load lifters he'd seen earlier.

After walking for about a minute, they came to a bank of lift tubes, these ones with regular, human-sized doors. The nearest one chimed and opened for them as they approached, as if Rovik had summoned it from a distance.

They walked inside, and the lift started upward with a barely-perceptible jolt of movement. Ethan's ears popped, and the lift opened, revealing another rooftop.

Smack. The rotting garbage smell was back. They walked out, and Ethan noticed that now they were much further from the trash fields with their glowing accelerator tubes. The noisy bustle of machines compacting and cutting trash had been reduced to a distant rumble.

Looking up, Ethan saw towering rows of apartment buildings stretching all the way out to the distant, hazy line of the horizon. The apartments were aglow with lights, and each one was painted a different color—blue, red, green, purple, yellow . . . It was an assault on his eyes.

Elevated streets ran along in front of the buildings,

connecting them to each other and providing easy access for pedestrians rather than cars.

On the far side of the residential complex, the side closest to the garbage dump, Ethan saw a high wall with glittering rows of spikes on top.

"What is this place?" Ethan asked.

"This is where the people you saw in the market live."

Ethan began nodding. "Subsidized housing?"

"Free."

"Who pays for it?"

"Omnius. The trash field used to be twice as large as it is today. Omnius reorganized the space to make room for a housing project. This is where Nulls come when they have no place left to go."

"I thought he doesn't care."

"You're mistaken. He cares too much, but we tie his hands and stop him from helping us."

"Why did you bring me here?"

"I didn't. He did. I suspect he wants you to know what he's doing, even for people that don't want his help."

Ethan frowned, unsure of what to say to that.

"There's one other thing you need to see before we go."

"What's that?"

Not bothering to reply, Rovik walked over to one side of the rooftop. Ethan followed. They came to a long staircase. It descended at least ten stories from their vantage point, all the way down to the highest level of streets running between the apartment buildings. Blue Cape led the way. By the time they reached the street level, Ethan was short of breath and his legs were shaking. He felt nauseated again. "Hey!" he gasped, leaning over a railing to catch his breath.

Rovik turned to him. "Come, Ethan. Your wife is awake

and asking for you. She is not happy. I suggest you don't delay."

Ethan grimaced and started after the Peacekeeper again, trying to ignore the way the world felt like it was tilted on one end and he was about to slide off. That kick to the side of his head must have upset his sense of balance.

They walked down the street, passing apartment building after apartment building. People's front decks were lined with glowing green plants and some basic furniture. A few residents sat outside, drinking or smoking something fragrant and sweet. Dark eyes watched him as he hurried by.

A railing ran along the side of the street to his right, and walkways led to people's homes on his left. Most of the apartments were bright and occupied, but the glass was blurry to preserve people's privacy. A few of the apartments had holotext signs hanging above their doors and in their windows, describing services that their residents offered—everything from hair cuts to more exotic things that had no place being advertised on a public street.

"You know someone down here?" Ethan asked, catching up to walk beside Rovik rather than behind him.

Again, no reply, but just a few moments later the Peacekeeper stopped and turned to walk down one of the walkways to a particular apartment. This one was painted a bright sea green. The house number was 1050C. A blurry yellow light shone out from the front windows, pooling on the apartment's narrow front deck.

Rovik knocked on the door. Ethan stopped beside him and leaned over the railing of the walkway to look down. Elevated streets and apartment buildings fell away below in a dizzying swirl of light and color.

Rovik knocked again, louder this time.

Ethan heard footsteps approaching the door from the other side. "Just a minute," a gruff voice said.

At the sound of that man's voice, a tickle of recognition shivered through Ethan's brain.

Then the door swung wide to reveal a young man—maybe thirty-something—with hard brown eyes and straight, short brown hair. He had a strong, square jaw, a chin dimple, and sunken cheeks.

"Can I help you?" he asked, his eyes on the Peacekeeper.

Again, that voice sounded familiar, but Ethan couldn't figure out where he knew this man from. "Do I know you?" he asked.

The man turned to him and looked him up and down quickly. His brown eyes widened, and he shook his head, stumbling back a step. "It can't be ..." he whispered. "Ethan?"

"How do you know my name?"

"Well, I ought to know it," the younger man replied. "I gave it to you."

CHAPTER 13

Bretton Hale's heart thudded in his chest. There was a Peacekeeper in Sutterfold Mine. Did that mean the resistance had been found?

"Hello, Master," Bretton said, resorting to the default honorific for people from the Uppers.

The Peacekeeper stalked toward them and gestured to the unconscious Imperial they'd brought with him. "Did you know your friend there is unlisted?"

Bretton forced his eyebrows up, feigning surprise. "Really?" Of course the man wasn't listed. Donali had crash-landed on Avilon, and his personal data had yet to be uploaded to the Omninet.

"Yes. Really." The Peacekeeper stopped a few paces away from them and gazed down on Donali with a thoughtful frown, his glowing amber eyes unblinking. "What's wrong with him?"

Bretton shrugged. "Tripped and fell down an old mine shaft, I'm guessing. We found him down here while we were doing our inspection. We're trying to get him back up so we can take him to a med center."

"I'd better take him for you. They won't treat an unlisted Null without some convincing. What did you two say you were doing down here?"

Bretton pointed to the Gencore emblem on his jacket. "We're investigating reports of a dymium gas leak."

The Peacekeeper smiled at that. "In that case, you'd better come with me."

"What?" Farah burst out. "We haven't done anything wrong and you're going to book us?"

Bretton was faster on the uptake than his niece. He placed a hand on her arm and replied to the Peacekeeper's smile with one of his own. "So you're the new security system."

"Avilon's finest. Who's going to pick a fight with a Peacekeeper?"

Bretton let out a long sigh. "You had me for a minute."

Farah's eyes darted from Bretton to the man in the glowing armor and back again, but she said nothing.

"I'm going to need you two to submit to a quick scan."

Bretton nodded and watched as the Peacekeeper removed a wand-shaped tool from his utility belt. He clicked something on the wand and it sprang to life, the tip glowing brightly with a shimmering fan of light that swiftly swept down to their feet and back up to the tops of their heads.

"You're clean," the man said, and then turned to use the wand on Donali. "So what's this guy's real story?"

Bretton chose that moment to explain, before the sentry found the same thing that Dag had found: a cloaked alien implant sitting right beside his regular Lifelink. "He's not what he looks like."

The guard turned to them with a frown. "And what does he look like?"

"Human."

"I'm listening."

Bretton went on to explain about the battle and the fact

that Commander Lenon Donali had come to Avilon aboard one of the warships involved in the fighting. Then he explained about the Sythian implant Dag had found when they'd tried to de-link him, and what their mind walk had subsequently revealed about Commander Donali and the Sythians.

"That's quite a story."

"Now you can see why we have him stunned."

"If all of what you just said is true, you've brought us something that not even Omnius has."

"I wouldn't count on that. His Lifelink was working when we found him."

"So why didn't Peacekeepers find him and pick him up before you did?"

"I'm guessing because he's spent most of his time on Avilon unconscious. For at least part of the time that he wasn't, Omnius was busy fighting a war."

The guard shook his head. "Doesn't add up. Omnius doesn't miss things like this."

"And yet he did."

"Might be a trap."

Bretton frowned. "We checked him. He's not broadcasting anything on quantum or regular comms."

Wordlessly, the guard finished scanning Donali with his wand and then he looked up, staring at nothing in particular as he studied something projected on his ARCs.

"Well?" Bretton pressed.

"I think I know why Omnius didn't find him . . ."

"Why's that?" Farah put in.

"He has two implants, just like you said, but neither of them are from Omnius."

That news hit Bretton like a bucket of ice. *"What?"*

"One of the implants is an Avilonian design, but its an old one. Very old." The guard turned his glowing eyes on them. "This refugee of yours might even predate Omnius."

"How's that possible?"

"I don't know. It's possible that he's an old Avilonian who somehow managed to leave Avilon before Omnius was created. You made a copy of the data on this implant?"

Bretton nodded, his hand absently finding the breast pocket inside his coat where he'd tucked the holo card that Dag had recorded with the contents of Donali's brain.

"We'll need to take a look at that." The guard returned the scanner wand to his belt and then opened a compartment beside it and removed a thin metallic strip. He clasped it around Donali's neck and then removed two more matching strips of metal and started toward them. "You ready?"

Bretton nodded. When the guard clasped the circlet of metal around his neck, he staggered slightly. His head felt suddenly light and airy and his eyes were heavy. He'd been through this before, so he knew what to expect, but the sudden onset of inescapable fatigue was always a shock.

He sunk to his knees on the cold floor of the station platform. It felt so good to rest, like he'd been running sleep deprived for a week. He yawned and said something that not even he could make sense out of, and then he lay down on the floor and drifted off into darkness.

As he slept, he dreamed of floating through the air, weightless, and then of a roaring wind that tore at his clothes and carried him into a place that was so bright it seemed to be made of light. In the midst of that light he saw a familiar face. Small mouth and bright, intelligent blue eyes ... dimpled cheeks and a ragged mop of dark hair. He was tall and lanky for an eight-year-old, but Ciam was just the way Bretton remembered him.

"Hello, Dad!" Ciam said, smiling at him from the blinding brightness.

Bretton's mouth cracked open, but he found he couldn't speak. Only strained whispers came out.

Ciam frowned. "When are you going to come visit me?"

Again, Bretton tried to say something, but the words got stuck in his throat.

Ciam's expression turned hurt and angry. "You left me! I waited for you to come, but you never did. You left me to die!"

Bretton shook his head. "No!" This time he managed to scream, but his son turned away, disappearing into the blinding light as if he hadn't heard a thing.

The fuzzy black abyss returned, and he was consumed with rage and grief. After that, he felt like he spent a lifetime crying in the dark, not caring if anyone heard, or if he ever saw the light again; he just wanted it all to end.

But the darkness began to lighten with the first strokes of dawn. The light wasn't as blinding as before, but it was back, and he could hear voices calling to him from it, calling as if from a great distance . . .

"Wake up, Bretton . . . wake up . . ."

* * *

"Wake up!"

SLAP!

Bretton's eyes shot open and he gasped from the pain that stung his cheek. He squinted up at a bright ceiling light and he saw Farah appear, her face silhouetted with a bright golden halo. Behind her, a Peacekeeper stood by the door.

A Peacekeeper!

Bretton sat up suddenly, only to find that he was lying on a sterile metal table and surrounded by blinking and beeping equipment. His heart rate accelerated and he heard some of the beeping accelerate with it.

"Relax," the guard at the door said. "You're among friends."

"Relax? What is this?" he asked, finding an IV line trailing from his wrist. "Where am I?"

The room where they had him and Farah was equipped with half a dozen tables like his. Rather than the sterile white walls of a med center, here the walls were dull and gray— bare bactcrete, the lights were a harsh, artificial yellow, and a faint, musty draft wafted through the room, apparently coming from a dirty grate in the ceiling. A dark window on the far side of the room, beside the door, looked like it might be made of old-fashioned two-way glass. Bretton's gaze found their guard once more. He looked like the same one they'd met on the tram station platform.

"Why are we being held here?"

The door swung wide and in walked a tall, stunning woman with short, straight black hair, wide glowing silver eyes, and a honey brown skin. All of that was wrapped up in a familiar black uniform with white piping and the gold star of a *Captain.*

"You're not being *held* here," she said as she approached. "New decontamination protocols. Don't worry; you're clean. We've just been waiting for you to wake up before we take you in for debriefing. The collar must have given you too much sedative." The woman stopped to stand in front of them, hands clasped behind her back, her posture military straight.

"Where did you get that uniform?" Bretton asked, his eyes wide and staring.

"Old navy surplus."

"Not from Avilon's navy . . ."

The woman answered that with a small, secretive smile.

"You're from the Imperium," he said.

She shook her head. "No, I was born on Avilon."

"Then . . ."

"You'll see for yourself soon enough."

Bretton began shaking his head. "This is all new to me," he said, looking around the room again. His eyes landed on her once more, marveling again at the uniform she wore. "And so are you."

"We've had to increase our security protocols pretty much overnight, so everything is still in flux. I'm Marla Picara," she said, sticking out her hand.

Bretton shook it with a thoughtful frown. "Why all the changes?"

"Omnius killed over five thousand Nulls the night before last."

"What? Why?"

"They were reportedly members of a rebellion that tried to kill everyone in the Uppers."

"Is that even possible?" Farah asked.

Marla shrugged. "The virus was meant to overload their Lifelinks and fry their brains. Do that to everyone in the Uppers and corrupt the databases at the same time, and they're not coming back. Not ever."

"How did Omnius kill the rebels?" Bretton asked.

Marla made a flicking motion with one finger, as if to turn off a switch. "Same way. The Lifelinks."

"That doesn't make any sense," Bretton said. "No rebel in his right mind would still have a working Lifelink."

Marla nodded. "Exactly."

"So . . ."

"It wasn't us, if that's what you're wondering. The Lifelink databases are far too hard to slice into, and even if we could, we wouldn't be that stupid. Suppose we got it right—Omnius wouldn't just roll over and play dead because we killed all of his precious children. He'd sic the drones on us and we'd be next."

"Then it's a cover up."

Marla nodded. "The most obvious lie we've ever seen. Either the rebels responsible are still out there, or, more likely, they never existed in the first place, and Omnius invented the rebel plot as an excuse for why he had to make an emergency shut down—an emergency shut down that conveniently coincided with a Sythian attack."

Bretton shook his head. "You're saying Omnius let them in on purpose."

"Maybe."

"Why? I thought looking after his chosen ones was his primary purpose, the almighty reason behind everything he does."

"No one really died in the attack. Besides all the Nulls who got hit by falling debris, of course. Maybe Omnius wanted to impress upon us all the seriousness of the Sythian threat."

"By destroying his own fleet—the same fleet he needs to fight them."

Marla shook her head. "I don't pretend to understand his reasoning, but if we can prove he shut down on purpose and there never was any rebel threat, we'll have what we've been looking for."

"Proof of that might be hard to find."

"Maybe, but this lie is proof enough of one thing—Omnius is getting sloppy."

"Or he just doesn't care about preserving his *holier than thou* image anymore." Bretton smiled. "It would save us a lot of trouble if he exposed himself."

"But what happens next? We turn everyone on Avilon against Omnius and then he sics the drones on us and we're all dead. The Resistance has the same end point as that so-called rebel plot."

"What are you saying—that we've just been wasting our time and we shouldn't even bother trying to expose him?"

"No, I'm saying that it's time to start thinking about our next steps."

"How about some food and sleep for next steps?" Farah chimed in.

Marla turned to her.

"We've been running short on both. Might be a nice way to show your appreciation for us bringing in that Sythian agent."

"Yes, about him ..." Marla trailed off and Bretton watched her turn back to him. "By now the analysis of the Lifelink data you brought us must be finished. Follow me."

Farah's mouth dropped open. Her plea for hospitality had been ignored. She began to say something about it as they followed Marla out of the room, but Bretton elbowed her in the ribs. "Not now," he whispered. "There'll be time for rest and recovery later. There's something big going on here and I want to know what it is."

"What, just because miss prissy pants is wearing an old Imperial uniform?"

"Yes."

Farah snorted. "She's not from some lost fleet. You heard what she said—born on Avilon."

"Call it a hunch, then."

Marla led them down a long corridor. The door swung shut behind them with a noisy *click,* and Bretton turned to see the guard following them out. More bare bactcrete lined the corridor. A matching floor and exposed pipes overhead made Bretton think of a bunker. A few flickering glow panels were there to remind him how badly the Resistance needed the funds from commissioned members like him. At the end of the corridor was another door. Above it hung a glossy black sphere with a dim red photoreceptor that looked like a drone's eye. Marla stopped there and waited. A fan of red light flickered out and passed over all of them from head to toe. Once scanned, a loud beep issued from the door, and the eye in the black sphere glowed green.

They walked through into a circular chamber lit with a dim red light. In the center of the room was a familiar glossy dome. "What is that?" Bretton asked in a startled whisper, even though he already knew the answer. The dome began to rise on shimmering pillars of light as they approached, confirming his suspicions.

"You stole a quantum junction!" Farah said.

Marla cast a grin over her shoulder. "We'll never have to worry about anyone finding our headquarters again."

Bretton stopped at the edge of it, his hand lightly brushing the smooth surface of the dome as it rose. A kind of reverent awe settled over him, and he whistled slowly. "If Omnius knew you had this, he'd turn the Null Zone inside out just to find it. You could jump straight into the Zenith Tower—or better yet, send a proton bomb into Omnius's core."

"Unfortunately, he's already thought of that. Everything important in the Uppers is already shielded with disruption fields. We can get off-world if we want to, though."

"You have the power for that?" Bretton asked, surprised.

"We have more funds than we like to admit."

"So let's go!" Farah said. "What are we waiting for? This is exactly what we need! Let's run as far as we can from here and never look back."

"And leave countless billions of Nulls to Omnius's mercy?" Marla asked, arching an eyebrow at them.

Bretton frowned. "We could take some of them with us."

"Not nearly enough."

They walked under the dome to the middle of the glowing green circle in the center. The guard in Peacekeeper's armor stood outside the dome, watching them leave. Marla raised her hands and swiftly dropped them, and the dome fell with a *boom*. A rising *whirr* started up, quickly becoming a deafening roar as air whipped around inside the dome. The walls began to glow and Bretton shut his eyes before they turned blindingly bright. The brightness blazed through his closed eyelids, and with it, he remembered the little boy from his dream.

Ciam.

Through the deafening roar of wind and the painfully bright glow inside the dome, Bretton did something he usually tried not to do—he remembered.

The memories flooded back, running backward in time—happy memories for a change . . . They went all the way back to the beginning, and he saw his wife, Karie Hale, looking younger and more beautiful than he remembered her, smiling and crying with joy as they were reunited in Etheria. She'd been waiting a little over a month for him to join her on Avilon.

"*I have a surprise for you, Bret,*" she said, withdrawing from their embrace.

He arched an eyebrow at that. "*You've already surprised me enough for one day.*"

"Then maybe someone else should surprise you." She said, smiling and placing his hand on her belly.

He frowned and shook his head, wondering what she was on about. Then he caught the meaningful look in her gaze, and his eyes flew wide. "*That's not possible! We were . . .*"

"*Together on Advistine. Four months ago.*"

"But you . . . You died, Karie."

"*So how am I here speaking to you now?*"

When the light and sound vanished and the dome rose once more on shimmering pillars of light, his recollection faded, and Bretton opened his eyes. He found himself back in darkness.

Marla led them out from under the dome, into another circular chamber lit with dim red lights. They stopped at a door and another black eye scanned them with a fan of light. Then the door *swished* open, and they walked out into a bright, bustling operations center.

Bretton blinked against the sudden glare of the lights, trying to make sense of the chaos. Before them lay a gleaming catwalk, at the end of which was a broad bank of viewports cluttered with stars, and in the middle distance lay a familiar table with uniformed men and women gathered around it. To either side of the gleaming catwalk were control stations with more people in uniforms sitting behind them.

The whole scene was a blast from the past. Bretton's heart skipped a beat and seemed to freeze in his chest. His eyes burned with emotion and he shook his head, feeling certain that he was asleep and this was all just a lot of wishful thinking.

"Where ..." Bretton trailed off, unable to finish that sentence.

Farah was more eloquent. "Holy frek! You found a working venture-class cruiser?"

Marla grinned broadly at them, but her eyes quickly found Bretton's. "Welcome back to the ISSF, Captain Hale."

CHAPTER 14

Ethan couldn't believe his eyes. "Dad?"

The younger man nodded, confirming Ethan's suspicions. "Come inside," he said, holding the door open for them.

Ethan walked through first, and Rovik followed behind him. The apartment was a small, open concept space with living room, dining room, kitchen, and what looked like a bedroom and bathroom at the back.

"It's not much," Preston said, but it's home."

The floor was a dull matte gray, the walls plain white. The living room furniture was solid blue, and the dining room table solid white with gray chairs. It was all utilitarian and uninspiring to look at, but the space was tidy and warm, much warmer than the air outside. Preston Ortane directed them to sit in the blue living room furniture.

"Drinks?" he asked, already on his way to the kitchen.

Ethan sat down in an armchair that looked to be made of several interlocking pieces. It was surprisingly comfortable. "What do you have?" he asked.

"Beer. Water."

"I'm fine, thank you," Rovik said, taking a seat on one of the room's two couches. The cushions squeaked noisily against his armor and he sunk deep into the couch, making him look as though he were a midget with giant legs. Ethan surmised that the Peacekeeper must weigh a lot with his armor on.

"Beer," Ethan replied.

Preston returned with two bottles of a dark-looking beer and passed one to Ethan. Preston turned and eyed Rovik with a frown. "You better not break my couch."

"Why? Was it not free?"

"The pieces were, sure, but putting them together costs a lot of sweat." Preston flicked the cap off his beer and sat down on the other couch, as far from the Peacekeeper as he could. "Don't tell me you came to Avilon looking for me?" he said, his eyes on Ethan as he took a long gulp from his bottle.

Ethan flicked the cap off his own and tried the brew. It was bitter, flat, and awful, but he tried not to let that show on his face. At least it was cold. "Actually, I came looking for my son."

"Ah, right, little Atty . . . he must be all grown up now. He died in the war, I guess?"

Ethan shook his head, and Preston's dark eyebrows swiftly rose. He finished that look of surprise with a heavy frown. "What do you mean? He actually found a way here as a mortal?"

"Him, and a bunch of others, including my wife and I."

"So where's Destra, then?"

"Not Des . . . Alara. We're newly-weds with a baby girl on the way. It's a long story."

"I see. Well . . . you shouldn't have come. Especially not with a pregnant wife."

"The rest of the galaxy isn't a great place to be either."

Preston shrugged and took another gulp of beer. "Grass is always greener or bluer someplace else. Then you get there and find there ain't any grass at all. I'm guessing you're stuck here now."

Ethan nodded.

"So why come visit me? Old times' sake?"

"Actually, I don't know why I'm here," Ethan said, glancing at Rovik. "Omnius wanted me to come."

"He did, did he?" Preston's eyes turned to the Peacekeeper, too. "Well, what is it the big ol' eyeball wants from me?"

Rovik shook his head. "Please show more respect, and he doesn't want anything. He just wanted the two of you to find each other and catch up."

Preston snorted and jumped up from his couch. "Ain't that something! The eyeball doing me a favor out of the kindness of his . . . core. Doesn't have a heart, now does he?" Preston laughed at his own joke.

Ethan watched his father start pacing around the room with his beer, emptying it in two quick swigs. He tossed the bottle aside, and it bounced and rolled to a stop in one corner. "Want another?" Preston asked, his gaze suddenly sharp and insistent as he turned to Ethan again.

"I'm all right, thanks."

"Well, I wouldn't mind another."

Ethan eyed the bottle in the corner of the room, wondering how the apartment could be so clean if his father had a habit of throwing his garbage on the floor. He tried another sip of his beer and grimaced at the flavor of it. It went down with a warm tingling sensation that made him think it probably had a much higher alcohol content than the average brew.

As he sat back in his chair, the buzz began to burn in his veins, but rather than make him feel relaxed and pleasantly numb, he felt more alert than usual. Little noises he hadn't noticed before became loud. The scratching of a bug's legs as it scuttled across the floor drew his attention to one side of the room where, sure enough, a small insect was making a hasty dash for the fallen beer bottle. Ethan found his mind felt clearer than usual, and he felt happier, more focused, more at ease in his own skin. He felt like he could conquer the world!

Rovik was watching him carefully.

"What?" Ethan asked.

"Give me that bottle," he said, reaching out for it.

Ethan withheld his beer, sheltering it with his other arm. "Why?"

"Just trust me, Ortane," the Peacekeeper said.

"Frek that!" Ethan took a long swig.

His father returned with another beer, already open. This time he didn't sit down to drink it; instead he paced over to the fallen bottle and cap he'd tossed aside previously, as if it suddenly irritated him to see them lying on the floor. On the way he made a hasty sidestep to crush the bug scuttling across his floor. He picked up both the remnants of the bug and his empty beer bottle and cap and carried them to a wide pipe running down the wall from ceiling to floor. There was a bulge halfway down the tube. His father opened a hatch in the side of it, revealing an empty compartment. He placed the bug there and shut the hatch. No sooner had he shut the door than the bug was sucked away with a noisy *slurp* of air.

Preston carefully placed his empty bottle and cap on an adjacent bar counter, as if he planned to reuse them later. Then he returned to the couch and sat down with a broad grin. Ethan could relate. He felt indescribably happy to have found his father again. They'd never had a great relationship, but now on Avilon, maybe that could change.

"I'm thinking about moving out of here," Preston said, looking around the room, slowly bobbing his head. "Get myself a bigger place in a nicer district."

Ethan found himself nodding along with that. "Sounds like a good idea."

"Yea, just have to get my brew business going and I'll be set."

"Your brew business?"

"The beer. How'd you like it, son? That's some of your old man's finest."

Ethan turned the bottle over in his hand, looking at it as if for the first time. The bottle looked old and there wasn't any label on it, but he found the flavor was growing on him. He took another sip and savored the warm tingling sensation that coursed through him. "Best I've ever had."

"That's what I thought."

Ethan noticed Rovik stand up from the couch. He stretched leisurely, revealing a glowing palm. Ethan realized what that meant and he grabbed the bottle with both hands. Rovik yanked Ethan out of his chair and onto the floor. Then the Peacekeeper stepped on his back, pinning him painfully to the ground and forcing him to release the bottle.

"Thank you."

The pressure on Ethan's back eased, and he responded by reaching out with both hands and grabbing Rovik's foot. He pushed up and twisted, flipping the Peacekeeper off his feet. Rovik landed beside him with a ground-shaking *thud*.

Ethan heard the neighbors below them wake up and start asking each other about the noise. He bounced to his feet, his eyes flashing as he stood over the fallen Peacekeeper. "Give it back," he said, reaching for his drink.

The Peacekeeper responded with a smile and tightened

his fist around the bottle. It exploded with a *pop!* sending a dark rain of beer and glittering shards of glass cascading over his fist.

"No!" Ethan yelled, leaping onto the man's chest and raising his own fists to hammer the Peacekeeper's face. Rovik's visor shimmered to life in preparation for the blow, and that gave Ethan pause. He knew he couldn't punch through a shield, so he just sat there panting, furious, and unable to imagine why the Peacekeeper had stolen his drink only to *waste* it. "What's wrong with you?" he demanded.

Rovik's expression was inscrutable behind his glowing blue visor. "I could ask you the same thing. You attacked me over a beverage, and somehow you found the strength to knock me off my feet. My armor alone weighs more than a hundred pounds. You haven't stopped to wonder why you were able to do that?"

Ethan clambered off the Peacekeeper's chest, feeling suddenly stupid about his outburst. He held out a hand to help Rovik up.

The Peacekeeper ignored it and pushed himself off the ground to point a finger at Preston. "Bliss is illegal. What are you doing putting it in beer?"

"What, so now Peacekeepers are being sent to do Enforcers' work? Mind your own business, *Non*."

"I should report you."

"You should leave."

"What's Bliss?" Ethan asked, even though the word had already dredged up a definition in his brain, courtesy of the information Omnius had fed them all while they slept. Bliss was a performance enhancing stim that made people stronger, faster, and smarter—the stim to end all stims—and one in every five Nulls was addicted to it.

Ethan turned to his father, suddenly seeing him with new eyes. Preston was agitated all right, his hands clenching and unclenching, his eyes darting, his lips twisted into an angry sneer. He looked ready to explode at any moment.

Ethan felt some of that same restless, angry energy flowing through his veins. The clarity of mind and euphoria he'd felt earlier had come at a price. Forcing himself to calm down, he took a few deep breaths and shook his head. "Dad," he managed.

"What?"

"Why are you living down here?"

"In the Null Zone? Because Omnius is a control freak who wants everyone to be on their best behavior all the time."

"No, I can understand *that*, but why are you *here*. This is free housing, your furniture is free, your food is free. You don't pay for anything do you?"

"Sure I do. You think that brew you wasted didn't cost something to make?"

"Do you sell any?"

"Well ... I'm not set up for mass production. Not yet. Have to perfect the recipe first. You could help me!" He took another hasty gulp of his beer, part of which missed his mouth and dribbled down his chin.

Ethan shook his head, feeling violated. "You should have warned me you were giving me stims."

"Then you wouldn't know what I'm talking about! You wouldn't get how important this is." Preston walked up to him, his eyes wide and wild. He held up his half-empty bottle and shook it in front of Ethan's face. "This stuff is better than what you'll find on the streets. Fewer side effects! Tastes better, too! We could make a fortune! You and me, son! Think about it!"

"I need to go, Dad."

Preston's eyes flashed angrily, but then they darted sideways to the Peacekeeper, and he nodded, offering them a tight smile. "You'll be back," he said, turning away, and then—*"He'll be b-back ..."* Preston whispered to himself, stuttering like a pro.

Ethan felt himself being pushed and shoved back the way they'd come. He felt a fiery flash of annoyance at that, but he resisted the urge to turn on Rovik again.

Once outside his father's apartment, Ethan turned to the Peacekeeper and asked, "Why didn't *you* warn me?"

He shook his head. "I didn't know. Omnius only told me after you'd had your first few sips. I suspect he wanted you to know what it feels like."

"Why? So he can make me an addict, too?"

"No, so that when you choose to become a Null you don't end up like your father."

That cooled his jets. Ethan looked away quickly and made an irritated noise in the back of his throat. "Let's go. My wife's waiting."

"Of course."

All the way back to the mansion where he'd been staying at the top of Destiny Tower, Ethan tried to convince himself that he would never end up like his father. He told himself that the entire trip had been a waste of time. Just because he'd been a stim runner in the past didn't mean he would become a stim *user*. That was entirely different.

He was different.

One in five nulls is an addict, he thought, remembering the statistic that was apparently common knowledge on Avilon. *Why so many?*

Ethan didn't want to dwell on it, but his mind was still

clear as crystal and working twice as fast as usual, so ignorance wasn't an option. If Bliss made a man stronger, faster, and smarter than he'd otherwise be, it stood to reason that regular citizens would have a hard time competing with all the Bliss-doped addicts, and that would force more people to start using. In a world as overcrowded as Avilon, having a competitive edge wasn't just good business—

It was key for survival.

CHAPTER 15

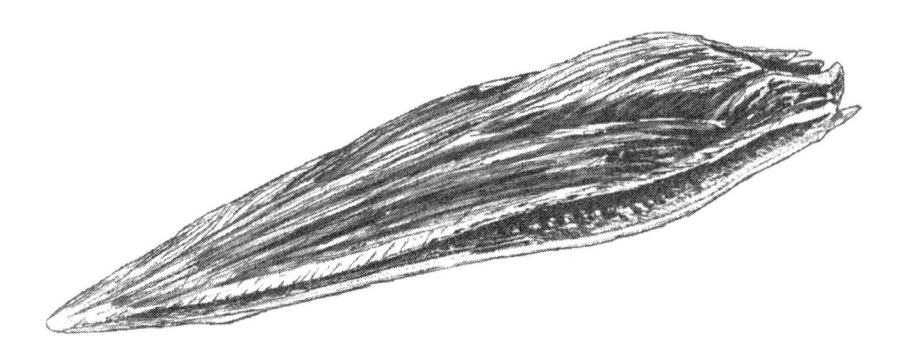

"We detect incoming vessels, My Lords!" One of the diminutive Kylians called out in a high, reedy voice from the crew pit below the command deck.

"Report!" High Lord Kaon hissed from where he sat in Lady Kala's seat aboard the mighty *Kyra*—her command ship. Rather than wait for the report, Lady Kala herself *flew* down to the crew pit and spoke quickly in hushed tones with her sensor operator.

Kaon's wide blue eyes narrowed swiftly. He had commandeered Lady Kala's ship, but clearly her crew was still more loyal to her than him.

A moment later Lady Kala flew back up to retake her seat beside him on the command deck.

"Our reinforcements arrive," she said.

"So sssoon?" Lord Shondar asked from Kaon's other side.

Kaon brought up a star map and watched the red friendly blips begin melting out of the icy nebula at the entrance of Dark Space. Wave upon wave of Sythian cruisers poured out of the nebula until space was crowded with warships.

Kaon felt his twin hearts accelerate, flushing his skin with a pale lavender heat. Beside him Shondar bared his black teeth and hissed with pleasure.

"Make contact with the new clusters, and have them join our formation," Kaon said.

"Yess, My Lord," the comms operator said. "We establish contact. . . . They request to look upon us."

"Transmit a visual," Kaon replied.

The starlight shining in through the bridge's star dome was replaced by a dark view into another bridge deck, almost identical to the one where they sat. In the center of it sat a small Sythian in an over-sized command chair. "Greetings, I am Queen Tavia," she said in a smooth voice. "I trust I am not too late to save you from the terrifying humans." Tavia's papery black skin and bright red eyes were trademarks of her sub species. She was a Kylian like Lady Kala, but she was no mere *Lady*, she was the queen of her people. Tavia smiled, revealing two neat rows of needle-sharp teeth.

Kaon's eyes began to itch. He did not appreciate being condescended to, but when faced with the queen of all the Kylians, he had little choice but to accept the shame her words brought to him. "You are not late, My Queen."

"Good. As you might guess, I am here at Mighty Shallah's request . . ." She trailed off, letting that sink in. "To replace you, of course."

"Of course," Kaon replied, bowing his head. "We have made many preparations for the enemy already, but I am sure that with your superior leadership we—"

"Forget your preparations. I come to you with a weapon that shall make all of your plans obsolete."

"A weapon?"

"Yess. The Avilonians have cloaking shields, just as we do, yet it would appear that they can see through ours, and we cannot pierce theirs. This has since changed."

"We can detect cloaked vessels?" Kaon's mind whirled as he considered the tactical advantage that would give them. The Avilonians would fly in assuming they were invisible when in fact they were not.

"They shall come expecting to have the element of surprise, when in fact they fly blithely into our trap. We must hurry to install these new sensors in your existing clusters. How long do we have before the Avilonians come for us?"

"I do not know," Kaon admitted. "We do not even know for certain that they do come. I have been unable to contact my agent in Avilon."

"I see. Well, if they do not come, then we shall go to them." Queen Tavia smiled her needle-sharp smile once more. "For glory," she said.

"For glory!" Kaon replied.

Kaon risked glancing up, and he noticed that something had caught Queen Tavia's attention. Her head had turned as if she were looking past them. "Interesting," she said, and her eyes found Kaon's once more. "I appear to have found the fleet you lost, Lord Kaon."

At that, Kaon's gills flared and he sat up straighter in his command chair. "Where?"

"Right above your head, and they are with a cloaked human vessel ... no ... *three* human vessels," Tavia said, looking past them again, no doubt studying a star map. "They are oblivious to the fact that we can see them slinking away."

"We must strike!"

"You shall do nothing!" Queen Tavia spat at the screen, her red eyes shining fiercely in the purplish gloom of her bridge. "Nothing, but watch and learn," she went on, her voice becoming smooth and calm once more. "I wouldn't want you to lose another command ship."

The contact ended, and Kaon was left blinking in shock. Lady Kala shot him a look. Her expression was inscrutable, but he felt certain she was being smug. He had commandeered her command ship, but her queen had just commandeered Kaon's entire armada.

* * *

Bretton gaped at the scene before him. "I don't understand . . ." They had been on Avilon in the heart of the Null Zone just moments ago. Now they were on the bridge of an old venture-class cruiser.

"What's not to understand?" Marla asked.

Bretton turned to her and studied her black ISSF uniform. "You're a captain," he said, his eyes once again finding the gold star emblazoned on her shoulder.

She nodded once. "And so are you."

"I *was*," he corrected. "That was a long time ago."

"You know more about these ships than any of us. We need you."

"Wait . . . *ships*?" Bretton's eyes widened appreciably. "You have more?"

"Only two. This beauty here is the *Tempest*. Our other ship is the *Emancipator*, but she's still being refitted."

"You're in command of this one?"

"Technically this is Admiral Vee's ship, but I'm in command whenever she's not on deck."

"Admiral Vee?"

"You haven't met her yet. She's with the prisoner."

"This is ridiculous," Farah said. "You're all out here playing soldier, building your little fleet so that you can do what exactly? Swoop in to save the day and liberate the Nulls with all *two* of your ships?"

"Never despise humble beginnings, Commander," Marla replied.

"I'm *not* a commander," Farah said.

"That's up to you."

Bretton heard his niece snort, but she left it at that.

"Come with me," Marla said. "The admiral would like to meet you."

They followed her back the way they'd come, walking back through the circular chamber with the quantum junction to a familiar bank of lift tubes. They'd set up the junction right outside the bridge, no doubt so resistance members could jump directly in and out of the ship's nerve center rather than waste time with lift tubes and long corridors. A few seconds later, they found themselves in just such a lift tube, and after that, walking down one of those long corridors.

Bretton passed the time wondering where they might be in space. Where would the resistance hide an illegal fleet? Better yet, where in the netherworld had they found it?

They reached the ship's med center and hurried through a pair of sliding transpiranium doors. A corpsman waited for them on the other side. He saluted briskly and told them to follow him.

Another long corridor brought them to one of the ward

rooms. The door *swished* open and they walked into a room crowded with medical equipment both old and new. In the center of the room was a stretcher with their prisoner laid out and strapped down. He was writhing and frothing at the mouth as if he were in great pain. Clustered around him were no less than three officers and two medics. One of the officers, Bretton noted, was wearing a Supreme Admiral's uniform, with four gold stars arrayed in a diamond on her shoulder.

Bretton approached the table cautiously and stopped to salute the admiral when she turned to see him. "Ma'am," he said.

"At ease, Captain."

The admiral was no less stunning than Captain Marla Picara. Her refined features, and large, faintly glowing green eyes belonged to a young model, not a battle-hardened admiral, but Bretton assumed that she, like him, had descended from Etheria, and her physical beauty was just an unwelcome reminder that some vital element of her humanity had long ago been stolen. Her blond hair was tucked up under an admiral's cap that he had to struggle to remember. As an Avilonian, she couldn't have known the hat that went with her old Imperial uniform was reserved for formal occasions and not daily wear.

"I trust you've already briefed Captain Hale?" the admiral asked, turning to Captain Picara.

The other woman nodded. "Yes, Ma'am."

On the table before them, Donali stopped writhing long enough to shout something unintelligible at them.

"What did he say?" Bretton asked.

"I believe he's cursing at us in Sythian. He's been trying to call home ever since we woke him up, but this ship is fitted with quantum disruptors, just in case Omnius figures out where we are and tries to jump a battalion of drones on board."

Bretton's eyebrows shot up, wondering why they would need *quantum* field disruptors to stop him from contacting the Sythians. "I hadn't realized Sythians have quantum tech."

"Just comms," Admiral Vee said, turning to him. "We analyzed the data you brought us. He's a Sythian all right, but there's a lot more to it than that."

Bretton waited for her to go on, but he noticed the admiral's gaze slip past him to his niece. "Miss Hale, would you please excuse us for a moment?"

Farah looked up, wondering why she'd been singled out. Then she caught on. "Oh sure, keep your secrets. I don't care."

She left in a huff with the corpsman who'd escorted them to Donali's room leaving with her. Neither of them had the clearance to hear what the admiral was about to say. Bretton watched Farah go with a frown, wondering why she was still treating the resistance like a lost cause even after learning about their access to a quantum junction and their hidden fleet.

"Captain . . ." the admiral began.

It took a moment for Bretton to realize she was speaking to him. "Yes, Ma'am?"

"This agent you brought us was the right hand man of a distinguished admiral in the fleet, perhaps you knew him—Admiral Hoff Heston."

Bretton blinked. "He was my commanding officer. I was attached to the 5th Fleet when I died." He glanced over his shoulder to the door by which his niece had left. "Both of us were."

"I know. Commander Donali—back then Lieutenant Donali—knew both of you by name."

Bretton shook his head, not catching the significance of that.

"Admiral Heston was actually an immortal Avilonian, living in exile in the Imperium."

"What?" Bretton couldn't believe that. "That doesn't make sense. He was *old*."

"A long time ago, things were different in Avilon. People were immortal not because their bodies were engineered to live forever, but because they cloned themselves over and over again, always transferring to a new clone before they died."

"Back when Heston lived on Avilon, Omnius didn't exist, and neither did the nulls. Everyone was immortal, and it was believed that allowing mortals and immortals to coexist would have disastrous consequences. When Heston proposed that the council was wrong about that, they tried to kill him and he fled to the Imperium. His XO here—" Admiral Vee turned to indicate Commander Donali. "—found out that he was an Avilonian. Rather than find a way to shut him up, Heston made Donali immortal, too, which is why he has an older version of a Lifelink implant. The Sythian implant sitting beside it is some type of quantum transmitter. We believe the Sythians are using it to keep in touch with their agent."

"He should have a Lifelink from Omnius, too," Bretton said. "Everyone in the Imperium was implanted. How did Donali escape that?"

"At the end of the war, Heston's fleet ran and hid along the edge of the galaxy for several years. The original Lieutenant Donali was killed by Sythians during that time, and his clone obviously never received one of Omnius's implants."

Bretton's eyes widened with understanding. "That explains why Omnius didn't find and capture him before I did."

"Yes, we are lucky you found him first."

Bretton still felt like he was missing something. Abruptly he realized what that was. "Wait a minute. That means the original Donali who died . . ."

"Is somewhere on Avilon right now, but he's not a Sythian spy, so we don't have to worry."

"No, I suppose not," Bretton agreed.

At that, Admiral Vee's eyes seemed to drift out of focus, and Bretton realized she was studying something that had appeared on her ARCs. Her smooth forehead wrinkled with concern, and her eyes focused on him once more.

"We need to get to the bridge."

"What's wrong?"

Admiral Vee and the pair of officers accompanying her were already on their way out of the ward room. "Keep the prisoner sedated!" she called over her shoulder as she left.

One of the medics attending Donali nodded. Captain Marla Picara turned. "We'd better go," she said.

They hurried to catch up with the Admiral.

Farah was waiting for them outside the med center. "*Now* can we get something to eat?" she asked, her eyes on Captain Picara. Again, the captain ignored her.

"Hey!" Farah said.

The admiral and her entourage broke into a brisk jog, and Bretton ran to catch up. "What's the hurry?" Farah called after him.

He jogged up beside the admiral. "Ma'am, what's going on?" he tried again.

"Sythians, that's what. They're on the move."

"*Sythians?* They're here?"

Admiral Vee shot him a look. "Do you even know where *here* is, Captain?"

He shook his head. "No, Ma'am."

The admiral smiled, and her green eyes glittered. "We're in Dark Space, surveilling the enemy fleet."

CHAPTER 16

Atton peered over the rim of his cup of caf, eying the Peacekeepers sitting opposite him. According to his ARCs, it was 0530 hours. The sun was already up and rising, although Atton supposed the difference between day and night became a slight one when you only had to sleep for four hours. Before the Imperials had been resurrected in Etheria, Sync had taken less than an hour. Omnius was still expanding himself to deal with the increased demands of governing more citizens. Atton assumed Sync would eventually return to its former status as a minor blip in the lives of Avilon's citizens—the ones who lived in the Uppers anyway. Mortals like him still needed a good eight hours of regular *sleep.* And that was something that no one had managed to get last night.

The nightmare of experiencing a very real death and resurrection on Avilon by reliving Strategian Rovik's memories was enough to wake all of them up as soon as Sync ended and Omnius released them from their induced sleep.

Ethan had apparently been the first one up, and he'd gone on an unscheduled tour with Strategian Rovik in the early hours of the morning. Now he was back in his room with Alara, reflecting on whatever it was that Omnius had shown him. When Atton had seen him come in, he'd been very pale, looking like he'd seen a ghost. Of course, on Avilon there were plenty of those.

Beside him, Ceyla got up from the table and went to put her dishes away. Atton watched her go, not too sleepy to appreciate what he saw as she was leaving. Without warning she turned and caught him looking at her. He cleared his throat and smiled, not bothering to hide his interest. She arched an eyebrow and smiled wryly back, which he took for subtle encouragement. Ceyla Corbin came from a conservative Etherian background, but she obviously wasn't averse to flirting.

"Are we ready to go?" a familiar voice asked. Atton turned to see Strategian Rovik standing in the hallway leading from the dining hall to the entrance of the mansion. The morning sun sparkled off the Peacekeeper's armor as it streamed in through the wall of windows beside him. "Day two," Rovik said. "It's time to tour Etheria, where hopefully you'll all be living soon. You have fifteen minutes to meet me at the front door. Don't be late."

"Ready," Atton said, pushing out his chair and standing up. He took his dishes to the kitchen, scraped them off into a collection tube, and then stacked them neatly in an oversized dishwasher.

That done he returned to his room to gather his belongings. It wasn't much, just his ISSF flight suit and uniform. Both still smelled of acrid smoke from the Sythians' attack on Avilon. His current attire—a shimmering white robe—was much more comfortable, but everyone seemed to wear the same thing in Celesta, and that made him feel uncomfortable, like he was just one of a trillion other faces—not unique or special in any way.

"Hey handsome," Ceyla said, popping up behind beside

his ear and dropping a sweet-smelling kiss on his cheek.

He turned to her, wide-eyed with surprise. She'd never done *that* before. "Hey ..." he replied, whispering in a voice that was more seductive than he'd planned.

She blushed and looked away. "We need to get going."

"Right."

Minutes later they were all gathered in the foyer downstairs. Atton noted that his father still looked unwell, his skin waxy and pale. His gaze moving on from there, Atton saw a pair of Peacekeepers at the front doors, but Strategian Rovik was nowhere to be seen. Atton went to check in with his father. His eyes met Alara's as he approached.

"Is he okay?" Atton asked, stopping beside her.

She bit her lip and eyed her husband worriedly.

"I'm fine," Ethan managed, but Atton noticed that he was sweating even though the air inside the foyer was fresh and cool.

"What happened this morning?"

Ethan gave no reply, but Alara leaned over to whisper in Atton's ear. "They took him to the Null Zone to meet his father—your grandfather."

Atton withdrew and stared at Alara in shock. That was when Master Rovik chose to show up. He stopped to speak with the guards at the entrance for a moment before turning to address the group. Atton noticed on his ARC display that the Strategian was more than ten minutes late.

"My apologies," he said. "I was called away for an emergency session of the war council. The Sythians are reinforcing their numbers in Dark Space, and it would appear that we are running short of time. The Choosing must go on, but I've been told to cut it short. You will now have just one day—today—to make your choices."

Atton heard people gasping and murmuring all around him. His own eyes grew wide and he began shaking his head. He'd had an idea about what he was going to choose, but having just one day to make that choice suddenly threw him into a swirling pool of doubt. What if he made the wrong choice?

Strategian Rovik went on, "Today we will tour both Etheria and the Null Zone, and by tomorrow morning I expect you all to be ready to begin your new lives on Avilon. Tomorrow night, the entire fleet is going to war, and I hope to see some of you flying out with me when that time comes," the Strategian finished, his eyes roving over the group.

"Hey!" someone said. "Why do we have to hurry up and choose just because *you're* going off to war?"

Atton turned to see *Razor*, Guardian Five, the only other surviving pilot from his squadron besides him and Ceyla.

"Because there will be no one left to supervise your choosing," Rovik explained, his tone suggesting that the answer should have been obvious. "We need every Peacekeeper we have to fight the Sythians."

Atton blinked, only now realizing the seriousness of the situation—the Avilonians were afraid they might actually *lose*. With that realization, he made up his mind. His hand shot up before he even realized he'd raised it.

"Yes, Atton?" Rovik asked, pointing to him.

All eyes turned to him and he felt suddenly less certain about his choice. "I'd like to sign up to fight, sir."

"Without even having seen Etheria?"

Atton nodded, and the Strategian smiled.

"Take note of this boy's courage *and* his faith. He is an example to you all. He's willing to accept, without having seen, that he will be better off in Etheria living under

Omnius's rule. Take a good look at him. If he keeps that up, someday he'll be ruling over all of you at Omnius's side."

Atton noticed that several of the glances turned his way were now filled with suspicion and resentment. One gaze stood out from all the rest and cut straight through the confidence he'd had in his decision, filling him with regret. Ceyla Corbin's blue eyes were full of hurt and shock, as if he'd just rejected her right along with the possibility of a life in the Null Zone. He realized that because of her beliefs, that was exactly what he'd done. Ceyla would never accept that Etherianism had actually come from second-hand knowledge of life in Avilon. Etherus was Omnius, and the people that she believed had died and gone to Etheria were actually Avilonians.

Atton started toward Ceyla, hoping he could find some way to comfort her. Maybe after the war he could join her in the Null Zone. Before he'd taken two steps, a firm hand gripped his shoulder and spun him around.

"What the *frek* is wrong with you?" It was Ethan. He still looked pale, but his green eyes were blazing and full of life. "I didn't spend ten years mourning your death only to find you alive and well just in time to watch you *kill yourself!*"

Atton frowned. "I won't be dead."

"Are you *sure* about that?"

"No, but I *am* sure that if we don't defeat the Sythians, they'll kill all of us, not just me."

Ethan stared at him for a long moment, revulsion and shock warring on his face.

"The boy's right," Strategian Rovik interrupted. "And *you* of all people should not be attacking his faith, Ethan. Would you care to share what Omnius showed you in the Null Zone this morning?"

Ethan turned to face the Peacekeeper. "No," he said, "because *Omnius* showed it to me. He's been trying to sway my choice ever since I got here, and I'm not about to let a rambling AI with a god complex decide my fate."

"Very well. It would appear that in this case like father is very much *not* like son. Atton, Omnius smiles upon you as well as all of those here who think as you do, but as I mentioned earlier, the Choosing is not optional. Please follow me. We are already late for our tour of Etheria."

Atton watched Strategian Rovik turn and head not for the front door of the mansion, but rather to the back of the foyer, cutting through the group of refugees to get to the stair case they'd all descended a few minutes ago. They followed him up past the second floor landing, and up another flight of stairs to a third floor that Atton hadn't even noticed until now.

The third floor landing led down a long hallway running beside an equally long balcony. As they walked to the end of it, Atton walked up beside Ceyla and reached for her hand. She jerked it away and shot him an angry look.

"Ceyla..." he began.

"I'm not talking to you," she replied, looking away.

Suddenly there was a painful knot in his throat. They came to a door, which Master Rovik opened for them. Beyond that lay a familiar golden transporter dome ... a *quantum junction.*

Atton watched it rise on dazzling columns of light, thinking to himself, *Next stop Etheria ...*

Somehow that word held less hope and anticipation for him now that he knew without a doubt that Ceyla wouldn't be joining him there. But even more than he needed her, humanity needed soldiers to fight the Sythians. Atton's lips curved into a bitter smile. It seemed like duty would always come before his own personal needs.

He supposed it was some consolation that soon he'd have all of eternity to make up for that.

They walked under the dome of the quantum junction and huddled together inside the glowing green circle on the floor. Moments later the dome began to glow and it fell with a *boom*. The air began whipping and roaring around them and the light inside the dome became blinding.

Next stop Etheria . . . look out skull faces, here I come.

* * *

Destra sat in the viewing gallery anxiously watching as the *Baroness* slipped unnoticed through the Firean system. Atta was bouncing up and down beside her on the row of bench seats where they sat. Destra turned to her with a smile. The innocence of youth shielded Atta from the significance of this moment. Here—now—was where they would say their final goodbyes to a once great empire, and with it, civilization. The Imperium of Star Systems, as they all had known it, was about to disappear forever. What came next would be a long and treacherous time for humanity and their Gor allies. They would either stay hidden and thrive, or they would be discovered by the Sythians and slaughtered once and for all.

Destra's eyes roved between the bright, twinkling stars. Her gaze stopped here and there to study clusters of much brighter points of light that lurked between those stars.

Atta's innocence shielded her from more than just the melancholy nostalgia of the moment, but also from the potential danger. Traveling unseen with them, their ships likewise cloaked, was an entire fleet of Gors, and together they were all flying past the noses of hundreds, if not thousands, of Sythian warships.

Theoretically there was no way that they could be detected through their cloaking shields, but a cynical part of Destra wondered if the Gors had successfully managed to remove all traces of the Sythians' locator beacons from their ships. If not, this would be a much shorter trip than anyone anticipated.

Destra had to remind herself that they'd been running ops together in Dark Space for months since the Sythian occupation of the sector, and the Gor fleet had yet to be detected.

"Mommy, look at that star there!" Atta bounced up and pointed out the viewport.

Destra frowned, trying to see what her daughter was pointing at. It didn't take long to find the silhouette of an enormous Sythian warship glinting in the red light of the system's sun.

"Is that another galaxy?" Atta asked.

Destra smiled and nodded, unable to give voice to the lie. Based on its size, that had to be one of the Sythians' thirty-kilometer-long command ships. A behemoth-class. They were usually cloaked and hidden behind the fleets they carried into battle, but this one was sitting brazenly out in the open, as if the Sythians had suddenly lost the fear of death that had driven them to use slave crews for their smaller warships. More likely they weren't hiding now because they knew they had nothing to fear.

As they flew onward, Destra spotted more of those massive warships, each of them sitting in the center of its own cluster of smaller ships. By the time she'd counted the eighth command ship, a dark frown had wrinkled her forehead, and she was reaching up to her comm piece to make a call.

"Stay here, Atta," she said, getting up from the bench seats.

"Where are you going?" Atta asked.

"Nowhere, darling. I just need to make a call." Destra walked to the far corner of the room and leaned up against the bulkhead to watch her daughter from the shadows. The lights were turned down low in the viewing gallery to make it easier to see the stars.

"What is it, Councilor?" a gruff voice answered as her call went through.

"Captain," she began, whispering into her comm. "I just noticed the number of ships out there ... There's more than seven command ships."

"I know."

"There were only seven in the entire invasion."

"*Were* is the operative word, Councilor," Captain Covani replied. She imagined his tangerine eyes narrowed to unhappy slits.

"How many are there?"

"We're cloaked, so passive scanning only, but visual estimates would suggest there are more than twenty."

"*Twenty?*" Destra couldn't believe it. "That's more than double what they used to defeat the Imperium!"

"Good thing there's no Imperium left for them to defeat."

She thought about Avilon, where her son, Atton, had gone to get reinforcements, but she didn't want to mention that in case the captain decided to take them there. Hoff had warned her that the Avilonians wouldn't welcome so many refugees, particularly not *Gor* refugees. "How far are we from the jump point?" she asked.

"Nearest one is fifteen minutes out. The one I've set is about half an hour."

"What? Do you have a death wish, Captain? Use the nearest one!"

"There's a lot of risk jumping too far from the out-system gate. We want to avoid running into in-system debris and ships. Besides, jumping out parallel to the old gate will help us to avoid obstacles in the Stormcloud Nebula. The lane should still be clear."

"I don't like it," Destra replied.

"We're cloaked, Councilor. What are you afraid of?"

"Suppose one of their fighters accidentally runs into us and they realize we're here?"

"The odds of that are slim. Space is vast."

"We should jump out now, Captain, while we still can."

"Your suggestion has been noted."

"It wasn't a suggestion."

"Leave the military decisions to me, Ma'am. That's what I'm here for."

Destra thought about arguing further, but she had to pick her battles, and this one wasn't worth fighting. "Very well. Keep me informed."

"Of course. Speaking of that, you might like to know the prisoners you rescued are almost aboard."

"They're *what?*"

"Coming aboard. You asked to be notified . . ."

"I know *that*. You should have waited to transfer them. How did you even coordinate that without giving our position away?"

"The Gors are telepaths."

"And how do they know where our hangar is without some type of comm beacon to guide them in?"

"We're using a Gor-piloted shuttle to aim for a Gor-occupied hangar. They can telelocate, too, Ma'am . . ."

Destra didn't appreciate the Captain's condescending tone. "Very well. Which hangar?"

"Port ventral."

"I'll head down there now."

"See you there. Covani out."

The comm went dead, and Destra fought the urge to punch the bulkhead. Hopefully the captain's attitude was provoked by hunger from the emergency rationing rather than by true insubordination.

Destra let her frustration out in a sigh. A sudden draft stirred the air. Turning to see what had caused it, she heard a sibilant hiss. That was when she noticed the dark shadow sitting beside her, yellow eyes glinting in the dark.

Destra cursed and jumped backward, slamming into the bulkhead with a painful *thud*.

"The captain showss you little ressspect. You should eat him."

Destra's heart thudded in her chest. "Torv? What are you doing here?"

"I come to rest my eyes and to be free of my shell for a time."

"Your shell?"

"That which protects me from the heat and brightness that you humans prefer."

His armor. She realized then that he wasn't wearing it. As her eyes adjusted to the gloom, she also saw that he was sitting cross-legged on the deck, his back propped up against the cold duranium bulkhead behind him. "How long have you been sitting there, Torv?"

"Long enough to see how much you care for your daughter. She knows nothing of war, even though it is all around her. Does that not inspire you?"

Destra nodded. "It does."

"Peace is something my people can only dream of, until recently."

"You mean freedom," Destra suggested, thinking that peace was still an elusive goal for all of them.

"Are they not the same? Without freedom there can be no peace, and without peace there is no freedom."

"I suppose you're right."

"Peace comes at a price," Torv mused.

"It always does."

"The Sythians slaughter my people for it. Humans do, too."

Destra smiled ruefully. "Not anymore," she clarified, in case she'd missed something in the present-tense-only translation. "We're allies now. And don't forget that the Gors slaughtered us, too. It's a happy little circle of death."

Torv nodded his big head and he looked away, turning to watch Atta, still sitting patiently on the benches along the gallery viewport. After a moment, he spoke again, "If the Sythians took your crecheling from you, what would you do?"

"I'd go get her back, and then I'd kill the ones who took her."

"You would do anything for her. Even if it meant risking

your own life."

"Yes."

"Then humans are not so different from my people. We, too, would do anything to keep our young ones safe." Slitted yellow eyes found Destra again. "They are alive, you know."

"Who?"

"Our young ones. The crechelings on Noctune."

"What? How can you possibly know that? They're a galaxy away from us."

"They do not communicate with us, if that is what you wonder."

That's exactly what she had been wondering. The ability to communicate between galaxies without SLS comm relays and waiting weeks or months for an answer was a technology that humans had yet to develop, let alone the supposedly savage Gors.

"I know it," Torv went on, "because my inner voice tells me this."

"Your inner voice."

"Yes. The same voice that tells me to trust humans even after they lie and kill my people. Even after they torture the lords of my creche."

"The lords of your . . . your *parents*," Destra decided.

"My creche lord desires to ask you something. He regrets that he is not here to ask you himself."

Destra recalled that Roan was Torv's creche lord, as well as the leader of the Gor fleet. "What would he like to ask, Torv?"

"He asks you to convince the captain to go to Noctune, so that we can rescue our young ones. As a Matriarch to your own young one, he thinks you must understand, but after what I hear and see between you and the captain . . ." Torv hissed and went on, "I am not sure your understanding matters."

Destra frowned. "If the Sythians claim to have killed all of the Gors on Noctune, what makes you think your young ones are alive?"

"The creches are far below the surface of our world. Until crechelings grow older, they are susceptible to the cold, so we raise them deep below the ice, where it is warmer."

"How deep?"

"As far as this ship is long, and farther still."

"Three hundred *meters?* Your people dug that deep into the ice?"

"The creches are below the ice."

Destra shook her head, shocked by what she was hearing. If the Gors' homes were dug that far beneath the surface, there actually was a good chance that some of them had survived the Sythians' bombardment. "Do the Sythians know how far your homes go below the surface?"

"I do not think so. They do not care to know about the Gors. We are too little important to them."

"If that's true, then you might be right."

"Speak with the captain for us. Remind him there are many worlds close to Noctune that humans would find pleasant."

Destra's brow furrowed. "I still don't understand that part. If we'd find them pleasant, the Sythians should be there, too."

"I do not know why they are not, but I know it to be true."

"Why do you need us to go? If you want to go back to Noctune and look for your young ones, you are free to go, Torv. We are not your masters."

"If we go, we do not return. Our ships do not have the fuel for it."

"I understand. We will miss you."

"A Matriarch and the lord of her creche are both strong and can defend themselves, but if one of them dies while their crechelings are still young, then there is either no lord to hunt for the creche or no Matriarch to defend it. The crechelings are eaten by predators or die of hunger."

"What are you saying, Torv?"

"Humans are like the Matriarch. Gors are like the creche lord. We are the hunters, and you stay home to defend the creche."

Suddenly Destra understood. "You're saying we have a better chance of survival if we stick together."

"You speak truth."

Destra nodded. "I will do everything I can to convince the captain we should go. If you're right about there being empty worlds in your sector, it's probably the last place the Sythians would think to look for us. If not, at least we'll be cloaked, and we'll be able to stay hidden long enough to explore and find another suitable place to start a colony."

"May it be so, my Matriarch."

Destra accepted that honorific with a nod. "I'd better go, Torv. I have to see the prisoners we rescued."

"May the Mighty Zarn and Kar go with you."

"You're going to stay here? Doesn't the captain need you on the bridge?"

"The captain has ears but he does not use them, and I do not trust myself not to eat him for his disrespect."

Destra gave a shadowy smile. "I know the feeling."

* * *

Bretton Hale watched on the captain's table as a group of several hundred vessels ran through the Sythian fleet. Most of those warships were identical to the Sythian ships, except for the fact that they appeared on the gravidar as shadowy outlines rather than solid icons. That meant they were cloaked. Thanks to Avilonian upgrades to the *Tempest,* they could see through those cloaking shields. For a moment Bretton didn't understand what he was looking at. It seemed like the cloaked fleet was just another part of the Sythian one. There was a human cruiser with it, but that didn't mean anything, since there were dozens of other human ships in formation with the enemy. From what he'd learned walking through the traitor's mind, he knew that Dark Space had surrendered to the Sythians and the humans living there had been enslaved. So why was part of the fleet cloaked and making a dash for the edge of the system?

"They're Gors," Admiral Vee supplied, as if she'd read his mind.

"Gors?"

The admiral explained about the distinction between the Sythians and their slave soldiers, and about the recent Gor rebellion that had resulted in the Gors stealing an entire fleet of ships.

"That's impossible!" Farah said.

"It's not common knowledge that the Gors are actually slaves of a race we've never seen," Admiral Vee explained. "Omnius probably knows, but he hasn't seen fit to tell Nulls like us."

Bretton was equally shocked. "Forget Omnius, *we* should have known about them. We fought the Sythians for almost a year before the retreat and exodus to Dark Space. How could we miss noticing that we were fighting two different species?"

"Actually more like eight. The Sythians are made up of seven interrelated sub-species. As for how they hid themselves during the war, that's easy. You only ever fought the Gors. The Sythians stayed cloaked behind the lines and let their slaves fight. Now they're using human slaves from Dark Space because the Gors rebelled. Our most recent news from the Uppers suggests that Omnius is planning a counter attack here in Dark Space, and he's going to try to free the slaves so he can bring them to Avilon."

Bretton shook his head slowly, still reeling with shock. "They'd be better off fighting for the Sythians."

"So that fleet there is a rebel fleet," Farah said, pointing to the cloaked ships racing toward the out-system jump gate.

"Yes," the admiral replied.

"So what about the second fleet?"

"What second fleet?" Admiral Vee asked, searching the grid.

Captain Marla Picara was the first to point it out. "There!"

They all watched as another, larger group of cloaked ships broke formation with the rest of the Sythians.

"That's curious . . ." the admiral said, watching both fleets for a moment. "They're both cloaked, but the second fleet is matching trajectories with the first."

"They're following them," Bretton said.

"Yes, but how?"

"I thought Sythians don't have cloak detectors," Farah said.

"Not that we know of," the admiral replied.

"Then?"

"Either that's changed, or our rebels have a Sythian agent on board. Either way, the rebels are in trouble."

"We have to warn them!" Farah said.

"They haven't noticed us," Bretton added, noting that their position on the grid wasn't attracting any groups of cloaked Sythians.

"No . . . which makes the traitor theory a lot more likely. All the same, we should make sure we don't get too close to the enemy."

"The rebels are going to jump out . . ." Farah interrupted. "Aren't we going to do something?"

Admiral Vee turned to her with a smile. "Yes, that's a good question." Turning to Bretton she said, "What do you think? Are you ready to assume command of the *Tempest*?"

"You want *me* to command her? It's been a long time, Admiral."

"I'm sure it's just like riding a hover cycle. Besides, who better for the job than a real venture-class captain?" With that, she turned to Farah. "The same goes for you, Commander. We need you both."

Bretton turned to look at Farah, and he was surprised to find a hesitant grin tugging at the corners of her mouth.

"What do you think?" he asked.

"I was late with my rent payments anyway." Her grin popped out of hiding, and he matched it with one of his own.

"We accept," he said.

"Good. Just in time, too." The admiral pointed to the grid, where the rebel fleet had been only a second ago.

"Where'd they go?" Farah asked.

"Jumped out," Captain Picara replied.

"Did someone record their jump heading?" Bretton asked, raising his voice to ask the entire crew.

Picara shook her head. "We don't have to." She gestured to the star map rising from the captain's table and it zoomed out until all the contacts on the grid became just one big red dot. Further out, seen speeding away at several times the speed of light, was another dot, a green one. "There they are," Picara said.

Bretton smiled. "Quantum tech. Got to love that." Range on quantum scanners was rated in the *light years* rather than klicks. "I'm assuming we have quantum drives, too?"

"And comms," Picara replied.

Bretton tried to imagine a venture-class equipped with quantum technology. It would be more or less equivalent to an Avilonian judgment-class cruiser, but slightly larger, with a slower sub-light drive and weaker shields.

"What kind of range do we have on these scanners?" he asked.

"They'll drop off the grid at about a thousand light years out," Captain Picara replied. "Tracking them won't be hard, but we'll have to wait until they drop out of SLS before we know where to jump to follow them, and depending how far away they are . . . jump calculations could take a while, since we don't have Omnius to do them for us."

Bretton ran a hand along his jaw, stubble rasping audibly against his fingers. "Hopefully they drop out of SLS soon, then."

As they watched, the second cloaked fleet jumped after

the first. That gave a lag time of just a few minutes between the rebel fleet and the pursuing Sythian one, which meant they'd have to be quick if they were going to warn the rebels before the Sythians found them and attacked.

"I suppose you'd better take this time to get me acquainted with my command," Bretton said, speaking to Captain Picara, whose ship the *Tempest* had been previously. "No hard feelings I hope?"

"Not at all. Once you're done training me, I'll head back here to command the *Emancipator*. By then the refits should be finished."

"Training you?"

"You're the one who knows about Imperial warships, sir. I can brief you on the refits and the crew, but that's about it."

"Right."

"Well, I'm going to leave you all to handle this situation," Admiral Vee said. "Admiral Hale, I expect to find my ship in one piece when I return. Your orders are to engage the enemy only if necessary, and only with extreme caution. Don't go playing the hero on the Resistance's tab."

Bretton turned to salute her. "Yes, Ma'am."

"Good. Carry on then."

They watched Admiral Vee turn and start back down the gangway at a brisk pace. Bretton found himself admiring her figure as she left. "She's a Null?" he asked.

"Yes."

"She doesn't look like one."

"Looks can be deceiving," Picara replied. "I don't look like a Null, and neither do either of you."

Bretton turned to her with an appraising look. "So she came from the Uppers at some point. Like us."

"Could be."

"What do you mean *could be*? It's obvious she wasn't born below the Styx."

Picara smiled a pretty smile. "We're not allowed to know much about her, for our safety and hers. Suffice to say, the Admiral could even be a *he* under that bio-synthetic suit."

"Bio-synthetic . . ." Farah trailed off.

"She's wearing a disguise," Bretton clarified.

"The best money can buy. She'll even pass biometric scans and surface level DNA analysis."

Bretton turned back to watch the admiral as she left, thinking to himself that there was no way she was a *he*. Wide hips and narrow shoulders would be hard to fake without holographics, and that was something any sophisticated scanner would easily pick out. As for her perfect skin and teeth, her long blond hair and blue eyes . . . all of that could easily be fake. "What's she really look like?"

Marla shook her head. "No one knows."

"So she could be anyone," Farah said.

"That's the idea," Picara replied.

Bretton nodded, his brow furrowing all the way up to his wavy brown hair. He knew that the rebel leader hiding her identity made sense, but he couldn't help feeling suspicious. If he didn't know who Admiral Vee was, then he couldn't be sure he could trust her.

The doors at the entrance of the bridge *swished* open and then shut behind the admiral, punctuating his thoughts.

"How far up the command chain is she?" Bretton asked, turning back to Captain Picara.

She raised her hand up as high as it would go above her head. "All the way, sir."

Bretton nodded. "Interesting."

* * *

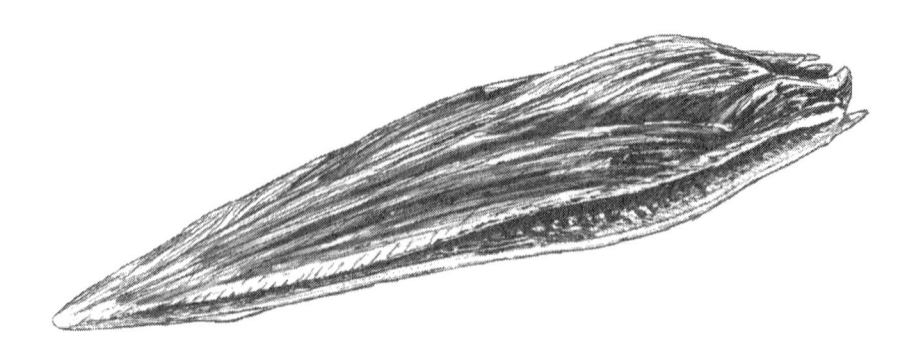

Lord Kaon studied the star map. Friendly and enemy contacts were highlighted red and purple respectively. The purple enemy ones winked off the grid as he watched, and he hissed, pounding the armrests of his command chair with his fists.

"They escape! Why does Queen Tavia let them escape?"

"She does not *let* them," Lady Kala replied. "She follows them with one cluster."

"Yess, but by now they should be dust in the cosmic wind!"

Lady Kala turned to him, her red eyes glittering. "You dare to second-guess your queen?"

Kaon thought to remind her that Tavia wasn't *his* queen. She was the ruler of the Kylians, not all seven sub-species of Sythians, but he decided against that. Queen Tavia was still far above him in rank, and he didn't want her or Shallah to hear his thoughts about whose queen she was and wasn't.

Kaon turned away and called down to the comms operator. "Put a call through to Queen Tavia."

"Yes, My Lord."

"You wish to second-guess her to her face?" Lady Kala asked with a warble of laughter. "You are a fool, Lord Kaon."

Kaon was about to reply to that, but the queen's visage

appeared before he could. Her papery black skin was wrinkled with disdain, and Kaon's stomach turned. As an aquatic species, his skin was perpetually moist and smooth. Wrinkles meant desiccation and death to him. "My Queen," he said, bowing his head.

"What is it, Lord Kaon?"

"I am merely curious, why do you allow the human fleet to escape?"

"I am following them."

"But you could have their heads stuffed and mounted by now."

"And risk showing these Avilonians of yours that we can now detect cloaked warships? No. We would be giving up our advantage too soon. This must come as a surprise, Lord Kaon."

Suddenly he understood the queen's patience, but he wasn't sure her caution was necessary. "My Queen, how would they ever know?"

"How does an enemy ever know anything before they should? By spying on you. I trust you have noticed that two of the cloaked enemy vessels remain in this star system."

Kaon rubbed his rubbery lips together as he struggled to remember the position of all the contacts on the star map. "I confess I do not notice this."

"Then you know why Shallah replaced you with *me*. Those vessels are here watching us, Lord Kaon."

"Then they saw your fleet leave, chasing the Gors, so you are already revealed to them."

"Indeed, but what do they make of that? We do not attack the fleet we follow. For all they know, both fleets are ours."

"Ahh, I see."

"Patience, Lord Kaon, we must wait until we have all of

the fish in our net before we make our move."

Kaon wasn't sure he appreciated the analogy to fish, since his sub-species, the Quarn, was much closer to a fish than humans were.

"I defer to your wisdom, Queen Tavia."

"As you should. Do nothing to show the other two vessels that we can see them. Our trap must come as a complete surprise, one we spring upon the enemy at precisely the right moment, or we will be the ones with our heads stuffed and mounted."

Kaon bowed his head once more. "Yes, My Queen."

CHAPTER 17

ASCENDANCY

The quantum junction rose overhead, and Ethan walked out into Etheria, straight up to a broad viewport that was shaped like the inside of an inner tube. Through the curving bottom half he looked down, down, past a dizzying swirl of traffic, streets, and colorful holo signs popping out the sides of the buildings. There were at least two separate levels of streets and traffic. Below that was the faint blue shimmer of the Styx, looking like a luminescent river.

Around him, the refugees gasped and shook their heads in awe. Alara grabbed his hand, using him as a lifeline as she leaned toward the bulging windows to peer down. She sucked in a quick breath and took a quick step back. Ethan smiled, despite how ill he felt. The dose of Bliss he'd received from his father had made him dizzy and sick. Peacekeeper Rovik had explained to him on the way back up that the first few doses of Bliss were always a shock to a person's system — something about rearranging neurotransmitters and receptors. Users and pushers alike called it *Initiation Sickness*.

Etheria was much more colorful in the urban sense than the majestic upper city with its vast stretches of low-rise buildings and cultivated parks. As they had seen while staying at the top of Destiny Tower, Celesta was designed so that the people living there could sometimes forget they were living in a planet-wide city. Not so in Etheria. Here metropolitan life was celebrated and emphasized. The city was bright with the neon lights of holo ads and glow panels, bustling with multiple layers of air traffic and elevated streets, and variegated with pedestrians dressed in all kinds of clothes, not just Celestial whites. Here things weren't so alien, and Ethan actually felt like maybe the people walking the streets were real humans.

Alara squeezed his hand and whispered beside his ear, "Look up!"

Ethan did, and that's when he noticed something strange. The distance above their heads was at least as far as the distance below, but despite there being another two levels of both streets and traffic between them and the Celestial Wall overhead, Etheria was bright, not cloaked in dark shadows as one might expect. The reason for that was hard to miss. The bottoms of the streets above them were plated with broad glow panels that shone so dazzlingly bright Ethan found it hard to look at them. Then there was the Celestial Wall above that. It was equally blinding, and brighter than he remembered seeing it from the air above Celesta.

"Looks like Omnius built a pipeline to the sun," Ethan muttered.

"Very bright for such a vertical city," Atton agreed.

He turned to see his son standing on the other side of him. Beside Atton, the Peacekeeper, Rovik, stood with a hand on the boy's shoulder. That man's gravelly voice was the next thing that Ethan heard:

"In Etheria Omnius simulates the rise and fall of the sun with artificial illumination. Paradise would not be paradise if it lay in darkness."

Ethan shook his head, remembering the deep, depressing gloom in the Null Zone. "So why don't they do that below the Styx?"

Rovik turned to him, his blue eyes bright with with all the light that the Null Zone didn't have, as if the Peacekeeper had personally stolen it from them.

"We don't say that the Nulls live in darkness just because they have chosen a dark path. It is also literal. They don't have light in the Null Zone because it is too expensive to produce that much illumination, and the Null government cannot afford such waste. What daylight they can afford to generate is reserved for growing food."

Ethan scowled and looked away, back out the viewport, gazing down to the bottom of Etheria far below.

"Come," Rovik said. "Our tour bus is waiting,"

They followed him to a pair of broad doors on one side of the room. Standing to either side of the doors were two more of Omnius's drones. *Omnies*. Ethan eyed them curiously. Then the doors slid open and everyone walked through. The Omnies didn't react to their passing. They just stood there like statues. Curious, Ethan stopped between them and stared at the nearest one.

"Do you have a name?" he tried.

Nothing.

"Hey! Can you even hear me?"

Still no reaction.

Ethan walked straight up to it with one fist raised to punch it in its gleaming metallic chest. Seeing that the drone still didn't react to him, he cocked his arm back and swung.

Suddenly a sharp pain erupted in his wrist. The drone's movement was so fast that his eyes hadn't registered it at all. Maybe he'd blinked at just the wrong moment. Whatever the case, he saw that his fist had stopped mere inches from connecting with the drone's armor, and its spindly fingers were wrapped tightly around his wrist. The ball-shaped head rolled his way and its red eye fixed him with a bloody stare. The drone's grip tightened abruptly, and Ethan cried out in pain. His wrist felt like it was about to explode.

Then Rovik appeared, and the drone released him. Ethan gasped from the sudden release of pressure. He was left rubbing his wrist and staring accusingly up at the big red eye of the drone. "Frek! That thing almost broke my wrist!"

"What did you do to it?"

The drone looked away then, as if feeling guilty for its overreaction, but Rovik wasn't mad at the drone.

"Come on," he gritted, dragging Ethan through the doors. "You need to watch your step or you're going to die long before old age finds you."

"Frek it! Let me go," Ethan said, struggling.

"Then behave yourself." Rovik released him, and he almost fell on his nose.

Ethan glowered at the Peacekeeper's back. "I was just trying to get it to react. They stand there all day, doing nothing!"

"Their job is to react to *threats*, not small talk. Clearly you identified yourself as a threat. You're lucky it didn't kill you."

Ethan shook his head, outwardly annoyed, but inwardly shaken. He hadn't been expecting such a violent response when he tried to punch the drone. He couldn't do the drone any real damage by punching it, and he hadn't even meant to hit it very hard, but either the drone didn't know that, or *overreacting* to threats was part of its programming.

Ethan followed Rovik through the doors and out onto a balcony that led to a waiting air bus. He found Alara already seated inside. She shot him an angry look as he sat down.

"What were you thinking?"

"How do you even know what I did?"

"I was going to go save your ass until Rovik told me get on board and let him deal with it. If there weren't Peacekeepers around, you could have gotten us both killed!"

Ethan looked away. "Lucky for us they were here then," he replied.

"Ethan, I'm serious."

"So am I," he said, nodding slowly, and turning to look past her, out the side window of the bus. She looked out the window, too, making an irritated noise in the back of her throat after it became apparent that he had nothing else to say for himself.

As the bus began pulling out of the narrow alley where it had parked and into the vast chasm between buildings that they had been looking out on earlier, Ethan's mind wandered back to the drones.

From what he'd heard they were not sentient or independent. Omnius controlled all of them. Whatever independence the Omnies had was likely governed by automatic sub routines. No doubt a self-defense sub routine had been responsible for almost amputating his hand. Either that, or Omnius had been behind that display of force, and the AI was just itching to make an example out of him.

Whatever the case, the drones were a more direct extension of Omnius's will than the Peacekeepers would ever be. Peacekeepers followed orders almost without question, but they were still part of a grand society of people that all worshiped Omnius as god. They thought he was good and perfect. Ethan doubted the truth of that, but since everyone else was suckered into believing it, the AI definitely had some appearances to keep up. *Which means he can't order his Peacekeepers to do something atrocious, but with the drones he can be himself—whatever that looks like.*

I wonder what your drones are up to when no one's watching?

The inner voice that Omnius had occasionally used to speak to him since arriving on Avilon was strangely quiet, as if the AI knew the jig was up, and there was no point hiding himself from Ethan anymore.

I'm on to you, he thought, but still there was no reply. Ethan watched the lights of passing holo signs streaking past the air bus. He listened with half an ear as Rovik stood in the aisle between the rows of seats in the bus, describing what life would be like in Etheria. Ethan couldn't be bothered to listen. Whatever life was like here, he knew it wasn't for him. Having Omnius watching his every step . . . telling him what to do, even invading his dreams at night . . .

That was no way to live.

* * *

Atton watched the neon lights of the city blur past the air bus. Animated holo signs caught his eye, each one seeming to leap out at him as he focused on it—no doubt a trick of the ARCs he wore. He watched pedestrians walking on the streets and bridges below, glancing up now and then to keep from getting dizzy. Rows of colored windows streamed by, highly reflective and impossible to see through in the bright, artificial daylight of Etheria. Up ahead Atton saw endless lines of red tail lights stretching out to the horizon, as well as the bright white headlights of oncoming traffic. There were four lanes running in each direction, making the space between the buildings wider than Atton had first suspected. Given the amount of traffic and the risk of collisions, he guessed that the cars were all running on autopilot. Master Rovik confirmed that just a second later, explaining that Omnius controlled all of the cars in Etheria in order to avoid accidents. In his next breath, Rovik said that was not the case in the Null Zone, and accidents were a frequent occurrence there.

Atton turned from watching the sights to focus more squarely on what their tour guide was saying.

"Among the many advantages to life in Etheria, jobs, medical care, and education are all freely available. Even natural abilities can be altered or enhanced via gene therapies. Like Celesta, Etheria is a place of equal opportunity where you can rise as far as your own merit takes you."

"So, I could be a professional grav ball player?" someone asked.

"I'm not sure what grav ball is, but if you mean to ask whether you can be a professional athlete, the answer is yes. You can be anything you want, but certain jobs are in greater demand and less supply. As a result the the training for certain jobs will cost more, while other jobs will not even be available to you at your citizenry rank. Because a person's training and education can change overnight via their Lifelink implants, it's not uncommon to start your career with various undesirable jobs, working your way up until more appealing options become available to you. As refugees, you will all start at the bottom of our society and live just above the Styx."

"Doesn't sound equal to me."

"In a lot of ways it's easier to gain favor with Omnius, and thus gain rank, when you are at the bottom, because less is expected of you, and those around you are often worse than you and have been stuck there longer. If you are truly of equal merit to say, a high-ranking Celestial, it will not be long before you become his neighbor."

"What's your idea of merit?" the same naysayer asked. Atton pegged the man as a former sentinel from the *Intrepid*.

"It's not my idea of merit that counts, but Omnius's. Your merit is represented by your citizenry rank. Your rank is determined by how well you follow Omnius's commands."

"So what are these so-called commands?" Atton recognized his father's voice this time.

"The first command is simple. Serve Omnius above all else, and the second one tells you how to do the first: treat others as you would like them to treat you."

"All well and good, but what if I'm the only one doing that? Then I get frekked," Ethan said.

"No, you get promoted, so you move up in our society, figuratively and literally. Then the people around you will be like-minded, and they will treat you just as well as you treat them—sometimes better."

"That's all easier said than done," someone else said. "We're not wired to think about others all the time."

Master Rovik smiled. "That is what Avilon and Omnius are for. The more you learn to put others first, the more successful you will become."

Atton frowned at that, seeing the flaw lurking in that design. He waited for a break in the conversation before adding his thoughts, "If we're not thinking about personal gain, we won't push ourselves, and we'll never reach our full potential. For example, if I give all of my money to the poor, I'll probably stop working as hard to earn it—maybe I won't even be aware that I'm slacking off, but I'll still do it, and then I'll start making less and giving less, too. Eventually I'll have nothing to give and I won't be a productive member of society anymore. At least from an economic standpoint, some kind of balance between selfishness and putting others first makes sense."

Master Rovik turned to look at him, his glowing blue eyes bright, his lips curving in a faint smile. "Young Master Ortane has just highlighted for you all the reason behind capitalism and a free market economy, but Omnius is well aware of how humans are wired, and a healthy balance is exactly what it takes to succeed in the Ascendancy. If you give all of your money away, you will be neglecting your own family, and you may also stop pushing yourself to do well in your job, both of which will keep you from ascending very far. Despite your generosity, you will be seen as neglecting your social responsibilities. And in case you think about denying yourself for selfish reasons, delaying gratification of self in order to appear less selfish than you are, remember that Omnius knows you better than you know yourself. He can see straight through our motives and he knows when altruism is genuine. Here, you are better off being honest about your flaws and working to improve yourself, because you won't be able to look any better than you are."

"That makes sense," Atton said, "But if Etheria is a paradise, I assume that means there's no poverty, so isn't charity unnecessary anyway?"

"No one in Etheria goes without their basic needs being met, not even the lowest ranking citizens, but there are always those less fortunate than yourself, and charity, as you call it, is not given to a particular person, but rather to Omnius. We call this tithing. Omnius sees that the money goes where it is needed most. Tithing replaces taxes as you know them, and it is entirely voluntary. Inevitably, those with greater ranks and greater merit than you will both earn more and offer more in tithes."

Atton blinked, shocked by these revelations. It *did* seem like the perfect system, but he was beginning to see why no one had ever implemented such a thing in the Imperium. It took an all-knowing, and incredibly intelligent entity to administer such a system effectively. Without which, there would be no way to accurately judge merit, and no way to properly reward it in order to incentivize the system. He made a guess about something else, and said, "Etheria uses a planned economy, doesn't it?"

"Yes."

"So nothing is privately owned?"

"No, everything is privately owned, but technically Omnius is the real owner, and he can seize your assets or give someone else the job of administering them if he so chooses. Rest assured, however, seizures are very rare, and changes in administration are typically voluntary, occurring when the present owners and administrators move to a new type of job."

"Then Omnius is not only your god and head of government, he rules over every area of your lives!"

"Right down to who we should court and marry, how we should treat them, and how we should share responsibilities within our homes. Omnius does not force us to listen to Him, but as an Etherian, you will find it expedient to do so, and to seek His will as often as you can. The more that you seek Him, the more He will help you to make the right choices for your lives."

Atton heard his father grunt with disapproval.

"You have something on your mind, Ethan?" Master Rovik asked.

"Damn right I do. Omnius is controlling everything, forcing a square peg into a round hole to make us all well-behaved little bots. He's making us extensions of him with no minds of our own! No wonder that little girl in the Null Zone called you guys *Nons. Non-humans.* You're not humans, because you have an AI determining everything for you! Where's the variety? The individuality?"

"Unlike in your culture, Ethan, individuality is not prized here. It is a way of saying you don't want to obey Omnius, and that is another way of asking to become a Null."

"So what if I want to be an Etherian but I don't want to follow the rules? Suppose I'm just stubborn, but I like what you've done with the place, so I don't want to go down where I belong. What then? Omnius kicks me out?"

"If you repeatedly try to do harm to others, perhaps. If not, then you will simply never ascend. People will be able to see your rank and how long you have held it. From that they will know to stay away from you. You will become a social pariah, and your only escape will be to become a Null."

"Nice, so I get treated like a freak because I'm different. That's real benevolent of you guys."

"It has nothing to do with being unfeeling. No doubt some will try to help you see the error of your ways. They will be rewarded if they succeed, but most will want to stay away to keep you from being a bad influence on them."

Atton nodded along; it all made perfect sense to him. In fact, now that he understood better how life worked in Etheria, he was more determined than ever to make his choice. Where was the down side? Etheria promised a world with no poverty, no death, no disease, no suffering, no unemployment, no boredom, no unfairness, no crime ... the list went on and on.

So why was his father so determined not to be a part of it? And what about Ceyla? Surely by now she could see enough parallels between life on Avilon and the after life the Etherians had preached about that she couldn't deny it anymore. This *was* the Etheria that her codices described. Omnius was the benevolent god who was supposed to resurrect everyone after the apocalypse. That apocalypse had come with the Sythians, and life eternal was *here*.

"I have a question," a new voice asked. The voice was soft and feminine, and Atton realized belatedly that it belonged to Ceyla. He turned to look behind him so he could make eye contact. Rather than sit with him on the bus, she'd opted to sit on the other side, a few rows back. She was obviously still angry with him.

"Yes, Miss Corbin?" Master Rovik growled, sounding as though his patience were being strained with all the questions.

"If this is Etheria, where are all the people who died?" Ceyla's expression was mild and there was a faint smile on her soft, ruby lips. Her blue eyes contrasted sharply with them, her gaze hard and angry.

"I'm not sure I understand ..." the Peacekeeper slowly replied. "Everyone is here, alive and well." He gestured outside the bus to the endless rows of skyscrapers flashing by to either side of them.

"No," Ceyla shook her head, and now her lips parted in a tight smile that curved contemptuously up on one side. "I mean the ones who died before the Sythians invaded—my grandparents, and great grandparents. Where are they?"

Master Rovik sighed. "They are not here, nor are they anywhere else. We've been over this Miss Corbin. The afterlife you are looking for does not exist. If it did, we'd at least be able to see whatever it is that links us from this plane of existence to the next. There would be some evidence of that link."

"Maybe you just don't know how to look yet. We didn't know how to see past cloaking shields. Your very own Omnius exploited that and implanted us all without our knowledge. What if something bigger than Omnius puts a different kind of implant in all of us at birth? What if its something that's cloaked even from Omnius? If Omnius could fool us because he's so much smarter, it stands to reason that an entity even smarter and more powerful than him could do the same thing."

The silence that followed those arguments was palpable. Atton turned back to look at Master Rovik and the rest of the peacekeepers sitting at the front of the bus. Some looked annoyed or angry, but none more so than Master Rovik himself. The man's blue eyes were full of something that looked all wrong and out of place.

When he'd turned around, Atton had half expected to find the man's gaze full of compassion and pity for Ceyla's ignorance and inability to accept the truth. Instead what he saw was raw, raging hatred. There was enough of a threat lurking in the Peacekeeper's steely blue gaze that Atton was reminded of a deadly predator backed into a corner and ready to pounce.

As the silence wore on, Atton's insides clenched up in anticipation of something terrible. His heart beat erratically in his chest, and his palms began to sweat. He felt a sudden need to defend Ceyla from the Peacekeeper.

His father beat him to it. "So that's what you look like when you don't have all the answers. You don't look very happy, Blue. Down right crushed. Just watch how you throw that tantrum you're fantasizing about right now. You touch one hair on that girl's head and I swear I'll mess up your pretty face so bad you'll never want to see a mirror again."

For a few more seconds, Rovik didn't so much as twitch, but then he seemed to snap out of it, and the bloody gleam left his eyes as his gaze left Ceyla's face. "You'd be dead before you even touched me, Martalis," he said, turning to Ethan.

"Hey, you remembered my name! Martalis. I get it now, Blue. Means *mortal* in Versal, just like you said. That's what you call the Nulls, isn't it?"

"No," Rovik replied. With that change in topic the last vestiges of cold hatred burning in the Peacekeeper's eyes seemed to disappear. "By calling you Martalis, I am being polite, referring to you as I would refer to any child in Etheria or Celesta—the word simply means you are not yet immortal because you haven't made your choice. Calling you a Null, however, is a way of denying your very existence. The word means the same thing to us as it means to Omnius—nothing. A null byte is a byte with the value of zero, and that is exactly how much value you will have once you become a Null."

Ethan replied with a snort, and Master Rovik smiled ruefully. "You are as lost as anyone I have ever met, Ethan, but Omnius isn't through with you yet. He is more patient than you realize." The Peacekeeper's gaze swept back to Ceyla. "That goes for you as well, Miss Corbin."

"The feeling's mutual, Glow Stick."

Atton had to suppress a laugh at that. The Peacekeepers

were strangely bright to look at, thanks to their glowing armor and eyes.

"Cute," Rovik replied. "Now if you'll excuse me, I must get on with your tour. No more questions please." For the most part, the rest of their tour through Etheria passed in silence. Atton watched the sights of the city pass them by, listening with half an ear as Master Rovik described them and explained what they were. He was too distracted to pay much attention. For some reason, he couldn't get Ceyla's arguments out of his head.

What if there was a way to prove the existence of something more, some other life beyond the one they were all busy living?

Yet if proof of an afterlife existed, surely a vast super intelligence like Omnius would have found it by now. He'd already been around for thousands of years, and he'd never found anything to suggest that there could be a life after this one. At least, if he had, he hadn't thought to share that discovery with his people.

But if he truly cares about us, he wouldn't hide that. And hadn't Omnius already proven his love for people by saving them from the Sythians and by building a utopia for them?

Then there was the Null Zone—a large, impoverished, and unhappy group of citizens looking for ways to undermine the whole system. If Omnius didn't love people, he wouldn't give them a choice.

No, the lie made no sense. What possible motive could Omnius have to hide the real nature of the universe from people? Atton couldn't think of one. It was easier to accept that Omnius was exactly what he claimed to be, and that he wasn't hiding anything.

CHAPTER 18

"What are you hiding, Mr Cavanaugh?" An ugly threat lurked in Captain Covani's voice.

Destra eyed the big, broad-shouldered man, known so far as Cavanaugh. He stood before them, his hands already bound behind his back with lengths of stun cord. His nose was bleeding, and a set of bloody gashes were torn in his baggy orange prison garb, revealing one muscular upper arm with matching furrows carved into his skin, while the other sleeve was torn away entirely, revealing the shiny silver shell of a cybernetic prosthesis.

Destra thought about the man's bloody nose and the gash in his arm. She didn't have to wonder where he'd received those injuries. The gash was consistent with claw marks. Her eyes narrowed on the Gors. At least they hadn't taken a bite out of him.

"Please, call me Darron," the broad-shouldered man replied in a breezy tone. "None of my friends call me Cavanaugh."

"I'm not your friend," the captain replied.

He shrugged. "Maybe I'm not yours, sir, but you broke me out of prison, so that makes you mine. You'll come around." He flashed a big smile. "I'm irresistible."

"Cut the krak. You compromised our rescue operation on Etaris in order to rescue unauthorized persons. I want to know who you really are, and what the frek you thought you were doing," Covani said, looming close to the prisoner. The effect was no doubt intended to intimidate, but it merely looked comical due to the vast difference between the two mens' sizes.

The big man's cheer abruptly vanished. "I already told you who I am."

"Then you're going to need some proof, because the man who was supposed to be in your cell was one Edgar Framon, murderer and rapist, serving two consecutive life sentences. I suppose the other prisoners you rescued are equally depraved low-lifes?"

Cavanaugh's brow furrowed and he shook his head. "If you think I'm Framon, why the frek would you bust me out of there?"

"We only rescued you because the Gor who broke into your cell got the cell number wrong."

"Seems like it's my lucky day then."

"Start talking."

"Name's Darron Cavanaugh, just like I told you, *sir*. *Framon* along with his crimes is an identity they made up for me when my commanding officer burned us and threw us to the bureaucrats. Have you even thought to look up the name *Darron Cavanaugh* in any of your databases? Surely you still have *some* records from the old Imperium."

Covani frowned. "We did look you up, but we didn't get a match."

"Really? Not even if you check Sentinels' databases? The kakards must have done a better job covering up than I thought."

"Covering up what?" Destra asked.

"You ever hear of the Black Rictans? The *Blackies?*"

Destra blinked and her eyes widened as that unit name connected to meaning in her head. Back before the Sythian Invasion and the war, the *Blackies,* or the Black Rictans, had been the most famous squad of sentinels in the Imperium. They had been splashed all over recruitment posters, and their unit was *the* unit to be in. The faces changed over the years as soldiers died or got promoted and moved on, but the squad had stayed the same, with the same reputation.

Suddenly, Destra found herself scanning the others standing with Cavanaugh. They were all equally big and tough-looking, which was consistent with a squad of elite sentinels. There was just one problem—the Black Rictans had gone down in a blaze of glory during the gener riots on Alista. The Alistans had been fighting over ethical and societal objections to engineering genetically superior children.

"You all died," Destra said quietly.

"So everyone keeps telling me. Try looking me up again. Sergeant Darron Cavanaugh, serial number 24-1556-6179-8858."

Captain Covani snapped his fingers to an aide standing beside him.

"Sir?"

"Go find a holo pad and look up that serial number."

"I have one here, sir. Could you please repeat the number to me, Mr Cavanaugh?"

The broad-shouldered man repeated the string of numbers, and the aide spent a moment tapping them into his pad. Once he had the result, he shook his head and turned the pad so Covani could see. Destra peered over the captain's shoulder to get a look.

"Name, *classified*," Covani began, reading the dossier aloud. "Division, ISSA, Sentinels. Rank, Master Sergeant. Unit, *classified*." Covani looked up with a patient smile. "You know what that tells me, *Cavanaugh?* You knew a Sentinel, and somehow you got him to tell you his serial number."

"Can someone reach into my pants?" Cavanaugh asked.

"You think this is a joke?" The captain gestured to all of the other prisoners standing with them in the hangar. "You put all of these men's lives in jeopardy with your actions. I'd let them decide your fate, but I don't want to encourage their darker sides any more than I have to." At that a few angry looks turned Cavanaugh's way.

"It's no joke, Captain. Release my bonds and I'll show you what I mean."

Covani's eyes narrowed quickly. After a brief pause he gave a quick nod and took a long step back. "Release him." Destra and the others retreated to a safe distance with the captain, and watched warily as a pair of sentinels stepped forward, their weapons drawn and ready. One of them aimed a small remote at Cavanaugh and pressed a button. There came a *click* and the man's stun cords clattered to the ground, deactivated and inert. Cavanaugh relaxed his arms and took a moment to roll his big shoulders.

"Get on with it, Framon," the captain said.

They watched as he reached into his pants and fiddled around for a moment. Covani didn't look amused.

"There we go . . ." the prisoner said, and he produced a small, shiny silver chip. Destra recognized it as a soldier's ID tag. Wrist-embedded Identichips were ubiquitous to everyone in the Imperium, but Sentinels also wore a secondary piece of ID around their necks that was nearly indestructible. ID tags contained a few bytes of basic data hard-coded into their molecular structure, rather than digitally encoded in a more fragile format. That was in case, say, a plasma grenade burned the sentinel in question to atomic ash and his regular identichip didn't survive.

"My ID tag," the prisoner said, holding it out to the captain. One of the sentinels stepped forward and cautiously took the tag, his eyes and weapon on Cavanaugh the entire time. The sentinel retreated, backing up until he could pass the tag to the captain.

Destra watched as the captain's aide scanned the chip with his holo pad. Another few lines appeared on the pad.

Cavanaugh
Darron A.
24-1556-6179-8858ISSA
Blood Type: O+
Religion: Agnostic

"Where did you get this?" Captain Covani demanded.

"With respect, sir, where do you think I got it?"

Destra shook her head. There was no way a prisoner had managed to create that tag to support his phony story. It was equally unlikely that he'd found a way to read it, or that the real Darron Cavanaugh had told Edgar his serial number before Edgar had killed him and stolen his ID tag.

"You said something about a cover up?" Covani asked, taking a step closer to the prisoner.

"That's right. Alista was just to get the public eye off us. We weren't even there. We went on a highly-classified mission instead. To the Getties Cluster."

Destra blinked. "When was this?"

"Oh, about five years before the Imperium built the space lane between the two galaxies. Six years before their official, inaugural mission went there and stirred up a krakload of Sythians."

"Why would anyone want to cover up your mission?"

"Because our mission went to a different sector of the Getties. Our report was used as the primary reason to open a space lane for Imperial expansion into the Getties. In the six months we spent exploring, we didn't find any Sythians. Or at least, we didn't think so at the time."

Captain Covani crossed his arms over his chest. "Go on."

"We found Noctune and the Gors, sir. Our exploration was limited to the sector around Noctune, but we found nothing to suggest civilization. Our xenobiologist classified the Gors as a type zero civilization. Primitive hunter-gatherers. We found evidence in our geological surveys to conclude that Noctune was once much warmer with a much brighter and stronger sun. Something catastrophic happened that diminished the power and likely the mass of their sun."

"Skip the Gor history lesson and get to the point, Cavanaugh."

"Yes, sir. As I said we encountered no sentient life besides the Gors. We explored several solar systems in depth and found most of them contained sterile ice balls even less habitable than Noctune.

"A few worlds had basic flora and fauna, but the Gors were the only intelligent species we found. Our long range probes found more of the same. The Getties was dark and cold, and unoccupied by any kind of advanced civilization that we could detect."

"Then explain the Sythians to me, Sergeant," Covani replied.

"I'm getting to that, sir. Based on our report when we returned one year later, the government began funding a space lane to connect the two galaxies. My recommendation was that another more extensive mission be sent before any conclusions be drawn about whether or not the Getties was safe and open for Imperial expansion. The brass ignored me, and rather than funding another mission, work began on the space lane to the Getties.

"But rather than put the lane through to Noctune and the system we'd already cleared as safe, some krak-for-brains committee decided we should put the lane through to a more habitable system that we had yet to fully explore. Well you all know the rest of the story. No sooner had we finished the space lane than we ran into Sythians on the other side."

Destra shook her head. "A testament to human arrogance."

Cavanaugh snorted and went on. "At the time our unit was assigned to another undercover op. We were recalled to join the war, but rather than join the fight, we were taken straight to Etaris without trial or explanation. We found out when we arrived that our identichips had somehow been altered and we were now convicted felons with false names. Suffice to say no one believed us when we arrived. Our uniforms and weapons were confiscated along with our ID tags. You don't want to know what I had to do to keep mine."

At that, the captain glanced distastefully at the metal chip lying in his palm.

"The prison warden was in on it, so he didn't let us say anything to anyone who mattered, and the guards figured we were all crazy."

"So someone buried you all to make sure no one ever held them accountable for letting the Sythians into our galaxy."

"That's right. I guess back then they still thought we might win the war." Cavanaugh flashed a nasty grin. "But the ones who burned us ended up dying in the war, while we all survived here in Dark Space. Irony's a kakard," Cavanaugh said, chuckling.

Captain Covani didn't look amused. "We're going to have to verify your story by running the serial numbers of the rest of your men."

"Not a problem," Cavanaugh said.

"If everything checks out, the Black Rictans will be officially reinstated with a public pardon—public in this case being the officers on this ship."

"That's more than I could have hoped for, sir."

Covani nodded and Destra watched as he turned to speak to the entire group of prisoners they'd rescued. "As for the rest of you, you will be riding in the brig under close watch until we can determine who, if anyone, should receive a pardon for their crimes. You will also all be subjected to medical examinations and interrogations to ascertain whether or not you have yet been brain-washed into becoming Sythian slaves. If you are cleared, you'll soon pay your debt to society by helping us rebuild on a new world. That will be all." Turning back to Cavanaugh he said, "Unfortunately, Sergeant, you and your men will also have to go through the exams."

"I understand, sir."

"Good. Dismissed." Covani saluted the sergeant and turned on his heel to head back the way they'd come. Destra caught up to him a second later.

"Sir," she whispered.

"What is it, Councilor?"

"I need to discuss something with you."

"Can it wait? I'm running short on sleep, and I'm long overdue for a hot meal."

"So am I. I could join you in your office for a meal and we can discuss our next steps."

"Very well. Meet me there in fifteen, but whatever it is, let's keep it short."

"Agreed."

Fifteen minutes later they sat down in the captain's office. A low-ranking sentinel brought in two plates of food, each with an identical portion of re-hydrated ration blocks. A small pinkish chunk of meat, a greenish chunk of vegetables, and a stale dinner roll lay steaming on Destra's plate. The smell was appetizing, but that was probably only because she was so hungry.

While they ate, Destra explained what Torv had said about Noctune and the Gors' desire to search for survivors there. The captain greeted that news with a frown, so Destra tried sweetening the deal by referencing what they'd just learned about Noctune and the surrounding systems from Sergeant Cavanaugh.

"I'll admit Cavanaugh's report makes the Gors' case stronger, but this will be a one way trip. Do you really want the future of our civilization to depend on staying hidden right under the Sythians' noses? We might manage it for a few generations, but what happens after that? It would just take one passing Sythian scout to find us. If they found and enslaved the Gors on Noctune, it is likely they will find us and either enslave us or wipe us out."

"More likely than them finding us in this galaxy after they cleared it for future expansion? At least the Getties won't be subject to any active exploration, because they already know what's in their backyard. A passing scout won't easily detect us, unless we're trying to communicate with it, or unless we've already reached a significant level of civilization. Hopefully if we become that advanced we'll also be cautious about broadcasting things into space."

Covani frowned. "What's your point, Councilor?"

"My point is that for the foreseeable future it could actually be easier to hide in the Getties. Besides, if we don't help the Gors now, they will leave us. Can we afford to start over without them?"

"It might be nice to have fewer mouths to feed. Besides, just because we're allies now, doesn't mean the Gors won't become our enemies in a hundred years, or even a thousand. For all we know they'll be our ultimate undoing, not the Sythians."

"That's a lot of supposition, Captain, but I have another suggestion. We're already aware that there are a number of extra-galactic planets and star systems lurking in the nebula between our two galaxies, and those star systems are even less likely to be found and explored by Sythians than systems they have already explored in their own galaxy. While we travel to Noctune, we can stop off and check out some of the extra-galactics that the Imperium already cataloged.

"Cataloged but not explored," Covani clarified. "We don't know what's out there."

"Exactly! If *we* knew about those systems for countless centuries without even bothering to explore them, it's because we had plenty of other systems to explore closer at hand. We went to the Getties before we explored the systems lying along the way."

Covani looked thoughtful. "That is actually a promising place to start."

"Of course it is! So ... do you want me to tell Torv the

good news, or are you going to?"

"I'll sleep on it."

"You'll..."

"Madam Councilor, we are in no position to be making such crucial decisions about the future of the human race when we haven't slept more than a few hours in the last two days."

Destra opened her mouth to object, but Covani waved her objection away while chewing his last morsel of rehydrated meat. "We'll reconvene here one hour before reversion to real space. By then I should have an answer ready for you and the Gors."

"Captain, may I remind you that the Admiral left me in charge?"

"And the admiral is not here. Nor will he ever be here again. I am sorry for your loss, Ma'am. I have nothing but respect for the admiral, but his widowed wife has no business making tactical decisions that affect the survival of our species."

"Widowed wife ..." Destra's face turned red and the veins began standing out on her forehead. "I'm also the Councilor of Karpathia and the next in line for command of the Imperium."

"*Councilor* is a civil rank, not a military one. The Imperium no longer exists, but my ship does, and you have no business commanding it. I might also point out, *Miss* Heston, that you were only recently *appointed* to office, and it may be argued that the only reason you were appointed at all was because your late husband was ruling the Imperium at the time."

"How dare you!" Destra rose to her feet, her hands balled into fists. "And it's still *Mrs* Heston, thank you."

"Ma'am. Please return to your quarters and get some sleep. I will announce my decision one hour before reversion. Dismissed."

"You can't *dismiss* me. I'm not one of your crew."

"At this point, Ma'am, even the prisoners are a part of my crew, and I can dismiss whoever I like." He rose to his feet, his tangerine eyes glittering in the low light of his office.

Destra glared daggers at him. She considered popping his self-important bubble by telling him that the surviving remnants of humanity were a lot bigger than him and his ship, but Avilon and its location was her secret weapon, and it wouldn't be wise to reveal that yet.

"Good night, Covani," she said, and turned to leave his office, her head full of bitter thoughts.

* * *

As the tour of Etheria ended, the air bus left the main stream of traffic and began dropping straight down. Ethan watched out the window as they fell past countless dozens of floors. Shadows crept as they descended, flickering past the bus like living things. Darkness gathered despite the dazzling light pouring from the bottom of each level of elevated streets. Soon Ethan could see the fuzzy blue glow of the Styx swelling up beneath them. That hazy blue shield wall was noticeably dimmer than the one above them, as though Omnius didn't want to give the Nulls any more light than was absolutely necessary.

The bus came to a sudden stop, which they all saw, but none of them felt thanks to the vehicle's inertial management system.

They sat in an apprehensive silence, waiting. Ethan listened to the faint hum from the bus's grav lifts, to the air *whooshing* from climate control vents overhead. The only sign of life inside the bus was the occasional rustle of fabric from the white celestial robes they all still wore. Master Blue Cape had long since stopped pointing out the sights, which Ethan found to be a relief. The man's gravelly voice was almost as irritating as he was.

"What's the delay?" someone asked, breaking the silence.

"We have to pass a customs check to make sure our vehicle isn't carrying any illegal items into the Null Zone," Blue Cape replied from the front of the bus.

Silence reigned once more.

"What did you see down there?" Alara whispered beside him.

"I already told you," he replied. "It's like Dark Space, but worse. Omnius took me to some place called the *Grunge*. Everyone down there was living in free housing, living off free food and other things that Omnius recycles from the city's garbage."

Alara nodded absently, and Ethan looked out the side window of the bus—only to find that something was looking *back* at him. A silver ball with one bright red eye in its center hovered just outside the window, watching him.

"What the *frek*?"

All around him others were having similar reactions, and Alara, who was sitting closest to their window suddenly leaned as far over into his lap as she could.

"What is it?"

"Do not be alarmed," Rovik said. "They are the drones who will scan our vehicle before we are permitted into the Null Zone."

Up till now Ethan had only seen Omnius's drones—or *Omnies*—in their vaguely humanoid form. Now, as he looked more closely, he realized that these bots were identical to the other ones, or rather, to their *heads*. Apparently they could detach from their bodies and fly around for greater mobility.

Suddenly the red eye staring at them burned bright red, dazzling Ethan's eyes. His ARCs adjusted a second too late, polarizing to protect his eyes. Red light flickered through the bus, and Ethan turned to see more drones looking in from the other side. He felt his skin grow warm and begin to tingle, and then the light was gone, plunging the inside of the bus into a sudden darkness. His ARCs brightened once more, but by the time the spots cleared from his vision, the drones were already gone.

The bus began descending, and Ethan leaned over Alara to get a closer look out the window. He saw that the hexagonal segment of the shield directly below the bus had been deactivated to let them through.

Moments later they passed below the shield and the segment flickered back to life overhead. The light emitted from the bottom of the shield was a dim blue, unlike the dazzling brightness they'd seen from beneath the Celestial Wall.

In an attempt to make up for that, lights from passing windows and strips of external glow panels shone out from the buildings, casting the under city in a dim, multi-colored gloom.

"Welcome to the Null Zone," Rovik said. The bus continued slowly downward, and the Peacekeeper launched into a description of life in the Null Zone. Ethan had already guessed at most of it. Unlike the upper cities, the Null Zone did not benefit from free health care, education, or equal opportunity. It was run by an elected government, and the economy was free market and privately-run. Unemployment was high—about 10%. Birth rates were low, and the population would be shrinking without immigrants from the Uppers. Despite that, rent was not cheap, and space was at a premium. Organized crime was creeping in at the lowest levels, taking over abandoned sectors. Making matters worse, the upper class was hogging all the more desirable space higher up in the Null Zone.

Social programs and charities, funded and put in place mostly by Omnius, were what people fell back on if they couldn't look after themselves. Reference was made to what Ethan had already witnessed—recycling programs that made food and other basic necessities freely available to even the poorest citizens.

Crime was on the rise. Local enforcers—the Nulls' version of the Peacekeepers—were corrupt and underpaid, and they tended not to patrol below level ten. If they did, it was with one eye shut. Anything below level ten was considered a red zone, and the sub levels were either abandoned or home to various crime lords and their gangs. A tenuous balance existed between law-abiding citizens and criminal organizations.

Underpinning all the crime was the distribution and sale of a super drug, a synthetic performance enhancer called *Bliss*.

Ethan grimaced as he heard that. He'd already had a taste of the stuff, and based on the way it had made him feel, he wondered why anyone would ever want to take it again.

"Despite Bliss being illegal, you'll find plenty of users are respectable citizens living in the upper levels. The drug makes them better at what they do, so they keep using, but every now and then someone stops taking it because they can't afford to keep dosing. Go too long between doses and you damage your brain. Do that enough, and you'll wind up no better than a simple-minded beast."

Ethan wasn't surprised that the rich had a lock on Bliss, but in a way it made them responsible for all of the crime and corruption in the lower levels. Without users there'd be no demand and no one would bother to illegally traffic the supply. King-pins and their organizations would shrivel up and die. Of course, that was just a fantasy. People wouldn't stop using Bliss just to eradicate crime.

The bus continued drifting down, and a level of elevated streets came into view below them. Ethan noticed that the street was lit with glow lamps, and the pedestrians all seemed to be well-dressed. The faces of the buildings were neat and recently painted, and the architecture was suitably grand and ornate. He felt a spark of hope lighten his spirits. Maybe living in the Null Zone wouldn't be so bad?

As they dropped below that level, however, things quickly became worse. Paint peeled from walls, curtains took the place of the more expensive reflective coating on windows, allowing them to see straight into a few apartments. Cheap, ugly-looking black bars caged every window, and balconies disappeared entirely.

Ethan wondered how far down they were, and his ARC display reacted to that thought by producing a small cross section of the Null Zone showing their current location. The bus was represented by a green dot, seen descending slowly past level 21.

As soon as they reached level 15 a dense, dirty gray fog crept in, making the city even darker than it had been before. Ethan grimaced. The light shining out from the windows of nearby buildings became all but lost in the swirling clouds of gritty moisture. As they dropped below level 10, the light diminished even further, and only the occasional fuzzy white or golden glow still bloomed through the mist. Either not many people lived down here, or the residents were afraid to advertise that they were there.

Ethan estimated that another minute or two passed with them drifting down through the fog before something changed. Suddenly the window he was looking out turned a blurry blue, and the fog peeled away, as if blown by a giant's breath. The fog stopped retreating at a set distance of just a few meters from the bus. There, holding it at bay, was the blurry blue barrier he'd seen before. It was a shield of some kind. The ground swirled into view, and fog billowed out beneath the bus as the shield pushed it away. Then they stopped and hovered just a few feet above the ground.

Rovik turned to them and said, "Whatever you see, please remember, we're perfectly safe in here."

With that warning, the bus began moving forward again. Alara's nails bit into Ethan's arm. He reached for her hand to keep her from doing any serious damage.

The bus went slowly, giving their imaginations time to populate the shifting shadows with hideous monsters. The occasional fuzzy glow bloomed in the darkness, giving just enough light to paint more shadows against the swirling clouds of gray mist. Ethan was sure the shadows were just his imagination, until he began to see those shadows *converge*. They swarmed toward the bus. Ethan's heart beat faster, and the bus *slowed down*.

"Ah, Blue . . ." Ethan said.

Around them others were murmuring with concern, and Alara was back to digging her nails into his arm—this time with both hands. "Hey, Blue!" Ethan said. "Any particular reason why we're slowing down?"

"Do not be alarmed," Rovik replied. "Omnius wants you to see this."

Then, as if it had all been perfectly staged, the shadows took form, and the bus's running lights splashed them with color. Bedraggled masses of people came wandering out of the darkness, blinking against the light, stumbling about as if in a daze. They were a disorganized mob dressed with ragged scraps of clothing, a sea of bony arms and legs. They came toward the bus like moths to a flame, mesmerized by the light. Ethan watched them approach, horrified by the sight of them. He'd seen Psychos before, but not like this, not so close.

"Ethan . . ." Alara began, her grip tightening still further.

He winced, suddenly reminded of what it felt like to hold a pregnant woman's hand while she was in labor. "Relax, we're safe in here."

"Then why are they still coming?"

Ethan shook his head, unable to answer that. Despite the shield, they saw the bedraggled masses step right through it, as though it were nothing.

"Blue, your shield's not working . . ." Ethan said, his eyes on an old hag with stringy gray hair and wild-looking yellow eyes. Those eyes found his, and she licked swollen lips.

Ethan shuddered. "Rovik!"

"The shield is only to hold back the fog, Martalis, not the wildlife."

"Wildlife?"

"I mean the Psychos, of course," Rovik said.

Ethan could have sworn there was a touch of humor in the man's voice, but whatever had the Peacekeeper so amused wasn't tickling Ethan's funny bone at all.

He eyed the old crone as she stumbled toward them. Alara leaned away, all but winding up in his lap. "What does she want?" Alara asked, sounding desperate.

The bus slowed to a complete stop, and the old woman walked straight up to their window. Dozens more crowded around her, each of them fixated on their own subject within the bus.

The old woman stood a few inches away from the window, watching them. She was at least sixty, but disfigured and scarred, with several open sores that they could see. Dirty fragments of cloth clung to her in all the wrong places, revealing jutting bones and dirty skin. She pressed hands that were black with dirt to the glass. Then came her nose, pressed up and pushed back like a pig's snout. She began steaming up the glass with her breath, all the while staring at them with those wild yellow eyes. There was something in her gaze that inspired pity, and for a moment Ethan was almost fooled.

Then a few more bedraggled humans crowded around her. One of them, a younger man, rapped on their window with a long, impossibly thin arm.

"They look hungry," Alara said. "Do we have any food we can give them?" she asked, raising her voice to be heard over the rising tumult inside the bus.

Rovik replied, "You might not like their idea of food."

"What do you mean?"

The old woman licked her lips once more, and suddenly Ethan understood. "Because they think they've just stepped up to the buffet table," he whispered.

More knuckles rapped on the window, and this time the sound echoed all around them. Psychos pounded on the sides of the bus, rocking it on its grav lifts.

A woman screamed.

"They can't get in here, can they?" someone asked. Ethan recognized the voice as Atton's.

"No, don't worry. We're safe," Rovik replied.

"I think we should get moving," Ethan said.

"Not yet."

"I'm going to have nightmares tonight," Alara whimpered, turning away from the scene and burying her face in his robes.

Ethan looked on, afraid to look away in case one of those clawing hands should find a way into the bus. The faces pressed against the glass were all dirty and ugly. If these people had been normal once, there was no sign of it now. A few of them were foaming at the mouth and spraying the window with spittle.

Then something new happened.

Ethan saw the middle distance behind the Psychos flash with a ball of blue light that sparkled and then swelled quickly to three times its size. At that point it burst and the world became a blinding sea of brightness. A deafening *boom* rattled the windows and the bus rocked violently under them. The fact that this time they could *feel* the movement told Ethan something was wrong. The lights flickered and died; then the bus suddenly dropped and hit the ground with a bone-jarring *crash*. People screamed. Ethan held tight to Alara, waiting for the lights to come back so he could see what was going on.

He felt a cold brush of something against his arm and jerked reflexively away from it. The lights came back a split second later. Everyone was thrashing to get back into their seats, the majority having fallen into the aisle. Ethan turned to look out the window, and he saw that the crowd of Psychos had left. There were no bodies on the ground where the explosion had occurred.

"What the frek?" he wondered aloud.

Rovik shouted something to the driver, and the bus leapt off the ground, lurching into motion again. This time they were going *fast*.

Another flash of blue light bloomed beside them. Ethan looked away to shield his eyes. It exploded a split second later, rocking the bus once more.

The shield bubble around them suddenly brightened and contracted, drawing much closer to the sides of the bus. The fog swirled back in, and Ethan was even more blinded than before.

Another blue light flashed on the other side of the bus, followed by another, and another. The explosions rumbled around them like thunder, and the bus rocked as though it was adrift over stormy waters. Ethan looked up to see Rovik come stalking back through the bus. He looked furious.

"What's going on?" Ethan asked.

"Isn't it obvious?" he replied. "We're under attack."

"I thought you said we'd be safe down here!"

"You are. Nulls are not supposed to have access to pulse weapons."

"Pulse weapons?" Ethan caught the Peacekeeper by the arm.

Rovik twisted out of his grip easily and stood staring at him, his glowing blue eyes blazing. "Weapons that interfere with the conversion and distribution of energy."

Another flash of blue light went off behind them, taking

with it the Peacekeeper's patience. He hurried on down the aisle.

"What the frek is that supposed to mean?" Ethan called after him.

"It means they are trying to disable us, Mr Ortane! They want us alive."

Ethan blinked, suddenly curious. They *who?* He watched as Rovik reached the back of the bus. Once there, the Peacekeeper waved his hands and an emergency door slid aside. Unsavory smells began wafting in. Rovik raised his arms to fire back at whatever was pursuing them, using weapons built into his suit. For a moment it looked like he was taking an inordinate amount of time to fire on their unseen enemy. He kept repositioning his arms as if to get a better angle on some unseen target. Then he dropped his arms, as if he'd given up altogether. A second later, bright orange explosions began to blossom out of the fog behind them. The explosions peppered some unseen surface and then flowed together like an amorphous ball of plasma. When that bright orange glow was all they could see, it went off with a mighty screech of rending metal, and a sound like breaking glass. The brightness of the explosion was dimmed enough by the fog and the contacts they all wore that Ethan didn't have to look away this time. Rovik turned away from the door and it shut automatically as the Peacekeeper strode back to the front of the bus.

As he breezed by them, he said, "Your tour is over!"

Alara breathed a sigh of relief and looked up. Ethan noticed that her cheeks were wet with tears, and he regarded her with a frown. "Are you okay?" Usually she had a better tolerance for danger.

She shook her head and returned to sitting upright in her

seat. "Must be my hormones."

He squeezed her hand and sent her a lopsided grin. "Don't worry, I was scared, too."

Alara shook her head. "I wasn't scared."

"Then . . ."

"I can't help thinking about those people we saw, reduced to barbarism, starving to death down here in the dark. I can't imagine a worse way to die."

Ethan shook his head. "They're not even human anymore. You heard what Rovik said. They're brain damaged cannibals. Someone should put them out of their misery."

"Maybe they're not human anymore, but they used to be . . ." She trailed off, shaking her head. "They used to be someone's mothers, daughters, sons, and fathers."

Ethan frowned. "What are you getting at?"

She turned to look at him, her face distraught. "I don't want our daughter to end up like that, Ethan."

"She won't."

"No? Can you promise me that? One in five Nulls is addicted to Bliss!"

"We'll raise her right."

"And what if that isn't good enough?"

"You're getting way too far ahead of yourself. She's not even born yet." He squeezed her hand. "We'll warn her every chance we get. Besides, you heard Master Blue—it's just the rich that have to worry about Bliss."

"No, Ethan. It's just the rich that don't have to worry about becoming Psychos. People like us, we might just get desperate enough to start using for a chance at a better life, but what happens when we can't afford another dose?"

Ethan didn't have an answer for that. "Let's take one day at a time. For now, it's good enough that we know what we're going to choose. The rest will work itself out. It always does."

Alara nodded and looked away, back out the window of the bus. Although she gave no reply, Ethan could read her thoughts as clearly as if they were his own. She wasn't sure about what she was going to choose anymore, and that frightened him more than anything they'd seen lurking in the shadows of the under city.

CHAPTER 19

Destra sat in the mess hall with her daughter. The ship's intercom crackled to life and Captain Covani's voice rasped through the room.

"Attention all personnel, this is your captain speaking. We are one hour away from our scheduled reversion to real space, and the time has come for us to decide where we should go from there."

A sudden hush fell in the mess hall as the noise of conversations and cutlery scraping plates ceased.

"I've met with my advisers and councilors and we have discussed the matter at length. Every possible option was discussed."

Destra's eyes narrowed at that, and she wondered if there had been a meeting that she hadn't been invited to. She and the captain had only discussed one option at length, which was for them to go to Noctune and help the Gors look for survivors.

"Our galaxy was ruled out, since the Sythians wouldn't have been so relentless about killing every last one of us if they planned to share the galaxy with us. They'll be looking for us here, and if we stay, eventually they will find us again.

"We discussed going to The Getties Cluster, but logic compels us to ask the question—if the Sythians came here because they ran out of space in their galaxy, will there be any room for us there to hide?"

"Thus, the third and final option becomes the only one still available to us. We must go somewhere so remote that no one would bother to look for us there.

"With that in mind, our destination is The Devlin's Hand Nebula. We will search for rogue stars and habitable planets lying between the Adventa Galaxy and the Getties. Our ETA to the first such star is approximately three months. Food and supplies are scarce, so all non-essential personnel will be placed in stasis and only awoken when we arrive. There will be two crews of ten officers who will rotate in and out of stasis while we travel. If you haven't already been told that you are one of those twenty, you should make your way to the med bay for stasis prep as soon as possible.

"For those of you who are wondering, the Gors are leaving us. They will go to Noctune to look for survivors from the Sythian assault on their world. We will stop briefly at our next reversion point to transfer the ones we have on board to their fleet.

"The road ahead of us is a long and treacherous one, but if we stand together, we will prosper. Ruh-kah!"

Silence reigned for just a moment longer as everyone in the mess hall processed the Captain's announcement. Then people snapped into action. Chairs slid out from tables, pivoting on articulated arms that kept them anchored to the deck. Trays and cutlery banged and clattered into collection bins. A hundred different voices rose at once, everyone arguing over the Captain's decision.

Destra took Atta by the hand, carrying their trays in the

other. She stopped to drop them in the nearest collection bin, and then hurried on for the exit, all but dragging her daughter along.

"What's the hurry?" Atta asked.

"We're going to see the Captain."

"Why?"

"Because I want to talk with him."

"About what?"

"Quiet. Let Mommy think."

Atta remained quiet for a moment, and Destra ground her teeth together as she considered the captain's orders. She hadn't been notified that she was one of the twenty individuals who would be awake for the coming journey.

Clearly Captain Covani had decided to negate her authority entirely and make himself the uncontested ruler of humanity. Worse, he was prepared to lose the Gors as allies!

Destra could barely contain her rage. She wasn't going to let him do that without a fight.

* * *

Atton stood on the balcony of their communal quarters on level 30 of Destiny Tower—almost halfway down to the mist-choked netherworld on the surface of the planet. Up here the city was noticeably safer and more civilized. Just five floors below, Atton could see and hear the noisy bustle of pedestrians walking along the Null Zone's well-lit, elevated streets. Pedestrian hover trains periodically *whooshed* by on both sides of those streets, leaving a broad gap between the buildings where streams of air traffic could be seen rising and descending vertically between the upper and lower levels.

Atton watched the crowds of pedestrians, his eyes darting from one person to another, searching for psychos. There was the occasional beggar standing on a street corner, but nothing consistent with the sub-human dregs they'd seen on the surface. It was hard to imagine that one in *five* people walking those streets was already well on their way to becoming a psycho.

Atton breathed a deep sigh, his nose wrinkling as he took in the musty odors of the city. He looked up at the Styx. The shield wall shone a dull, hazy blue overhead, a poor substitute for the sky. They'd begun touring Etheria in the early morning, and since then, Atton estimated that no more than six hours could have passed, meaning it was still the middle of the day, but it looked like the middle of the night.

He shook his head. The contrast between Etheria and the Null Zone was striking. There was no question that life would be better in Etheria, making it pointless to argue about whether or not individual freedom was really a good thing.

He turned away from the view and walked back inside the living area of their suite. The Peacekeepers had left the suite soon after arrival with the excuse that they were needed elsewhere. They'd warned that drones had been posted outside in case any of them started causing trouble. But no one seemed to have the energy for trouble. Everyone was lying around on couches and chairs, exhausted from the events of the past few days. Omnius's nightly intrusion on their dreams hadn't helped. Nightmares in Avilon were much worse, because you knew upon waking that it had all been real, and that your dreams definitely *did* mean something.

Atton meandered over to the dining area where a group of officers and non-coms were sitting and talking in hushed tones. On his way there, he passed his father and step-mother sitting together in an over-sized armchair. Alara was passed out, asleep on Ethan's chest, but Ethan was very much awake, and he glared as Atton walked by.

Atton considered stopping to speak with his father, but then he saw Ceyla watching him from the other side of the living area, her blue eyes hurt and pleading, and he looked away quickly, suddenly unwilling to linger.

He reached the dining table and pulled out a chair beside the former venture-class captain, Loba Caldin.

"Ma'am," he said, waiting for her permission before he sat down.

Caldin nodded. "We were just discussing what's next while we wait for dinner," she whispered.

Atton caught the hint and whispered back, "You've all already made up your minds," he said. It wasn't a question.

"Yes," Caldin replied.

Atton's eyes flicked around the table. He noticed the other Nova pilot from his squadron besides Ceyla—Guardian Five, *Razor*. Then there was Caldin's XO and chief engineer, Cobrale Delayn, sitting beside Lieutenant Esayla Carvon, the *Intrepid's* ebony-skinned gravidar officer; filling the rest of the seats at the table were a handful of sentinels.

"So . . ."

"We're going to rejoin the fight," Caldin said. "The Sythians aren't defeated yet, and until they are, not even Avilon will be safe."

Atton nodded. "I agree. All this concern over whether or

not we die when we're resurrected will be pointless if the Sythians conquer us here. Besides, death is more academic to us. We're used to putting our lives on the line. Weigh the chance that we do actually die while transferring to our new bodies against the near certainty that we'll die in combat, and it seems like a good bet to make. Besides, even if I die tomorrow when I resurrect, I'd still like to give my immortal clone a chance to do what I couldn't and make the Sythians pay for what they've done."

Murmurs of agreement spread around the table and more heads bobbed. "Ruh-kah," one of the sentinels said. "Never thought I'd be agreeing with a Nova jock, but there you have it."

Atton smiled. "And I never thought I'd be having a heart to heart with a stomper."

"Stomper, huh. You better watch it or I'll train up as a pilot this time just so I can shoot you down."

Chief Engineer Delayn raised a new concern, "That's a good point. Didn't the P's say we could join the fight for Dark Space if we choose to become Etherians? I thought they're leaving soon. How are they going to train us in so little time?"

"The P's?" Atton asked.

"Peacekeepers," Caldin supplied. "I think if Omnius could teach us Avilonian while we slept he can teach us just about anything else the same way."

Atton considered that. "The Imperium developed that tech already. Never works out. You implant a skill and it's only ever a shadow of the real thing."

Caldin shrugged. "Maybe they've found a way to get closer to the real thing. That would explain how education in Etheria is free."

A new voice joined their discussion, "Well, isn't this a

nice little gathering." Atton turned to see his father standing behind the captain, his arms crossed over his chest. "Captain Loba Caldin . . ." Ethan began. "I suppose I have you to thank for indoctrinating my son."

"Hello, Mr Ortane," Caldin replied, twisting around to address Ethan. "Atton is more than old enough to make up his mind for himself, which he evidently already did before arriving at this table. But you already know that, so why are you looking for a scapegoat now?"

"Maybe I just don't like your face. Good thing you're going to change it soon." Atton watched his father's gaze rove around the table. "So you've all decided to go through the meat grinder . . ."

"The meat grinder?" Caldin asked. "What are you talking about?"

A nasty smile crawled onto Ethan's face, and his gaze returned to her. He affected a more nonchalant pose, uncrossing his arms for an eloquent shrug. "What do you think they do with all the bodies? Your old ones. I bet they go through a meat grinder to make tasty little sausages for all those starving Nulls. Waste not want not. Seems to be Omnius's policy. What you throw away today could be on your plate tomorrow!" Ethan laughed.

No one else laughed with him. Atton rose to his feet. "That's enough, Dad."

Ethan turned to him with a dark look. "I'm sorry, did I ruin your appetite? Cause you sure the frek ruined mine."

"Dad, I'll still visit you in the Null Zone."

"No you won't."

"I promise, I will."

"Frek your promises, Atton, you won't even *be* you anymore. Anyone else thinking about dying for the cause?"

Ethan turned in a slow circle to address the whole room. "Omnius doesn't need you to fight the Sythians. He can just make another billion Omnies and send them in your place, and they'll probably do an even better job than you will!"

"Dad. That's *enough*. Let people make up their own minds."

Atton reached out to grab his father's arm, but Ethan shrugged him off and shot him a cold look. "I've said what I had to say. The captain's right, you're an adult so you can do whatever you want, but know this—" Ethan raised a finger and jabbed him in the chest with it, forcing him back a step. "You join them and you're dead to me."

"Dad . . ."

"I'm serious, Atton. Dead. I don't want to see you again unless I can be sure that it's really you."

Atton's jaw dropped and he watched, speechless as his father returned to where he'd been sitting with Alara. Atton took one hesitant step to follow, but a strong hand grabbed his arm and pulled him back toward the table.

"Leave him, Atton. He lives for himself, and he'll die for himself. I don't think your father has ever fought for something bigger than his own small world, and he never will. Not willingly anyway."

Atton was about to sit back down when he noticed Ceyla staring at him. She was close enough that he could see the tears shimmering in her blue eyes. His father's rejection had hurt, but this was agony. He'd never loved a woman before, never had the chance, but Ceyla already cared enough about him that she was actually *crying* for him. No sooner had his eyes met hers than she looked away and stood up from the couch where she was sitting.

She hurried from the room, passing quickly down the

dark hallway leading to their quarters.

"Excuse me, Captain," Atton said. "I need to go say goodbye."

"I understand."

Atton hurried after Ceyla. In the hallway he noticed more abstract light paintings like the ones they'd seen in the mansion on the top level of Destiny Tower. Unlike those ones, which he'd seen as a series of smiling, joyous faces, these paintings depicted lurid scenes of naked bodies writhing in ecstasy. Atton eyed them curiously. Destiny Tower had been built with Avilonian children in mind, not adults. It seemed inappropriate to put such paintings here.

He wondered where Ceyla had gone, and his ARC display obligingly pointed the way by showing which rooms were occupied and which ones were not. Only one of the rooms was occupied, and he could actually see Ceyla through the nearest wall, painted as a bright blue silhouette. She was sitting down, her head in her hands.

Atton frowned as he stopped before the door. He was about to knock, but the door *swished* open for him. Ceyla sat on the edge of the nearest bed, her face buried in her hands, sobbing quietly.

She didn't even look up as he approached. Maybe she hadn't heard him come in. "Ceyla?" he asked as he sat down beside her.

She flinched and looked up suddenly. Then recognition flashed in her bloodshot eyes. "What do you want?" she asked.

"I wanted to know if you're okay."

"Of course I'm not okay! Atton, why? Why are you so ready to throw your life away?"

He shook his head. "We don't know that's what I'll be

doing."

"*I* do. We could have been so happy," she said, shaking her head.

"We?" He took her hand and held it between both of his. "I didn't realize you had feelings for me," he said, swallowing thickly past that lie.

"Don't be a skriff, of course I do! You're not like the others, Atton. You pretend not to care, but you do. Iceman ..." She snorted, shaking her head as she recalled his call sign. "You saved my life up there. I'll never forget that."

It felt like forever ago. During the battle over Avilon he'd chosen to rescue her instead of his own wingmate, Gina Giord. Gina had subsequently succumbed to enemy fire and died, while Ceyla had punched out and lived. Atton remembered looking into the accusing eyes of Gina's clone, and he shuddered.

"Ceyla, I—"

She didn't let him finish that sentence. Instead she pulled him close and kissed him. Her tongue forced his lips open and her hands ran quickly through his hair, raking over his shoulders and back. Before he knew what was happening, she'd pulled open his Celestial Robes and pushed him flat against the bed where they were sitting. She crawled on top of him, still kissing him. He reveled in the sweet fragrance of her breath and lost himself in a sea of bliss that had nothing to do with drugs.

Then something occurred to him, and his eyes opened and flicked sideways to the door where he'd come in. There were at least half a dozen other beds in the room, and someone else could come in at any moment.

"Ceyla ..." He began to object.

But she shook her head and pulled open her own robes.

He gaped at her for a moment, suddenly distracted by the sight of her half-naked body.

Her lips and tongue met with his once more. The heat of her kisses and the salty tang of her tears were electrifying. Before he knew it, he'd rolled her over and he was kissing *her*. His hands fumbled to remove her underwear beneath her robes. Then their naked bodies met, finding each other with surprising familiarity, as if they used to be one and were only now returning to that state after a long time apart. It wasn't what he'd expected.

It was better. Ceyla gasped and her eyes rolled as he went in. For a moment he thought she was in pain, but she silenced his objections with a fierce kiss, biting his lip and running her hands through his hair once more.

Time ceased to have all meaning and Atton lost himself in her, for the moment forgetting about The Choosing, the Sythians, Omnius, Avilon ... everything. In that moment he would have given anything just to be with her, like this, forever. Somewhere in the back of his mind, a small voice insisted that he could, and that he already knew what to do in order to have her with him for eternity.

Atton smiled as her body arched against his and the world exploded in bright streaks of light. Her nails scratched fiery lines down his back, and then they lay together breathless and spent.

"I love you, Atton," she whispered in his ear.

For a moment, he didn't know what to say. He felt something powerful stirring inside of him, but was that love?

He wasn't even sure he knew what love was yet, but he said it anyway, and after that, they made love again. Dinner was forgotten, and the night—or day, Atton wasn't sure which—stretched out endlessly with the two of them caught up in the novelty of one another until they were too exhausted to do anything but lie in each other's arms. Ceyla fell asleep with her head on his chest, and Atton lay staring up at the ceiling, trying to work out a way that he could convince her to join him in Etheria.

Maybe she won't need convincing, he thought. *Maybe I'm enough.*

* * *

That night Ethan went to bed with a heavy heart and an empty stomach. He hadn't been lying when he'd told Atton that he'd lost his appetite, but it wasn't just because of Atton's choice. He was secretly even more worried about Alara's.

She hadn't spoken much since the tour had ended, and they'd eaten dinner in silence. He remembered at some point noticing that Atton and Ceyla didn't join them, but he was also smart enough to know why. Ceyla was using the one thing she had left to sway Atton's decision, and Ethan wasn't about to let anyone interfere with that. He'd noted which door they'd both taken, and hinted to the others that that room should be off limits until Atton and Ceyla worked out their differences.

Ethan hoped it worked, but now he had to worry about a more immediate concern. Neither he nor Alara had spoken about what was coming, and they were out of time to make up their minds. Rovik had come in at the end of dinner to remind them all that they would be making their choices early tomorrow morning.

Now Ethan was desperate to know what Alara's choice would be. He watched her go to bathroom and take a shower. Once again, because they were married they'd been assigned a private room. When Alara returned from the bathroom, he was sitting up on the bed, waiting for her.

"Hey there beautiful," he said.

She shot him a wry grin. "Not tonight."

"What, just because a guy compliments you, you automatically assume he's after something?"

"I just know my husband. A brick could fall on your head and you'd still be trying your luck."

Ethan grinned. "Only with you, darling."

"Better be, otherwise I'll be the one dropping that brick."

Ethan chuckled and smiled as she climbed into bed next to him. "You're the best wife a man could ever have."

"Really? I'm your second."

"Exactly, so I should know what I'm talking about."

"You always have the right answers."

"Yeah ... I do. Mostly. I hate to spoil the mood—especially when I'm about to get lucky for being so damned charming—but there is one answer I don't have that I could really use right now."

"What's that?"

"What are you going to do tomorrow?"

Alara arched an eyebrow at him. "You're not seriously asking me that."

"I am."

"What are *you* going to choose?" she countered.

"I asked first."

"Fine. I already know what you're going to do, and you're right. I know you're right, but I'm scared. I want what's best for our daughter, and I want that so badly that I can't really think about myself, or even us, but when she turns eight she'll have to decide for herself anyway."

"So..."

"So, I'm not leaving you, Ethan. Not now, not ever. We made promises to each other, remember? I can't leave you for a better life in Etheria any more than I could leave my own skin."

"Actually, you *can* leave your—"

She stopped him with an upraised hand. "I know, not the best analogy."

He smiled tightly, touched by her commitment to him. "You and me, Kiddie," he said, grabbing her hand.

"You, me, and Trinity," she replied, placing his hand on her belly.

Ethan lay back with a sigh, his hand still on her belly. "We're going to be okay, Kiddie. I promise. I'll do whatever it takes."

"I know," she said, and turned out the lights with a verbal command. She rolled over and he wrapped his arm around her, molding his body to hers.

As they fell asleep, Ethan wondered whether she was agreeing that everything would be okay, or that he would do whatever it took to make things okay. Then he began wondering whether he would be able to keep that promise...

His thoughts floated away in a dreamy haze, and he saw Alara in his mind's eye, naked and beckoning. Some part of him absently noted that it was a dream, but for once it wasn't one of Omnius's instructional nightmares, so he decided to go with it. Besides, the way things were going, he wasn't about to find another time to be with his wife.

Alara straddled him on the bed, and he found her breasts in his hands. She kissed his lips passionately and he kissed back, but by the time she withdrew, he saw that it wasn't Alara straddling him, but some other woman. She was unusually stunning, with hair like black silk and bright turquoise eyes, the color of a tropical sea, but she wasn't his wife.

Ethan's eyes grew wide with horror at that realization. He shook his head quickly. "Get off," he managed.

The other woman's lips curved wryly. "Why? Don't pretend you don't like it." She kissed him again. A part of him surrendered to it, but then he found the strength to resist once more, and pushed her off.

She began laughing. "It's too late to push me away now. Alara will never forgive you."

Ethan had to restrain himself from slapping the grin off that woman's face. He'd never hit a woman before, but in that moment, he was sorely tempted.

Suddenly she was back on top of him as if she'd teleported there. She pressed her body against his in all the right places, and he tried once more to resist, but this time he found that his body wouldn't obey his commands.

Instead, he focused on waking up, using his outrage and indignation to do so, but no matter how hard he tried, he couldn't open his eyes.

The woman smiled, as if she knew she'd won. "You like it, don't you?" she asked. "I told you."

Ethan was unable to deny that, but he hated himself for it, and he hated her even more. At last, just before he might have enjoyed himself too much, he woke up and lay staring up at the ceiling, feeling enraged and violated, bathed in a cold sweat, and painfully aroused.

As he lay there, a quiet voice ran through his head, *I told you you would cheat.*

CHAPTER 20

Destra arrived at the captain's office with Atta in tow. The guards standing there moved to block her way as she approached—yet another sign of Covani's defiance.

"I'd like to see the captain, please," she said.

The guard looked uncomfortable, and his eyes briefly flicked to Atta, perhaps noting the presence of a child as something out of place. Destra in turn noted that he was a high-ranking sentinel, a master sergeant.

"I'm sorry, Ma'am," he said. "The captain asked not to be disturbed. And you should be on your way to the ..." He trailed off and glanced at Atta again. "Well, I'm sure you know the way," he finished. Destra realized he was sparing her daughter the knowledge that they were going into hibernation, and maybe never coming out.

Destra loomed closer to the pair of guards. The master sergeant held his ground. "You realize I'm your superior, not to mention the captain's. I give the orders here."

"With respect, Ma'am, you are a civilian and have no rank."

"You and I both know that civilian branches of authority command the fleet. At least they did until recently."

"Yes, Ma'am. Times change."

"One person should not be solely responsible for commanding the last remnant of humanity," she insisted.

The sergeant took a breath and shook his head. "The command structure is clear, and my duty is clear."

"At least let me in to speak with him. If the captain doesn't change his mind, what's the worst that could happen? You can't be court-martialed. We're short enough on active personnel as it is."

"I could be sent . . . with you, Ma'am."

"So that's it? You're afraid? I can see this military dictatorship is already working nicely."

The sergeant pressed his lips into a firm line and hesitated. His eyes darted to Atta and back again. "Make it quick. He orders me to take you out, and I will. But I'd rather not make a scene in front of your daughter, Ma'am."

"Fair enough."

"I have to search you first."

She nodded and submitted to a pat down search as well as a thorough scan with a wand. After that, both sentinels stepped aside, and the sergeant keyed the doors open by waving his wrist across the scanner.

The doors *swished* open, revealing Captain Covani sitting in the dark behind a big, glossy black table. A holomap was rising from that table, bathing him and the room in a cold blue light.

"Covani," she said.

He looked up with a scowl. "What is she doing in here? I told you no interruptions! Take her to the stasis rooms!" Belatedly he seemed to notice Atta standing there, looking scared, and he frowned. "Mrs Ortane, please take your daughter and head below decks to the med bay."

"I'm not going anywhere until you've heard me."

"Then talk fast," Covani growled.

"You're treading on dangerous territory. Maybe you think you're best suited to leading us to safety, and maybe you're right, but what about the man or woman who takes your place? And the one after that? You're dismantling representative government, and with it, our foundation for the future."

"I'm not the power-hungry dictator you seem to think I am. As soon as we've found a place to settle, we will establish a proper government to take my place."

"Power is addictive. You would be better off making provisions for that government now."

The captain shook his head. "I won't cloud all of our decisions by subjecting them to debate. Just one wrong move could be the end of us. Emergency war measures exist for a reason, Councilor. You will be reinstated to help set up the new government as soon as there is room for one."

"You need your advisers now more than ever, Captain."

"Really? You want us to go to Noctune and save the Gors! I can't think of a more foolish way to squander our resources and our chances of survival! Yes, let's use humanity's dying breath to help the species that drove us to extinction."

"The Gors are as much the victims of this war as we are. But I think we can agree to a compromise. Let's set up a colony and *then* send the *Baroness*. We'll go as soon as we can afford to spare her."

"We don't have the fuel for a two way trip."

"The Gors do, if we re-allocate some of it. Their ships run on dymium, too."

"The dymium they use would take refining."

"To make it more efficient, not to make it work for our

purposes."

"We could lose the only vessel we have to defend ourselves—not to mention the only advanced technology we have left."

"We have the Gors. An entire fleet of protection and advanced technology. If we abandon them, we'll be on our own."

"Yes. Exactly! Your mistake is assuming that's a bad thing. What happens if the planet we find doesn't have room and resources for both humans and Gors to co-exist? It's more likely than not we'll end up fighting each other, and they outnumber us badly. Let them go to Noctune. Maybe the Sythians will kill what's left of them before they turn on us again."

Destra gritted her teeth and shook her head. "You're determined to do this your way."

"I am."

"Then I have nothing left to say."

"You shouldn't have wasted your breath to begin with." The captain stabbed a button on the table and the doors *swished* open behind her. "Sergeant!"

Destra turned to see the sentinel she'd been speaking with a few minutes ago.

"Sir?"

"Please escort these two to the med bay. Make sure they are placed in hibernation safely. We wouldn't want anything to happen to the councilor."

"Yes, sir," the sergeant said, stepping forward to take Destra by the arm and guide her out.

"I hope you don't regret the decisions you're making, Captain," Destra said on her way out.

The doors *swished* shut behind them, and Atta began

tugging on her other arm, making her presence known.

"Mom . . ."

"Yes, dear?"

"What's stasis?"

Destra grimaced but quickly covered it with a bright smile, which she used to regard her daughter. "It's like sleep, but better, because there are no nightmares in stasis."

"Oh. Why don't we always go to stasis then?"

"Because it's harder to go into stasis than it is to go to sleep. We keep it for special occasions."

"What's special about now?"

"We're celebrating the discovery of our new home."

"Really? What's it look like?"

"Nothing like here. There are forests and trees, rivers and lakes . . . Mountains. Blue skies and warm, sandy beaches."

"Wow. Like on Karpathia?"

Destra smiled. Atta had grown up on starships her whole life until just recently. She'd gone to live on Karpathia with Destra when Hoff had appointed her as the planet's high councilor, but their time on Karpathia had only lasted a few months before the Sythians had invaded again.

"Even better than Karpathia, sweetheart."

"I want to see it!"

"I know, dear, but you can't yet."

"Why not?"

"We have to go into stasis first. When you wake up you'll see it."

"Okay!" Atta beamed. There was a bounce in her step that hadn't been there before. The sergeant traded a grim smile with Destra as they reached a bank of lift tubes and waited for one to arrive. As soon as it did, Atta ran into the lift. Destra let go of her hand, giving Atta some time to get her energy out.

She wouldn't be able to bounce around while she was hibernating in a tube the size of a coffin.

The lift doors slid shut and the sentinel keyed in their destination. Looking out the small windows in the sides of the lift, she could see passing glow panels turning into blurry golden streaks as they raced down through the ship's 18 decks.

"Will Daddy be there?" Atta asked suddenly.

Destra turned to Atta, momentarily shocked by the question. A scene of her husband's execution flickered into her mind's eye—him kneeling in the airlock, his battered face and bleeding lips twisted into a broken smile as he saluted the camera recording his death, and then the outer doors opened, and a sudden violent wind ripped him off the deck and he became nothing but a dwindling speck against the starry blackness of space. . . .

She shook herself out of the memory and fought back the tears that threatened to give her away. "I don't know, darling," she said, affecting a smile. "Daddy is on a very important mission. We don't know when he'll be back."

"I miss him," Atta said.

Destra nodded. "So do I."

The lift came to a stop and the sergeant gently ushered them out. Ten minutes later they were being whisked through med bay and into the prep room for injections. Atta cried when she saw the needle. Destra had to hold her still for the corpsman. Atta screamed as the needle went in. Then they were ushered into one of the stasis rooms. Theirs was already crowded with at least a dozen others, all of them women. They were stripping naked and folding their clothes into neat piles for the attendants to place in nearby lockers. Then they lined up on both sides of the room in front of the stasis tubes and waited for the medic to finish configuring them.

Atta was still crying as she folded her clothes. She wasn't old enough to mind much about stripping naked in front of a bunch of strangers. The sergeant who had escorted them was waiting outside the doors to the stasis room.

"Mom, w-why do we have to sleep naked?" Atta asked, shivering, as the female corpsman attending them took her pile of clothes. The stasis room was cold. They always were.

"Shhh. No more questions for a while, okay, sweetheart?"

The corpsman took Destra's clothes next, and they were told to stand in line with the others. The medic in charge of configuring the stasis tubes guided the woman at the front of their line to an open tube.

Atta stepped out of line to watch. "We're going to sleep in those?" she said, a slight tremor creeping into her voice. "Why don't we get beds?"

"Because that's how stasis works."

"I don't want to go to stasis anymore," Atta said. "I'm going to sleep in my room." Atta was already on her way to the exit, so determined to leave that she was going without her clothes.

Destra took a long step to catch her daughter by the arm. "Atta, you can't leave, okay?"

"Let me go!"

Destra wrestled Atta back into line, and the female corpsman attending them suddenly reappeared, as if out of thin air.

"Is there a problem here?"

"Not at all."

"I don't want to go," Atta said, crossing her arms over her chest.

"I can give her an additional sedative," the corpsman

suggested, ignoring Atta.

"No, that's okay." Destra knew the risks. Too much sedative made waking up more disorienting and hibernation sickness more likely.

"Let me know," the corpsman replied, sending Atta a dubious look as she left.

As soon as the corpsman's back was turned, Atta tried to break free again, but Destra held her fast, squeezing Atta's arms until her hands hurt. "Stop it."

Atta settled for whimpering instead. They were almost at the back of the line, so it was a long wait. More people kept entering the room all the time, and soon they were at the front of another long line of women. When it was their turn to go, Destra insisted they take Atta first. She held her daughter's hand as long as she could, only letting go as the transpiranium cover began to swing shut.

"I'm scared!" Atta cried. They'd used thick restraints to hold her in place, pinning her arms to her sides. Now she was trying desperately to wriggle out of them. "I don't like stasis!"

"You'll wake up soon, okay?"

Atta shook her head and went on struggling. The cover shut and Destra placed a hand against it as a poor substitute for real human contact. Then the medic pressed a button and cold gas began hissing into the stasis tube, frosting the transpiranium cover. Atta's eyes rolled up in her head, and her body went limp.

"How long are we going in for?" Destra asked as the medic led her to the next tube in line and helped her inside. The medic buckled restraints over Destra's naked legs and torso. The straps were padded, but cold, and she gasped as they touched her skin. When it appeared that the medic wasn't going to answer her question, Destra repeated it.

"Indefinitely, Ma'am," the medic said without looking up.

Destra gaped at her. "Indefinitely? That's against fleet regulations!"

Her stasis tube cover began swinging shut with a slow groan, and Destra's heart began pounding *hard* in her chest. Each beat felt labored as adrenaline fought the stasis preparation they'd injected into her bloodstream.

"Captain's orders, Ma'am. We don't know when we'll arrive, and we can't risk people waking up too soon. Ma'am . . . please try to relax. Your vitals are spiking dangerously."

"Relax! How dare you tell me to . . ." She trailed off as a wave of dizziness and exhaustion swept over her.

The cover of the stasis tube met the frame with a muffled *thud*. Destra glared at the medic as she pressed the button. Close beside her ears came a hiss of frigid gas, and she shivered despite the pleasant numbness that was already creeping through her. Destra felt an overpowering urge to shut her eyes and sleep, but she fought against it as long as she could.

The last thing she saw as the transpiranium began to frost up was a faint flicker of movement along the far wall of the stasis room. A familiar gray, skull-like face appeared, and two slitted yellow eyes peered at her from the gloom. *Torv?* she wondered, surprised to see him there. She blinked and he was gone, as if he'd suddenly cloaked himself to avoid being seen.

She realized she was hallucinating. By now the Gors would all be on board a transport waiting to transfer to one of their own ships.

Her eyes drifted shut and she dreamed of the Gors taking over the ship and using the crew in stasis to augment their dwindling rations. She woke up in her dream, faced with the cadaverous face of a hungry, hissing Gor.

What she'd told Atta was a lie. There *were* nightmares in stasis; they were just limited to the first few minutes and the last few minutes.

The Gor went on hissing at her, and now he bared sharp teeth and prominent canines. She wondered if that meant he was planning to eat her, and if so, why he didn't just get on with it.... She braced herself for the sudden stabbing pain of teeth sinking into her flesh.

The Gor reached out for her with giant hands. She squeezed her eyes shut. Something groaned and snapped, and then a weight she hadn't realized was resting on her chest lifted.

Her eyes popped open and she saw the restraining belt that had been strapped across her chest dangling from the Gor's hands. Destra used her freshly-freed hands to fend off the monster.

Rather than tear off one of her arms, the Gor ignored her feeble efforts and bent down to rip out the belt that was pinning her feet in place.

That done, he stepped back and waited, hissing at her once more.

Destra blinked and shivered, her senses coming alive. Pins and needles prickled through her hands and feet. Suddenly she realized that this *wasn't* a dream, and the Gor standing before her was none other than Torv—the same one she'd thought she'd seen before succumbing to stasis. There were no medics or corpsmen anywhere to be seen.

Then she remembered her daughter and panic gripped her. She stumbled out of her stasis tube to the one beside it. Atta was still asleep behind the frosted glass, her cherubic face relaxed in sleep. Destra glanced at the timer. It was counting up, not down, since they'd been placed in an *indefinite* hibernation. The glowing red digits marked just *four hours, fifteen minutes, and twelve seconds.*

Destra turned to Torv and shook her head, for the first time noticing the bloody red emergency lighting in the stasis room. "What's going on?" Her gaze traveled to the exit and she found a trail of bodies leading there—medics and corpsmen as well as a few sentinels. None of them were moving. Destra turned back to Torv, wide-eyed. "What have you done?"

* * *

30 Minutes Earlier . . .

Sergeant Cavanaugh kept his ripper rifle trained on the Gors' backs as they crossed the hangar deck to their waiting transports. There were a few dozen *skull faces* in all. Captain Covani was adamant that they be confined to their transports while the *Baroness's* crew went into stasis, just in case.

They reached the nearest of three Gor transports, and stopped there, waiting as one of the Gors went to trigger the loading ramp.

"Get me a head count," Cavanaugh said.

Rictan Five replied a moment later. "Twenty-six skullies, sir."

"Twenty-six?" Cavanaugh asked. "There were meant to be twenty-seven."

Five nodded. "The Gor's liason, Torv, is still coming, sir."

"Without an escort?"

"Another squad is bringing him."

"Why am I only hearing about this now?"

"I thought you knew."

Cavanaugh grunted and put a call through to the bridge. "The Gors have reached their transports, sir."

The captain's reply crackled close beside Cavanaugh's ears. "Are all of them accounted for?"

"All except for *Torv*."

"What? I just received confirmation that he's with you."

Alarm bells rang in Cavanaugh's head. "From who?"

"His escort!"

"His escort never arrived," Cavanaugh replied, looking around quickly. His skin prickled, and hairs rose on the back of his neck. "That confirmation must have come under duress. There's no one else here."

"Stun them, Sergeant!"

Suddenly the air shimmered and the Gors were gone.

"Frek!" Cavanaugh said.

Ripper fired roared out from Cavanaugh's squad, tearing through the empty air where the Gors had been and plinking harmlessly off their transport.

Cavanaugh's pulse pounded in his ears. "Fall back!" He turned and ran for the hangar bay doors. They had to get there before the Gors did. Their only chance was to trap the skull faces inside the hangar.

Moments later, Cavanaugh heard a human scream. He turned to see Rictan Five dangling by one foot, help up by an invisible force. Cavanaugh aimed just above Five's foot and fired. Something *screeched* and *hissed*. Five fell on his head, but he was wearing a helmet, so he still got up and ran.

Cavanaugh laid down covering fire. "Come on!"

Another *hiss* sounded right beside his ear. He whirled toward it, spraying bullets in a wide arc. Something knocked the rifle out of his hands. He reacted instantly, drawing his sidearm and firing off four shots into thin air. Sparks flew as those rounds hit an invisible plate of armor. Then something grabbed his sidearm and wrenched it out of his hand. Cavanaugh saw the weapon floating in the air, the barrel turning to face him, and he knew he was in trouble.

He lashed out with his prosthetic arm, hammering his invisible opponent. His arm hit something solid and unyielding. Then he was lifted bodily and *thrown* across the deck. Cavanaugh skidded to a stop and scrambled to his feet. He saw the rest of his squad spread out and locked in their own struggles with invisible opponents. A steady stream of blue stun bolts came racing in from one side, hitting Rictan Seven, then Five, then Two. They crumpled to the deck, armor and weapons clattering as they fell. One of the Gors had stolen a sidearm and he knew how to shoot.

But why stun bolts? Cavanaugh wondered.

He didn't have time to come up with an answer.

The gunman fired on him next. Cavanaugh ducked and rolled. He came out of that roll sprinting for the nearest again for the hangar bay doors. One of his squad mates caught up beside him. Rictan Four.

They reached the doors. Cavanaugh passed his wrist over the control panel, and the doors *swished* open. "Go, go, go!"

They raced through and Cavanaugh sealed the doors from the other side. The doors slid shut, but didn't close. Something invisible was wedged in between, forcing them open again.

Rictan Four raised his ripper rifle and fired a burst into the gap. Sparks flew from invisible armor, provoking a *hiss* from the Gor who was forcing the doors apart. That alien retreated, nursing whatever injuries they'd inflicted, and the doors shut the rest of the way.

Cavanaugh's comms crackled. It was Captain Covani. "What's going on, Sergeant?"

"The Gors attacked! Four men down. We're on our way to the bridge!" Cavanaugh spun away from the doors. Rictan Four tossed him a sidearm, and Cavanaugh caught it in the air.

Then came another *hiss.*

Cavanaugh jumped with fright and spun toward the sound. He went flying into the doors, hit by an invisible enemy. Rictan Four fired blindly back. Then he got hit by the same thing and slammed into the ceiling. His ripper rifle clattered to the ground a split second before he fell on top of it. Cavanaugh recovered just in time to be slammed into the doors for a second time.

His ears rang with the impact. The sidearm was pried from his fingers and turned on him. Then came a stun bolt, fired straight into his chest. Cavanaugh collapsed, his muscles turning to jelly as he fell. Before his eyelids fluttered shut, and his eyes rolled up in his head, he saw the air shimmer, and a face appear—

A *skull* face.

It was Torv.

CHAPTER 21

"We've got a lock on the *Baroness*. She's just dropped out of SLS!" the *Tempest's* sensor operator called out.

Bretton turned and nodded down to the crew deck. "Helm, sequence our jump."

"Yes, sir."

"And get me an ETA as soon as you can."

"Approximately . . . ten minutes, sir."

Bretton grimaced. *Ten minutes!* By then the Baroness could jump somewhere else.

Bretton drummed his fingers on the captain's table while he waited. He was peripherally aware of Captain Picara and his niece, Farah, crowding him to either side.

A countdown hovered up before Bretton's eyes, projected mere millimeters from his retinas by his newly-acquired ARCs. At first he'd balked at the reminder of being a Peacekeeper, but these contacts were only networked to the ship, and he'd already been de-linked from Omnius, so the AI-god couldn't use the ARCs to read his mind.

After what felt like an eternity, the timer reached zero, and then—

The world exploded with a blinding radiance. An instant

later the light was gone, and everything was back exactly as it had been before, but now the star map on the captain's table was showing a different star system, and the pattern of stars beyond the forward viewport had been replaced with a dark, intermittently flashing gray nebula—the Stormcloud Nebula.

"Report!" Bretton called out.

"Jump successful, all systems green ..." the ship's engineer replied.

"The *Baroness* is dead ahead, sir! Twenty klicks," sensors announced.

"Good let's—"

"Sir! I'm detecting multiple contacts! Sythian hull types. They're moving to surround the *Baroness*."

Bretton scowled. "That was fast. Aren't they supposed to have slower jump drives than the ISSF? How did they get here at the same time as the *Baroness*?"

"Maybe they've been improving their jump tech," Farah suggested.

"Maybe," Bretton conceded. "Comms—please tell me you still have the old systems working."

"Old systems, sir?"

Bretton turned to regard the comms officer. "You expect to contact an Imperial vessel with quantum tech? There's a reason we never heard from the Sythians during the war. Quantum signals won't even register on their comms."

"I believe they are working, sir, but I'll check. Give me a minute."

"You've got thirty seconds. Gunnery—I assume we have some kind of ordinance on board ... ?"

"We have a few thousand dymium grenades, sir."

"*Grenades?* What are you going to do, throw them out the nearest airlock? What about torpedoes, missiles ... ? You must have ripper cannon rounds at the very least."

"The *Tempest* wasn't in good condition when we found her, sir, the original armaments were all non-operational."

"Okay, back to my original question—what are we going to do against the enemy with *grenades?*"

"We'll launch them with the quantum junction," Captain Picara put in.

Bretton gaped at her. "Assuming that works, we'll have just one launcher."

"Yes, but one that's capable of teleporting a lethal payload instantly to the target," Picara replied. "Sythians don't have quantum disruptors. They barely have quantum comms. They'll be defenseless."

"So what do we do about enemy fighters?"

"Keep our distance and stay cloaked."

Bretton was incredulous. "This is the resistance's secret weapon? A warship without guns? I feel like I'm the captain of a garbage hauler!"

"We can't hope to defeat either Omnius or the Sythians in a straight fight," Picara replied.

"No, I can see that."

"I meant that it won't make a difference how many guns we have, Captain. It'll never be enough."

Bretton shook his head.

"Sir! Conventional comms are working, but I can't hail the *Baroness* without revealing us to the enemy," the comms operator interrupted.

"Are we out of range of the enemy?"

"A few ships have been drifting closer to us since we arrived. They're not far out of range," sensors replied.

Bretton's eyes fell on the glowing blue star map projected above the captain's table. "Drifting closer?" He eyed the disposition of enemy forces on the grid. Suddenly he noticed what the sensor operator was talking about. A small group of Sythian warships had broken off from the main formation and was taking a very circuitous route to get to the *Baroness.* If Bretton didn't know better, he'd say they were maneuvering to get closer to *his* ship.

"Sensors, get me vectors on those ships."

A moment later vector lines appeared on the grid. Current and projected headings appeared as green and red arrows respectively. Those arrows turned slowly around the red icons of enemy contacts like the hands of old-fashioned clocks. It didn't take more than a few seconds for Bretton to see that the vectors were all subtly shifting in their direction.

"That's impossible," Captain Picara whispered. "There's no way they can see us."

"They can't detect their own ships when cloaked, let alone ours," Farah added.

"So how are we detecting them?" Bretton replied. "Obviously the tech is out there to be discovered. Omnius has it. Maybe now the Sythians do, too. It would explain how they followed the *Baroness* from Dark Space. We *assumed* they have a traitor on board. I wonder if there isn't a simpler explanation."

Picara shook her head. "We've been hiding under their noses for months. We *still* have a ship hiding in Dark Space. The *Emancipator* should have come under fire by now if the Sythians could see her."

"Maybe, or maybe they've just been watching us to see what we're up to. It's not like *two* ships are much of a threat to them. In either case, we need to know if the enemy can see us. Engineering—please confirm the status of our cloaking shield."

"Engaged at 100%, all sub-systems green."

"Are we releasing any radiation? Comms? Engines?"

"Nothing that's getting by the shield, sir."

"The enemy is launching fighters!"

Bretton saw a large swarm begin pouring out from the main formation, zeroing in on the *Baroness*. A smaller swarm poured from the ships vectoring in on them.

"Why haven't they jumped to SLS?" Farah whispered, her eyes on the *Baroness*. "They've had more than enough time."

"There's a lot of obstacles in this nebula," Captain Picara said. "It's playing havoc with sensors. Maybe they don't want to risk running into something."

Bretton began nodding. "That, and they don't know they've been followed. The Sythians are still cloaked. Sensors—how long before the enemy reaches firing range?"

"ETA five minutes for the first squadron," the sensor operator replied. "The others aren't far behind...."

"If we power energy shields now, they'll see us for sure," Captain Picara said. "We might be jumping at shadows."

"Any chance the traitor that *we* brought on board is communicating with the enemy to give our position away?"

"We would have detected that. Besides, he's sitting in the middle of a quantum disruption field. Nothing's getting in or out of that. It's your call, Admiral," Picara said, "but we may not survive a volley from them even with our shields raised."

Bretton eyed the approaching contacts on the grid. "Gunnery! Can we remote detonate those dymium grenades of yours?"

"No, sir, but they have proximity sensors."

"Good enough. Find a squadron of Shells that isn't moving around too much, behind the leading edge of the fighter wave, and then launch a handful of grenades as close as you can get them to the target."

"Yes, sir."

"Two minutes to firing range!" the sensor operator declared.

Bretton watched the grid without blinking, his eyes intent upon the enemy as he waited.

"You're going to fire the first shot," Farah said, slowly nodding.

"I don't see how that helps us assess their threat level," Captain Picara put in.

"It might get them to open fire prematurely," Farah explained. "Right now, they're trickling out towards us. The fighters will reach firing range before their capital ships. If they think the jig is up, those Shells might start firing right away rather than wait for the big guns to get into position first. We'll survive some small arms fire from the Shells with our shields down, but the big guns could take us out in one volley.

Bretton turned to regard Farah with a smile. "Exactly. When did you get so good at reading my mind?"

"About the same time I became a wise ass, sir."

Bretton gave a snort of laughter.

"Grenades away!" gunnery reported.

Bretton watched the grid intently. A small burst of light flared in the middle of the enemy fighter formation, taking almost a dozen Shell Fighters off the grid as it faded.

"Nine down!" sensors reported.

Bretton held his breath, waiting.

"The first squadrons have reached firing range with us," sensors reported.

Long seconds passed and nothing happened.

"Guess they can't see us after all . . ." Farah said.

Then, suddenly, the onrushing waves of enemy fighters de-cloaked and the grid came alive with sparkling purple waves of Sythian Pirakla missiles.

"Frek me!" Farah exclaimed.

"Shields!" Bretton bellowed. "Helm—take evasive action! Comms—see if you can hail the *Baroness*. By now they should have detected those enemy fighters, but at least let them know who we are and ask them if they need any help. Maybe this time we can agree on jump coordinates and set up a rendezvous."

A chorus of *Yes, Sirs*, reached his ears. Bretton watched with a grimace as red enemy contacts began brightening all over the grid. The Sythians were all de-cloaking and powering their shields. The cloak and dagger phase of this engagement was over, but Bretton couldn't take any satisfaction in that. The *Baroness* and the *Tempest* were horribly outnumbered.

Bretton's eyes skipped to the *Baroness*, watching a much larger wave of fighters rushing toward them. The enemy wasn't in range of them yet, but they would be soon.

Suddenly he noticed something. The Baroness's icon on the grid was still dark.

Farah was the first to voice that concern. "They haven't raised their shields yet. What are they waiting for?"

Bretton made an irritated noise in the back of his throat. "Comms—are they responding to our hails?"

"Negative, sir. Nothing yet."

"They're not maneuvering or accelerating, sir," sensors added.

"What, you mean they're derelict? What do they think they're doing?"

"As far as we can tell, they are still under power, sir,"

sensors replied.

Bretton waited a few more seconds. Veins pulsed in his temples. He felt an impatient heat rise around his collar. "Come on . . . raise your shields, damn you!"

"The first fighters are in range of the *Baroness*. Opening fire!"

Bretton watched, breathless, as waves of sparkling purple missiles raced toward the unshielded hull of the *Baroness*.

And still they didn't raise their shields.

"They're going to be obliterated if we don't do something."

"Frek it . . . Helm! Plot a micro jump into the path of those missiles."

"Yes, sir."

"You can't be serious," Captain Picara said. "They're not responding or maneuvering. For all we know they're dead. You plan to sacrifice us for a ghost ship?"

"No, I'm going to buy some time while I teleport over there and take command of the *Baroness* myself."

"What if the ship has suffered a catastrophic failure? There's no quantum junction on the other end. You'll be trapped on board as she goes down."

"The resistance needs a real ship, Captain. One with real weapons. We can't afford to lose the *Baroness* without a fight."

"Even if you get her working, with just two ships against an entire Sythian fleet, we don't stand a chance."

Bretton was already turning to hurry down the gangway and off the bridge. Farah hurried to keep up beside him. "Helm, how are those jump calculations coming along?"

"Almost ready, sir. . ."

"I need an ETA!"

"Thirty seconds!"

The timer appeared before Bretton's eyes and he nodded in approval. "Good." He reached the doors leading off the bridge and stopped there to turn to Captain Picara. She was just half a step behind him. "You're in command while I'm gone, Picara. With any luck I'll be back soon."

"Don't do this, sir. Even if you can save her, we can't beat an entire fleet of Sythians with just two ships. We have to go now. The *Baroness* is forfeit."

"The *Baroness* isn't on her own, Picara. I've been crunching some numbers in my head. Based on how long it took for the *Baroness* to drop out of SLS and how far she travelled in that time, she was deliberately traveling slower than she needed to. That's how the Sythians caught up to her so fast. They haven't improved their jump tech."

Picara shook her head, still not getting it.

Bretton saw the timer reach ten seconds and decided to cut his explanation short. She'd have to connect the dots for herself. "The *Baroness* was flying out of Dark Space with an entire fleet of rebel Gors, Captain, and none of them had any reason to suspect that they'd been followed, so why should they outrun their allies?"

Bretton turned back to the bridge doors. He snapped his fingers to the pair of guards standing there. "You two, with me. We don't know what we're going to find on the *Baroness*."

The timer reached zero and a bright flash of light suffused the deck. Bretton waved his wrist over the door scanner and the bridge doors *swished* open to reveal the glossy golden dome of the quantum junction.

"Incoming!"

"Brace!"

Bretton braced himself on the door jamb and turned back to see a swarm of purple stars come spinning out of the flashing gray clouds of the Stormcloud Nebula. They had just enough time to gasp before those missiles slammed into the bridge. The explosions were blinding, and a simulated roar rumbled through the sound in space simulator. The deck shuddered underfoot.

"Shields at 67%!" engineering reported.

Bretton winced. "Gunnery! I assume you're in charge of the junction? Get me onto the bridge of the *Baroness. Now!*"

He didn't wait for a confirmation of that order, instead he rushed into the dimly-lit concourse outside the bridge. A split second later the golden dome of the junction rose on four shimmering pillars of light, and he ran in. Once Bretton was standing in the center of the glowing green circle beneath the dome, he turned in a quick circle to see who was standing there with him. There was Farah, checking the charge on her sidearm, flicking off the safety; and the two guards he'd ordered to join them, both hefting old Imperial ripper rifles and looking nervous. Bretton unstrapped his own sidearm and then the quantum junction began to drop over their heads.

"Ruh-kah," Bretton whispered in Imperial Versal.

The guards, both Avilonian-born gave him curious looks, but Farah sent him a tight grin, and replied in Versal, "Just like old times, Captain."

"Hoi, that's *Admiral* now, Commander."

"With all due respect, frek you, sir."

* * *

"Torv ... What is this?" Destra gaped at the bodies strewn across the deck.

He spoke to her, but again, all she heard was alien hissing. Reaching up to her ear, she found it as naked as the rest of her, and she shivered, noticing how cold it was in the stasis room.

"Give me a second," she said, and hurried over to the lockers. Her translator would be there with her clothes. She kept half an eye on the Gor as she went, half-expecting him to attack her at any moment. What had he done? She hoped it was some big misunderstanding.

Destra reached the locker with her stasis tube's number on it, and opened it. She pulled out a neat stack of her clothes and personal items. The first thing she did was fit the combination translator and comm piece into her ear; then she began hurriedly getting dressed.

While she was still getting dressed, Torv stalked up to her. Destra's heart pounded in her chest, even though she knew that the Gor would have eaten her already if that had been his intention.

"Torv, please explain this," she tried again.

More hissing. This time it was accompanied by a translation. "I tell you already, my Matriarch. We are forced to take control of this vessel."

"You killed them?!"

"They sleep."

Destra shook her head. "You turned on us."

"We have no choice, Matriarch. Your people refuse to honor you as they should. Their disrespect is a dishonor to their creche and all who belong to it."

"What did you do to them?"

"We steal weapons and use the sleep setting. Now they sleep."

"You stunned the entire crew?"

Torv heaved his mighty shoulders. "All who resist. Others choose not to. We watch them while we wait for you to take command."

"What about the captain?"

"He kills several Gors who try to reason with him. I take his life myself. He can no longer disrespect you, creche mother."

Destra swallowed hard and nodded. "What is our position in space?"

"We are no longer in the light stream. My creche mates arrive soon."

Destra spared a glance for her daughter, still trapped in a stasis tube, the glass frosted so that she could only make out a hint of Atta's face. All the other stasis tubes in the room were likewise occupied. The Gors had timed their coup well, waiting until the majority of the crew was already asleep.

"We need to get to the bridge, Torv," Destra said. Waking Atta would have to wait for a more convenient moment.

"Lead us, my Matriarch. I make sure no harm comes to you."

Destra took off at a run, dodging the fallen bodies of

stunned corpsmen, medics, and sentinels on her way to the exit. She grimaced as she accidentally stepped on one man's leg. He didn't even stir. Passing her wrist over the door scanner, she ran out and down the corridor. Glancing over her shoulder, she was just in time to see Torv cloaking himself. She grimaced and looked away, feeling her skin prickle with unease.

The Gors had seen Captain Covani as a threat and taken matters into their own hands, effectively taking over the ship so that they could put her, a Gor-friendly leader, in command. She should have felt flattered, or maybe encouraged by that vote of confidence, but she couldn't help thinking about the late captain and wondering...

Am I next?

Destra felt a stab of regret for Captain Covani. She hadn't been responsible for his death, but she felt guilty anyway. She'd argued the Gors' case, but as it turned out... He'd been right to fear them.

Destra reached the nearest bank of lift tubes and rode them all the way up to the bridge. As she left the lift tube and hurried down a short corridor to the bridge, she listened for Torv's footsteps. The only ones she heard were her own. Maybe she'd lost the Gor along the way...

As she reached the doors to the bridge, the deck shuddered under foot, and something below decks groaned ominously. Destra's eyes flew wide and her breath froze in her chest—

They were under attack.

She passed her wrist over the scanner, and the doors *swished* open. The scene that greeted her on the other side was shocking. A huddled group of officers stood at the Captain's table surrounded by half a dozen armored Gors. A few glossy black helmets turned her way; the sunken eye sockets of their skull-shaped helmets glowed bright red in the dim emergency lighting.

Destra hesitated, arresting her momentum before she stumbled into them. Were they expecting her? Then the air shimmered ahead of her and Torv appeared. His unarmored gray torso blocked her view, and she heard him begin hissing at the others.

"The Matriarch arrives! Show her the respect she is due!"

The armored Gors bowed their heads to her as she approached.

Encouraged by that, Destra squared her shoulders. "Release them," she demanded, pointing to the huddled group of officers. If she was supposed to be an authority figure for the Gors she would have to act the part.

The circle of Gors opened up and their human prisoners walked cautiously out, eying their captors.

Destra stopped one of them, grabbing him by the arm. "Where is the captain?" she whispered.

The man regarded her with wide, glassy eyes.

"Lieutenant!" she snapped.

He blinked and turned to point at a bloody corpse lying on the deck beside the captain's table.

Destra eyed Covani's body with horror. He looked like he'd been mauled by wild animals.

The deck shuddered again, and a damage alarm sounded, bringing Destra back to the moment. "Everyone to your stations!" she called out, clapping her hands together.

The crew scrambled down from the gangway. Destra turned to Torv and gestured blindly to the Captain's corpse without looking at it. "Have your men clean up their mess, please Torv. It's bad for morale."

Torv turned to hiss something at the armored Gors, and they carried Covani away.

Destra turned in a quick circle, surveying the crew. Fortunately the captain was the only one dead, so she wasn't missing anyone. There didn't appear to be an XO on deck, however. She walked up to the Captain's table, trying to ignore the sticky smears of blood around it.

"Report!" she called out. "What are we looking at?"

"Sythians, Ma'am . . . an entire fleet of them!" gravidar reported.

"Aren't we cloaked? How are they shooting us?"

"I don't know . . . we're not radiating anything our sensors can detect, Ma'am."

"Well they have to be able to see us to shoot at us, so we must be radiating something!" As if to emphasize her point, the deck shuddered once more. "Raise our shields and take evasive action!" Destra said.

"Yes, Ma'am!"

Destra studied the grid rising from the captain's table, trying to make sense of the mess of red and green contact icons there. She had zero experience with command. Suddenly she understood Covani's point about him being better equipped to lead them to safety. Despite her lack of experience, she did notice one thing that seemed odd. As she watched, a green friendly contact appeared out of nowhere, right beside the *Baroness.*

"Contact!" gravidar reported. "She's friendly, venture-class! Looks like she's shielding us from the bulk of the enemy fire!"

"They're trying to hail us," Comms reported.

"Well hail them back!" Destra shook her head, feeling overwhelmed and bewildered. She leaned heavily on the captain's table, studying the friendly warship. It lay in the enemy's line of fire, sacrificing itself to shield them from harm. Destra wondered about that. The ship's designation flagged it as the *Tempest*.

She didn't recognize the name.

Suddenly one of the crew began yelling and shouting. Those exclamations were soon echoed by others on deck, and Destra spun around, trying to find the source of the fuss. Everyone was staring at the entrance of the bridge, where the air was shimmering as though something were de-cloaking there. A sound like rushing water roared through the air, and then came a strong gust of wind. Destra was staggered by it, but even more staggered by what she saw next.

A group of four officers appeared out of nowhere—three men and one woman, all of them wearing ISSF uniforms, and their eyes were *glowing*.

Destra blinked a few times quickly. Recovering from her shock, she started toward them with a scowl. "Who are you and what are you doing on my ship?" As she drew near, she noticed that one of the men was wearing two gold stars on his uniform, marking him as an admiral.

Suddenly all four of them raised their weapons and took up a defensive stance, their backs to each other's, their eyes and gun barrels warily tracking through the room.

The admiral spoke, "Tell those skull faces we can see them skulking around, and we *will* open fire if they don't stand down and reveal themselves immediately!"

Destra called out. "Torv! They're friends!"

The air began shimmering again, but there was no accompanying noise or blast of wind. Gors appeared all around the bridge. Torv was standing right beside her, thick arms crossed over his chest and slitted yellow eyes scanning the quartet of newcomers.

"Who are you and how did you get on board my ship?" Destra demanded as the newcomers relaxed their defensive stance.

The admiral breezed by her without a word of explanation, hurrying toward the captain's table.

Destra caught up to him. "Hoi, I asked you a question!" she said.

"I'm taking command of this ship," he said.

"Not without the Matriarch's permission," Torv hissed.

The admiral turned to regard him. "What did he say?"

"He said you'd better ask nicely first," Destra explained.

The deck shuddered again, and engineering reported, "Hull breach on deck twelve! We're not going to take much more of this!"

"Seal it up!" the admiral ordered. Turning to her, he pointed out the forward viewport and said, "We don't have time for pleasantries or explanations. I know what I'm doing. Let me save you first, and then I'll tell you whatever you want to know."

She hesitated just a split second longer before she nodded and gestured to the captain's table. "Be my guest."

The admiral turned and walked up to the captain's table, frowning as he stepped over the bloody smears Covani had left to mark his passing. "What happened here?"

"We don't have time for explanations, remember?"

"Very well. Helm, plot a blind jump out of here."

"Yes, sir."

"We have a fleet of Gors with us. They can't follow a blind jump," Destra objected.

The deck shuddered once more.

"Shields at 74%!" engineering reported.

"And you can't survive much more of this. Comms—contact the *Tempest,* inform them of our plans and tell them to make their own jump out."

"You intend to leave my people behind," Torv said, stepping up on the other side of the table.

Destra translated.

"Multiple contacts inbound!" the gravidar operator interrupted. "It's the Gors!"

Destra watched the unidentified admiral and Torv glaring at one another across the captain's table.

"Your people communicate telepathically—directly from one mind to another—don't they?" the admiral asked.

Hiss.

"Yes," Destra translated.

"Then you can tell them where we end up. If we don't leave now, they'll be on their own anyway, because we'll be dead."

"Very well. Do not jump further than the distance that light travels in ten orbits or I cannot contact them."

The admiral looked to her once more, and Destra translated for him.

At that, the Admiral called out, "You heard the skull face! Make that blind jump a short one."

Destra winced. "Don't call them that," she whispered.

The admiral shot her a bewildered look, but said nothing. She could read his expression easily enough. His eyes said it all. The Gors would always be *skull faces* to him.

"The *Tempest* just jumped away, sir! We're exposed again!"

The deck began shuddering in earnest. Destra's gaze fell upon the grid once more and she saw flashing streaks of purple light streaming out from the enemy fighters and slamming into their aft section.

"Aft shields at 67%!"

"Helm! Where's that jump I ordered?"

"Our SLS drives are still spooling, sir!"

"What? What have you all been doing out here? You should have had your drives spooled long ago!"

"We were otherwise occupied," Destra put in.

The admiral shot her a glance.

"Incoming missiles!"

"Take evasive action!" the admiral ordered. "Why aren't our gunners firing back?"

"They're in stasis," Destra explained.

"Stasis? What are they doing in stasis?"

"Brace for impact!" gravidar called out.

They all grabbed the captain's table, and Destra fiddled with the emergency grav field generator on her belt, just in case artificial gravity failed. The lights dimmed and a loud roar of simulated explosions filled the air.

"Damage report!"

"Aft shields holding at 43%! Minor hull breach on four! Coolant leak in the reactor room. We're down to 75% power."

"Helm! We need to jump!"

"One more second!"

"Here comes the next wave!"

Destra scanned the grid and she saw a sparkling wall of Sythian missiles rushing toward them from one of the larger Sythian warships. The first missile reached them with a titanic *boom!* Ten more followed, one after another.

Boom!

Boom!

BOOM . . . !

"Helm!" the admiral bellowed to be heard over the

roaring of the explosions. "Where's that jump?"

"Aft shields at two percent!"

"Jumping!"

Destra looked up and saw the flashing gray clouds of the nebula turn to a blurry gray streak as they jumped to SLS.

"Stay in SLS for half an hour. Project our exit coordinates and start plotting a second jump from there. We don't want the Sythians tracking us from our jump trajectory. We'll have to confuse them with multiple jumps." Destra saw the Admiral's brow grow lined as he turned to look at Torv. "The Sythians could follow your people to us. Their jump drives are the same speed as yours. Ours are twice as fast, so we can lose them. You can't. We can't afford to rendezvous with your people."

Torv hissed loudly and looked away from the admiral. His slitted yellow eyes bored into Destra's instead. "You lie to me! You say we follow, but you leave us to die!"

Destra translated that, and the admiral shook his head. "I didn't lie. I simply didn't have enough time to think about it in the heat of battle."

Torv's expression flickered and his eyes seemed to darken. Destra had a premonition of violence, and she took the admiral aside.

"Sir, we can't abandon the Gors. They're our only allies, and their fleet is too valuable to sacrifice."

"What would you have me do? Better that we lose them than all of us die together."

A loud hiss drew their attention back to Torv. He bared razor sharp teeth in a terrifying grin. "You repay our sacrifice by taking us to Noctune."

"What did he say?"

Destra translated.

"What?" The admiral shook his head. "That's in the Getties! Why the frek would we go there?"

For the first time Destra heard one of the other men who'd come with the admiral say something. She was shocked when she realized that he wasn't speaking Imperial Versal.

Suddenly the questions she'd been holding back since they'd mysteriously appeared out of thin air all came flooding back. The admiral replied to his subordinate in kind, using the same language.

"Who are you?" Destra whispered, momentarily ignoring Torv's hissing.

The admiral turned to her. "We're in the middle of a diplomatic negotiation. Try to keep up." He turned back to Torv. "We will take you and the other Gors on board this ship to Noctune, if that's what you want."

Torv went on hissing at them. As soon as he was done speaking, he looked away—from both of them this time. Now even *she* was unworthy of his sight. Turning to the admiral, Destra translated, "Torv says that will be good enough, but that humans have no honor and cannot be trusted. The alliance is at an end." There'd also been a more personal note about her not being worthy of the title of *Matriarch*, but she chose not to translate that part.

"Fine with me," the admiral grunted, turning away. "Engineering, how are repairs coming along?"

"They're not. Our crew is in stasis, sir."

"*All* of them? Someone had better start explaining *something* soon."

"We're critically low on supplies," Destra said. "Stasis was a way to make them go further."

"I see . . . and the blood stains?" he stamped the floor

under his feet.

"The Gors didn't see eye to eye with our captain. They wanted him to take them to Noctune."

The admiral's head came up suddenly and he fixed Torv with a deadly look. For his part, the Gor still wasn't looking at them.

"The captain refused, and they killed him."

Destra nodded. "I was in stasis at the time, but they tell me he killed a few of them first."

"So where are the bodies?"

Destra shrugged. "The captain's was here when I arrived. I asked the Gors to take him off the bridge."

The Admiral's gaze turned to her and she felt suspicion pouring off of him. "So you were the one calling the shots after this little mutiny of theirs?"

"They ... wanted to put me in command, since I was willing to take them to Noctune. They called me their *Matriarch*. Until now."

"I see, and who are you?"

"Councilor Heston."

The admiral blinked at her. *"Heston?"*

"Yes."

"You're not by any chance related to Admiral Hoff Heston, are you?"

"I'm his wife."

"His wife?" the admiral asked, surprise evident on his face.

"You knew him?" she asked, wondering at the man's sudden interest in her.

At that, he stuck out his hand. "Admiral Bretton Hale. It's a pleasure to meet you, Ma'am."

Destra eyed his hand a moment before taking it; they

shook briefly. "A pleasure to meet you, too . . . whoever you are," she said, releasing his hand to cross her arms over her chest and regard him with a skeptical frown. "I was under the impression that my husband was the last surviving admiral from the Imperium."

"I fought beside him in the fifth fleet, during the exodus. Back then I was a Captain. My ship became . . . *separated* from the rest of the fleet during our evacuation from Roka Four."

Destra's eyes lit with sudden understanding. Then she recalled something she'd witnessed a moment ago, and her frown was back. "Your accent is Imperial, but you speak another language. I've never heard it before."

Admiral Hale nodded. "We're from a place called Avilon. Perhaps your husband told you about it?"

That news went through Destra like a lightning bolt. Her pulse raced; her palms began to sweat; she broke out in goosebumps all over. "Avilon? It's real? Has anyone arrived there recently? Imperials?" The admiral began shaking his head, but Destra barreled on, "A young man, by the name of Atton Ortane. He's a fighter pilot, a—"

"I'm afraid I wouldn't know, Ma'am."

The woman standing behind the admiral shot him an impatient look. "Sir, we don't have time for this."

Destra sent her a scowl. "You have children?"

"No, Ma'am."

"Then you wouldn't understand."

The woman's cheeks bulged for a hasty retort, but she let that breath out with a sigh, obviously thinking better of it. The admiral turned to her, "You have command for now. Leave the crew in stasis. With all of the recent changes in command we could have another mutiny on our hands if we're not careful."

The woman eyed him for a moment longer before nodding reluctantly. "Yes, sir."

Destra saw the Admiral's eyes flick to Torv and from him to the other Gors standing around the bridge, leaning against the walls and watching them all from the shadows. He said something else to his executive officer then, but it was whispered and spoken in that foreign language of his. To that, she nodded, and she began eyeing the Gors, too.

Admiral Hale turned back to her and said, "We have a lot to talk about, Mrs Heston. Is there somewhere more private we can speak?"

Destra nodded. "Follow me."

She led him off the bridge, down the hall to the Captain's quarters. Once there, they locked the door behind them, and both sat down—her behind the desk in the captain's chair, him in front of it. Destra listened for what felt like an eternity as the Admiral told her the most impossible story she'd ever heard.

He told her all about an AI god called Omnius and his resurrected empire of humanity. They were interrupted a few times as the woman the admiral had left in charge of the bridge called them on the intercom to ask for further orders.

By the time the admiral finally finished explaining everything to her, they'd dropped out of SLS not once but twice, and were now waiting for the *Tempest* to arrive at their rendezvous.

Admiral Hale went on to explain the difference between Nulls and resurrected Etherians, saying that Nulls were not networked to Avilon's AI god, so he couldn't keep an eye on them or tell them what they should and shouldn't do. When he explained that he and the others with him were part of a Null resistance movement, something occurred to her, and she interrupted him.

"If I have a Lifelink implant like everyone else, then is Omnius watching me, too?" Destra asked.

That question seemed to take the admiral by surprise. "I suppose he can, yes ... You make a good point. We'll have to get you and the rest of your crew de-linked before I end up in front of a firing squad. Excuse me ..."

Destra waited while he contacted his XO again. The two of them had a heated discussion in their language. Unable to understand what they were saying, Destra took the time to process everything that she'd learned. It seemed too good to be true. Everyone who died in the war had been resurrected on Avilon? Did that mean Hoff was still alive?

As soon as the admiral finished speaking to his XO, he rose from the desk. "We need to go."

Destra rose with him. "Your first officer didn't sound happy. What's wrong?"

"Besides the fact that Omnius could be tracking us right now because we're in the company of a bunch of *martales?*" He shook his head. "The *Tempest* is here, and we need to take your Gor allies to Noctune before they do to me what they did to your previous captain. How many do you have on board this ship?"

"A few dozen, I believe."

"There were only seven on the bridge. Where are the others?"

"I've been in stasis, Admiral."

"Well, it doesn't matter. We can't afford to fight that many of them in close quarters. We'll take too many casualties. The easiest will be to give them what they want."

"I'm not sure I would call that *easy*. The Getties is a very long way from here."

The Admiral regarded her with a small smile. "It'll take about a day to make the calculations, but otherwise we'll be able to travel there instantly."

Destra blinked, shock running through her. *"Instantly?"*

"Instantly," the admiral confirmed. "Having a super intellect guide human progress hasn't been all bad." The admiral's glowing blue eyes seemed to flare suddenly brighter, and Destra shivered.

"Is something wrong?" he asked.

"No, it's just a lot to get used to all at once . . . I'm having trouble believing it."

He nodded. "I know just how you feel."

But it wasn't just that. Destra was busy thinking about Omnius, and the resistance movement that Admiral Hale belonged to. She wondered whether she should be on their side, or Omnius's. From there her thoughts turned to Atton, and a stab of worry lanced through her heart.

Be safe my son. I'll be there soon. . . .

CHAPTER 22

ASCENDANCY

An alarm woke Atton at exactly 0400, right after Sync was supposed to end. He blinked, his eyes still bleary with sleep. He couldn't remember having dreamed anything in particular last night. For the first time in what seemed like forever, he felt rested.

Atton lay awake and staring up at the ceiling, waiting for the room to snap into focus. As it did so, he saw a wan golden light slowly rising in the room, like an artificial sun. He yawned, and tried to cover it with the hand lying on his chest. When that hand didn't move, and his real one encountered a pair of naked breasts, he realized that he hadn't slept alone.

He rolled to that side and came face to face with Ceyla. Her blue eyes were wide and bright in the light of her ARCs.

Suddenly the events of the previous night came back to him, and he smiled. He couldn't remember waking up with a smile on his face . . . ever.

"Hey," Ceyla said in a small voice.

Atton cleared his throat. "Hey."

Her lips were a tempting target. Despite the night they'd had, desire was already stirring inside of him.

"How are you feeling?" he asked, leaving the good morning kiss for later. He hoped there would *be* a later.

"I'm okay. What about you?"

Atton hesitated. Small talk wasn't going to get them anywhere. He wasn't sure how much time they had, so he just went for it. "Come with me. You're a pilot, Ceyla, a fighter. You won't be happy living a civilian life, and you can't join the Peacekeepers as a Null."

Ceyla's eyes flashed angrily and she sat up, turning her back to him in one smooth motion so that he caught only a glimpse of her breasts before she shut her robe.

Atton's heart sank. Her reaction said it all.

Ceyla turned to him then, her shimmering white robe now sealed all the way up to her neck. "You used me."

"What?" He blinked. "You threw yourself at me!"

"Because I thought maybe you needed a reason to live! I was stupid enough to think that *I* could be that reason."

"I'm going to live. I'm going to live forever."

"That's what you say."

Atton reached for her hand, but she withdrew it and stood up from the bed.

"Ceyla..."

"You can't have it all, Atton! You have to choose—me, or ..." She gestured helplessly to their surroundings and her lips twisted into a bitter smile. "Or Omnius's lies."

"He's not lying to us, Ceyla. He's just telling us everything he knows as honestly as he can. He can't tell us that we might have souls or that there might be a life after this one if he has no proof of that. *That* would be the lie. He's still a bot at heart, and he's too logical for such a thing as faith."

"Faith can't be reasoned, Atton, only felt."

"Ceyla..." Atton took a deep breath. "Is there any way you would agree to come with me?"

"Even if I did, it wouldn't be me that goes, and I'm not

willing to commit suicide."

"Then wait for me. I'll be back. You can at least be sure of that. Once Dark Space is free and the Sythians are defeated, I'll join you in the Null Zone. I'll leave it all behind. Until then I'll visit as often as I can."

Some of the anger left Ceyla's gaze, and she sunk back to the bed, her eyes shimmering with tears. She bit her lower lip and shook her head. "No, Atton. Don't. I can see how that looks like a big sacrifice to you, and maybe even a fair trade—me for eternity. But the truth is it's not fair to either of us. If your clone has a chance to live forever, he shouldn't give that up for me, because he won't have a chance to see me in the next life. As for me, whoever I decide to marry, I don't just want to be with them here and now, I want to be with them in the next life, too. You'll be dooming me to an eternity of loneliness and despair. You won't be able to join me where I'm going."

Atton frowned, confused by her reasoning. "How do you know my clone won't have a soul? Maybe the Etherus you believe in will take pity on us."

"And allow two different versions of you to live in Etheria? Why not ten? Or twenty? In fact, what's stopping Omnius from cloning you a million times? Then would all one million of you get to spend eternity in Etheria when you do eventually decide to die?"

"I don't think Omnius would clone any one person that many times simultaneously, but hypothetically—why not? We'd all be unique individuals, having departed from the version of me they were cloned from at the moment they began living parallel lives. If this Etherus of yours is a good god, then he'll judge each of us on our individual merit."

"Okay, so which one of you do you suppose I'll be with in

Etheria? Maybe I'll just choose the one with the personality I like best. What if that one isn't *you?* Even if I just have to choose between just two of you—the original, and the clone, which one do I pick? Who's the real Atton? Maybe I spend eternity with both of you and you'll have to compete for my attention."

"I..."

"There are a lot of paradoxes and dilemmas along the lines of what you're about to do, and none of them end well for you. In the end they all make your existence look and sound hollow. All the clones living on Avilon are more like organic bots than real living humans."

"I'm not doing this for me, Ceyla. I'm doing it so that someone else won't have to. The Sythians need to be stopped. If your Etherus is as good as you seem to think he is, he'll see my sacrifice, and he won't allow me to be punished for it."

Some of the tears shimmering in Ceyla's eyes spilled to her cheeks and Atton winced. He reached out and wiped one of them away with his thumb.

Ceyla's lower lip began to tremble and she shook her head. "You said you loved me. How can you just leave me after that? Frek the Sythians, Atton! Haven't they taken enough from you?"

Something inside of his chest began to ache and Atton swallowed thickly. "The war is all I know. I won't be able to settle down and live my life until it's over. I wake up every morning feeling like a failure and go to bed every night expecting to wake up to people screaming and dying all around me. I still remember the invasion like it was yesterday."

"What you're talking about is post-traumatic stress. You need counseling for that, not more trauma and stress."

Atton shrugged. "It helps me sleep at night to know I'm doing my part to end the war."

"The war might never be over, Atton. There's countless trillions of Sythians out there."

"Then I'll have all eternity to defeat them."

"I won't be around to see that."

"Yes, you will. I'm not leaving you down here. *Please* come with me."

"You can't take me with you, and I don't want to go."

He shook his head, and she leaned in toward him. Her hands found his face and her lips found his in a soft, fragrant kiss that smelled like *her*. He lost himself in that moment, breathing her in desperately. Then it was over and something inside of him broke. His eyes began to burn, and the world grew blurry.

"Goodbye, Atton." She rubbed his cheeks and smiled ruefully at him. "I guess you're not made of ice, after all."

Before he could reply to that, the door to their room opened, and a familiar-looking Peacekeeper poked his head in. "It's time," Master Rovik said.

Atton nodded. "Just give us a minute."

"I've already waited ten. The two of you are breaking Omnius's heart. He had hoped things would turn out differently."

Ceyla flashed the Peacekeeper a sardonic grin. "Really? I thought he already knew how we're going to choose?"

"Just because you can read any part of a book doesn't mean you want to start by reading the end. Now come. The others are already making their choices."

* * *

The choosing ceremony was not what Ethan had expected. They were all whisked away to a large, circular chamber with high, vaulted ceilings. On the walls all around the circumference of the room were more light paintings depicting different scenes, what looked like snapshots of human lives. Each painting had one human figure as a subject, but it was just their silhouette, a shadow. The rest of the scene was painted in bold strokes of color. There were scenes of glory and triumph on colorful alien fields of battle, men and women standing together in arms amidst thousands of unidentified bodies. Others showed the scenes from the bridges of giant star cruisers, enemy ships exploding all around. Still others depicted happy families, and scenes of domestic bliss. A few showed scenes of loneliness and despair, of death and privation. Each scene was animated with a few frames to convey its nature.

Ethan's eyes fell on a particular painting. There was a male silhouette sitting on a street corner with his head in his hands and an empty bottle beside him. As Ethan watched, the painting came alive. Rain poured down and people passed by, glancing at the man on the curbside. Then a flash of lightning washed the scene away, and suddenly it showed that man lying in bed in the arms of a woman. Ethan stared at the painting, spellbound by it.

Suddenly the man's black, featureless face took form—it was *his*. The woman lying beside him opened her eyes, and he saw a flash of bright color in her irises—not violet, but turquoise, like those of the woman from last night's dream.

A hand found his and squeezed. The spell broken, Ethan shivered and looked away.

Alara's violet gaze was full of concern. "Are you okay?"

He shook his head. "Not really, no. I had a bad dream last night."

"So did I."

He tilted his head to one side. "What was yours?"

They heard approaching footsteps from the direction they'd come and turned to see Rovik walk in. Atton and Ceyla came in behind him. Ethan's eyes flicked to Atton then Ceyla, and he realized that they weren't walking next to each other and they weren't holding hands. That either meant he'd been wrong about what they'd been doing last night, or it hadn't worked. Either way, he was about to say goodbye to his son.

Ethan turned away with a furrowed brow, and Alara shook her head. "I'll tell you later."

Rovik walked to the front of the group. Behind him lay a shadowy section of wall with no light paintings hanging there. As the Peacekeeper stopped and turned to face them, that dark section of wall became suddenly radiant with light. Two doors appeared, one beside the other. One was narrow and glowing bright gold, while the other was wide and glowing a bloody red. To either side stood a pair of Omnies, the red eyes in the center of their heads glowing to life.

"Welcome to Choosing Day," Rovik said. "To your left lies the way to the Null Zone. To your right lies Etheria. All around you, hanging on the walls, are scenes that Omnius has drawn from your probable futures, based on the decisions you've all already made. No doubt one painting in particular has already caught your eye. That is no coincidence. That scene is yours, drawn from your future. For some of you, it is Omnius's last warning, while for others it is something to look forward to. Whatever the case, be sure that you choose wisely. Some people go to the Null Zone and die the next day. Others go to Etheria only to leave soon afterward. I hope that all of you will be satisfied with your choice, and I wish you all the best in your new lives. This is the end of our journey together.

"It has been my pleasure to watch some of you grow and open your minds to the possibilities of life in Avilon. Be sure that you don't later lose your way. Take it from one who has ascended and fallen and then returned to the truth."

Rovik turned and gestured to the gold-glowing door on the right. "Those of you who have chosen Etheria, please approach the door. Single file."

For a moment nothing happened, but then the group of refugees surged forward. Ethan watched, horrified as roughly two thirds of the group formed a long line toward the door. Atton lingered near the back of the line, his eyes on Ceyla, one hand held out to her. She refused to even look at him. Ethan grimaced and shook his head. Then Atton caught his eye.

"You'll be happier," Atton said.

Ethan shook his head. "Save it, Atton."

His son looked away, and the line began to move forward. As each of them reached Rovik, he shook their hands and welcomed them with a smile before ushering them toward the narrow, golden door. That door swallowed each of them with its dazzling light, making it impossible to see where they went.

When it came to Atton's turn, his son cast one final,

backward glance at the people he was leaving behind. He waved. Ethan winced and looked away once more.

Then they were all gone, off to kill themselves so they could live forever.

Rovik turned to the remaining people, his eyes skipping over the scattered group. Ethan noticed that besides him, Alara, and Ceyla, there were just two others. He didn't recognize either of them. Ceyla was hugging herself as if she were desperately cold. Ethan frowned, about to ask her to come stand beside them, but Alara beat him to it, leaving his side to go get the other woman. They stood together. Alara held one of Ceyla's hands and said, "You're not alone."

Rovik fixed them with a steely gaze. "I had hoped none of you would choose the Null Zone. It's not too late to change your minds. Now that you know who has left, you can choose to go with them."

Ethan noticed that the Peacekeeper was looking at Ceyla as he said that. "No thanks," Ethan said for all of them. "Let's get on with it, Blue."

"Very well." Rovik turned to the glowing red door on the left. "The Null Zone awaits you."

Their little group started toward the door. Ethan was first in line, but Rovik put up an arm, blocking his way. "What's going on?"

"One at a time," he said.

"What?" Ethan's eyes narrowed, feeling suddenly suspicious. "I'm not going in without my wife."

"You'll see her in just a few minutes, assuming neither of you changes your mind."

"I thought we get to make our choice by going through the door."

"No, that's just the first step. After that you make your

choices in private, in order to avoid any pressure from your peers."

Ethan shook his head. "And what exactly do we see through that door?"

Master Rovik shrugged. "That is different for everyone. Omnius usually issues warnings about the future to help you avoid making certain key mistakes."

"And tries to convince us to go to Etheria."

"Perhaps."

"That's not fair. If he really cared about giving us the freedom to choose he wouldn't try to bias our choices."

"Biasing someone with the truth isn't really bias. If you knew your wife were going to die in an accident tomorrow, would you tell her, or let her die?"

"That's a stupid question," Ethan growled.

"If you didn't love her, you would keep quiet. It is the same with Omnius. He cannot allow you to walk into disaster if he loves you, but by becoming Nulls you are telling him to leave you alone. Before he does, he will warn you one last time."

"All right that's enough preaching," Ethan growled. He turned to Alara and took both of her hands in his. "I'll go first. You already know I'm not going to change my mind, so all you have to do is join me."

Alara looked torn, but she nodded, and he turned back to the Peacekeeper. "I'm ready."

Rovik gave him a grim look and shook his head. "No, you're not."

CHAPTER 23

Rovik lowered his arm, and Ethan walked cautiously toward the broad, red-glowing door. It cast a bloody light on him as he drew near. The drone standing beside the door turned its matching red eye on him, watching his every step as he approached. Upon reaching the door, it hissed slowly open, revealing a corridor as dark as death. Ethan waited, trying to pierce the gloom and see what lay beyond the door. His ARCs responded by amplifying the available light in the room, but that only made the red glow coming from the frame of the door brighter. Whatever lay beyond the threshold remained cloaked in shadows, as if Omnius wanted to scare them away. Ethan started toward the unknown.

"Ethan, wait!" It was Alara.

He turned to her with a lopsided grin that was meant to be reassuring. It did nothing to diminish the panic in her eyes. He blew her a kiss. "I'll see you soon."

"I love you," she replied.

"Me, too."

Ethan walked into the darkness. No sooner had his foot crossed the threshold than something *grabbed* him and pulled him off his feet. He cried out, taken off guard. He felt himself being carried—no, *floating*—down an impossibly dark corridor.

A deep, resonant voice spoke out of the darkness. "Hello, Ethan."

"Omnius," he replied. "You can put me down, you know. I can walk."

"Can you? You're in utter darkness. You can't see where you're going."

"I'm sure I'll find my way."

"As you wish."

Ethan felt a brief falling sensation—

Smack.

He hit the cold hard floor; his teeth clacked together, and he bit his tongue. Then came the ferrous tang of blood. Ethan cursed and pushed off the floor. "You could have let me down gently."

This time there was no reply.

He scowled and started forward, his hands outstretched and groping in the dark. At first it was disorienting, but each time his hands found walls, he turned the other way, and soon he stopped running into them.

"Where's this go?" he asked.

Again, no answer.

He went on, picking up the pace, impatient to get out of the dark.

Suddenly Ethan's feet touched air and he tipped forward. He put out his hands reflexively but they touched air, too, and he began to tumble as he fell. His stomach lurched and wind rushed past him in the dark. He screamed despite himself. "Hey! You sick frek!"

Suddenly his momentum began to slow, and he saw a dim red light begin growing all around him. With the light he could see that he was falling down what looked like an open lift shaft. Ethan's eyes narrowed as he floated to a stop at the bottom. Intellectually he knew that he was caught up in some kind of grav field, but it was still disconcerting to see himself floating above the ground, suspended by an invisible force field.

A pair of transparent doors opened in front of him and he floated out into a vast chamber with a domed ceiling and a single, glossy black chair in the center of the room.

"You'd better not try that with my wife," Ethan growled.

"I thought you said you could find your way?" Omnius replied, his deep voice echoing through the chamber.

"Very funny."

"It's not funny, Ethan. If I hadn't caught you, you would have died."

"Yes, but you're also the one who left me in the dark, and you're the one who opened that lift tube so I could plummet to my death."

"The darkness and the fall are an analogy. You and I both know that you have a habit of getting yourself into trouble, and you are fond of blundering around in darkness. I won't be there to catch you in the Null Zone."

"I got by just fine in Dark Space. Doesn't get much darker than that. I think I can look after myself."

"But can Alara?"

Ethan looked accusingly up at the domed ceiling. It was glowing—pulsing—a faint red, providing the only illumination for the chamber.

"Cut it out and get this over with. I've made my choice, so stop trying to change my mind. You value our free will enough to make us choose in the first place, so respect my choice now and go find someone more gullible to listen to you."

"Very well, but know this, Ethan, without my help you will lose everything you hold dear."

"Like my son? Too late, you already took him, didn't you? I'm beginning to think you predict the future by making your predictions come true."

"No, Ethan, I'm talking about your daughter. And your wife. They're both going to leave you. They're going to go to Etheria."

Ethan's heart began thudding in his chest. "What are you planning to do to convince Alara? I suppose you're going to tell her the same thing—that I'm going to leave her and go to Etheria."

"I don't lie, Ethan."

"No? Well, you're blackmailing me with my family. That's worse."

"I'm telling you what's going to happen so that you can do something about it before it's too late. That's not blackmail. It's compassion."

Ethan didn't buy it. Alara wouldn't leave him. Especially not after she'd promised to follow him last night. And if Omnius was talking about something that was going to happen in the far future, well, not even he could predict that with any certainty. The Peacekeepers had said more than once that Omnius didn't add the Nulls to *Sync* and his simulations of the future. That meant that he and Alara were about to be thrown into a sea of unknown variables, and any one of those could change the future that Omnius was predicting now.

Ethan's eyes narrowed. "If you already know what I'm going to choose, why do you keep trying to convince me to change my mind?"

"So that the Ethan of the future won't ask me why I didn't try to stop him from going to the Null Zone."

"All right, then give me a hint. When is she going to leave me?"

"If I tell you that, you will know what she is going to choose now."

"So?"

"That would defeat the purpose of your choice."

"You're using her to blackmail me anyway! What's the difference?"

"Without certainty of the facts, you have to trust that I know what's best for you, even without understanding why."

"You're talking about faith."

"I am."

"You are one twisted frek, Omnius. You're a bot, not a god. Why should I need faith to deal with you?"

"Because I am smarter than you are, and neither of us have the time for me to walk you through the reasons for every little thing I say or do. It is much easier for you to simply believe that I am looking out for your best interests and obey my commands."

"Sounds like a convenient way of telling me not to ask questions. That's also a convenient way of hiding a lot of krak."

"Please sit in the chair."

Ethan turned from gazing up at the ceiling to stare at the glossy black chair in the center of the room. Suddenly, that chair looked sinister to him. He hesitated there, wondering about Alara and second-guessing himself. What if Omnius did convince her to leave him? Would she really break last night's promise?

"Wait," Ethan said.

"Yes?" Omnius replied.

* * *

Alara waited for what felt like an eternity before Master Rovik nodded to her. She was gratified to see that his eye had turned a nice shade of purple.

"You can go now, Mrs Ortane," he said, his voice surprisingly neutral considering that she was the reason his eye was busy swelling shut. She'd heard Ethan screaming on the other side of the door, and she'd run right up to it, pounding on it with her fists. Master Rovik had pulled her away from the door, and she'd punched him in the face. Then he'd explained that he'd been trying to prevent one of the two drones guarding the doors from identifying her as a hostile target. She'd felt bad after that, but only a little. Master Rovik had gone on to explain that Ethan would not be harmed in any way, and that his screams were from surprise, not pain.

Now free to follow him, Alara ran toward the door. It opened before she reached it, sliding aside with a loud *hiss*. The corridor beyond was so dark that she almost tripped over her own feet, but then she felt herself lifted off the floor and carried forward.

"Hello, Alara," a deep voice said.

"Hello? Omnius?"

"Yes, my child. It's me."

"I'm going to become a Null. I'm not your child."

"Are you certain of that?"

Alara frowned in the dark. "Yes. I won't leave my husband."

"How do you know he didn't choose to go to Etheria?"

Alara felt her momentum shift, and she began descending in the dark. Her eyebrows drew together. "What did you tell him?"

"Nothing but the truth."

"As you see it. You're saying you changed his mind?"

"I'm saying you need to make your own choice, for your own reasons, not simply follow your husband wherever he goes."

Alara felt herself slow to a stop and she saw a pair of transparent doors slide aside. She floated out into a large, circular room. The ceiling was pulsing with a faint red light and in the center of the room sat a glossy black chair. Alara eyed it curiously.

"What will you do, Alara?"

"I made Ethan a promise. I can't go back on my word. He'll never trust me again, and he'll hold it against me, so I'm going to the Null Zone. But you already know that . . . don't you?"

"Yes."

"Then why are you trying to convince me to change my mind?"

"To save you the heartache that's coming. Your daughter will go to Etheria when it comes time for her to make her own choice."

"You can't possibly know that."

"You will follow her, but Ethan will stay. Before he changes his mind, he will cheat on you with the first woman he can find."

"He wouldn't do that."

"Just like he thinks you wouldn't leave him?"

Alara frowned. "If our daughter left, we would talk about it and come to a decision together about whether or not to follow her."

"And if he didn't agree with your decision? You saw the way he treated his son. Atton is dead to him, and yet he is more alive than Ethan right now."

Alara's mind reeled. She felt like someone had gone into her head and turned everything upside down, taking away everything she believed in and making her doubt everything she trusted the most. She shook her head to clear away the creeping poison of doubt and despair. "You already know what I'll choose, so why are you trying to convince me otherwise?"

"If I didn't try, one day you might wonder why a supposedly loving god wouldn't warn you about what was coming."

Alara felt her resolve begin to flicker. Was it possible that Trinity really would choose to go to Etheria? Would she follow their daughter with or without Ethan? Would Ethan respond by cheating on her? Alara supposed the real question was whether or not Omnius could predict all of that before Trinity was even born.

"Please sit in the chair, Alara."

"What else have you seen? I thought you can only see a day into the future?"

"To know everything with absolute certainty, yes, but there are some things that I can see many years in advance, and some people are more predicable than others."

"But you can't be one hundred percent certain, can you? Especially not for Nulls. You don't even try to predict their behavior, so the entire Null Zone is filled with millions of unknown variables that constantly change and defy your expectations."

Omnius remained silent for a long moment.

"Admit it, you don't know. You're just guessing."

"It would take too long for me to explain how I know what I know, and you wouldn't believe me even if I did."

"That's a convenient answer."

"Right now the only answer you need to worry about is yours, Alara. What will you choose, and why?"

"I can always choose to go to Etheria later, can't I?"

"If you are still alive, yes."

"Will I live long enough to see my daughter go through her own choosing?"

"If you want to know with certainty how your life will turn out and that all of the outcomes along the way will be the ones you hope for, then you should choose to go to Etheria."

Alara chewed her lower lip, thinking fast.

"Have you made your choice?"

"Yes."

CHAPTER 24

30 Minutes ago . . .

"Wait."

"Yes?"

Ethan eyed the chair in the center of the chamber.

"A Null can choose to ascend to Etheria whenever they want, right?"

"That is correct."

"So if I choose to be a Null, at least I can undo that if it turns out to be a mistake."

"Yes."

"Then I'm standing by my choice."

"Very well. Please sit down, Ethan. There are others waiting for you."

He started slowly toward the chair. "What's it do?"

"Here you will get to select your professional training, which you will use to make a living for yourself in the Null Zone. The knowledge will be downloaded and then your Lifelink will be disabled. Choose wisely. Any change of careers after this point will require you to learn all of the necessary skills the old-fashioned way."

Ethan reached the chair and eased into it. He heard a

humming sound and looked up to see a glossy black dome descending overhead. Somehow he hadn't noticed it hovering above the chair.

The dome touched the floor with a *thud* and Ethan's ARCs brought up a glowing table of text and pictures. Each entry showed a picture representative of some type of training. Beside it was a text description, and in the third column was a list of possible jobs he might find with that training as well as the hours and monthly income for each job. Ethan quickly realized that he had no way of knowing what was a good job in the Null Zone, or even how much money he would need to survive. He began scanning the list for the highest salaries. There wasn't a lot of variation—just a few hundred *bytes* and usually with a corresponding change in hours. He began wondering about the difficulty level of each job as well as possibilities for advancement. Among the jobs listed were *building maintenance, law enforcer, custodian, night watchman, security guard, personal assistant, desk clerk, sales agent, receptionist, firefighter, bouncer, bartender* . . .

Ethan frowned as his eyes skipped down a very long list of possibilities. They weren't bad jobs, but none of them was particularly well-paid, and all of them had one thing in common—they were easy to train for. If he'd had to train for any of those positions in Dark Space the training program wouldn't have been longer than six months. He didn't really need to *download* new skills to do any of those things. "Ah . . . could you show me some better-paid jobs? Maybe with some more complex skills and training?"

"I cannot."

"What do you mean you *cannot?* You could train me up to be a medic—some kind of cyberneticist that makes more money in a year than I've seen in my entire life."

"I could, yes."

"So what's the trouble?"

"The Null government has placed restrictions on what types of training I can offer to people emigrating from Etheria. These are the best opportunities I can give you."

"The best ..." Ethan shook his head. "Let me get this straight. I came to Avilon with my own *ship,* and now I'm going to be stuck cleaning bathroom stalls for the rest of my life?"

"Yes, about your ship. There was a museum that wanted it. All of your personal effects have been removed and they will be forwarded to your new address as soon as you choose a place to live."

"Great. How much does that get me?"

"You managed to decrease your government debt by more than fifty thousand bytes. Now you only owe a hundred and fifty five thousand."

"My what?"

"Your government debt, Ethan. Please try to hurry up. There are others waiting."

"Yeah, yeah, just hold on. If it's a *government* debt, why do I have to pay?"

"Because your wife is pregnant, and that's how much it costs the government for you to have a child. Breeding licenses currently cost 205,000 bytes."

Ethan's cheeks bulged. "You can't charge me for that! We got pregnant before we came here."

"That doesn't change the expenses that the Null Government will incur on your behalf. You can always terminate the pregnancy if you can't afford to pay."

"Terminate the pregnancy? You're talking about my daughter, you dumb frek!"

"To you she is your daughter. To any other Null she is an expensive luxury that they can't afford. It's also illegal to breed without first buying a license, but since you couldn't have known that, it would be unfair to put you in prison and terminate the pregnancy for you. Instead, you'll be given a preferential interest rate on your breeding loan. You'll only have to pay two percent per year. The usual rate is five and a half."

Ethan couldn't believe what he was hearing. His throat was suddenly painfully dry. He shut his eyes and the room began spinning around him. He felt like he was about to be sick.

"Please try to calm down. It's not as bad as it could be."

"How could it be worse?"

"You could be having twins."

Ethan scowled. "You're enjoying this!"

"No, I'm not. I'm trying to help you. It's not too late to go to Etheria, Ethan."

"I'll pass."

"You are nothing if not stubborn. Would you like help selecting the best training program from the list in order to fit your personality and your particular financial situation?"

Ethan couldn't summon the strength for a reply. A moment later the long list of jobs and training programs narrowed down to just two.

Driver's training.

Law Enforcement.

He thought about how dangerous the Null Zone was and about how corrupt the Enforcers supposedly were, taking bribes from crime lords just to stay alive. He'd had enough of dealing with organized crime while trying to make a living as a trader in Dark Space.

"I'll take the driver's program."

"A good choice. Now select a job."

Another list appeared before his eyes, this time jobs with descriptions and salaries.

Air taxi driver.

Air bus driver.

Air truck driver.

Courier.

...

Taxi driver made the same per hour as any of the others, but the hours were flexible, meaning he could work when he wanted and as long he wanted, making some extra money in the process. He focused on the first option for a second and the rest of the list disappeared. Being a taxi driver didn't sound so bad. At least he'd more or less get to be his own boss.

"That is what I would have chosen for you," Omnius said. "It will take some time for you to get your own car, but there are a number of different companies you can work for, and we already know that you have the natural ability for the job."

"I'll take that as a compliment."

"Please close your eyes. This will only take a moment."

Ethan deliberately disobeyed that command, trying to keep his eyes open, but after just a few seconds he found he was unable to resist. His vision grew blurry, and his eyes drifted shut. . . .

When he opened them again, he found himself lying down on a gurney. From the way it rattled and shook, he realized he was in the back of a moving vehicle. A medic was attending him on one side.

"What happened? Where am I?" he croaked. His heart

began to pound. His head throbbed painfully with every beat.

Ethan remembered choosing a driver's training program and then choosing to become a taxi driver . . . but that was it. When had he left the room with the glossy black chair? How had he wound up lying in the back of a . . . an ambulance. He swallowed thickly and began checking himself with his hands.

"Don't move, please," the medic said.

Ethan rocked his head from side to side. With that movement he felt a painful stabbing sensation go through his neck, but it quickly faded. He winced and something pulled tight on his forehead. He reached up and found a thick bandage there. Horrified, he began to pull on it. The pounding in his head intensified, and he felt something warm trickle down beside his ear.

"I said don't move!"

"What happened?" Ethan demanded, trying to sit up. Strong hands forced him back down.

"You were in an accident," the medic replied.

An assistant appeared on the other side of him with a syringe.

"Alara? Where's my wife?"

"She didn't make it," the assistant said. "Her injuries were too severe. She . . . chose to go to Etheria."

"You idiot, are you trying to send him into shock?" the medic said.

"Alara died?" Ethan rocked his head back and forth again, feeling nauseated. He broke out in a cold sweat.

"He deserves to know. He might want to follow her."

A life signs monitor that Ethan hadn't noticed before began to squeal with an alarm.

"He's going into shock!"

Ethan's field of vision narrowed, and soon he was looking down a long, dark tunnel. Alara appeared at the end of that tunnel, beckoning to him, her expression joyous. "Ethan! I miss you! Come *with* me."

His extremities lost all feeling and a pleasant numbness began creeping through his body. Voices screamed and yelled around him unintelligibly as if he were underwater; he felt an incredible pressure on his chest, but at least his heart had stopped its painful thudding. He was peripherally aware of the medic injecting him with something, but he barely felt the prick of the needle. He reached out for Alara, trying to touch her beautiful face . . .

Suddenly his heart began pounding painfully again, and his eyes flew open. Alara disappeared, and something like fire surged through his veins. Now he was someplace else, staring up at a bright light. That light was coming from a medic's flashlight, checking for pupil dilation.

"He's awake," someone said.

"Good. Get him off the gurney. We've got others waiting."

"Yes, sir. Up you get!" Ethan felt someone trying to lift him, but his limbs were heavy and limp. "Come on! He's not responding, sir."

"How much sedative did you give him?"

"Twenty cc's . . ."

"No wonder! I said twelve, not twenty!"

"I—"

"Get out of the way."

Someone slapped his face, and Ethan scowled sleepily.

"Wake up!"

Then came a sharp prick, and again fire went shooting through his veins. He sat up suddenly, blinking and squinting against the bright lights in the room.

"Alara!" he yelled, and leapt off the gurney.

"Well, that got him up."

Ethan whirled toward the speaker and found a medic standing next to him with an empty syringe. "You!" he grabbed the man by his lab coat and shook him until his teeth rattled. "Where is my wife?"

"I'm right here, Ethan . . ." A sleepy voice said.

Ethan whirled around again. He saw his wife lying on the other side of the room, on another gurney. She lay under a fuzzy blue blanket, her stomach bulging noticeably beneath the sheets. He walked up to her, almost afraid to ask. "I . . ." He frowned, trying to understand what was going on. "What just happened?"

Alara turned to him with a smile. "We became Nulls. They just finished de-linking us and syncing us one last time. You were having some kind of nightmare . . . . You called out my name a few times."

A dream. It was just a dream. "There was an accident. You . . ."

Alara's brow grew lined. "I died."

Ethan felt a jolt go through him. "How did you know that?"

"Because I had the same dream, Ethan."

* * *

Atton sat down in one of the glossy black chairs. His chair faced more than a dozen others like it, arranged in a circle on the floor of the domed chamber. The ceiling glowed a bright gold overhead. Others came and took their seats.

"Hello, my children!" a deep, resonant voice boomed.

"Hello, Omnius," a few of them replied.

"Here you will choose what you will become in Etheria. I have narrowed the options for you all to just a few, based on your personalities, natural abilities, and the opportunities available to you. The training programs I've chosen are all equally good choices. Some of you already know what you want to do, and you will be either pleased to find that I agree with your choices, or surprised to find that your desired profession is not on the list. In the latter case, trust me when I say I know you even better than you think you know yourself."

A *humming* noise began to rise in the room, and Atton noticed glossy black domes dropping down from the ceiling all around him. There was one for each chair. Atton looked up, watching as his descended. It hit the deck with a *boom*, and there was a moment of utter darkness. Then a holographic display flickered to life, bathing the inside of his capsule in a dim blue-white light. Atton saw a table with pictures and text descriptions of training programs. Just three had been selected for him—

*Business Administration.
Law.
Political Science.

Atton's brow furrowed. None of those training programs came with a commission. Atton shook his head. "Omnius? Why can't I join the Peacekeepers?"

"I've determined that you would be better suited to a civilian career."

"The entire reason I became an Etherian was to join the Peacekeepers!"

"Are you saying you doubt my wisdom, Atton?"

"No, I'm saying that I can't sit behind a desk and watch while others fight. The Sythians took everything from me, and I won't rest until they're defeated."

"So you're motivated by revenge."

"Justice."

"It would be justice if you were impartial, but you're not."

"Fine, revenge. What does it matter?"

"It matters, because revenge is not the Etherian way. You will not get far here if you let revenge motivate your actions."

Atton thought about Ceyla and everything he was leaving behind for this. With the thought of her, a painful lump formed in his throat, followed by a dull ache in his chest. Steeling himself for further rebuke, he shook his head. "Either you let me be a Peacekeeper or I'm going to the Null Zone."

"I'm sorry you feel that way, Atton."

The table of career options faded and was quickly replaced by another one. This time all the options fell under the heading, *Avilonian Peacekeepers*.

*Pilot's Training.
Assault Training.
Command Training.
Crime Prevention.

The top option had a star next to it, marking it as Omnius's choice for him. It was his choice, too, so that made things easier.

"I'll take pilot's training."

"Very well. This will take just a moment . . ." The table faded, plunging the inside of the capsule into darkness once more.

Atton felt his eyelids growing heavier and heavier . . . after just a few moments he couldn't resist. He shut his eyes.

What seemed like just a split second later, he opened his eyes, but now he was somewhere else, lying in a bright room, surrounded by beeping machines with blinking lights and holographic displays. A medic appeared wearing a glossy white jumpsuit with the Avilonian crest emblazoned in black on his shoulders. A shiny, gold crescent insignia marked his right breast. The man's name and rank appeared on Atton's ARC display, hovering above his head in a bright blue font—Templar Tyron.

Atton tried to sit up.

"Easy there, Pilot," the medic said, helping him to sit.

"*Where am I?*" he tried to say. What came out instead was something like "Wharr awwm ayy?"

"You're on board the *Dauntless*. Strategian Heston's ship."

"*Hoff* Heston?" Atton asked, forcing his tongue to cooperate.

"The same."

Atton jumped off the gurney and almost fell on his rear. His knees buckled and wobbled under him, as though his legs didn't remember how to hold his weight.

"Careful. Your muscle memory is still impaired. Transfer is hard on the mind."

Atton shook his head. "Yeah ..." *Muscle Memory? Transfer?* "You mean I've already ..."

"That's what you signed on for, isn't it? New life, new body, and a chance to give the Sythians a taste of their own medicine."

Atton blinked. He'd expected some kind of warning—a memory of the procedure at least. *Something.* Instead, he'd closed his eyes in his old body and opened them in his new one, with no idea how much time had passed in between.

"You want to see yourself? There's a mirror over there."

Atton turned to look where the medic was pointing. On one side of the room lay a wall of mirrors. He caught a distant view of himself and curiosity drove him onward.

While he was still a dozen feet away, his footsteps slowed. The reflection there wasn't his. It couldn't be. He was too tall, his skin too perfect, his hair too full. He also had a width and strength to his frame that he wasn't used to. He'd been just over average height and build before, but now he was on the large side—not fat, though it was hard to tell beneath the baggy blue patient's gown.

"You can ditch the gown," the medic said.

Atton untied the strings and let it fall around his ankles.

He did a double take when he saw himself naked in the mirrors. He'd always been in decent shape, but now he looked like he spent his life in the fitness center. Out of nowhere he had beefy, well-defined arms, legs, and chest. Abdominal muscles rippled across his midsection. His ribs were visible, but only because there were thick ridges of muscle covering them.

"Holy frek."

"Language, Pilot. I don't want to have to report you on your first day out."

"Sorry. I'm just . . . is it my imagination or am I taller than I used to be?"

"Avilonian ideal is around six two. Everything is designed for that height for men. Five seven for women."

Atton nodded, poking his stomach and finding it rock hard to the touch. Below the waist there'd been some improvements, too, but he didn't feel like asking the medic about that.

"Now what?"

"You need to report to the operations center. The Strategian is waiting there to brief the new officers before we jump to Dark Space."

Atton spent another moment staring at himself before bending down to pick up his gown.

"You can leave it there. I have a uniform waiting for you in the closet."

"Okay, where . . ." With a *swish* the mirrors swiveled open in sections, revealing a long wall of hanging uniforms and equipment. The radiant armor he'd seen Peacekeepers wearing wasn't there, instead there was a rack of dark blue fabric uniforms. He selected one, pulling it down and holding it up in front of himself to measure it. The uniform was huge, even for his new, over-sized body.

"Seems too big."

"The fabric adapts to you."

"Huh," he nodded, still studying the uniform.

It was a glossy, midnight blue, and the Avilonian crest

glowed bright white on the upper sleeves.

"Hurry up, Pilot Ortane. Don't keep the Strategian waiting."

"Yes, sir."

A timer appeared on his augmented reality display. It was counting down from fifty minutes. Below it read: *Time to Jump.* He didn't even know what unit he was attached to, let alone what his role would be in the coming battle. Atton hurried to put on the jumpsuit. It peeled open along a seam at the back and slid on effortlessly. No sooner had he pulled his arms through the baggy sleeves than the fabric began to contract, hugging itself to his skin. He flinched as it pulled tight over his body. Atton tried plucking at it with his fingers, but it refused to detach from his skin.

"How do I get out of it?"

"It's bio-active. It will sense when you want to get undressed."

"*Sense?* Like read my mind?"

"More like your body language." The medic came up to him and slapped a shiny silver crescent on his right breast. His rank insignia.

As Atton focused on it, glowing blue text materialized before his eyes. Rank—*O-2, Pilot.*

"Hurry along. We don't have much time for processing. Follow the arrow at the top of your ARC display."

At that, a green arrow appeared, pointing to the room's only exit. Atton turned to the medic and offered a quick salute. His hand made it only halfway there before he realized that he was supposed to do something else.

"We don't salute each other here, Pilot. We raise one hand to Omnius. Like this—"

Atton watched as the man's arm shot out straight, raised

at an angle from his body, palm flat and held up to the sky. "Hail, Omnius!" he said, his voice too loud for the small room.

Atton nodded and mimicked the gesture. His own *Hail Omnius* was noticeably quieter.

He hurried from the room, following the green arrow. The door *swished* open for him and he passed out into a long, white corridor with glowing green trim lines. He noticed that the arrow turned whenever he turned his head, always pointing in the same direction regardless of which way he was facing. Below it read a textual cue—Op. Center.

Atton's eyes began to burn as he ran. The overhead lights were too bright, but he supposed his new eyes were just as unused to seeing light as his muscles were to movement. He walked briskly, not running, but his legs were threatening to buckle, and he had to concentrate not to trip over his own feet.

Atton passed more medics and orderlies along the way. A few stopped and hailed Omnius as he ran by. He nodded back. He didn't have time for that.

The corridor ended in a large, empty waiting area. A quick look at the jump timer revealed it was down to 45 minutes. Feeling surer of his own feet, he sprinted toward the double doors along the far wall. They *swished* open and he found himself in another crystal white corridor with glowing green trim. This corridor was much broader than the one in the med center—made for more foot traffic, he supposed. Thankfully out here the light was a softer gold as opposed to the bright, sterile white of the med center.

One corridor ran into the next, branching and winding, and he ran past countless officers, dressed just like him— except their uniforms glowed all different colors along the seams. He raised his arms and was surprised to notice the same glowing trim had sprung to life on his uniform. He wondered if it was really glowing, or some type of ARC overlay. His trim lines were glowing white. That of the officers he passed varied—the majority were green, but some glowed white like his, while others were blue, or red, sky blue, or gold.

He wondered about that and the answer came to him as if he'd always known it—the colors corresponded to the destination of each officer, and each color represented one of the ship's six crew decks. White, Atton's color, represented the *Command Deck*. Green was the med bay.

The arrow he was following made a sudden right turn, and he turned with it. The corridor broadened into a semi-circular room with gleaming, semi-transparent tubes lining the far wall from floor to ceiling. Each of them was half open and pulsing with racing bands of light. There were six of them in all, three going up, and three going down.

Atton knew without having to wonder this time that the tubes were used to travel between decks. They read people's ARCs and Lifelinks to determine where they were going and took them there as quickly and efficiently as possible. No waiting for lift tubes.

Atton ran for the nearest of the three tubes marked with up arrows. He jumped inside and immediately he felt an invisible force field catch him and begin accelerating him up to a blinding speed. He looked down, noticing the long drop below his feet. He estimated there were at least twenty decks below. Looking up, there appeared to be roughly a dozen more.

Atton came to an abrupt stop and floated out into another semi-circular room full of transporter tubes. On this level the trim was all glowing white—the color of the *Command Deck*.

Atton broke into a run again. This time he saw a few armored Peacekeepers. He wondered about their armor and the answer came unbidden to his mind—they were Assault Troopers. Fleet Officers wore uniforms like his except when going into combat.

Atton was vaguely surprised to realize that he knew everything there was to know about life aboard an Avilonian Starship. He supposed that went along with the Pilot's Training he'd selected.

Before long the green arrow at the top of his ARC display led him to the Operations Center. Two assault troopers guarded the doors. Seeing him running toward them, they moved to block his way, but just as quickly they moved back.

They'd just used their ARCs to check whether or not he had the clearance to enter the *Op Center*.

The doors *swished* open and Atton breezed in. Strategian Heston was waiting at the head of a long, white table. There were a few others there with him. Most were armored Assault Troopers, but two others were dressed exactly like Atton, with the same silver crescent insignia. He recognized the man as *Razor*—Guardian Five—and the woman as Captain Caldin. His gaze lingered there a moment. She had always been a pretty woman, with delicate, feminine features and short blond hair, but now she was truly striking and only vaguely recognizable. She smiled at him as he walked in, flashing a perfect set of teeth. He noted that her rank insignia was the same as his—*pilot*. Atton turned to raise his arm to the Strategian. "Hail Omnius," he said.

His mind was bursting with questions that he hadn't thought to ask before. Hoff had died in Dark Space, and then he'd come back to life here. That had been just a few weeks ago, but his insignia—three *platinum* crescents—marked him as a Strategian, equivalent to a *captain* in the ISSF. How had he risen in rank so quickly if Captain Caldin had been reduced to a low-ranking officer?

Hoff nodded to him. "Sit down, Ortane."

Ortane. Maybe it was the Admiral's tone, or the way Hoff had chosen to address him, but something was off. Hoff was his stepfather. Atton had expected more of a personal greeting. Maybe Ceyla was right—maybe they really weren't the same people anymore.

Atton shivered and took a shaky step toward the nearest empty chair. It slid out automatically, swiveling to face him. He sat down, and the chair tucked him under the table.

"That's all of us," the Strategian said.

"I'm the last one to arrive?" Atton hadn't thought he'd been that slow. He'd run the entire way.

"There were some problems with your transfer."

"Like what, sir?"

"You died during transfer."

"I *what?*" Atton's heart began thudding in his chest and his palms began to sweat. A numb sense of unreality swept over him. He could hear his pulse pounding in his ears.

"Death is the wrong word for it. Our bodies can die, but our essence lives on, stored in our Lifelinks. Your autonomous functions ceased during transfer, but your mind was preserved and successfully transferred."

"How is that possible?"

"Transfer is hard on the mind. Sometimes your brain overreacts and kills you."

"Don't you use life support or something?"

"We do, which is why you didn't experience any brain damage. Your brain activity also ceased, however, plunging you into a coma. That made transfer more delicate, and time-consuming, but as you can see, there were no further complications. Rest assured, now that you've done it once, it will be easier in the future. There are fewer variables when transferring from one clone to another."

Atton slowly shook his head. Horror wormed through his gut, making him feel ill. "Why didn't they just . . . jump-start my brain or something?"

"I'm not qualified to answer that. The bio drones handle transfer. You'd have to ask them. Not that I expect they'll answer."

"What about our medics? I woke up in a room with a medic. I could ask him."

The admiral shook his head. "The medics deal with waking you up, checking vitals, and orienting you once you've already been transferred. They won't know anything about the process. If you're concerned, you should ask Omnius; I'm sure there's a reason no one tried to get your brain activity going again. Probably because they don't have to.

"Now—we don't have much time, as you can all see from the jump countdown, so I'd like to officially welcome you all aboard the *Dauntless*, and quickly explain a few things you might still be wondering about.

"Your units have already been designated. You can check them via your ARCs. Although you might be nervous about performing your duties, your ARC displays will tell you anything you don't already know, and you'll find that almost everything comes to you automatically anyway. You're all starting out as low-ranking officers. All enlisted personnel are drones. You will be their superiors.

"The drone decks, which make up the majority of

Avilonian ships, are off limits unless we need to help make repairs or fight off assaulting enemies. Those decks have no life support, and they act as extra armor on our ships. The *Dauntless* has 52 decks. That's 46 drone decks, 23 above your heads, and 23 below the lowest crew deck, Green Deck, or *Med Bay*.

"Now that I'm explaining this, you should realize that you already know what I'm talking about, so I'll stop there. If you ask the right questions, you'll find the right answers are already waiting for you, implanted in your brains. That said, do any of you have any questions that you can't answer for yourselves?"

Atton nodded. "Just one. How come you're a Strategian and we've all been busted back to O-2?"

"I was about to ask the same thing," Loba Caldin added.

"I died many years ago. The Admiral Heston you all knew was a clone. Now that there are no more living clones of me elsewhere, Omnius has allowed me to choose whether or not to combine my memories with those of my subsequent copies. I decided in favor of that option."

A flash of insight rippled through Atton's brain. *That* was why Hoff was acting colder than usual. He was essentially two people, fused together. His memories of Destra, Atta, and him would be more impersonal, almost as if they belonged to another person—which they had.

"So . . . you're a Strategian because you've been here in Avilon for years already."

"That is correct. I started out with the Peacekeepers as a *Pilot*, just like you, Atton."

Atton took that in with a smile. "For some reason I can't imagine you flying a starfighter."

The Admiral—*Strategian*, Atton corrected himself—

returned that smile and then his gaze moved on, his eyes roving around the table to address all of them. "Any other questions?"

People shook their heads.

"Good." Strategian Heston rose from the table. "Consult your ARCs for your current orders, and follow the green directional indicators at the top of your displays. There's thirty-five minutes left on the clock, so I suggest you all hurry. Dismissed."

Everyone rose from the table and hurried for the exit. The doors *swished* open, and people jogged back to the transporter tubes. Atton noticed *Razor* jog up beside him.

"Couldn't convince her, huh?"

"I'm sorry?"

"Ceyla. She stayed in the Null Zone, didn't she?"

Atton's chest began to ache again, but he pushed the feeling down. "Yeah."

"Don't worry. I hear a lot of Nulls recant before long."

Atton frowned at the religious connotation of that. *Recant. Recant what? Their choice? Their beliefs?* "I'd rather not talk about it," he said, hoping to forestall further conversation.

"Sure, sure. No problem."

Silence came. Atton listened to the sound of their footsteps pounding down the deck as they all jogged together. In the distance the bank of transporter tubes appeared. The group slowed to a stop and then shuffled forward, entering the transporter tubes three at a time, all of them heading *down* to their various destinations, since the *Command Deck* or *White Deck* was the topmost of the six.

Atton looked around, noting the trim colors of their uniforms had changed. His, Caldin's, and Razor's were all now sky blue—the color for the flight deck and storage level.

The rest of their group were armored Assault Troopers. They didn't have trim lines, but an ARC overlay limned their armor with a colored outline.

As they shuffled forward, Razor broke the silence once more. "Hey, do you think Gina's still mad at you?"

"What?" Atton turned to the other pilot with a frown.

"You know, for abandoning her and saving Ceyla instead . . ."

"What does it matter?"

Razor's eyebrows floated up. "You mean you haven't checked our unit roster yet?"

Atton shook his head. As he thought about it, the roster appeared in a small window at the top of his ARC display. He focused on that window and it grew large enough to read. Two names on it were familiar. *Pilot Gina Giord and Pilot Horace Perkins*. They were in his flight group, but thankfully neither one of them was his wingmate.

"Great," Atton said.

"Yep. Just like old times. Except this time the Captain's in the thick of it with us. Just don't ditch her like you did Gina."

Now that Razor mentioned it, Atton saw that Loba Caldin, his former captain, was now his wingmate. The squadron leader was someone Atton didn't recognize—Chevalier Davellin.

"See you on the Flight Deck," Razor said. There came a *whoosh* of air and Atton looked up just in time to see Razor speeding down one of the tubes.

Atton was next in line. He hesitated just a second before jumping in. The force field grabbed him, accelerating him downward even faster than the ship's standard gravity. The ship's inertial management system took care of any sensation of falling, but not the feeling of being trapped in a narrow space. Feeling claustrophobic, Atton crossed his arms over his chest and closed his eyes.

Bright rings of light from other decks flashed through his eyelids like strobe lights. In between flashes, he saw Gina's face come swirling out of the darkness. Her amber eyes were bloodshot, her face skeletal. *"You killed me,"* she whispered in a thready voice.

Atton's eyes sprang open just in time to see himself floating out onto a deck with sky blue trim lights. Caldin and Razor were already running down the corridor up ahead. Atton hesitated a moment before running after them.

It was time to face the skeletons in his closet.

CHAPTER 25

Ethan turned to glare at the medic attending him and his wife. "I thought Omnius was going to get out of my head if we chose to become Nulls."

The man blinked and began shaking his head. "What do you mean?"

"My wife and I just had the same dream. I'm assuming that was Omnius's doing. . . ."

"Don't worry; you won't have any more of those. No doubt Omnius wanted to warn you both one last time."

Ethan was about to give a scathing reply when he felt Alara grab his arm. He turned to see her sitting up slowly on her hover gurney. She clutched her pregnant belly as she did so, and Ethan felt a stab of alarm go shooting through him.

"Are you okay?" He remembered the medics talking about administering sedatives, and making a mistake with his—giving him too much. He turned to glare at them again.

"She and the baby are both fine."

"No thanks to you." Ethan turned and helped his wife down from the hover gurney. As he did so, the door *swished* open and an armored Peacekeeper breezed into the room. In his hands he carried a neat stack of clothing.

The Peacekeeper walked up to them and handed each of

them part of the stack. "These are your clothes."

Unlike the shimmering white robes they'd worn until now, these clothes were drab and made from more conventional materials. Ethan eyed the Peacekeeper for a moment, waiting for further instructions. When none came, he said, "You expect us to strip down in front of you?"

"Modesty. Of course. Forgive me, I'm used to dealing with Etherians. There's a restroom down the hall," he pointed over his shoulder to the door. "You can change there. As soon as you're done, you'll go to choose your new living quarters."

Alara nodded and took Ethan by the hand. He let her guide him out and down the hallway to the restroom the Peacekeeper had indicated. Once inside, Ethan locked the door behind them and leaned against it for good measure.

"I'm so glad to see you, Kiddie!" he breathed. "Omnius almost had me convinced that you were going to choose Etheria."

"I made a promise, remember?" she said as she stripped out of her patient's gown and got dressed in her new clothes.

"Yeah, I remember. No regrets?" Ethan asked.

She shot him a worried look. "We owe a lot of money, Ethan . . ."

"He told you about that."

"Yes . . . what are we going to do? We have to choose a place to live; we're not going to be able to afford much."

"We'll figure it out."

"What if it's dangerous? You saw the Null Zone. Below level ten it's a war zone, and the criminals are in charge."

Ethan snorted and shook his head. "Sounds like Dark Space to me."

"I'm serious, Ethan."

He took a step toward her and lifted her chin with one

hand. "Hey, we'll be okay, Kiddie. We've been through worse together."

"Not with a baby we haven't."

"Trust me." He dropped a quick kiss on Alara's lips and enfolded her in a hug. "We're going to be just fine. So long as we stick together, Kiddie. You, me, and Trinity."

She pulled out of his embrace, forcing him to hold her at an arm's length. "What if we don't stick together? Omnius kept trying to warn me that I'm going to leave you and go to Etheria. I didn't believe it, but after that dream . . . I'm starting to wonder."

Ethan shook his head. "Don't let him mess with your head. He can't predict the future. Not for Nulls. The Peacekeepers said so, remember? Omnius is just trying to manipulate us."

"But why? What does he have to gain if we go to Etheria?"

"Maybe he's bored and his only fun in life is messing with us. I don't know, but it's not our problem anymore." Ethan pulled her close for another hug and whispered beside her ear, "Everything is going to be fine, okay? I promise."

Later that day, after they'd been forced by a tight budget to choose their living quarters on *level nine* of Sutterfold East—affectionately known as *East Grunge*—Ethan became less certain that *everything was going to be fine*.

They had to be escorted to the surface by an armed guard of Peacekeepers. Ethan stood shivering on the surface of Avilon, his eyes darting furtively, trying to pierce the thick, garbage-smelling mist.

"This is the place," the Peacekeepers' squad leader said, gesturing to a rust-colored door in front of them. Above the door a bar of neon green text read *Fort Carlson*.

"The doorman already knows to expect you, and the security system will recognize you both, so you can go on in. Take the lift up to level nine. Apartment 9G."

Ethan eyed the rusty door dubiously. The roving black eye of a security camera was mounted high above the door. He imagined a doorman sitting somewhere inside the building, watching the security feed.

"One last thing." Ethan turned, and the Peacekeeper handed him a gun belt with a sidearm already holstered. "You'll need this. It's not lethal, but it'll be enough to fend off a few Psychos and give you time to get away."

Taking the gun belt and strapping it around his waist, Ethan nodded his thanks to the Peacekeeper and started toward the door. Alara held tightly to his arm as they went. The rust-colored door groaned as it slid open and lights flickered on for them in a small vestibule. A second security door lay beyond that, with a glowing control panel. Ethan studied the control panel and realized that he was supposed to place his palm on it. He did so and saw a bright bar of light pass through the scanner. Then a fan of blue light flickered out from a small black iris above the door, scanning them both from head to toe.

"Why are there two doors?" Alara asked.

The front door groaned shut behind them, and then the second door slid open with a more fluid *swish*.

"I'm not sure," he lied, and his hand dropped to the butt of the sidearm strapped to his hip.

He knew exactly why there were *two* doors. The entrance was designed like an airlock. The outer door would have to close before the inner one would open, making it almost impossible to sneak inside without properly clearing the security checks.

Ethan was beginning to understand why they called this building a *fort*. He guided Alara through a small, dingy lobby to a pair of lift tubes.

"Looks homey," he said as he waited for the lift. The walls inside the lobby were cracked and peeling with old wallpaper. The floors were dusty. Glow lamps flickered. Something skittered noisily across the floor.

Alara said nothing.

After a short ride up the lift, they stepped out onto level nine. The hallway was dim and crowded with doors. They came to 9G, and faced another palm scanner like the one for the front door of the building. Ethan placed his palm there and again it scanned him. A split second later, the door slid open.

Lights flickered on for them, revealing their new home, and Ethan's spirits took an abrupt nosedive. Their apartment was cramped. Very cramped. It was one room—a bed, a closet, a door that led to a bathroom, an open kitchen with a few basic appliances, a window with bars over it above the bed, and a ceiling that radiated a bright, sky blue light that Ethan assumed was meant to simulate daylight.

Ethan tried to look on the bright side. The space was clean. The walls were painted and not peeling like the outer walls of the building had been. . . .

Nevertheless, he stood frozen in the doorway looking and feeling defeated.

Alara turned to him with a smile. "It's perfect," she said.

He shook his head, searching her face for some sign of the lie he felt certain she'd just spoken, but she seemed genuine. "Perfect?"

"Yes."

Something rose up inside of him then—

Determination.

He'd been kicked when he was down before, and he'd always found a way to get back up. This time wouldn't be any different.

"Well?" Alara asked. "Aren't you going to carry me over the threshold?"

Now he matched Alara's smile with one of his own. Sweeping her off her feet, he carried her into the room.

The door shut behind them, meeting the frame with a soft *boom*, as if to punctuate their choice.

They'd chosen this. Life in the Null Zone.

Better known as the Netherworld, Ethan thought as he carried Alara to bed.

* * *

Destra held Atta's hand while she sat in the examiner's chair, waiting to be *de-linked*.

"Will it hurt?" Atta asked the man with the funny, lop-sided grin and glowing honey-brown eyes. Unlike most of the others Destra had seen, their medic wasn't unusually good looking. He was short, balding, and overweight, but somehow his more conventional appearance was comforting. Everyone else was just a little too perfect. Couple that with their strange glowing eyes and they looked almost more alien than the Gors.

"Not at all," the man said. "You won't feel a thing. Now, please lie back and close your eyes. . ."

Destra watched as the medic conducted a scan of her daughter's brain with a glowing wand. That done, he turned and began entering inputs at a nearby data console.

The majority of the crew had been left in stasis aboard the *Baroness*, but everyone the Avilonians had taken with them to their ship had been forced to go through this procedure. Admiral Hale had explained something about Avilon's AI ruler being able to track anyone who wasn't *de-linked*. Destra wasn't sure how that was possible, or exactly what that meant, but for now she was just happy to find out that she and the rest of the crew from the Baroness weren't alone in the universe. Before leaving, she'd insisted they wake Atta and take her along to Noctune. The Admiral hadn't wasted any time arguing; he'd just told her that Atta would have to be de-linked, too.

Apart from the two of them and the bridge crew, who'd already been awake when the Avilonians had come aboard, the only ones they were transferring over to the *Tempest* were sentinels. Destra suspected the admiral was trying to even the odds against the Gors—just in case.

Destra watched as the medic finished de-linking her daughter, passing his glowing wand over her one last time.

"You can open your eyes, Atta," the man said.

"It didn't hurt at all!" she said, smiling up at him.

"You see? I told you it wouldn't."

Destra nodded to the man. "Thank you."

"No, thank *you*. It's always a pleasure to meet new recruits. Especially when one of them is so young."

Destra frowned at that, but decided not to comment. She

hadn't formally decided to join this so called *Resistance,* but at the moment she supposed there wasn't much choice. "Do you have any idea how much longer we have before the jump to Noctune?"

"The better part of a day, Ma'am."

"I guess that means there's time to get something to eat, then." Her stomach grumbled loudly in response to that thought.

"Oh, plenty of time," the medic replied. "If you'd like, I can get someone to show you the way."

"No, that's all right," Destra said, taking her daughter by the hand and helping her down from the chair. "This is a venture-class cruiser. I'm quite familiar with the layout."

Later on, as she and Atta were standing in line in the mess hall, waiting to be served, Atta's eyes grew wide with all of the food. "Wow," she said.

As it came to their turn to be served, the woman behind the counter asked what they would like. Atta pointed to one of the fresh bread rolls. "I'll have one of those, please," she said.

"Anything else?" the woman asked.

Atta hesitated, and Destra squeezed her daughter's shoulders. "Get something else, Atta." Destra's own stomach was growling painfully with all the fragrant smells of food wafting through the room.

"I'm allowed?" Atta asked, looking up at her.

Destra remembered the emergency rationing that had been in effect aboard the *Baroness.* Clearly there wasn't any rationing aboard this ship. She smiled, unable to help herself. "Yes, Atta. Eat whatever you want!"

* * *

"You're sure you want to do this, Captain?"

Picara nodded, running a hand through her short, straight black hair as she stepped into the glowing green circle beneath the hovering dome of the quantum junction. "She's my command, sir. Who better to fetch the *Emancipator* than I?"

"The Sythians have been toying with her. They may open fire when they realize you're trying to escape."

"Maybe, maybe not. They can't detect quantum drives powering or track a quantum jump. With any luck we'll finish the refits and jump away before they even realize we're trying to escape. I bet we'll be at the rendezvous before you even make it back from the Getties."

Bretton gave her a grim smile. "Unless the Gors eat me. In which case you'll be in command."

Picara's brow grew lined with worry. "Don't joke, sir. They're savages. If I were you I would have dumped them out the nearest airlock long ago."

"Yes, that might be wiser, but the enemy of my enemy is my friend, and we have precious few friends as it is. In any case, it's not much out of our way thanks to the *Tempest's* recent tech upgrades."

"Well, be careful, sir."

"Likewise." Bretton stepped back, beyond the rim of the

glossy black podium that formed the base of the junction. Picara raised her arms, palms up, as if praising Omnius, and the dome began to drop down over her head.

Bretton gave a stiff salute, and Captain Picara just managed to return it before the dome blocked her from view. Then he heard a roaring noise come from within the dome; a bright light shone around the base of it, and then the light vanished and a heavy silence fell.

Bretton turned, walking back to the bridge. The doors *swished* open, revealing a long, gleaming gangway to the captain's table. Farah stood there, hands clasped behind her back, watching the grid. Behind her, broad viewports lay draped with a shimmering curtain of stars. Bretton started down the gangway, scanning the crew stations to either side.

He reached the captain's table and nodded to Farah. "Any new developments?"

"Our engineers have finished looking over the *Baroness*; she's clean. No tracking devices or unscheduled commcasts have been detected. It should be safe to wake her crew."

Bretton breathed a sigh. "That's a relief, but no, we're not waking the crew just yet. Any one of them could be a Sythian agent."

"We can't just leave her derelict. What if the Sythians come along? The *Baroness* has guns, we don't. We should take advantage of that. I'd almost say it would be better to move our operations to the *Baroness*."

"Almost," Bretton agreed, "Except the quantum jump drives and comms aboard the *Tempest* are our golden ticket, and our only line back to Avilon. But you're right. We can't leave the *Baroness* defenseless. I was thinking of sending Captain Hale along with a skeleton crew to command our new ship."

"Captain Hale, sir? So now you're referring to yourself in third person?"

Bretton turned to Farah with a faint smile tugging at the corners of his mouth. His eyes sparkled. "I'm not the only *Hale* here, am I?"

"You want *me* to command her?" Farah's eyes grew wide, and she shook her head.

"Why not? You're more than qualified. How about it, *Captain?*"

Farah grinned. She took a quick step toward him, looking like she wanted to give him a hug, but then she recovered and settled for a brisk salute, instead. "It would be an honor, sir. But don't you have to clear that kind of thing with the Resistance first?"

Bretton shrugged. "They made me an Admiral. That should come with some autonomy. Besides, who else would they rather have commanding an old venture-class? Some textbook captain or a real venture-class veteran?"

Farah's grin remained fixed on her lips. "I'll leave the explanations to you."

"Good." Raising his voice, Bretton said, "Gunnery, calculate a quantum jump to the bridge of the *Baroness!* Comms, contact the bridge crew we found aboard the Baroness when we jumped over. Have them meet us at the junction."

Both the comms and weapons operators acknowledged their orders and Bretton took Farah gently by the arm, leading her toward the entrance of the bridge. As they walked together, her grin faded to a more subdued glow. By the time they reached the junction, the golden dome was already hovering on four shining pillars of light.

Bretton stood with his niece at the threshold, waiting for

her crew to arrive. "I'm afraid this is goodbye for a while, Fay," he said, breaking military protocol for the moment.

She nodded, matching his serious tone with a slight frown. "You're still planning to take the Gors to Noctune," she said. It wasn't a question.

"Yes. It's not a big deal to us. It's a big deal to them. Maybe some day they'll repay the favor. Either way, we know what its like to be pushed to the brink of extinction. That's not a fitting end for any sentient species."

"Don't go," Farah said.

"We'll pre-calculate the jump home, just in case. There's no risk that way. First hint of Sythians we see and we'll jump straight back."

"I'm serious, Bret. Anything could happen, and I can't bail you out this time. I'm going to be a galaxy away, at least six-months' journey from coming to the rescue."

"So don't. If I don't show up at the rendezvous, don't wait for me, and don't you dare go to Noctune. Take your crew and the survivors in stasis and go start a colony somewhere new. Get away from Avilon, and don't ever look back. It's a fresh start, just like you always wanted."

Farah bit her lower lip, considering it. "Not exactly like I always wanted . . ." she said.

In that moment, the door on the other side of the junction opened, and in walked the five officers they'd found on the bridge of the *Baroness*—not including Councilor Heston.

Bretton nodded to them and smiled. He turned Farah by her shoulders to face the waiting junction and her crew. "Nothing ever is," he said. "Now go."

Farah walked under the dome, meeting her crew in the center of the glowing green circle on the glossy black podium that formed the base of the junction. She turned to wave goodbye just before the golden dome dropped and whisked her away to her ship.

Bretton returned to the bridge. Back at the captain's table he studied the star map for a moment, waiting.

"Commander Hale reports she is safely aboard the *Baroness*," the comms operator announced.

Bretton nodded. "That's *Captain* Hale, now. Tell her to form up, and—"

"Sir! Picara is reporting from Dark Space. She says its urgent."

Bretton turned to address his comms operator. "Put her through."

The main viewport shimmered, and Captain Picara's face appeared in a larger-than-life holo projection.

She looked somewhat paler than before. "Sir!" she said, sounding out of breath.

"What's wrong, Captain?"

She shook her head. "The crew just finished a sensors test to verify that the upgrades are working. We detected something new. There's a cloaked fleet out there, sir."

"That sector is teeming with Sythians. I'm surprised only *one* of their fleets is cloaked. Ignore it. Just make sure they don't get too close to you."

Picara shook her head. "No, sir . . . that's not it. The fleet is Avilonian. They're Peacekeepers."

"Peacekeepers? What are they doing in Dark Space?"

"I don't know, sir, but they're advancing on the Sythian armada. What are your orders? Should we warn them?"

Suddenly Bretton understood Picara's dilemma. The Avilonians were cloaked, and they obviously thought that the Sythians couldn't detect them. Bretton and the rest of his crew had just proven otherwise during their engagement with the enemy, and that meant the Peacekeepers were flying straight into a deadly trap.

Bretton considered that. The Resistance had just been given a once in a lifetime chance to strike a killing blow against Omnius's Peacekeepers, and the best part of it was, all they had to do was sit back and watch. The Sythians would do all of the work.

There was just one problem.

Who was the bigger threat—Omnius or the Sythians?

"Do you have a way to contact Admiral Vee?" Bretton asked.

Picara shook her head. "I've already tried. She won't answer."

"Bad time to be away from the comms . . ."

In his mind's eye Bretton saw his eight-year-old son, Ciam, his expression tranquil, his eyes closed, just as they had been when Bretton had seen him in the casket. Omnius had forced Ciam to choose, just like everyone else. Ciam had chosen to become a Null of all things. Less than a month later, he'd been walking down the street with his friends on his way back to his boarding school when he'd been caught in the middle of a shootout between two gangs warring over territory.

Bretton tried to compare that tragedy to all the trillions of people that the Sythians had killed during the invasion.

There was no comparison. The choosing was bad, and Omnius's rigidly controlled-society was worse, but at least he wasn't trying to wipe out the human race.

"Sir, we don't have much time. . . ."

"Warn them, Captain, and then get the frek out of there. We'll wait for you to arrive at the rendezvous before we go to Noctune."

"Our jump drives aren't finished being upgraded, sir."

"Then use conventional SLS! Right now, while the Sythians are distracted, is your best chance to escape. Make sure you use it."

"Yes, sir."

PART TWO: TO THE BITTER END

CHAPTER 26

Atton raced across the flight deck, otherwise known as *Sky Deck* for the glowing sky-blue trim lining all the walls. Caldin and Razor raced ahead of him, all of them following the green arrows projected mere millimeters from their retinas by their ARCs. Atton found his new body didn't just look fit; it was fit. He ran as easily as he remembered walking in his former life.

Up ahead a bank of transporter tubes appeared, but rather than jump into them, both Razor and Caldin disappeared down a corridor branching off to the right. Atton's arrow turned the same way, and he followed.

More officers streamed into the corridor from the other side, all of them dressed in the same glossy, skin tight blue uniforms with matching sky blue trim. On either side of the corridor were broad, star-dappled viewports with portal-shaped doors staggered in between. Remembering the layout of the ship, with drone decks running all the way around the crew decks in a protective cocoon, Atton knew that those viewports were simulated. The portal-shaped doors, however, were real.

A glowing, gold-colored numeral appeared to hover in

the air in front of each door. Atton read twelve numerals in all. Each of the doors led to one of the ship's X-1 launchers.

Atton found his place beside Caldin at launcher number eight. Hers was number seven. He turned to her. "Looks like we're going to be wingmates," he said.

Caldin nodded. "Nervous?"

"Not at all. This time we can't die, and the Sythians can't even get to Avilon for reprisals. It's time for some real payback, Captain."

"It's just *Pilot* now, Ortane."

"Consider it a call sign then."

She smirked at that. "Very well, *Iceman*."

Atton grimaced and took a quick look around to make sure no one else had recognized his former call sign. Gina was around here somewhere. . . .

He found her standing down the ranks to his right, in front of launcher number ten. She hadn't noticed him.

Someone clapped their hands and called for attention. Atton turned to look down the rows of waiting pilots once more.

"Listen up!" a man at the other end of the corridor said, stepping away from his launcher so that all of them could see him. Atton supposed this must be the squadron leader, *Chevalier* Davellin. "In just a few minutes, we're going to jump into Dark Space. Intel suggests we're badly outnumbered, so we're going to use every advantage we've got.

"The big boys are going to sit behind their cloaking shields and fire quantum-launched ordinance at the enemy. If you're wondering where we fit into that picture, the answer is we don't. If that sounds boring to you, then you can go hit the rack for some extra sleep." The Chevalier waited a beat, but no one moved. He began to chuckle, his broad shoulders shaking in appreciation of his own joke. "No one? Good. This battle will *probably* be a moonwalk, but if war always went as planned, we could all jump home now and let the drones handle it by themselves.

"Orders are we stay in our cockpits and sit tight. Chances are we'll only be called out after the battle's already over to help mop up stragglers. Are there any questions?"

Before Atton could stop himself, he raised his hand.

"Yes, Ortane?"

Everyone looked his way—including Gina. He could have sworn her eyes narrowed when she saw him.

He winced and cleared his throat. "Isn't this a rescue operation? How are we going to rescue the slaves if we stay cloaked and fire bombs at the enemy ships?" His thoughts were on his mother as he asked that. She had been in Dark Space when the Sythians invaded. By now she had probably been captured and turned into a Sythian slave with everyone else. Supposedly Omnius's reason for attacking Dark Space was a mission of mercy to liberate the slaves and give them a chance to choose a life for themselves on Avilon.

"There's always one of you, isn't there? You new recruits do ask the stupidest questions! Aren't you supposed to be on red deck?"

Atton's brow furrowed in confusion. Red deck was the *battle deck*, where the gunners remotely controlled the *Dauntless's* weapon systems, but he hadn't selected gunnery training.

"Well? What are you still doing here?"

"I selected pilot's training, sir. I'm an X-1 pilot."

"Oh! It's just that with you asking stupid questions about which type of ordinance the gunners should fire at the enemy, I thought maybe you'd been assigned to my squadron by mistake. Are there any other questions?"

Gina flashed Atton a broad grin, and he scowled back. No one else raised a hand to ask a question.

"Good! Time to go boys and girls!" The Chevalier stepped back in front of his launcher. A split second later, all twelve portal-shaped doors swished open at the same time. Atton peered into his and found himself looking into a small capsule with a soft, padded black floor. Beyond that lay a thousand different flight controls and readouts that he'd never used before in his life. Despite that, he recognized every status light, switch, and dial. Just another part of Omnius's instant training, he supposed.

Atton realized he was staring into the cockpit capsule of an Avilonian X-1 Interceptor. The portal-shaped opening was the rear-access to the cockpit, which would form the backrest of the flight chair when closed. The cockpit capsule was detachable from the rest of the fighter, and it doubled as an escape pod for emergencies.

Atton crawled through the portal and into his cockpit. The rear-access cycled shut behind him and he turned to see the access door padded with the same black cushions as the seat he knelt on. Suspending himself by the armrests of the chair, he swung his legs out and into the bottom of the capsule. He settled back against the rear hatch. The cockpit was roomy enough, even for his recently enlarged frame.

Before Atton could wonder about flight restraints, a pair of them whipped across his chest, writhing over him like snakes. He fought against them for a moment before he realized what they were. Feeling stupid, he muttered to himself about the overly automated systems aboard Avilonian starships.

Pop out displays and tool tips crowded Atton's ARC

display. His ARCs interacted with the various controls and readouts in his cockpit, highlighting some and providing extra settings for others. He found that he could select those just by thinking about them.

Atton began going through a preflight check while his cockpit capsule rocketed down into the frame of its fighter. Seeing the wings and nose take up a fair portion of his view, he flicked a switch for enhanced visibility and the shiny, bluish frame of the fighter abruptly shimmered and vanished. Even the frame of the cockpit disappeared, giving him the disconcerting notion that he was hovering in the air, surrounded by floating flight controls. Only a vague outline of the interceptor's frame remained, giving him a nearly unobstructed view of his surroundings.

The cylindrical walls of the X-1 launcher were also semi-transparent. To either side, he could see matching launchers with more X-1 Interceptors locked and loaded inside. He could identify the pilots sitting in the fighters immediately to his left and right, their expressions grim, cast in sharp relief by the hard blue light of their displays. Atton realized then that none of them were wearing helmets, nor had they been given flight suits to wear. Their cockpit capsules would be what shot away if any of them had to eject. But what would happened if the cockpit took a hit and depressurized?

He supposed he'd wake up in the nearest clone room. That wasn't much comfort when faced with the prospect of a slow, torturous death in outer space. . . .

As he thought about it, Atton realized that small leaks in the cockpit would auto-seal, and under his seat he had a few hull patches and cans of sealant spray for the ones that didn't. For all intents and purposes, the cockpit capsule was his flight suit.

Looking down to the end of his launcher, Atton saw a small circular opening filled with stars slowly scrolling by as the *Dauntless* turned to orient itself for the jump.

Keeping half an eye on the jump timer on his ARC display—just ten minutes left—Atton went back to doing systems checks and inventories.

The X-1 was packed with two magazines of eight quantum-launched thunderbolt missiles as well as two phased red dymium pulse lasers—that meant they could be rapid-fired, or pulsed, charged for slower cycle times, or even depleted with one shot as high-powered beam weapons, the likes of which Atton had never seen on a fighter this small. Making them even more deadly, those lasers had 360 degree firing arcs from front to back.

For its defenses the fighter was equipped with both particle and energy shields, as well as an optional cloaking shield. There was also a miniature quantum disruptor to prevent quantum-launched weapons from getting close, a mine layer with three cloaking mines, and a dorsal-mounted auto-cannon with explosive rounds, designed to shoot down incoming missiles, or shoot back at pursuing fighters. All of that, combined with the X-1's lightning-fast acceleration, quantum sensors, comms, and jump drive made the fighter a deadly weapon, far superior to the Imperial "Nova" equivalent.

Making the pilot's job easier, there was a range of computer-assisted and automated functions. The X-1 almost didn't need a pilot, but hands-on human pilots tended to fight better than both drones and remote-flying humans. They were more creative than drones, and for some reason the threat of death made even immortal pilots fight better.

Atton's eyes skipped to the jump timer on his ARC

display and he saw that just five minutes remained.

Finishing his preflight checks, he set up the star map on the fighter's main display screen so that he could watch the coming battle.

One minute.

Speakers crackled beside his ears. "Take care of yourself out there, Iceman," a smooth female voice said.

Atton frowned and turned to look out the left side of his cockpit at his wingmate. Caldin saw him looking. She smiled and waved. That hadn't been her voice.

He waved back and then turned to look at his comms board. The speaker was designated as Gold Ten, Gina Giord. *Figures.*

"Hey there, Tuner," he said, using her old call sign. "We're good, right?" After all, she hadn't ended up dead, but rather resurrected in the body of an immortal clone. How could she hold that against him? She'd skipped right by *The Choosing*. If he'd known what was waiting on Avilon he wouldn't have fought so hard to stay alive during the battle.

"We're perfect," Gina said. "Where's your girlfriend?"

"My what?"

"Ceyla . . . Green V."

"She, uh, chose to be a Null."

Gina snorted. "Well, at least she had a choice."

There was definitely a note of recrimination in Gina's voice that time. Atton wondered if she was still out for revenge. He decided that it didn't matter. Omnius was watching both of them, now, and he would deal with Gina if she did anything wrong. Besides, what was the worst she could do? Kill him? By some people's definition, he was already dead.

The jump timer reached zero and a bright flash of light

washed the world away. An instant later it was back and Atton's eyes fell on the star map rising from the fighter's main display.

That three dimensional projection of space was suddenly so crowded with glowing red enemy contact icons that it looked like they'd stumbled into some type of crimson nebula. Atton wondered how many of them there were and an obscene number appeared in the bottom corner of the star map. There were almost ten thousand capital-class warships, and the number of enemy fighters was in the high six figures.

The Avilonian fleet on the other hand was just 42 capital-class and 492 fighters strong. Atton shook his head, stunned by the sheer mass of the Sythian force. Now they were finally beginning to see the true strength of the enemy. The Sythians had originally invaded with just seven fleets. Now they had dozens more, and there were probably still hundreds sitting in reserve in the Getties. Even with the Avilonians' technological edge, Atton began to wonder if their fleet could prevail.

It's a good thing they can't see us right now, he thought, watching as their fleet began advancing on the enemy formation.

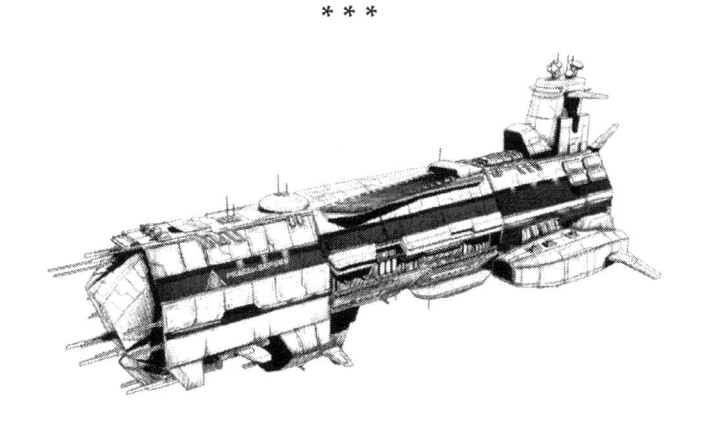

* * *

Hoff sat in his command chair on the bridge of the *Dauntless*, watching stars glitter like flecks of broken glass beyond the forward viewports of the cruiser. Then the jump timer reached zero, and everything disappeared in a blinding flash of light.

Space returned a moment later, but now the stars were hidden by a familiar gray nebula. Visibility was poor; shifting gray clouds of ice seemed to writhe like a living thing as the *Dauntless* sliced through them. The clouds were periodically lit up from within by bright, actinic flashes of light that came to Hoff's ears as thunder, simulated by the ship's sound system.

"Report!" Strategian Heston called out from where he sat in his command chair.

"Jump successful, sir!"

Hoff smiled to himself, nodding as he studied the star map on his ARC display. They were more than ten thousand klicks from the enemy formation. That put them at the edge of the Stormcloud Nebula, well above and behind the minefield that the enemy had laid for them around the old Imperial space gate. Clearly the Sythians hadn't got the memo that Avilonians didn't need to travel along physical paths between interstellar obstacles. Omnius had jumped them straight past the black holes that crowded the entrance of Dark Space.

Hoff noticed how vast the enemy armada was, but he knew it wouldn't matter. Sythian sensors couldn't pierce cloaking shields, and they couldn't shoot what they couldn't see. As soon as the Sythians realized they were being shot at with untraceable weapons fired from invisible ships, they would turn tail and run.

Omnius had already equipped the fleet for that eventuality, fitting their ships with SLS disruption fields.

Similar to the quantum variety, those fields would prevent the enemy from jumping to SLS within a certain radius of the generator.

Unfortunately, that meant they would have to get uncomfortably close to the enemy.

Orders came in from the Grand Overseer's ship—the *Justinian*—assigning each of the Avilonians' 42 capital-class warships with the task of snaring one of the Sythians' command ships. Once the command ships were snared in the SLS disruption fields, their fleets of slave-crewed ships wouldn't dare jump away and leave their masters to die. The entire armada would be trapped and forced to shoot blindly back at the Avilonian Fleet.

Omnius's plan was perfect.

The sensor operator highlighted their command ship on the map, and Hoff nodded down to the navigator. "Helm, full speed ahead!"

"Yes, sir."

Hoff sat back, studying the star map and watching as the range to their target swiftly dropped. After a while his thoughts wandered and he absently studied the rest of the Sythian armada. None of their vessels were cloaked, but they knew better than to try to hide after being surprised and losing one of their command ships at Avilon.

Lurking among the alien warships was a small group of captured human ships—what remained of the old Imperial fleet. Seeing a few venture-class cruisers there, Hoff eyed their names and ship ID codes, looking for one in particular and hoping against hope that he didn't find it.

Before he'd been executed, Hoff had left his wife and daughter hiding aboard a cloaked venture-class cruiser—the *Baroness*. He'd instructed Destra to wait for reinforcements with the rebel Gors. If reinforcements didn't come soon, they were to abandon Dark Space and take as many refugees with them as they could. With any luck they'd already left, and Hoff would be able to track them down later with Omnius's help.

He scanned a contact report that gave a breakdown of the ships on the map by class and hull type. He didn't see the *Baroness* among the handful of venture-class cruisers in the report, just a few older models that had been assigned to guarding various parts of Dark Space.

Then he noticed a name he didn't recognize. The *Emancipator*. The text was dim, meaning that one ship, of all the thousands of enemy vessels, was cloaked. They were trying to hide, but from who?

As he wondered where that ship was on the map, his ARC display responded, panning away from the Sythian armada to the far side of the system, to the ice world, Firea. The *Emancipator* wasn't sitting in the Sythian formation, rather she was all alone, cut off and hiding by herself. That, and the fact that it was cloaked, led him to believe that this vessel was not under Sythian control.

"Sensors, flag the *Emancipator* as neutral, and alert mission command. I believe we have a friendly in system."

"A friendly, sir?"

"Time will tell." Hoff eyed the venture-class cruiser as its icon went from enemy red to neutral yellow on the map. It wasn't the *Baroness*, but since the ship was cloaked, it wasn't actively broadcasting its ID code. And sensor profiles could always be mistaken without active ID.

Destra? he wondered, thinking about how he could hail that ship without revealing both it and the *Dauntless* to the Sythians. There was no way to do it with conventional comms, and neither the *Baroness* nor any other venture-class would have quantum tech.

Hoff resolved to teleport over there himself as soon as the battle was won to find out exactly who was on board that ship.

* * *

Captain Marla Picara stood aboard the *Emancipator*, looming over her comm operator's shoulder. "Well?"

"Just a minute, Ma'am."

"Make sure you don't transmit a visual from our end. And scramble our vocals. Sensors, is our quantum disruption field activated?" she asked.

"Yes, Ma'am. Nothing is getting on or off this ship. Not without using an airlock, anyway."

"Good." That was just an added security measure, in case the Avilonians somehow managed to identify them as Nulls despite their scrambled vocals and the lack of a visual on their end of the comm.

Marla tapped her foot impatiently, watching as the comms operator selected the largest ship in the Avilonian formation and hailed it using the *Emancipator's* recently upgraded comm systems.

"They're responding. Connection established, Ma'am.

Transmitting..."

Marla looked up, her eyes scanning the forward viewport. Suddenly, their view of space shimmered, abruptly replaced by none other than the Grand Overseer of Avilon, Vladin Thardris. His glowing silver eyes were just as unsettling as ever, seeming to flicker and dance like tongues of flame.

"Who is this?"

"You're flying into a trap," she replied. "The Sythians can see you through your cloaking shields."

The Overseer's eyes drifted out of focus as he appeared to consult something on his ARC display. "Then why haven't they responded to our arrival in system?"

"You mean why haven't they sprung their trap before you've closed to firing range?"

"What leads you to believe that the enemy can see us? I note that your vessel is also cloaked. There are no Sythians moving to engage you either. Why would you bother to cloak yourselves if you thought it wouldn't hide you from the enemy?"

Marla let out a frustrated sigh. "Trust me. They've already engaged us while we were cloaked. Right now they're leaving us alone because they don't want you to know they can see us."

"And who are you that I should trust you? If we were truly flying into a trap, Omnius would have warned me by now."

"Omnius doesn't know."

The Grand Overseer laughed and shook his head. "That is very presumptuous of you. Since you didn't ask me who Omnius is, I can assume you're an Avilonian."

Marla hesitated. "Yes..."

"And you're not a Peacekeeper, because I would know if

you were."

This time Marla gave no reply, seeing where the Grand Overseer's logic was taking him.

"There's no voice match, and you're not transmitting a visual. That means you're trying to hide your identity from me. I can only assume that you must be a Null who somehow escaped from Avilon. And you ask me to *trust* you? This conversation is over. I suggest you stand down and prepare for boarding. Your vessel will be dealt with soon. Thardris out."

The viewport shimmered once more and the Overlord's burning silver gaze faded to the black of space.

"You self-righteous son of a . . ." Marla calmed herself with a few deep breaths. She realized her crew were all staring at her, waiting for further orders.

"Get Admiral Hale back on screen," she said, nodding to the comms operator. "We're going to need a new plan."

CHAPTER 27

"What do you mean they didn't believe you?" Bretton said.

"The Grand Overseer deduced that we're Nulls, sir."

"So? What do you or any other Nulls have to gain by *warning* them that they're flying into a trap?"

"If I had to guess, sir, I'd say he thinks we're trying to get them to expose themselves and engage in a straight fight with a more numerous foe."

"More numerous, but not stronger. What are they afraid of? They have faster sub light drives and warheads that can be fired from extreme range with no chance of being intercepted. They just have to fly circles around the enemy, launching missiles at them until the Sythians are either all dead or realize it's futile and run away."

"I don't believe their purpose is to destroy or drive away the enemy fleet. Based on their heading, it looks like they mean to capture the Sythian fleet."

"What?" Bretton's mind boggled at the thought of Omnius getting his greedy circuits into a fleet of almost ten thousand warships—some of them, the behemoth-class command ships, over thirty kilometers long. If all of those ships were upgraded with quantum tech, it would certainly go a long way toward swinging the balance of power in humanity's favor.

Except that it would never happen.

The Sythians would wait until all the Avilonian ships had closed to firing range and then they'd open fire. With cloaking shields rather than energy shields raised, the Avilonians would be wiped out in just one volley.

"We can't just leave them to die, sir," Marla said.

"They won't. Only their fleet will, and last I checked ships don't die; they blow up."

"And if they do, it will leave Avilon defenseless. Now the Sythians have quantum sensors that can pierce cloaking shields. What if they develop quantum jump drives next? They'll jump right by our wall of grav fields, straight into orbit, and this time the upper cities won't be the only ones whose towers fall."

Bretton sighed. "Even if the Peacekeepers' fleet is destroyed there's still the drone fleet to defend Avilon, but I suppose I do see your point. What do you suggest we do? You said it yourself—they know we're Nulls, and that means they won't trust us no matter what we say."

"I think we'll have to *show* them that we're telling the truth."

"Show them?" Bretton shook his head, uncomprehending.

"Don't wait for me at the rendezvous, sir."

Bretton's eyes hardened. "Don't you do anything stupid, Captain!"

Bretton watched her raise her arm for a stiff salute. "Goodbye, sir," she said just before the visual vanished.

"Marla!" Bretton bellowed. "Where did she go? Get her

back on screen!"

"She cut the transmission from her end, sir," the comms officer reported. "I'll try to hail them again.... They're not responding, sir."

Bretton shook his head. *Damn you, Picara!* Unlike the stupid Peacekeepers, she and her crew actually could die.

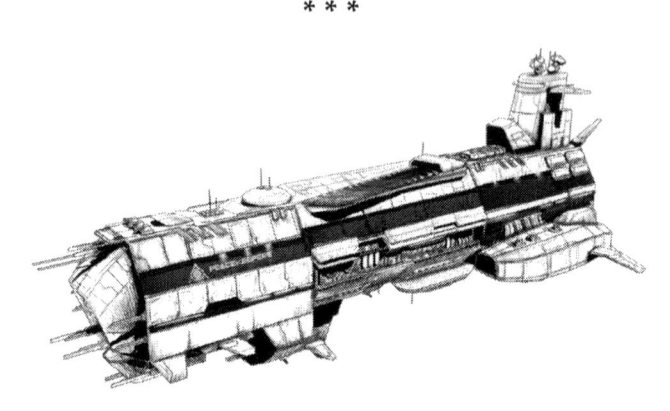

* * *

Hoff watched the star map without blinking for minutes on end. He was still curious about the venture-class cruiser lying mysteriously cloaked on the far side of the system.

Could it be the *Baroness?* Perhaps Avilonian databases were not up to date and the *Emancipator* was a previous name for the ship.

He was tempted to jump aboard them now and see for himself, but Omnius whispered to him, reminding him that his duty to Avilon must come first.

He tried asking Omnius for clarification. Surely *he* knew where Destra and Atta were, but all Omnius said was, *Trust me, you will be reunited with your family soon.*

That neither confirmed nor denied that they were aboard the *Emancipator.* Omnius was being as cryptic as ever.

As Hoff watched, something changed, and the *Emancipator's* glowing yellow icon abruptly vanished from the map.

Hoff blinked, for a moment too shocked to speak. "Sensors! Where is the *Emancipator*?"

"The what, sir?"

"The neutral ship!"

"Checking . . ."

Suddenly Hoff's view of the map panned over to the Sythian fleet, zooming in until he could see the mass of red enemy contacts as individual icons. There, in the midst of them lay one small yellow dot. Zooming in further, he was able to confirm that it was the *Emancipator*. She was just a few hundred klicks below the Sythian formation.

"What are they doing there?"

The question had been hypothetical, but his XO, Tactician Okara, answered. "I believe they used their jump drive to make a short hop, sir."

Hoff turned to her, his eyes narrowing swiftly. "I know *that*, I want to know *why*. Surely they don't mean to attack the enemy."

"They remain cloaked. Perhaps they have a plan?"

"One that will alert the Sythians to our presence. Comms! Advise the *Justinian* and ask them if they want us to do anything about that ship before they give us away."

"Yes, sir . . ."

Hoff waited for what felt like an eternity, watching as the *Emancipator* began accelerating toward the nearest Sythian command ship. His brow dropped a troubled shadow over his eyes as he tried to understand what they were doing.

"The *Justinian* just replied with a fleet-wide update. They're aware of the position of the neutral ship. We are to ignore them. They are not operating under Omnius's authority."

"I could have guessed that. If they were operating under His authority, then they wouldn't be trying to ruin His battle plan!"

"They didn't elaborate further, sir. Those are our orders. Would you like to send another inquiry?"

"No, never mind." Hoff continued watching the map on his ARC display, unable to tear his eyes away. As he watched the cruiser, awareness trickled slowly through him, and he began to sit up straighter in his chair, trying to get a better look even though the map was projected just a few millimeters from his retinas. His ARCs read his intentions and zoomed in on the neutral ship, providing extra details about its speed and heading.

"That's a collision course! What are they doing?" Hoff bounced up from his chair, his heart pounding and his brain buzzing with adrenaline.

He became gradually aware of his crew turning from their stations to stare at him.

"They're going to use their ship as a missile, sir," the sensor operator replied. "That Sythian cruiser isn't moving, so they won't be hard to hit. By the time the *Emancipator* reaches it, she'll be traveling dozens of kilometers per second."

Suddenly Hoff understood what they were doing. The Sythians couldn't see the *Emancipator* coming, and their command ship wasn't moving. That made them the perfect target. Given enough time, the *Emancipator* could accelerate up to a lethal speed. That much mass, moving that quickly . . . they would overload the enemy's shields and cut them in half.

"Sir?" Hoff's XO said, trying to catch his attention. "Our orders were to ignore them."

Hoff shook his head. "Who are they?" he wondered aloud, and hoped to Omnius that his family wasn't aboard.

Maybe that was what Omnius had meant when he'd said they'd be reunited *soon*. Maybe Omnius knew they were going to die and be resurrected on Avilon.

"Sir?" his XO tried again.

Hoff slowly sank back to his command chair, but he remained silent, watching until only seconds remained before the inevitable collision.

At the last possible moment, the Sythian command cruiser fired her engines at full burn to get away.

Hoff gaped at that. The *Emancipator* missed its target by just a few klicks. "They moved!"

"Sir? Who moved?"

"Wasn't anyone watching? That command cruiser *moved* just before the *Emancipator* could hit it."

"With all due respect, sir, we don't have time for—"

"Comms! Hail the *Justinian*. I want to talk with the Overseer."

"Yes, sir."

Hoff heard his XO make an irritated noise in the back of her throat, but he ignored her. Moments later the blazing silver eyes and chiseled features of the Grand Overseer appeared. He looked impatient. "What is it, Strategian?"

"Sir, I've been tracking the neutral ship, and—"

"I thought I ordered you to ignore them."

Hoff bridled at being cut off, but he rallied his patience. "Yes, sir. I was curious about their intentions, so I kept an eye on them. They set a collision course with one of the enemy command ships. The Sythians moved to get out of the way, sir."

At that, the overseer sighed and shook his head. "You think they somehow saw the *Emancipator* coming. Even through its cloak."

"Yes, sir."

"I'm going to let you in on a little secret, Heston. The ship we're talking about, the one you designated *neutral*, just finished contacting me to describe the same coincidence. They seemed equally surprised that they didn't die in a fiery explosion."

"They contacted you? Who are they?"

"They're Nulls, and this is the second time that they've tried to convince me that the Sythians can see through our cloaking shields. But the fact remains that the Sythians have yet to open fire on any of us—including the ship that just tried to ram them."

"How did *Nulls* get off Avilon?"

"Now there's a good question. Spend your time thinking about that, and let me know if you come up with any answers."

The overseer turned away, no doubt intending to end the comm call there. Hoff called out to stop him, "Wait, sir!"

"Make it quick, Heston."

"What if it's true? What if they can see us? We'll be flying straight into a trap."

"Why would Nulls warn us about that? They'd let us fly to our doom, laughing as they watched."

Hoff wasn't convinced. "It's still a big coincidence. We should look into it, sir."

"If there were a real threat, don't you think Omnius would be warning me instead of you? Or do you think your instincts are now better than His? He's watching this battle, too, Heston. I suggest you examine the situation more thoroughly before you go casting doubt on Omnius's plans. Otherwise, you risk making a terrible fool of yourself."

Hoff frowned. "Yes, sir."

"Thardris out."

The grand overseer's face vanished as the comm call ended.

"I tried to warn you, sir," Hoff's XO said.

He turned to glare at her. "Helm!" he called out.

"Sir?"

"Calculate a micro jump to the far side of Firea. Set a pre-defined course that will bring us to our objective, and leave our coordinates at the time of the jump as variable for now."

Tactician Okara fidgeted beside him. "Our orders are to—"

Hoff waved away her objections. "I know what our orders are, Tactician."

"You're planning to run. You doubt Omnius's plan will work?"

"I doubt nothing. I am simply being careful. If Omnius didn't need us to think for ourselves, He would command this ship Himself, don't you think, Okara?"

She had no reply for that. She looked away, and Hoff did likewise. He shook his head and went back to watching the star map. The Avilonian fleet flew onward, drawing ever closer to the enemy formation. It wouldn't be long before they came into range of the enemy's weapons. . . .

If they can see us, we're about to find out, he thought, frowning at the map. He hoped the next thing they saw wouldn't be a blinding wave of enemy fire, followed by a long, dark tunnel with a light at the end of it.

* * *

Dark Space V: Avilon

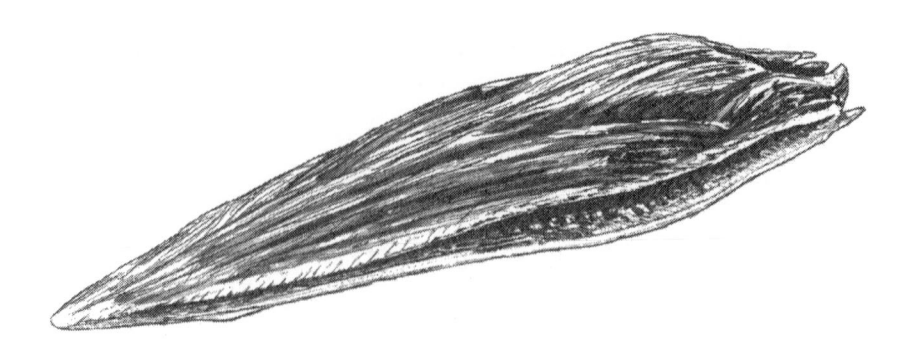

Lord Kaon watched the enemy ship enter the light stream and drop out a moment later—right on top of them. The gills in the sides of his neck flared with shock, and his twin hearts beat suddenly faster.

"What is thisss?" he hissed. "The humans send this puny vessel to taunt us!"

"It is cloaked, Lord Kaon. They don't know we can see them," Lady Kala replied from the command chair to the right of his own. "They must be trying to analyze our formation for weaknesses."

Kaon rubbed his translucent lips together, thinking. "No, that is not it. Look . . ." He pointed to the holographic star map hovering in the air in front of his command chair. "They are setting course to intercept us."

They watched together in silence. Lord Shondar spoke up from Kaon's left, "That is not an intercept course. They mean to collide with the *Kilratha!*"

Kaon's eyes grew even wider than their usual aperture. He studied the enemy ship's heading and ETA, querying the *Kilratha's* computer for a prediction of how fast the enemy vessel would be moving when it reached them . . . and how much energy it would impart in a collision. When he saw the answer, he hissed.

"We must shoot them down!"

"We cannot," Lady Kala replied, "not without revealing that we can see them."

"We cannot allow them to destroy us, either! Weapons! Track that ship!"

Lady Kala flew out of her chair—literally—flapping her glossy black wings and landing on the crew deck below. "Belay that order!" she shrieked.

Kaon gaped at her and slowly rose from his command chair, astonished that she would contradict his orders. This was her ship, but he was the ranking Lord. "You dare to defy me?" he said.

"This is not your battle, Kaon. Queen Tavia has command."

Kaon hissed and subsided to his chair. He had gone too long without a direct superior. He had almost forgotten what it was like to submit his plans for approval before acting on them. "You are right. The Queen must be informed."

Moments later the Queen's round face appeared projected in the air before his command chair. Tavia's glossy obsidian skin and glowing red eyes robbed the child-like impression that her visage gave. Being a Kylian like Lady Kala, the two of them were almost impossible to distinguish from one another.

"What is it, Kaon?"

"Have you noticed the enemy vessel that tries to collide with the mighty *Kilratha*?"

"Are you certain that is their intention?"

"There can be no mistake. We must open fire on them before they slice us in half, My Queen."

"You will do no such thing!"

"But, My Queen . . ."

"Where is Lady Kala?"

"She is on the crew deck, Glorious One."

A loud *whoosh* sounded behind Kaon and he jumped with fright.

"I am here, My Queen."

Kaon turned to see Kala land behind his chair.

"Good. You now have command of the *Kilratha*. I trust that you shall not ask me such foolish questions."

"I shall not."

"Good."

The queen's nightmarish face vanished as the contact ended from her side, leaving Kaon's eyes watering and itching with frustration. Lady Kala came to stand in front of him a moment later.

"You are sitting in my place."

Kaon rose slowly, woodenly from his seat of honor and command. His tail thrashed the deck as he stood aside.

"You do not have long to sit in it," he said, glaring down on Lady Kala. "The enemy draws near, and both you and your queen insist that we do nothing!"

Lady Kala ignored him. "Helm, begin evasive maneuvering! Full speed ahead."

Kaon's gills flared with surprise once more. "You mean to evade them? What is the point? You may as well shoot them! Either way they must know that we can see them."

"No, Kaon. Ships move. That is why they have drive systems, is it not? The enemy will see our evasion as coincidence, nothing more."

"Then they will try again to ram us."

"But by then we shall not be a stationary target, making it impossible to reach a lethal velocity. They shall splash harmlessly off our shields."

Kaon sat in the vice lord's chair that Lady Kala had

occupied only moments ago. His eyes continued to itch and water. Tears began streaming down his face as his frustration mounted. Why hadn't he thought of that? Perhaps Shallah, the Supreme One, had been right to send Queen Tavia to take his place. Had he lost his instinct for command?

"The enemy fleet is almost in range, My Lady," the sensor operator reported.

"Weapons! Stand by!"

Kaon hissed quietly to himself, hoping that Kala made enough of her own mistakes in the coming battle to eclipse his prior lapse of judgment.

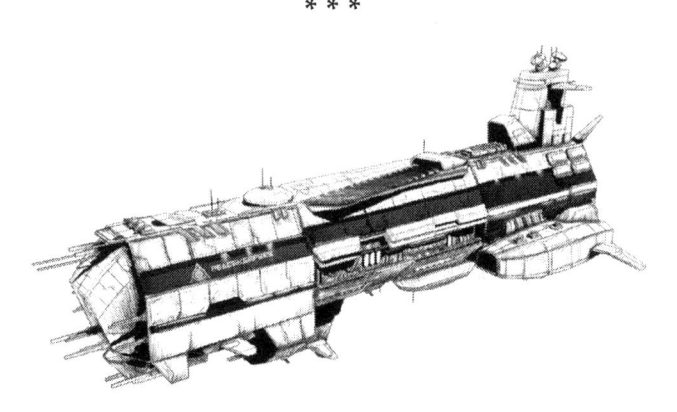

* * *

Hoff held his breath as they flew into weapons range of the Sythians' formation—

But nothing happened.

He had half expected them to open fire with a withering assault of missiles and lasers. The fact that they hadn't seemed to agree with the Grand Overseer's assessment that the Nulls aboard the *Emancipator* had been trying to trick them.

Hoff let out the breath he'd been holding, and continued watching while the Avilonians pressed onward, flying closer and closer to the enemy. They flew past the nearest warships and into range of hundreds more.

Dark Space V: Avilon

Still no response from the Sythians.

"It would appear your caution was unfounded, sir," Tactician Okara said.

Hoff didn't waste his breath on a reply. He sat there, stroking his chin as the Avilonian fleet flew to the center of the Sythian formation, where the enemy's command ships lay.

After just a few minutes, the navigator called out, "We're in position, sir!"

"Good. Hold steady. Start feeding our current coordinates and flight path into your jump calculations."

"Yes, sir."

"You're still worried that they can see us?" Okara asked. "If they could, they would have opened fire by now, sir."

"Transmission coming in from the *Justinian!* The fleet is in position. We are to power weapons and open fire on their mark . . . mark is set for one minute and counting."

"Gunnery!" Hoff called out. "Get your crews ready! Remember, shoot to disable. Helm—make sure we keep our distance as much as possible! We want to avoid any blind fire that gets directed our way."

Without energy shields raised they were dangerously exposed, but space was vast. It was unlikely that the Sythians would score a blind hit on any of the tiny specks now encircling their command ships.

"Crews ready and standing by, sir!" the gunnery officer reported.

Hoff nodded, his eyes on the countdown projected on his ARC display. *Ten seconds . . . nine, eight, seven—*

A bright flash of light illuminated the bridge. Hoff minimized his ARC displays to see what was happening.

All around them, space was alive with spinning,

sparkling purple stars that flocked and swarmed like a cloud of insects. The light show was dazzling and strangely beautiful to look at. Enemy lasers were faster to reach their targets, leaping out in blinding torrents and slamming into the *Dauntless* with perfect accuracy.

"Shields!" Hoff yelled to be heard above the simulated *roar* and *sizzle* of their hull melting out from under them. "Helm! Get us out of here!"

"Jumping in five, sir."

"Shields at 10% and rising!" engineering reported.

Then the first missiles began to hit them. The explosions sounded like thunderclaps, and they heard an ominous *shriek* that went on and on.

"Hull breach!"

The world turned white. For a moment Hoff was afraid that was it. Then stars and space returned. He saw a bright, snow-white crescent on the horizon.

Firea.

Hoff shook his head, trying to rid his ears of the residual ringing from the explosions. "Report!"

"Shields recovering at four percent. Hull breach on deck 22. No major damage."

One of the drone decks. Hoff nodded. Those decks were depressurized, so the damage wouldn't be critical.

Hoff eyed the star map, searching for the rest of the fleet. He'd been prepared, so they'd jumped away to the far side of Firea, but the rest of the fleet was still surrounded by Sythians, caught in the thick of the fight. Hoff saw two Avilonian cruisers simultaneously explode as they succumbed to enemy fire.

"They're being slaughtered," someone whispered beside him. Hoff turned to see that it was his XO, Tactician Okara.

Her jaw was slack with horror, her glowing green eyes fixed and staring as the Avilonian fleet was cut to pieces.

She looked as frightened as he felt.

"Orders, sir?" someone else asked. It was the ship's navigator.

"Engineering—what's our status?" Hoff replied.

"Shields at 25%."

Hoff came to a decision then. His ship, the *Dauntless*, was a covenant-class battleship—eight kilometers long with a crew of over 50,000 drones, and two thousand living crewmen. They had over a hundred thousand torpedoes on board. Those munitions could be quantum-launched from extreme range, and the *Dauntless* was much faster than her Sythian counterparts, so there would be no concern about return fire. Even without the rest of the Avilonian fleet to support them, the *Dauntless* would be a formidable foe.

Hoff mentally selected one of the Sythian command ships from the star map on his ARC display. "Gunnery! Open fire on that ship with everything we've got. Shoot to kill."

"Yes, sir!"

"Helm, keep us away from the enemy. Engineering—activate SLS disruption fields."

"Yes, sir," they said, one after another.

"Sensors! Get me a virtual rendering of the battle and put it on the main screen."

"Focal point, sir?"

"For now, our target. Comms—launch fighters! Have them fly cover for us. I have a feeling there's going to be a *lot* of Shell Fighters coming our way very soon."

"Yes, sir."

Okara turned to Hoff, her eyes still wide and blinking. "You're going to fight back?" she sounded confused.

"Did you think I would run?" Hoff smiled and slowly shook his head. "No, Okara. From what? They can't catch us."

The main viewport shimmered, and their view of Firea transformed into a virtual rendering of a Sythian command ship. It was a massive, teardrop-shaped cruiser with organic lines and a shining lavender hull. Explosions began sprinkling that hull with fire as torpedoes teleported straight to their target. The alien ship's shields flared brightly with the assault.

"Enemy shields at 84% and dropping!"

The Sythian cruiser fired its thrusters, turning to run, but there was nowhere they could go to get away from the assault.

After just a few moments, the glow of the Sythian command ship's shields began to darken and fade. The torpedoes tore blackened holes in her outer hull. Gunners fired over and over again at the same spots, digging progressively deeper. Explosions flashed *within* the enemy ship. Thick clouds of debris spun out into space. That went on for long seconds before the enemy command ship cracked in half.

A cheer went up from the crew. Even Okara looked revitalized.

"Good work!" Hoff targetted another command ship for his gunners to fire on. "One down. Thirty to go."

Okara sat up beside him. "We've got incoming!" she yelled.

Hoff mentally set the grid to center on their ship. A vast sea of red enemy contacts had appeared in orbit above Firea. They'd jumped straight into the *Dauntless's* path.

"Break orbit!" Hoff ordered. "Have our interceptors cover us."

"Yes, sir!"

Okara gasped. "There's over ten thousand fighters out there..."

Hoff was about to order the ship's gunners to begin firing torpedoes at them until he heard that. Ten *thousand*. Quantum-launching warheads at them would be inaccurate and highly wasteful. It was probably exactly what the enemy wanted them to do. They'd waste all their munitions on the enemy's fighters and be unable to do anything to their capital ships.

"Have our X-1's engage the enemy. Hit and run only. As soon as they're out of ordinance, come back and re-arm."

"Yes, sir."

"They'll be torn apart," Okara warned.

"Not if they're good pilots," Hoff replied. "All they have to do is drop their missiles and run."

"And then what? We have six squadrons—seventy two interceptors. It'll take hundreds of attack runs for them to take out all of those fighters!"

"It's going to be a long engagement," Hoff agreed.

The star map flickered with movement, and another sea of red enemy contacts appeared in front of the *Dauntless*, this time on her new heading. The Sythians had hemmed them in on two sides.

"Helm! Adjust course..." Hoff trailed off as another four groups of Shell fighters jumped in—starboard, aft, top, and keel. The *Dauntless* was completely surrounded.

"We need to plot a jump back to Avilon," Okara said.

"Adjust course to where, sir?" the officer at the helm asked.

"Calculate a new jump! Into the Stormcloud nebula. Transmit the coordinates to our fighters."

"Yes, sir!"

"Cloaking shields aren't the only way to hide," Hoff said quietly.

"They'll jump after us," Okara said.

"I'm counting on it. There's enough interference in that nebula to knock out their sensors and comms."

"Ours, too."

Hoff smiled and shook his head. "Ours are better. We should still be able to see their capital ships lying outside the nebula to shoot at them. The enemy, on the other hand, won't be able to find us, or even communicate our position to each other when they do. They'll dribble in randomly, and we'll take them out at our leisure."

Okara's eyes lit with understanding, and she began nodding. "It'll buy time. Perhaps enough to take a few more command ships down before we die."

"Jump calculated!"

"Begin sequencing," Hoff replied. He turned back to his XO. "Who said anything about dying? We're Avilonians. We don't die."

"I meant—"

Hoff's lips twisted ironically. "I know what you meant, Okara. But what *I* meant is that I'm going to win this fight."

CHAPTER 28

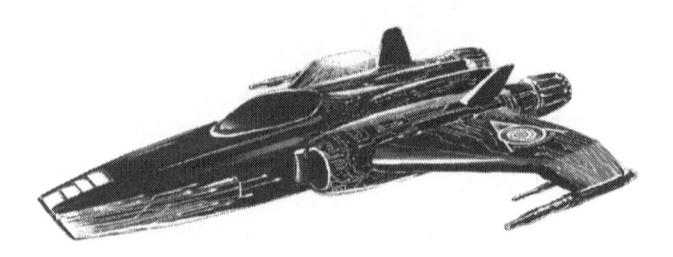

The order to launch came through the comms a split second before Atton saw his launch tube light up like the inside of a sun. His interceptor rocketed out into space, pinning him to the back of his flight chair. He'd set inertial management to 98%, so he could still feel his maneuvers. Stars burst to life as he left the launcher. The planet Firea stretched out below him, vast fields of snow shining a dazzling white in the distant light of the system's sun.

"Form up Gold squadron! We've got incoming!" Chevalier Davellin ordered.

Atton studied the star map. There were thousands of enemy fighters racing toward the *Dauntless* on the far side of Firea. The Avilonian fleet sat dark and derelict in the middle of the Sythian formation.

"There's too many of them! What the frek are we supposed to do against that?" Gold Ten said. Gina's voice.

"Language, Pilot," the Chevalier replied. "Orders are to engage the enemy, empty our Thunderbolts and mines, then head back and re-arm."

Atton did the math. Sixteen Thunderbolt missiles, times 72 interceptors. Assuming all of those missiles hit their targets, and none of the interceptors succumbed to enemy fire, they would all have to go back and reload at least ten times. It was absurd.

Then the grid flashed with incoming contacts, and things got worse. They were surrounded. The contact report revealed there were more than a hundred thousand Shells within a hundred klick radius.

"Seriously?" Gold Nine said.

"They really don't want to make this a fair fight, do they?" someone else put in.

"Cut the chatter," the chevalier said. "New orders Golds. We're jumping out. Transmitting jump coordinates now. Start calculating!"

The coordinates for the jump were inside the Stormcloud Nebula, at the edge of the star system. Atton shook his head, not comprehending Strategian Heston's plan.

"I thought we were going back to Avilon," he said.

"You thought wrong, Pilot," Gold One replied.

The comms crackled with a new voice—mission control. Orders were to keep enemy fighters off the *Dauntless* while they launched their ordinance at the Sythian command ships. They were going to use the nebula as cover and take advantage of their superior sensors to hunt down any Shells that accidentally stumbled into them.

Atton's jump finished calculating, and he began sequencing it. An audible countdown from five began.

When it reached zero, space disappeared with a bright flash. Then came the grasping gray tendrils of the nebula. Sensors were washed clean of enemy contacts. Gold squadron reappeared all around, along with the other five squadrons of interceptors from the *Dauntless*. The battleship itself lay large and majestic above Atton's cockpit.

In the distance giant chunks of ice swirled out of the gloom, appearing wraith-like from the nebula. The *Dauntless* opened fire with bright sheets of red pulse lasers, clearing a path. Ice shattered and exploded, vaporized by the assault.

"Now what?" Atton's wingmate, Loba Caldin, asked.

"Boost your sensor range and follow me," Gold One replied. "We're going to scout ahead and screen the *Dauntless* from enemy fighters. When they find her, they'll have to get past us first."

* * *

"Get us clear of the enemy formation!" Captain Picara ordered. "There's no point in us sticking around to watch them die."

"Yes, Ma'am."

Lasers tracked toward them. Hundreds of deadly bright streaks raced after them, impacting on their shields with a steady *hiss*.

"We're going to collide with something if we don't slow down!" the navigator warned.

"If they don't want to die, too, they'll get out of our way," Picara replied. "Keep accelerating!"

Lights flickered steadily overhead as the shields drew extra power to dissipate the energy from enemy weapons' fire. A thin veil of white smoke drifted through the bridge, bringing with it the acrid smell of burned circuitry.

Someone's control station gave up a shower of sparks and they cried out in alarm. Endless waves of missiles spun away to all sides.

"Shields at 74%!" engineering called out.

Picara eyed the enemy formation. They'd barely crossed half of it. The deck shuddered with the distant *boom* of a stray missile finding its mark.

"They're firing missiles across our path!" gravidar warned. "We're running straight into them!"

Picara grimaced. "We'll make it."

Another *boom*, louder this time. The bridge rattled around them.

"Shields at 67%!"

There wasn't anything to do but weather the storm. Impacts came fast and furious, one deck-shaking *boom* after another. Sythian warships raced by in a shiny, lavender-tinted blur, forming a tunnel around them.

Suddenly, whole squadrons of Shell Fighters began darting into their path, deadly glinting specks that would be no better to run into at this speed than an asteroid field.

"What are they doing?" Picara gripped the edges of the captain's table, her nails digging painfully into the glossy black surface of the holo projection plate.

"Brace for impact!" someone called out.

Explosions roared in Picara's ears, louder than ever. The Deck shook and shuddered and the lights flickered. Then the lights went out and all the noise became fading echos as the sound in space simulator lost power. Picara saw herself float free of the deck.

Smoke poured into the bridge, and a horrible groaning screech sounded somewhere deep inside the cruiser.

Then something big and bright went racing by them.

Picara blinked and squinted against the glare of it. Then she saw it for what it was—it was their ship, sliced out from under them. The bridge and the uppermost decks had been cleanly severed from the surrounding superstructure of the *Emancipator*. Picara gaped, watching as the larger part of their ship sailed on, its massive thrusters still glowing orange as it accelerated onward and slammed into another wave of Shell Fighters. Explosions peppered the ship's outer hull, ripping molten furrows through it. An instant later the ship broke up into dozens of jagged black pieces, and the thrusters sputtered into darkness, splashing fast-freezing streams of liquid dymium into space.

After that, a poignant silence fell on the bridge, with all of them drifting in zero G. They watched out the viewports as they tumbled through space along their original trajectory, shieldless and powerless, and moving at over forty kilometers per second.

All it would take was one more collision—just one more stray Shell Fighter or missile crossing their path at the wrong moment and they would be gone.

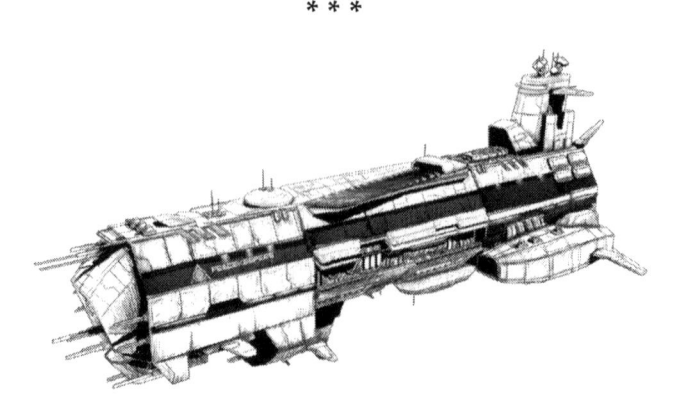

* * *

Another Sythian command ship cracked apart. Hoff's crew cheered, watching a rendering of its destruction on the main holo display. The interference inside the nebula had kept them from being detected so far, while their superior sensors still allowed them to fire out at the Sythians' largest warships.

Hoff smiled. His plan was working perfectly.

"We won't stay hidden for long," his XO warned.

"Let them come."

In order to find the *Dauntless*, the Sythians would have to use their hundreds of thousands of fighters to grid search the nebula. And even if that worked, they wouldn't be able to transmit their discovery from inside the nebula.

"Gunnery mark your next target!" Hoff roared, laughing.

Beside him, Okara frowned. "This is hardly a victory, sir. We were supposed to disable the enemy and board their ships, not destroy them."

"And we will—as soon as we've destroyed all of their command ships. Sythians don't like to mingle with their slaves, so our objective remains attainable."

"They'll run before we can destroy all of their command ships."

"*Run?* From just one enemy ship? You underestimate the Sythians' pride. No, they won't run. They'll stand and fight until their last command ship turns into a flaming ruin beneath their feet."

"If you say so, sir."

"I do."

"What are *Omnius's* orders?" Okara said. Hoff shook his head. "You haven't asked?" Okara's glowing green eyes grew wide with shock.

"Omnius has been strangely silent. Knowing Him, that means he approves of my plan."

"You *assume* he approves."

"It is only logical. My plan will result in a successful outcome. That is what we are here for—to defeat the Sythians and rescue their human slaves."

Hoff watched as a rendering of yet another Sythian Command ship came under fire.

Then it vanished.

"Where'd they go?" Hoff asked.

"They jumped away, sir," the sensor operator replied.

Hoff brought up the star map on his ARC display and he found the enemy ship again, along with the rest of their command ships. All of them now lay clustered together on the far side of the system, having retreated to what the Sythians probably thought was a safe distance.

Hoff's smile returned. "Resume firing!"

"From this range it will take longer to calculate jumps for our ordinance," the gunnery chief warned.

"We're not in a hurry," Hoff said, chuckling to himself once more.

"Incoming! Enemy fighters!"

"The found us already?" Okara asked.

"That was too fast," Hoff agreed, his brow furrowing as he panned the star map over to center on the *Dauntless*. A squadron of Shells fighters was racing in on their port side. As Hoff watched, they swerved suddenly, reacting to the appearance of the *Dauntless,* as if surprised to see it there. Then they opened fire with a steady stream of Pirakla missiles.

A second later the enemy was cut to shreds by X-1 interceptors.

"Brace for impact!"

Two dozen alien warheads splashed across their bow, causing the deck to shiver under them.

"Hull breach! Deck ten!"

Another drone deck. "Patch it up! That squadron was lucky to find us," he decided.

Okara turned to him. "That, or we're not as hard to detect as you seem to think, sir."

As if to prove her point, three more squadrons of Shell Fighters came swirling out of the flashing gray soup of the Stormcloud Nebula. This time they targeted the *Dauntless's* fighter escort.

"Sensors! How are they finding us so quickly?"

"I don't know, sir! Their ships must have better sensors than we thought."

Hoff grimaced. He supposed he should have guessed as much. The Sythians had upgraded their sensors to see through cloaking shields. That upgrade had probably come with other improvements as well.

Shell fighters winked off the grid in quick succession as Avilonian interceptors swarmed them. As Hoff watched, yet another squadron of Shells came streaking in, joining the original three. Zooming out, Hoff searched the nebula for enemy fighters. The ones their sensors could detect were flying randomly through the nebula, searching blindly for the *Dauntless* rather thank tracking toward them. That was a good sign.

Hoff considered raising cloaking shields to make things harder for them, but with all of the floating chunks of ice in the nebula, it would be too dangerous to drop their energy shields. Just one high-speed collision would be enough to rip them apart.

Another wave of Sythian missiles streaked out from the Shell fighters busy dogfighting around them. That volley hit the *Dauntless,* and the deck shuddered.

"Shields down to ninety two percent!"
"They won't get anywhere," Hoff decided.
"For now," Okara replied.

CHAPTER 29

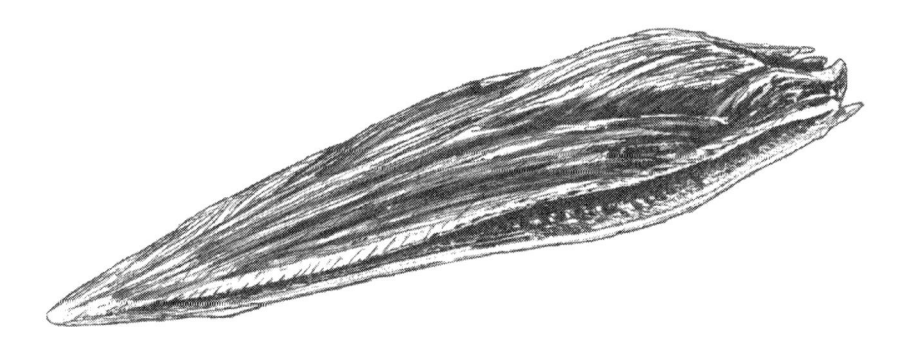

High Lord Kaon stared open-mouthed at the bird's eye view of the battle on his star map.

"They still fire on usss!" Lady Kala hissed. "We must flee!"

"Flee?" Kaon was incredulous. "Their fleet is disabled in our midsts! They have but one warship left, and you wish to run away, as if they defeat *us*?"

"We have lost two command ships, and they are killing a third!" Lady Kala shrieked.

Before they could argue any further, Queen Tavia's visage appeared, hovering in the air in front of them. Her red eyes gleamed, and her black skin wrinkled. "My Queen," Kala said, bowing her head.

"Kala, have your clusters jump into the nebula and follow them in."

"The nebula?"

"It is where the enemy hides."

"We shall lose contact with each other if we follow them."

"Yess," Queen Tavia hissed. "But with more of us looking, it will be harder for them to hide, and we need only stumble upon them with one command ship to deal with them effectively. They shall not remain hidden for long."

"For glory, My Queen."

"For Shallah," the queen replied.

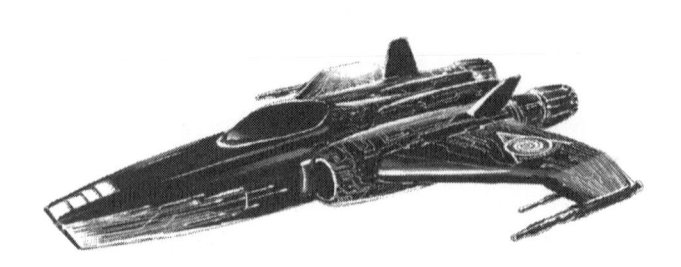

* * *

Atton's threat detection system screamed a warning, and he threw his fighter into an immediate spiral to dodge incoming fire. Bright purple streaks of Sythian lasers and missiles went racing by on all sides, creating a tunnel of flashing lights.

Speakers crackled to life beside his ears. "Gold Squadron, take evasive action!"

Atton glanced at the star map and grimaced. The nebula was a mess of streaking missiles and swarming enemies. Three squadrons of Shell Fighters buzzed around them like flies. As he watched, another squadron came swirling out of the nebula to join them.

"How are they finding us?" He knew there were a lot of enemy fighters out there, but this was ridiculous. Space was *vast*.

A warning siren sounded close beside Atton's ears, and he realized the enemy was targeting him. He dropped a cloaking mine and went evasive. Seconds later the inside of his cockpit flashed with the bright orange light of the mine exploding in his wake. The simulated roar of the explosion reached his ears, and two shell fighters winked off the map.

Mentally targeting the next nearest enemy, Atton pulled up hard and toggled his lasers for an automatic firing solution. Both lasers fired up at a 60-degree angle, shooting at his target before it even came into view. By the time he saw his target, its shields were sparking and failing, its thrusters peeling open like mechanical flowers.

Then the Shell's reactor went critical. A blinding flash of light lit up the inside of Atton's cockpit with a deafening *boom*. A speeding wave of shrapnel hissed off his shields, and then he was through the expanding cloud of debris and cruising toward a group of over a dozen Shells, all of them facing him and firing a steady, sparkling stream of Pirakla missiles. Before Atton could so much as twitch, those missiles went streaking by him and slammed into the *Dauntless*. The simulated *booms* of explosions rumbled distantly through his cockpit speakers.

"Let's see if we can make them blink, Iceman!" Caldin called out. Then came a *roar* and a bright golden glow of thruster emissions as her fighter went racing past his, looping and spiraling rather than heading directly toward the enemy.

A split second later, bright explosions blossomed in the distance, and six of the approaching Shells vanished in consecutive fireballs.

Finding another group of enemies on the grid, Atton followed Caldin's lead and tagged them with his own compliment of Thunderbolt missiles. He launched four in quick succession and five more Shells winked off the grid.

Atton was tempted to gloat, but with hundreds of thousands of enemy fighters still out there, it didn't seem to matter how many they killed—

It would never be enough.

* * *

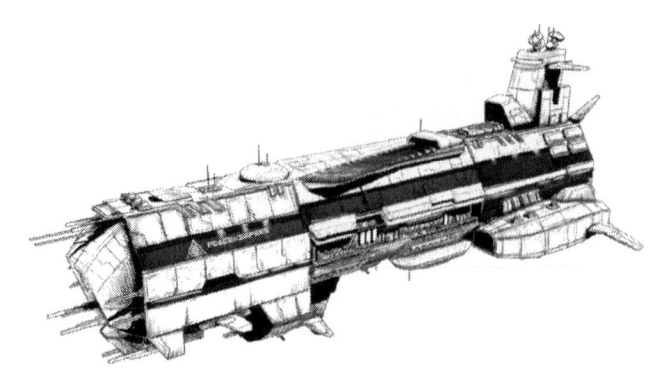

The deck shuddered and shook with a simulated roar of Pirakla missiles exploding against the *Dauntless's* hull. Return fire rumbled, the battleships's laser batteries flashing out in raging torrents and slicing enemy fighters in half. For every squadron of Shells that they killed, another one came racing in to take its place.

Hoff grimaced. It wasn't what he'd hoped for, but so far the nebula was doing its job. The Sythians had yet to amass a deadly force against them.

"Sir! The Sythian fleet just jumped away," the sensor operator reported.

Hoff blinked. "They ran?"

"I'm not surprised," Tactician Okara said.

Hoff glared at her. She may as well have said *I told you so.*

Then, moments later, the sensor operator exclaimed. "Contact! Dead ahead! Five Sythian cruisers."

"Range?"

"Twenty-two klicks, sir."

"Get me a visual!" Hoff bellowed. The main forward viewport shimmered, and a group of five Sythian cruisers appeared, dark shadows lurking within the flashing gray clouds of the nebula.

"Gunnery! Open fire!"

"Yes, sir!"

Bright orange fireballs lit those shadows on fire as quantum-launched ordinance wreathed their hulls in fire. Fat white beams of light lanced out from the *Dauntless*, filling the air with a resonant *hum*. One of the Sythian warships exploded, followed by another, and then two more. The last one died with a titanic *boom* that rattled through the bridge speakers. Moments later, a wave of debris *hissed* against their shields.

Then the deck shuddered violently.

"What was that?" Hoff asked.

"Nebular ice, sir!" the sensor operator replied. "With everything going on our gunners must have missed intercepting it."

"Damage report!"

"Breach on deck six," engineering replied.

"Seal it up. Gunnery! Tell your crews to wake up!"

"Yes, sir!"

Hoff sighed, watching as the remaining enemy contacts on the grid—all of them Shell fighters—were torn apart by the *Dauntless's* fighter screen.

"That was close, sir," Okara said.

"Let's hope no one saw those cruisers exploding."

The nebula grew calm. X-1 Interceptors flew back to point and flank positions.

Minutes passed.

The nebula impaired their sensors enough to hide all but the largest of the enemies ships—their thirty-kilometer-long behemoth-class command ships. Hoff was about to order his gunners to open fire on the next nearest one, when something happened.

One of those behemoths jumped in right on top of them. It

opened fire, and a dazzling wall of pirakla missiles came spinning toward them.

"Helm! Evasive action! Gunnery—give that ship everything you've got!"

White-hot beams lanced out, *humming* through space, and drawing fiery lines across the enemy cruiser's bow. Explosions peppered its hull as quantum-launched torpedoes reached their mark.

"Enemy shields at 82%!"

The enemy missiles drew near, and it became hard to see past all of the bright purple halos they cast in the nebular clouds.

"Brace for impact!" the sensor operator yelled.

Dozens of impacts roared against their hull, some of the noise simulated, some of it real. Bright purple lights strobed through the bridge as missile after missile impacted on the bow of their ship. Fire sprang up in a dozen places. Damage alarms wailed. The deck shuddered and shook.

"Forward shields at 25%! We have hull breaches on several decks!"

"Equalize shields!" Hoff roared. "Helm! Roll over and show them our keel."

"Yes, sir!"

Hoff watched the enemy cruiser on a display that was part real visual, part rendered. The command ship's hull gushed debris from ragged, molten craters all along its length. Those craters flashed brightly from within as the *Dauntless* launched more ordinance, straight past their shields and *into* their exposed decks. The port side of the command ship buckled and appeared to liquify as a raging ball of fire tore it apart from within.

Then, suddenly, the entire ship *bulged*, as if trying to

contain a mighty flood. A second later it flew apart with a deafening *boom.* Hoff was blinded by the explosion. The deck rocked under their feet as the shockwave hit. The debris were too dispersed to do much damage.

Hoff sat in his command chair, blinking and slowly shaking his head. "We didn't kill them," he said.

"No, sir! They appear to have self-destructed."

Hoff grimaced. "They sacrificed themselves to call for reinforcements."

Okara turned to him. "We need to get out of here."

"Helm! Calculate a jump back to Avilon."

"Too late," Okara whispered.

The grid came alive with enemy contacts jumping in on all sides.

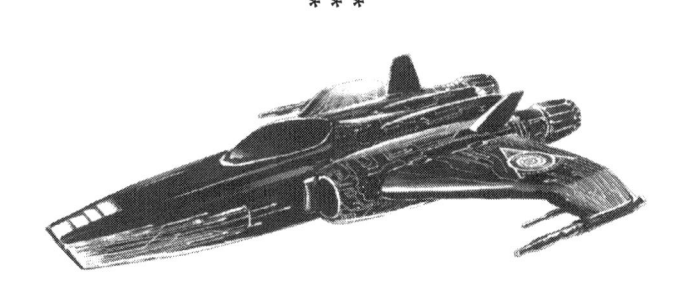

* * *

Atton saw the Sythian command ship detonate, spewing white hot flecks of molten alloy in all directions. Then the shockwave hit, and his shields hissed loudly with the assault.

"What was that?" Gold Two asked.

"They just did our work for us," Atton replied. "They blew their reactor."

"Why would they do that?" Gina asked.

"It's a beacon," Gold One said. "We're going to have company again real soon."

The Chevalier was right. Hundreds of fighters came swarming out of the Nebula from all sides, followed by dozens of Sythian cruisers and battleships jumping in.

"Here they come!" Gold Five said.

Two squadrons of Shells angled toward them.

"Tag your targets! We fire on my mark," Gold One said.

Atton tagged a pair of enemy fighters. His threat detection system screamed a warning and half a dozen Pirakla missiles spun out toward him.

"Mark!" Gold one said.

Atton pulled the trigger. Something *clunked* as his missiles shot away.

Explosions blossomed against the nebula, and a whole squadron of enemy fighters vanished.

"*Ruh-kah!*" Gina cheered, uttering the old Imperial battle cry.

"For Omnius!" Gold One replied.

The surviving Shells opened fire and bright lavender lasers came streaking out. Atton made his interceptor dance. He targetted the nearest enemy and toggled his own lasers for a charged shot. Taking careful aim, he lined up his target, doing his best to ignore the angry *hiss* of lasers hitting his shields. The targetting reticle flickered green. Atton pulled the trigger. Two dazzling red beams shot out, and his target disintegrated. He flew through the speeding debris, and the larger bits *clunked* as they bounced off his hull.

Atton's comms crackled. "Nice work, Golds! Form on me. Lets go back around for another pass."

Pulling up hard, Atton found his squadron already hot on the tails of the enemy fighter wave. Those Shells fired volley after volley of missiles at the *Dauntless*. Enemy cruisers and battleships did the same, closing to point blank range.

Atton watched helplessly as Strategian Heston's battleship was ripped open in a dozen different places. The

Dauntless fired back valiantly, but they were badly outnumbered.

The Sythians peeled them open like an overripe fruit.

CHAPTER 30

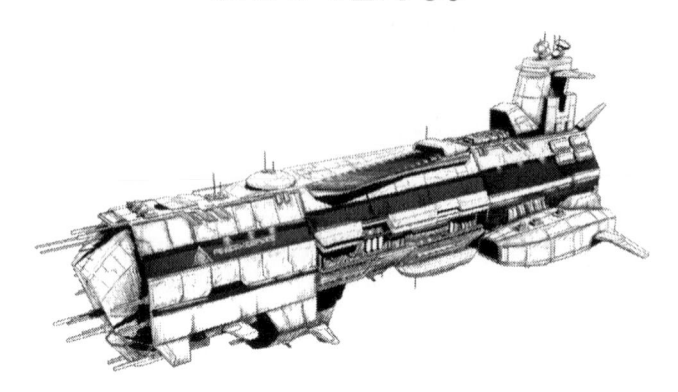

Hoff watched the scene unfold like something out of a bad dream. Explosions blossomed all around them, clearly visible through the simulated viewports running around the bridge.

"Shields are coming and going, sir!"

"Boost the power!"

The deck shook with a violent series of explosions, and the lights flickered out.

"Our power core is already ten percent past maximum output, sir! To increase the power draw any further would risk catastrophic failure of the containment field."

"So funnel the power from someplace else!"

Beside him Okara spoke through gritted teeth as another explosion rocked the deck. "There isn't anywhere to funnel it from!"

Hoff scowled and stood up from his command chair. He watched out the viewports as gleaming lavender starships circled them like carrion birds, firing steady streams of missiles and lasers.

Sirens wailed. Crewmen yelled at one another. The deck shook. Return fire *thumped* and *hummed* from the battleship.

The overhead lights came and went. Hoff turned in a slow circle, looking from one viewport to the next.

Suddenly something changed. The enemy switched from firing spinning purple stars to firing dazzling blue spheres.

"Sensors! What is that?"

"I don't know, sir . . ."

Just a few seconds later those weapons began impacting on their hull. The roar of exploding warheads continued, but this time the ship didn't shudder violently with every hit.

"Power levels are dropping!" engineering reported.

"Did they hit our reactor?"

"No, sir . . . something is interfering with energy conversion and transmission from the core. I think they're disabling us, sir."

"Helm! Where is that jump I ordered?"

"We have to stop maneuvering, or our calculations will be off! We could end up jumping into the middle of a planet or a sun!"

"Power output dropping below eighty percent."

Too late for a jump now. Hoff's eyes narrowed to deadly slits. "They're trying to capture us. Everyone to armory! Prepare for boarding!"

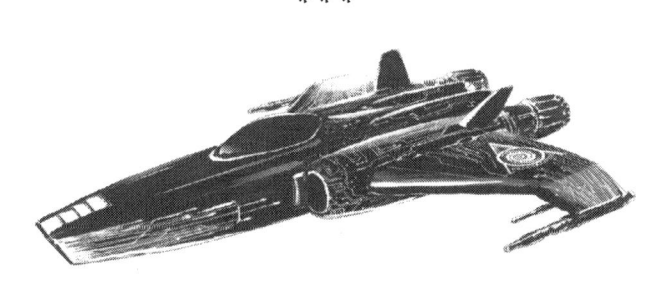

* * *

Atton saw the sudden shift in the Sythians' strategy, and he was the first to call out the alert.

"They're trying to capture us!"

No one argued with that assessment. Instead, Gold One ordered them to keep an eye out for any Sythian transports trying to get to the *Dauntless*. Maybe they wouldn't be able to win the fight for Dark Space, but at least they could draw it out and force the Sythians to suffer greater losses.

"I've got nothing yet! Just thousands of fighters," Atton said.

"Be patient," the chevalier insisted. "They'll be here soon. We need to buy time for our crew to fortify themselves. Save your Thunderbolts for the transports."

A pair of stray laser bolts hissed off Atton's shields, bringing him back into the moment.

"Watch it, Eight!" someone warned. "You've picked up a dozen Shells on your six!"

Atton dropped a cloaking mine behind him. A split second later, there came a flash of light and a titanic *boom*. His fighter rocked in the explosion, and two Shells winked off the grid. The others scattered.

"I've got transports, incoming!"

The coordinates were highlighted on Atton's star map, and he began tagging targets. The other members of his squadron did the same, broadcasting their choices to avoid overkill.

"Targets marked?" Gold One asked.

"Yes, sir."

"Affirmative."

"Locked in and standing by," Atton added.

"Open fire!"

Atton pulled the trigger three times fast, dropping ordinance two at a time. Half a dozen Thunderbolts went teleporting straight to their targets, and the grid lit up with fire. The first wave of enemy transports disappeared without a trace.

"Hah! Take that!" Gold Seven said.

A grim smile sprang to Atton's face as he realized that transmission had come from his wingmate, former *Captain* Caldin.

"Keep that enthusiasm, Pilot!" the chevalier said. "We've got more incoming! Same routine people! Mark your targets!"

"I've got enemy fighters on my six!" Gold Nine interrupted.

"Shake them off!" Two replied. "You're lightning compared to them."

"I . . . they're everywhere!"

"Twelve, go help Nine and Ten! The rest of you, stand by."

"Already on it . . . Sir!" Twelve replied, sounding like he was speaking through clenched teeth.

"I—"

A scream of static followed that transmission, and Atton saw both Twelve and Nine wink off the grid amidst dozens of Pirakla missiles. Atton saw Gold Ten go flying out the other side of that engagement, hounded by dozens of enemy fighters.

Gina. He eyed her fighter as it bobbed and weaved between enemy fighters, lighting them up with her lasers and ventral auto-cannon.

"Motherfrekkers!" Gina gritted out over the comms. "That's the second time you've killed my wingman!"

"Language, Pilot!" Gold One said.

"Frek you, sir!" Gina replied.

Atton felt a grim smile tugging at the corners of his mouth. *You can take the mortal out of mortality, but you can't take the human out of humanity.*

"Can I get a little help over here? Someone?" Gina went on.

"Stay on target!" the chevalier replied. "It's going to take all of us to stop this next wave."

Coming to a sudden decision, Atton began tagging the squadron of Shells still chasing Gina. He launched three thunderbolt missiles at them, and then he *slid* and *twisted* his flight stick to the left, engaging lateral thrusters and maneuvering jets simultaneously to bring Gina's fighter under his sights. Explosions tore through the group of fighters chasing her as his missiles reached their targets.

"How's that, Ten?" Atton asked, pushing his throttle to the max and racing up behind the other fighters still chasing her.

"Well, well, making up for lost time, are we, Iceman?"

"Better late than never."

"You two will be facing disciplinary action when we return to Avilon!" Gold Two reported.

Atton hassled the remaining fighters on Gina's tail with his pulse lasers, while she fired backward on them with the same. Two more Shells flew apart, and the remaining ones broke off their attack.

"I'm clear," Gina reported. "Thanks."

"No problem."

"Three transports got by us thanks to you!" Gold One continued. "Get back in formation now!"

"Yes, sir," Atton replied, banking back the way he'd come and firing his afterburners to catch up. The battle was a confusing mess to look at from afar, but the HUD projected over Atton's ARCs helped by bracketing and magnifying only the nearest enemy targets.

Atton handed his evasive flying over to the autopilot for a

moment and released the flight stick to flex his aching hand. Temporarily freed from having to think about evading all the random swarms of Shell Fighters and Pirakla missiles swirling around him, he turned to look over his shoulder at the *Dauntless*. Once a majestic covenant-class cruiser at over eight klicks long, she was now riddled with molten, jagged holes, her outer decks flayed open and exposed. She lay slowly drifting through fuzzy black clouds of her own debris. Absent was the subtle blue glow of energy shields, and her thrusters were dark and dormant.

As Atton watched, one of the holes leading into the ship lit up with small arms' fire, and three silvery specks were silhouetted in the flashing crimson light of those lasers.

The drones were firing on the three transports they'd let through.

"Incoming!" Gold One roared. "Another wave of transports! Get ready Gold Squadron!"

Atton grimaced and went back to hands-on flying. They encountered heavy resistance. A shimmering purple wave of Pirakla missiles raced out toward them, followed by dazzling streaks of laser fire. Hundreds of Shells concentrated their fire. As Atton watched, several streams of fire intersected on their targets, and at least half a dozens warheads found their marks.

Gold squadron evaporated before his eyes.

"Holy frek!" Gina said. "Where did that come from?"

Atton shook his head, stunned to silence.

Gina went on, "Looks like saving me was a good idea, hey Iceman?" That could have been you!"

Caldin's voice came crackling over the comms a moment later. "Listen up, Golds! There's just three of us now, and we won't last long if we stay out here!"

Atton was relieved to hear her voice. He spotted her fighter on the grid, racing toward the *Dauntless* with countless fighters on her tail. A siren screamed inside Atton's cockpit, and his ship's computer highlighted a wave of incoming missiles. Gritting his teeth, he waited until the last possible second, and then juked hard left, pushing down on the stick for a dorsal twist. The missiles went spinning by, so close that they bathed his cockpit in an eerie purple light. Atton finished the maneuver with an upward spiraling loop that brought him onto Caldin's tail. He pushed the throttle up past the stops, using afterburners to catch up.

"What do you mean *out here?*" Atton asked now that he had time to breathe. "All we have is *out here!* We're in space for frek's sake!"

"They're not firing on the *Dauntless* anymore," Caldin replied. "And if they want to capture her in one piece that's not about to change. Form on me, Golds, we're going in."

Atton shook his head.

"She's gone skriffy!" Gina said over the comms, as if Caldin couldn't hear. "You know how much debris is floating around that ship? We'll be lucky to survive the approach."

Atton was inclined to agree. Despite that, he didn't have any better ideas.

"*Ruh-kah,*" he whispered to himself in Imperial Versal. *Death and Glory.* Atton supposed now, thanks to Omnius, that battle cry was more like *resurrection and glory.* That was some consolation.

Maybe they wouldn't win the battle, but at least they couldn't die fighting it.

* * *

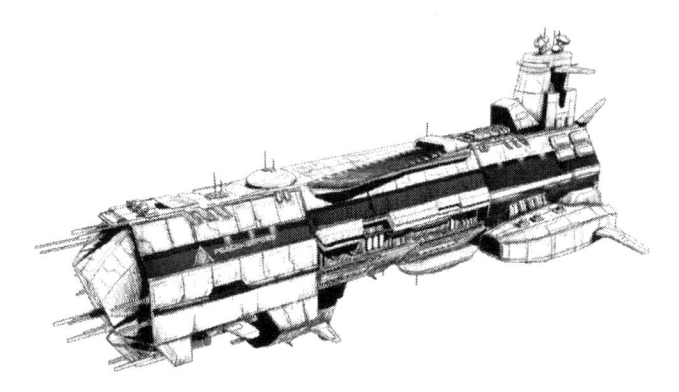

Strategian Hoff Heston stood behind a shattered bulkhead, wearing his assault armor and watching the crimson glow of lasers flashing in the dark. The drones were fighting valiantly, but Hoff knew they wouldn't be able to hold out forever. The Sythians had the numbers to suffer any amount of attrition and still keep coming.

"We should have blown the core while we had the chance," Tactician Okara said as she crouched down beside him. "Sooner or later we're going to die, and this ship is going to fall into enemy hands."

"Omnius could have blown the core at any time, Okara. The fact that he didn't means he's not worried about the Sythians capturing what's left of our fleet. Not only is this ship derelict, but without Omnius they can't hope to control it."

"They might not care. They'll have our technology to study. Given enough time they might be able to reverse engineer it."

"Now who's second-guessing Omnius?" he asked.

Okara frowned and turned away, her armored boots making soundless footsteps as she returned to her position. Drone decks were depressurized and airless by default to avoid explosive decompression of the ship's contents in the event that they were carved open—like they were now.

"They're breaking through!" someone warned.

Hoff watched as a trio of drones came backpedaling into view, firing forearm mounted pulse lasers as they went.

The enemy returned fire. Dozens of bright violet lasers crashed into the drones' gleaming chest plates, melting glowing orange holes in their armor. Two of them flew apart as their power cores detonated. Shrapnel hissed off Hoff's shields.

The final drone remained standing, somehow managing to raise his arm despite the withering assault. Wrapped tight in spindly silver fingers was a pulsing red sphere. *A splitter grenade.* The Drone made a move as if to throw it, but then its legs were blown out from under it, and it's torso went tumbling away in zero G, the grenade still locked in its grasp. That grenade began pulsing more rapidly. It was going to detonate behind their lines.

With only one direction open for escape, Hoff called out, "Charge!" He ran from cover, rounding his bulkhead and coming to a twisted and shattered deck. The ceiling had been ripped away, revealing nebular clouds thick and brooding overhead. Hoff's arms came up, palms outstretched, weapons charged. On his scopes he saw a dozen others running out behind him. Dead ahead lay a milling crowd of enemy soldiers. Then came a mighty shove from behind that ripped them free of the deck despite the artificial gravity fields projected by their armor.

Hoff went tumbling up toward open space. He drifted over the heads of *hundreds* of milling Sythian soldiers in their chitinous black armor. Glowing red eyes turned to gaze up at them as they flew overhead. Hoff opened fire and the rest of his squad followed suit. Streams of red pulse lasers shot out from their palms. A few of them threw grenades down on the enemy formation and they landed like bombs, picking up enemy soldiers by the dozen and tossing them out into space.

The enemy scattered and fired back, but Hoff's squad made short work of them. The trio of Sythian transports that had brought the enemy to their ship appeared below them, all three landed in the middle of a ragged hole that had been blown straight through half a dozen decks. Hoff briefly considered commandeering one of those transports, but what would be the point? Where would they go? It would be easier and faster to get home by fighting to the death. Hoff felt the warm glow of Omnius's approval ripple through him. Even for one who'd already been resurrected, it took considerable faith to put aside the fear of death.

Mentally activating his comms, Hoff said, "This area's clear. Let's get back into cover."

He used the grav guns in his gauntlets to grapple back down. The deck rushed up beneath him, and he bent his legs as he touched down. The rest of his squad landed all around him. All except for one.

"Where's Okara?" Hoff asked.

"Back on Avilon," the man beside him said. "She got hit by shrapnel on our way out."

Hoff grimaced. Now there were just fourteen of them. "Let's go," he said, breaking into a run.

Using his ARC display, he brought up a contact grid and zoomed out as far as his sensors could see. He ended up with a bird's eye view of the *Dauntless*, showing a radius of a dozen clicks around it. Red contact icons streamed into view, not far from their position. Hoff minimized the grid to better focus on his surroundings and look for cover. "We've got incoming," he warned as he ran out into another clearing.

The deck disappeared abruptly beneath his feet and he drifted down, falling past the jagged edges of four more decks before his feet touched solid ground once more. The others landed around him in quick succession, and Hoff stopped to look up through the top of the blast crater they'd fallen into. "Hold position," he said, squinting up at the nebula. A trio of dark specks were flying toward them, growing larger and closer by the second.

"Take cover!" Hoff yelled.

They scattered, diving behind broken bulkheads and doors. Hoff dashed through a floating cloud of shattered drones and ducked into an overturned supply crate.

"Activate cloaking shields!" he said, and watched as the rest of his squad went dark on the grid. Hoff hoped those incoming Sythians couldn't see through cloaking shields.

Peering up at the trio of approaching ships, Hoff saw that they had small, thin profiles that didn't correspond to either the Sythians' bulky shell-shaped fighters or to their teardrop-shaped transports and cruisers. A suspicion formed in Hoff's gut just moments before his comm crackled with a new voice.

"Don't shoot; we're friendly!"

Pleasantly surprised, Hoff replied, "Identify yourselves!"

"Strategian? Is that you? This is Gold Seven, reporting—pilot Caldin, sir. With me are pilots Ortane and Giord."

Hoff heard Atton's voice next. "Hey there, sir. I see they haven't managed to kill you yet—I mean *again*."

Relief washed over Hoff. He watched with a growing smile as three X-1 interceptors hovered overhead and then abruptly disappeared as they activated their cloaking shields. "How did you find us?" he asked.

"We followed your heat signatures," Caldin replied. "It's a good thing you've cloaked. There's a swarm of transports and fighters on their way here. You don't want them to pinpoint you the same way."

"Are they following you?"

"Maybe, but there's no room to land in here. I suspect they'll give up and head for more open areas of the ship. What are your orders, sir?"

Hoff crawled out of his supply crate and turned in a quick circle, watching as the others came out of their hiding places—translucent green shadows moving through the rubble. They were invisible to the naked eye, but his sensors revealed them on his ARC display. Hoff nodded once, as if coming to a decision. "We're going to take as many of them with us as we can. For Omnius!" he roared.

"For Omnius!" his crew echoed.

CHAPTER 31

After both Destra and Atta had eaten their fill, Destra's mind wandered to the Gors and their bloody revolution aboard the *Baroness.* She thought of Captain Covani, lying in a pool of his own blood on the bridge. He was the only one they'd killed. Knowing him, maybe he really had been the aggressor, and maybe the Gors' mutiny had been with all the best intentions. She tried to put herself in their position, slaves recently freed from their masters, only to have their home world brutally attacked out of spite. They were just trying to get home and see if any of their families were still alive, and Covani had been standing in the way of that. Now their fleet and what remained of their species was on the run, being chased across the galaxy by Sythians. It was beginning to look like humanity's killers would go extinct before they did.

On her way out of the mess hall, Destra saw one of the unnaturally handsome, young-looking Avilonians approaching. With his broad jaw, chin dimple, cheek dimples, and unreasonably perfect skin and hair, he was just a little too perfect. To top it all off, he appeared no older than twenty-one. After meeting Admiral Hale, however, with his equally handsome and young-looking face, Destra wasn't surprised.

She knew that most Avilonians looked that young, regardless of their actual age.

Destra grabbed the deck officer by one over-muscled arm as he was about to walk by her. He stopped and turned, looking annoyed. She noticed that his neatly-pressed black ISSF uniform bore the four silver chevrons of a deck officer. That meant he was part of the bridge crew. *Good,* she thought. *At least I'm talking to someone who'll know something about what's going on.*

"Officer, maybe you can help me? I'm looking for Torv."

"Torv?"

"One of the Gors, the son of their high praetor . . ."

The officer shook his head. "The Gors are in voluntary isolation on deck twelve, Ma'am," he said. "We have them all under guard until we reach Noctune."

"And when we arrive? What are we going to do with them then? We're just going to abandon them there and jump back?"

The man blinked his glowing green eyes and shook his head. "Isn't that what they want us to do, Ma'am?"

"Because that's all they think they can expect."

The man shot her a bewildered look.

"Who can I see about speaking with the Gors?"

"They're not talking to anyone at the moment. We've already tried communicating with them. They just hiss and spit at us. Ugly savages . . ."

Destra's eyebrows floated up. "Do you have a translator?"

The man frowned. "Not at the moment."

Destra scowled. "Then how do you expect to communicate with them? They understand us, but we don't understand them, and that's a one-way conversation. They always sound like they're hissing and spitting at you; that's how they talk, but I suppose you weren't aware of that."

"I still remember when a squad of them broke into my house and killed me and my family, Ma'am. Do you really think I care what they sound like when they talk?"

Destra shook her head. "You can't blame slaves for following their masters' orders anymore than you can blame a gun for firing when someone pulls the trigger."

"Maybe not, but you can lock away all the guns and make sure they're never fired again."

Destra snorted. "Good luck. Someone always finds the key and brings them out again."

"Right. Well, if you'll excuse me, I don't have much time for lunch. If you want to speak with the Gors, no one's going to stop you, but a word of advice . . ." The man's green-eyed gaze fell on Atta. "Leave the girl someplace safe."

Destra gave a thin smile and nodded, walking on to the nearest bank of lift tubes.

"Where are we going now, Mom?" Atta asked.

"To see a friend of mine," she replied.

"Your friend's a Gor, isn't he?"

"Yes, but don't worry, I won't take you to meet him."

"Why not? I want to say hi, too!"

They reached the lift tubes and Destra slapped the call button. She turned to Atta with a bemused expression. "They don't scare you?"

She shook her head. "Not anymore. One of them used to visit me at night."

Shock coursed through her at the thought of one of those hulking, gray-skinned monsters visiting her daughter at night. "What? When?"

"Aboard the *Baroness*. He used to come and sit beside the bed and watch the door with me until I fell asleep. He kept the monsters away."

Destra shook her head, unable to contain her horror. "What monsters, Atta?"

Atta shrugged. "All of them."

The lift *swished* open beside them and they walked in. Destra selected deck 12 from the control panel and leaned back against the nearest wall for support; her mind reeled. She realized just how much faith they'd placed in the Gors. They'd been given the run of the *Baroness* for weeks, all of them armed and armored, able to cloak themselves and disappear entirely from both sight and sensors. During that time, the ship had been rationing its food supplies, and the Gors had been slowly starving to death. Being carnivores, they could have turned on the crew at any time to sate their hunger, but they hadn't done that.

"He never tried to hurt you?" Destra asked.

Atta shook her head. "No."

The lift tube opened and a gust of frigid air swept in. Deck 12 was dark, almost pitch black, and a full squad of armored sentinels stood guarding the lift. Their helmets turned as Destra and Atta walked out. Their face plates were fogged with condensation.

Destra stopped beside the nearest soldier. "What's going on here, Corporal?" she asked, noting his insignia.

The man shook his head. "We're on guard duty."

One of the other sentinels turned and nodded to her. He was a sergeant. "Well, hello there, Mrs Ortane," he said. "What are you doing down here?"

Destra realized that she knew this man. He was none other than Sergeant Cavanaugh of the Black Rictans. She vaguely recognized a few of the others with him as members of his squad.

"What brings you to the Gors' balmy slice of paradise?" he asked.

"Balmy?" she asked, moisture steaming from her mouth as she spoke. Seeing that reminded her that it was *cold*, and she began to shiver.

"The Gors' idea. Soon as they got control of the thermostat on this deck they plunged us all into sub zero temperatures."

"I see."

"You brought your daughter here?"

Destra glanced at Atta and shrugged. "She wanted to come."

"The Gors are dangerous, Ma'am."

"So are we. May I see them?"

Cavanaugh hesitated. "I'll escort you there." He gestured to a pair of his squad mates and they took up positions on either side of Destra and Atta. "Follow me," Cavanaugh said.

They started down a long, dark corridor. There was almost no light for them to see by, so the sentinels turned on their helmet lamps. That was for her and Atta's benefit, since the soldiers could see just fine with their light amplification overlays and infrared.

The sergeant led them off the main corridor, to a pair of double doors with yet another squad of sentinels standing guard. Cavanaugh opened the doors for them, revealing a large, shadowy room with high ceilings and plenty of open space. It looked like it had been a supply room at some point.

The sentinels stopped just inside the entrance and swept their helmet-mounted glow lamps around, revealing a group of large, black objects arranged in a circle on the far side of the room. Glowing red eyes turned their way.

"There they are," Cavanaugh said.

Destra walked up beside him with Atta. She scanned the huddled group of Gors. They didn't look very threatening, all sitting on the floor with their knees drawn up to their massive chests, like school children gathered around and listening to their teacher tell a story. Then she noticed they were *watching* something.

"What's that in the center of the group?" she asked.

Cavanaugh passed his glow lamp over a large, gray-white lump lying on the floor in the center of the group, and it immediately began to writhe, hissing and screaming. A few of the armored Gors rose to their feet and moved to block out the intruding light. Destra blinked, shocked and confused by what she'd seen.

"What was that?"

"I don't know," Cavanaugh replied, sounding revolted.

A loud hiss sounded beside Destra's ear, causing her to jump. Atta flinched as well and began hugging Destra's leg. To her credit she didn't cry out in alarm. The translation to that hiss sounded in Destra's ear a moment later—

"That, is the future of our creche."

Destra shook her head and turned toward the sound. She couldn't see anything.

"Stop hiding you skriffin' skull face!" Cavanaugh said. "That was the deal. We give you your privacy, and you don't cloak."

Another hiss. *"And yet you are here, invading our privacy."*

"What'd he say?" Cavanaugh asked.

"He said you're not keeping your end of the agreement, so why should he?"

"Really? I oughta put a bullet between his—"

"Shhh." Destra showed him her palm to shut him up. "Torv?" she asked.

Another hiss, close beside her ear. *"Yesss?"*

"Torv, I've come to speak with you about what happened on the *Baroness*."

"Then speak."

"Why did you do it?"

"We did not want to kill. Your captain started it."

"But why did you take over the ship?"

"You are the Matriarch, and the captain does not show you the proper respect."

Destra sighed. Gor logic. "I suppose I meant to ask what was so important about getting us to cooperate? You had your own fleet. You could have taken your ships and gone without us. Why insist that we take you there?"

Torv was silent for a long moment. Then he said, *"Because . . . we do not know the way."*

Destra blinked. "You don't know how to get to your own home world?"

"Most of us are taken when we are very young."

Suddenly the air shimmered in front of Destra and Torv appeared. His sunken cheeks and protruding ribs made him look like a giant skeleton wrapped in a thin gray sheet.

"Motherfrekker!" Cavanaugh said, and his ripper rifle snapped up for a head shot.

Torv's skeletal head turned and he hissed at the sergeant, baring razor-sharp teeth.

"Stand down, Cavanaugh!" Destra said.

"It's Bones!" Atta cried. "Hi, Bones!" she said, raising a skinny arm to wave at him.

"Bones?" Destra turned to her daughter with a frown.

"He's the one who was keeping the monsters away."

Another hiss.

"Hello, little human," Torv said.

"Where have you been?" Atta asked. "I was looking for you when they made me go to *stasis*. You weren't there to scare away the monsters. They could have eaten me!" She crossed her arms over her chest.

"I am there, little human. I watch you as you fall asleep."

Suddenly Destra remembered her hallucination from just before she'd succumbed to stasis. She imagined that she'd seen Torv there, lurking in the back of the room.

"I didn't see you," Atta replied, sounding skeptical.

More hissing. *"Just because you do not see a thing does not mean that it isn't there."*

Destra frowned, about to tell Atta to stop interrupting, when she realized that something was wrong. Atta wasn't wearing a translator. She whirled on her daughter in shock. "You understand him?"

Atta looked up at her with big blue eyes. "You do, too."

"I'm wearing a translator, Atta!" Destra grabbed her daughter and backed away from Torv.

"Do not be alarmed, human. I did nothing to her."

"How the frek does she know what you are saying?"

"Mommy! Frek's a bad word."

"Quiet, Atta!"

"I speak with my thoughts. All Gors do. We also listen to yours. The translators you give us help to avoid misunderstandings, but we do not need verbal language."

"Then why can't I understand you without a translator?"

"Your daughter's mind is open enough to hear my thoughts. Yours is not."

Destra gaped at him, unable to decide whether or not she should believe him.

"It's true, Mommy. That's how he told me he was a friend and that he wouldn't hurt me. He told me he's scarier than any monster, so I wouldn't have to worry about them anymore."

"You've been visiting my daughter at night?" Destra asked, her eyes accusing.

The sentinels who'd come in with them were all still aiming their weapons at Torv, their eyes wide and staring behind their helmets.

"Her fear is so powerful that I can smell it from a great distance. You all reek of the same fear now. It is not a pleasant smell. Once I convince your daughter that I can keep the monsters away, her fear disappears, and I can breathe again."

"See?" Atta said. "Told you."

Suddenly they were interrupted by more hissing, this time high-pitched and keening, as if one of the Gors were in great pain. Destra's eyes darted around the room. "What was that?"

"I tell you already," Torv replied. *"That, is the future of our creche."*

Destra shook her head. "The future? What do you mean?"

"A new Matriarch is about to be born."

* * *

Atton sat in his cockpit, waiting. His interceptor was cloaked and running in a low-power mode, easy to mistake as just another piece of debris floating inside the *Dauntless*. His hand flexed around his flight stick; his ears strained for the slightest sound. He both heard and felt life support blowing barely-warm air across his face with a soft *whooshing* sound. Despite the comforting warmth of the uniform he wore. The icy darkness of space was ever creeping in. Low power mode meant even the small space heater inside the cockpit had been throttled back.

An endless field of stars glittered overhead. More than a few of them were Sythian warships, but Atton tried not to think about that. He took a deep breath, rallying his patience, and noticed for the first time that the inside of his interceptor had a fresh, citrus tang. Breathing deeply of it once more, he felt his fatigue melting away. His eyes grew just a little wider and he sat up straighter in his chair. The air was laced with some type of stim to keep him from falling asleep.

Atton studied the star map on his main display. Yet more Sythian transports were busy landing inside the ruined outer hull of the *Dauntless*. The firefight in space had ended. The battle was over. For all Atton knew, his squadmates and the strategian's crew hiding in the rubble below were the only ones left alive from their side of the engagement.

Hoff and his crew had moved rubble around, putting up barricades and walls, creating a bunker for themselves with their backs against a caved-in corridor. No one could come up behind them. They just had to hold the line as long as possible and make their stand count for something.

The three interceptors lying cloaked in the jagged shadows and floating clouds of debris above the deck were tasked with providing air support.

"I'm detecting movement on the far side of the crater," Gina breathed over the comms.

Their sensors were much better than those of the soldiers on the ground so they were also lookouts.

"Probably just a few stragglers," Atton said, watching the

same thing on his scopes.

"Nobody open fire," Caldin reminded them. "The strategian wants to save the big guns for last."

Moments later, two small, black-armored specks came stumbling out into the clearing below. Atton watched them with external cameras, not daring to fire maneuvering jets, even though his X-1 was safely cloaked.

Two bright lances of red laser fire shot out from the Strategian's bunker. One of the enemy soldiers crumpled and fell, his grav field obviously still working to keep him pinned to the deck, while the other one dove behind cover. A brief firefight ensued.

Atton saw the enemy's arm shot clean off with a spurt of red, human blood, and he tried to remind himself that these humans were Sythian *slaves*, and killing them would be doing them a favor. Once they died, they would wake up on Avilon, resurrected by Omnius.

"There's going to be a lot more where they came from," Strategian Heston warned over the comms.

Atton glanced up, out the gaping hole to the stars above their heads and hoped the Sythians didn't decide to deal with the newfound threat by firing more ordinance at the *Dauntless*.

Moments later, the grid came alive with movement. Atton zoomed in to watch in greater detail. A seething mass of tiny red dots began flowing toward their position.

"Looks like you *really* got their attention, sir," Gina said. "They're all on their way here."

"Good. Keep us posted," Hoff replied.

Atton eyed the grid, watching for long minutes while the enemy ran through the *Dauntless* to get to them. The first wave of enemies approached their crater.

"Here they come!" Caldin called out.

A dozen or more slave soldiers boiled out onto the deck below, jumping over fallen beams and twisted bulkheads, their weapons and glowing red optics scanning the starlit shadows in the bottom of the crater.

All of them were out in the open and exposed, but none of Heston's men opened fire. Suddenly a bright orange mushroom flowered in the enemy's midst, sending them flying in all directions. One was impaled on a jutting beam. The rest slammed into the broken bulkheads and lay still, while another went tumbling out into space. Atton heard a *thunk* as that one bounced off his fighter, and he grimaced, hoping the enemy soldier wasn't alive to notice that he'd just bumped into something invisible.

A few of the enemy soldiers stumbled to their feet. Then came a withering barrage of laser fire, and they were burned back down.

A cheer rose over the comms from the officers huddled in their bunker below. "There goes the first wave!" one of them said.

Atton smiled, but he decided to save his breath. There were thousands more where those had come from.

Another wave of enemy soldiers came rushing into the clearing below, but this time they knew where to shoot, and they opened fire on Hoff's bunker straight away. A few of them launched grenades and anti-personnel rockets that chipped away at the officer's hastily-constructed fortifications. When no return fire immediately came from the bunker, Atton heard, "Gold Squadron! Take them out! Use your auto cannons!"

Atton took manual control of his auto-cannon. An under barrel view appeared on his main display and he used his flight stick to control it. He lined up the first target, and pulled the trigger. A bright yellow streak shot out, tracer alloy activated by the accelerator coils in the barrel of the cannon. A small explosion bloomed on the deck, blowing his target apart with a gory rain that fell *up* instead of down. A few chunks *thunked* against his hull on their way out. Grimacing, Atton lined up another target and opened fire. Matching yellow streaks joined his own, and dozens of black-armored bodies flew apart, one after another. The enemy formation was thrown into confused chaos with all of them diving for cover and looking around stupidly for the source of the fire that was taking them out.

By the time all the enemy soldiers were down, there was a fine, frozen red mist drifting over the deck, along with bits and pieces of black armor. At least that's what Atton hoped they were.

"We've taken out more than fifty already," Caldin said. "They're not going to keep running out like that. We need to think about finding a new position, one that's less exposed."

"No," Hoff replied. "Omnius wants us back on Avilon. He's about to make an important announcement."

Atton's brow furrowed as he heard that. "So Omnius wants us to hurry up and die?"

"He wants us to make our stand and get out. We can't make a significant difference here."

"I disagree," Atton said. He felt a sweaty surge of anxiety with that statement, and he realized that what he was feeling was Omnius's disapproval. He shook his head and went on, "We could take out a few thousand of them at this rate."

"If Omnius thinks we're not doing any good down here, then I'm sure there's a reason for it," Hoff replied. "We're going to make this next wave our last," he said. "Arm your splitter grenades, one in each hand. We're going to charge out and take them with us when we go!"

Atton blinked, shocked by what he was hearing. A suicide charge?

"Gold Squadron—you can either join us, set your power cores to detonate, or run out and see how many Shells you can take down with you."

"We'll see you off first, sir," Caldin replied, sounding as dubious as Atton felt.

"Suit yourselves."

The next wave appeared, this one much bigger than the previous two. Rather than boil out into the crater, this time the enemy came creeping up behind cover, two at a time, trying to outflank the strategian's bunker. Growing tired of their skulduggery, Atton targeted the enemy with his auto cannon and took out two of them in a puff of red mist. The others looked up, this time noticing where the fire was coming from. Soldiers began streaming into the clearing, firing blindly up at them with a constant barrage of dazzlingly bright violet lasers.

A few random shots found Atton's fighter, causing it to shudder.

Atton fired back with a steady stream from his autocannon. This time both Gina and Caldin joined him. Then Atton saw Hoff and his men go running out into the fray, heedless of friendly fire.

Atton noticed the small pulsing red spheres they held in their hands—*splitter grenades*—and he grimaced. The strategian hadn't been joking.

Enemy fire shifted, turning toward the onrushing Avilonians, and Atton braced himself, waiting for a series of explosions to light up the deck. Then something impossible happened.

The enemy soldiers all suddenly crumpled to the ground and stopped firing. The Avilonians slowed their suicidal charge, and turned in confused circles to stare at their mysteriously fallen enemy.

Atton didn't understand what had happened. Was this some sort of strange new Sythian tactic? Play dead?

Then the Avilonians fell in like fashion, crumpling to the debris-strewn deck as one. Their splitter grenades detonated, washing away the bodies in a flash of blinding light. Atton blinked spots from his eyes. His ARCs polarized, and he glanced at his sensor display to see that his scopes were suddenly clear.

Before Atton could connect the dots, his eyes rolled up in his head. He went racing down a long, dark tunnel, heading toward a bright light. As soon as he arrived, the light overwhelmed him, and out of it came a voice like thunder—

"Welcome back, Atton," it said.

* * *

Lord Kaon watched in horror as the Sythian fleet suddenly stopped maneuvering. They lost contact with their landing parties. Their slave-piloted fighters and cruisers flew mindlessly onward. The star map flashed with explosions as fighters slammed into their carriers, missing their approach corridors by wide margins.

"What is happening?" Kaon demanded.

Lady Kala hissed at him. "I do not know. Our fleet does not respond."

A moment later, Queen Tavia appeared, her terrifying visage hovering in the air before them. "Why are your vessels not responding, Lady Kala? They are colliding with each other!"

"I do not know, My Queen!"

"The Avilonians have done this," she decided, her gaze flicking sideways to study something they couldn't see.

"What have they done, My Queen?" Kaon asked.

"Your human slaves are all dead."

"How is that possible?"

"I do not know how, but sensors do not find any lifeforms on your ships. Only mine, which do not have any slaves."

Kaon's eyes burned, and he began opening and closing his mouth soundlessly, like a fish. The queen glared at him, and he promptly shut his mouth.

"Lord Kaon."

"Yes, My Lady? I mean—My *Queen*," he corrected himself quickly.

"You are responsible for slaving these humans. It is your decision to do that rather than simply kill them. The shame of their defeat rests with you."

Kaon's mouth dropped open once more. "They are not dead because of any failure of mine."

"No, your failure lies in making them our slaves in the first place. The Avilonians are defeated. I shall finish capturing their ships with my troops. Then I shall exterminate all the humans who yet live in Dark Space. Let humanity cower in Avilon and know that they are all that remains of their pathetic species. Soon, we shall come for them, too."

Kaon bobbed his head agreeably. "May it be so, My Queen. For glory."

"Shallah wills it," she replied as her cherubic black face and glowing red eyes vanished.

Shondar sent Kaon a quick glance from the other side of Lady Kala, but Kaon ignored him. He was not in the mood for pity.

CHAPTER 32

"A new Matriarch? You mean a baby Gor?"

Torv's slitted yellow eyes glittered in the bright lights of the sentinels' helmet lamps. *"Yess."*

"Can I see her?"

"Come," Torv said. He turned and started toward the circle of armored Gors behind him.

Destra left Atta with the sentinels. "Stay here, Atta," she said.

"But I want to see the baby, too!"

"No. Stay here and don't move, okay?"

Atta crossed her arms over her chest and huffed. "Okay."

As Destra approached the circle of Gors, she began to make out the thrashing gray limbs of a monster lying on the ground in the middle of the circle. She saw a glimmer of a skull-like face contorted in agony, lips peeled back from razor-sharp teeth. Torv walked up to his creche mates and hissed for them to move aside, making a space for Destra to stand with them and watch. Glowing red eyes turned to her as she approached the circle. Torv, tall even for a Gor, stood behind his brethren, watching over their heads. The small gap that appeared in their ranks was for her. Through that narrow aisle, she could now see clearly that the thrashing gray monster on the deck was a naked Gor, a female with a grossly protruding stomach.

"Isn't someone going to help her?" Destra asked. She felt more eyes on her, quietly staring.

"We cannot help her," Torv explained. "She shall die. They all do."

"What? How does your species survive if all mothers die in childbirth?"

"She carries many crechelings."

Destra gaped in horror, watching the death throes of the pregnant Gor. Her limbs were thrashing more weakly now, and a glistening pool of translucent fluid had appeared, slowly spreading beneath her. "You can't just stand here and watch!"

"We honor her with our sight. She is worthy of it. Hers are the only crechelings that we now know of, and she the last Matriarch."

"The last ..." Destra looked around, her eyes skipping over the odd two dozen Gors standing in a circle around the thrashing, pregnant female. "You mean she is your last surviving leader?" Destra asked, turning to find Torv now standing behind her and looking over her shoulders for a better view.

"No," he hissed. "I mean she is the only surviving female."

Destra's jaw dropped. "That's what you meant when you said she's the future of the Gors."

"Her crechelings and the female in her belly who is to replace her must form the next generation of Gors. If we are not careful, it shall also be the last."

"What about your fleet, Torv?" Destra asked. "You must have another female aboard one of those ships."

"Our fleet is almost gone. The Sythians chase and kill my

people. But even should they survive, there are no females aboard those ships. Only the males go to war. My creche mother is the first and only Matriarch to travel beyond Noctune, and she only does this because your people come and take her from her home. She is the one who convinces the Gors to rebel against our masters. They would only listen to a Matriarch. The Sythians are wise that they do not allow any Matriarchs to be in their fleet, but you humans change that and set us free.

"Now my creche mother is dead, and my sister dies to give life to new crechelings. We have just one female left—she who is about to be born. The last Matriarch."

"Your sister? That's your *sister?*" Destra asked, pointing to the dying female.

"Yess," Torv replied.

Destra wondered why she'd never seen or heard of this pregnant Gor before, especially since she was Torv's sister. "You said your sister is pregnant with many crechelings. How do you know that only one of them will be female?"

"Because, only one of them ever is. For a Matriarch to give birth to more than one female is rare, just as it is rare for her to survive the birthing. Those who do survive are blessed, chosen by the gods to lead us as high praetors."

"Your creche mother . . . *Tova,* she was one of them?"

"Yess, she survives the birthing, but she gives birth only to me and my sister."

Suddenly Destra understood why the Gors wanted so badly to get to Noctune. They had just one female left. If they found even one more alive on their home world, she would become invaluable to their species.

Destra looked on, watching as the female Gor gradually gave up the fight and stopped her writhing. As soon as she lay still, her bulging belly began to move, her skin stretching and protruding strangely in several different places at once, as though fists were punching her from the inside—*or like little heads trying to butt their way out....*

Destra's stomach did a queasy flip, and she looked away, shuddering. Then came a wet tearing sound, followed by loud, high-pitched hissing. The circle of Gors broke and they started toward the dead female and her monstrous babies.

Torv stayed by Destra's side, watching her carefully. *"You look away as if our crechelings offend your sight. Why?"* a deadly threat lurked in that question, and Destra forced herself to turn back and watch as the crechelings were pulled one at a time from their dead mother's ruined belly.

"I mean no offense, Torv. My stomach is weak, and I am not used to seeing something this gruesome."

"Is birthing not gruesome for humans?"

"Yes, but not deadly."

They watched as two dozen armored Gors took turns comforting and cradling the crechelings. One of the adults brought a hissing, gasping little creature to Torv and he took it in both of his hands, holding it up before him and the other Gors. He grinned and said, *"Behold! Your Matriarch!"*

The Gors all roared and hissed, holding up the other crechelings. The female that Torv was holding abruptly stopped hissing, and she opened two wrinkly yellow eyes to look upon her subjects.

Destra studied the Gor baby curiously. It was about the size of a human baby, but its skin was a sickly gray. Its face and body was fuller than that of an adult Gor, but her nose was flat and bony, and her ears were just two small holes in the sides of her head.

"She's beautiful," Destra lied.

"Yesss!" Torv said after a moment. He turned back to her and cradled the baby against his massive chest. "They must eat soon," he said. "They are already starving."

A sudden, horrible suspicion formed in Destra's gut. "Eat what? Don't tell me they're going to eat . . ." Bile rose in her throat as her eyes flicked to the body of the dead female.

"No, to be eaten by ones creche mates is a great dishonor, and Tava does nothing to deserve this. We feed the crechelings, but we cannot feed them from the food you give us. They must eat fresh meat, and plenty of it."

"There isn't any," Destra said.

Torv hissed with displeasure. *"Perhaps you have some humans who do not deserve to live?"*

Destra blinked at him, shocked by the suggestion. "No."

"Then let us hope that we reach Noctune soon."

* * *

Captain Picara had expected to die a quick death; she had been waiting for the severed bridge of the *Emancipator* to collide with something else and disintegrate, but that never happened. Instead Sythian cruisers clustered around them, as if herding them to a specific destination. Moments later she realized that was exactly what they were doing. Their destination appeared in the distance—one of the giant, behemoth-class cruisers.

Picara broke the deadly silence on the bridge to speak to her crew.

"They're going to capture us," she said. That realization came with as much relief as it did trepidation—they weren't going to die. At least not yet. Picara wondered whether being captured by Sythians might be worse than death.

The enemy command ship grew until its shiny lavender hull was all they could see.

"What are they going to do with us?" someone asked.

Picara shook her head and reached for her sidearm. "Whatever they're planning, we don't want to be a part of it. Ready your weapons! They're not taking us alive."

When the distant, gleaming hull of the enemy ship became the gaping maw of a hangar bay waiting to swallow them whole, apprehension shuddered through Picara. The inside of the ship was dark, barely lit to a dim purplish glow. No sooner had they crossed the threshold of the hangar than they felt the sudden tug of gravity. Going from weightless to her full weight in an instant, Picara gasped. Her stomach leapt into her throat and there was a horrible moment of falling. People screamed.

Smack.

She hit the deck. Others landed around her with ringing *thuds*. Some of them stumbled to their feet, while others merely stirred and groaned. Marla Picara was among the latter group. She sat up and looked around, watching her crew rise as dark silhouettes against the alien glow shining in from the forward viewports. She tried to hold her gun steady, but from the way it flopped uselessly in her hand, provoking sharp grinding stabs of pain, she realized that she'd broken her wrist. Using her left hand to pry the gun from numb fingers, she trained it on the doors at the back of the bridge, waiting for Sythians to come boiling in.

That moment never came. Instead, they spent what felt like forever in darkness and pain, nursing painful bruises and broken bones.

Picara's XO walked up beside her. "Ma'am," the other woman said.

"Commander," Picara replied, nodding to her.

"What do you think they're waiting for?"

A sudden *clank* sounded on the other side of the doors, interrupting them. It was followed by a *whirring* screech as drills began boring through the doors. "Looks like they're not waiting anymore. Get ready!" she called out.

But the doors never opened. Instead, a loud *hissing* noise filled the air, and Marla began to smell something acrid that made her head swim.

"What the . . ." She flopped onto her side, a dreamy haze filling up her head like cotton. She drifted away, down a dark, endless tunnel.

Eternity passed in a heartbeat.

Picara's eyes flew open with a violent stab of pain. Black, featureless faces milled around her, red eyes glinting in the dark. One of them hissed at her, and to her surprise she found she could understand what it said.

"You are awake. Good."

Picara's heart thudded in her chest. Her palms began to sweat, and she felt a terrible pressure inside her head. "Where am I?" she replied, trying to get up, only to find that she was tied down and couldn't move.

Her hands were free, but her broken wrist had been immobilized. Picara's mind spun. The fact that they'd set her wrist showed that they were concerned for her welfare. But *why?*

"What are you going to do with me?" she asked.

One of the black faces drew near and she saw a mouth full of needle-sharp teeth. Broad, papery black wings spread from its back and refolded themselves. Picara watched in horror.

"You must help us to understand your technology," the creature replied. "We shall need it to reach Avilon."

Picara's eyes widened with sudden realization. Her crew had been busy making quantum tech refits to the *Emancipator*, but the components had all been ready-made, stolen and smuggled from the upper cities. Her crew wouldn't know how to recreate any of them. "Good luck," she said, spitting at them. "We don't even know how our tech works."

The creature hissed at her. "Then you will learn with us."

Picara smiled. "Learn from what? You destroyed the Avilonian fleet."

The creature bent close to her ear and she felt its warm, rancid breath on her face. "We do not destroy their ships. We *capture* them."

Suddenly Picara understood the real intention behind the Sythians' trap. They hadn't lured the Avilonians in just to kill them. They'd lured them in to disable their ships and study them. If they managed to reverse engineer quantum jump drives . . .

Visions of endless hordes of Sythians swarming into orbit around Avilon danced through Picara's head. Defeating Omnius didn't seem to matter anymore. When compared to the survival of the human race, freedom seemed like a pointless luxury.

* * *

After a rocky night's sleep and spending the morning seeing the Gors and their newborn crechelings to their transports, Destra stood on the bridge of the *Tempest*, watching as Admiral Hale readied the ship for its jump to Noctune. She marveled at the idea that they could jump directly from one galaxy to another. Avilonian technology was clearly far more advanced than anyone had ever thought possible.

"Engineering!" the admiral called out. "Are our shields raised?"

"In the blue, sir, 100% charged and ready."

"Good. We don't want anything to surprise us on the other end. Helm, do we have our jump back pre-calculated?"

"Yes, sir. As long as we remain at the exit coordinates, we will be able to jump back here without delay."

"Good. Then we're ready. Start the countdown!"

An audible countdown started from sixty seconds, and Destra squeezed Atta's hand.

"We're about to see the Gor's home world," she said.

"I know," Atta replied. She shivered and said, "It's going to be cold, though."

Destra smiled. "Don't worry, we aren't going to the surface."

Admiral Hale came up beside them. "Are the Gors all aboard their transports?"

Destra nodded. "I still think we should send a ground team with them."

"No means no, Ma'am," the admiral said, referring to their previous discussion. Last night she'd gone to tell the admiral all about the Gors' plight. He'd listened patiently to her, and then she had requested permission to join them on Noctune in their search for survivors.

"There's a difference between helping someone because you feel you owe it to them and helping them out of genuine empathy," she reminded him. "The Gors are facing extinction. If they don't find another female, their species probably won't survive. They could use our technology to help them find any survivors. Let me go with them. At the first sign of danger, you can pull me out."

"I want to go, too!" Atta put in.

Both Destra and Admiral Hale glanced her way, then back to each other. The admiral shook his head. "We don't know if you'll encounter Sythians down there, or for that matter if we'll run into them in orbit. We may not have time to extract you before we're forced to jump away. So the answer is still *no*."

"*No* to sending me, or *no* to sending any ground team at all?"

"No period, Ma'am, and that's final."

The countdown reached ten seconds and they all turned to look out the forward viewports.

As soon as the countdown reached zero, the world around them washed away in a blinding sea of brightness. It reappeared just as suddenly, with a new pattern of stars spread out beyond the viewports. These ones were somehow dimmer and farther apart than what they were used to seeing in Dark Space. The Getties Cluster was known for being colder and darker than the Adventa Galaxy—yet another reason why the Sythians might have wanted to expand from their over-crowded galaxy. *The grass is always greener somewhere else,* Destra thought.

"Report!" the admiral called out.

"Sensors clear!"

"All systems green! Jump successful."

"Excellent. Launch the transports," he said. "As soon as we confirm they've landed, we'll jump away."

"Yes, sir."

Destra noticed a small, bright orb in the distance. "Is that it?" she asked, pointing to the icy-blue speck.

"That's it," the admiral confirmed. "It's a good thing the Imperium's star charts had the coordinates, or we never would have been able to take the Gors here. I can't believe they don't even know where their own home world is," he said, shaking his head.

"The Sythians probably thought if they didn't know the way home, they'd be less likely to try to get back there."

"Probably," the admiral agreed, turning and walking over to the captain's table. Destra and Atta joined him, watching as the Gors' transports launched, carrying the last of their species home. The admiral panned their view over to Noctune and zoomed in on it. The surface was mottled white and blue with thick glaciers. The skies were clear and frigid, devoid of any clouds.

"There doesn't appear to be any sign of an orbital assault," the admiral mused.

Destra nodded. "Maybe the Gors have tunneled so far under the ice that an assault wouldn't be very effective."

"So our battle-shy Sythians landed on Noctune and killed all of the Gors themselves?"

"They must have."

"Even knowing that the Gors would cloak and hide, and stalk them in the dark? How many Sythians do you think they killed like that? Thousands? *Millions?*"

Destra began to see where the admiral was going with that. "You think the Sythians wouldn't risk that kind of bloodshed. Not if they were the ones who stood to die."

"Exactly. That's not their style. So either they lied about exterminating the Gors, or . . ." He shook his head.

"Or what? You said it yourself. There's no sign of an orbital bombardment. The ice is pristine. It would have boiled off and precipitated back to the surface."

"Perhaps it did, and that's why the ice is so pristine. Sensors! Get me a full volume scan of the planet. Image the result and project it on the main holo display. I want to see just how deep the Gors' tunnels go.

They both watched the main forward viewport, waiting for it to display the results of their scan. A moment later the planet appeared, and the layers of ice became a translucent blue. The planet's rocky surface appeared below that in a more solid gray. Trapped in the ice and woven throughout were jagged, oblong chunks of rock. Admiral Hale frowned, studying something Destra couldn't see, projected on the inside of the glowing contacts he wore.

"What is it?" she asked.

"Sir . . ." someone said, sounding alarmed.

"I see it," the admiral replied.

"See *what?*" Atta tugged on her sleeve. "Not now, Atta."

The admiral continued staring off into the distance, his eyes flicking back and forth behind his contacts.

"Mom . . ." Atta tugged her sleeve again, pointing up to the scan of the planet.

"What? What is it?" Destra replied.

"Is that the Gors' city?"

"The Gors don't have a . . ." Destra trailed off, suddenly realizing what she was looking at. Those weren't chunks of rock trapped in the ice.

They were skyscrapers.

CHAPTER 33

Bretton eyed the scan of Noctune as it slowly rotated before their eyes. The planet's thick layers of ice and glaciers had been peeled away by the *Tempest's* scanners, revealing not rocky terrain as he had expected, but a vast and ancient empire, the ruins of which lay buried deep beneath the ice.

Beside him, Destra Heston gasped and shook her head. "The Gors are a primitive civilization. Where did those cities come from?"

"I'm just guessing," Bretton replied, "but I'd say those glaciers are millions of years old, and Noctune used to be a much warmer planet than it is today."

"So where did the water come from? I can imagine oceans freezing, but kilometers of ice suddenly burying the surface?"

The ship's chief engineer replied, "The water must have been in the atmosphere, Ma'am. Based on the position of the ruins, the amount of ice, and the current lack of moisture in the air, we have to assume that the Admiral is right. Noctune used to be much warmer, perhaps even a little too warm, and the humidity had to have been near a hundred percent. Squeeze all the water out of that much air, and suddenly you have a world covered in thick sheets of ice."

"Kilometers of it?"

Bretton traced his finger over the rotating scan of the planet. "There are high mountain ranges surrounding those cities. This used to be a very rocky planet—something like Roka Four in the Imperium. As the climate changed and the air cooled, water precipitated out and flowed into the valleys, forming the glaciers we see now. The highest peaks are only covered with a thin layer of ice. Some of them are probably even exposed."

The ship's engineer chimed in once more, "Based on the type of ruins, the climate change was either very rapid, or the inhabitants died while their cities remained standing. Otherwise they would have built better shelters from the cold. You'd see domed habitats designed to focus sunlight and trap heat, not freestanding skyscrapers with plenty of space around them."

"A global catastrophe," Destra replied, nodding. "Do you think they were humans?"

Bretton considered that, putting it together with what he'd learned about the Sythians from the human traitor, Donali. "Yes. In fact . . . if I had to guess, I'd say the Sythians aren't the only ones that evolved from humans. The Gors probably did, too."

"Except that their race is primitive and barbaric, while the Sythians are advanced."

"True," the admiral agreed. "I wonder what secrets from our history lie locked away beneath the ice. . . . This place is an archaeologist's dream."

"Still sure you don't want to send a team to the surface?" Destra asked, raising her eyebrows.

"I want to go, too!" Atta reminded them.

Bretton regarded them both with a frown. "It would be

very risky. Volunteers only. We may have to jump out with no warning and leave them behind."

"I volunteer," Destra said.

"So do I," the admiral replied, smiling.

"You're the Admiral. You should stay here. We can set up a live holo feed to the surface so you can see what we see."

He held her gaze for a long moment and then sighed. "You're right, of course, but the child should stay, too."

Destra shook her head. "Not a chance."

"She'll be safer aboard the *Tempest*, Ma'am."

"I already had to leave one child because it was supposed to be *safer*. I'm not going to make the same mistake twice."

"Yay!" Atta said.

Admiral Hale regarded her with a frown. "Very well. Get down to the hangar. I'm sending Sergeant Cavanaugh's squad with you. He told me the Black Rictans were the first ones to explore Noctune. Now that experience is going to be of significant use to us."

"I'm not sure that's such a good idea."

The admiral arched an eyebrow at her. "Why not?"

"Because Sergeant Cavanaugh is hostile toward the Gors. He still remembers them as our conquerers. He could start a war down there."

"I've had him guarding the Gors' aboard this ship long enough to know he doesn't have a twitchy trigger finger. He won't attack them unless ordered to."

"Just because he hasn't done anything yet doesn't mean—"

"This is my operation, Ma'am. If you don't like how I'm running it, you can stay out of it."

Destra sighed. "Very well."

"I'll alert the Gor transports that our team is joining them on the surface. You'll explore *with* the Gors, that way if you do run into any survivors, at least they'll know you're friends and it won't turn into a bloodbath."

Destra nodded. "I'm sure the Gors will be happy to have us along."

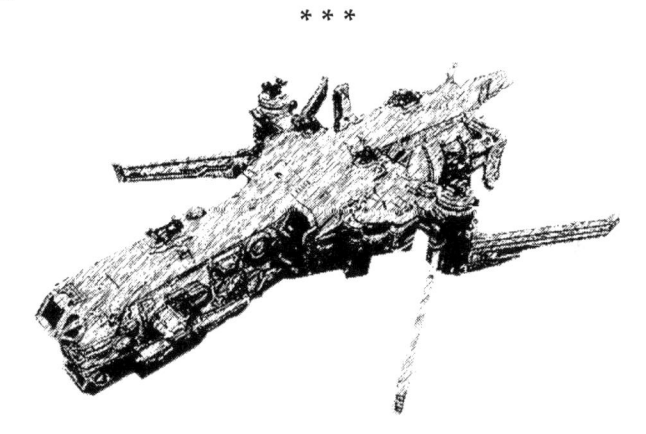

* * *

The transport rattled and shook around them. Destra stood with Atta, strapped in along one wall, surrounded by six Black Rictans. Cavanaugh and his squad were encased in the shiny black armor of Zephyr light assault mechs. Destra wore an insulated black vac suit, stolen from the *Tempest's* old Nova pilots' lockers. Atta wore her custom-sized bright yellow vac suit.

The atmosphere on Noctune was breathable, but too cold to comfortably inhale, so it had to be filtered and heated by climate controls inside their suits. The temperature was forty below freezing, and that was during the planet's dim, daylight hours. The night side sat at a cozy seventy-five below.

Destra watched on the opposite side of the transport as Sergeant Cavanaugh checked his weapons. His features glowed blue in the light of the displays inside the Zephyr's helmet. All of the Black Rictans were armed with two primary weapons—one ripper rifle, and one cutting beam to help them dig through the ice. In addition to that, they had drills to carve tunnels, and plenty of explosives to blast their way down.

Admiral Hale had identified one place in particular where he and his engineers had determined the ruins were in the best condition and not too far below the surface.

The Gors had been rerouted to that location, and now all of them were going to land together on the ice field, some fifty feet above the ruins.

Cavanaugh finished checking his weapons, and he looked up. "Listen up," he said, his external helmet speakers crackling to life. "Our Zephyrs can't detect cloaked skull faces, so we're at their mercy. By now you've all met our exalted diplomat and translator. She is our first and only line of defense while we're down there, so keep your fingers far away from your triggers, and hopefully we'll all live through this. Councilor Heston, is there anything you'd like to add to that?"

Destra smiled, feeling suddenly more hopeful about this expedition. "The sergeant is right. If I had my way, we wouldn't even be armed, but the admiral feels that since the Gors are a race of warriors, they will respect us more for having brought our weapons with us."

The transport shuddered and began bucking under them. Destra paused, waiting for the turbulence to pass.

"Soon we'll be landing on the surface. Our purpose on Noctune is different from that of the Gors. The admiral wants us to excavate a path down to the ruins as quickly and safely as possible. The Gors, on the other hand, are looking for survivors. They have agreed to leave one of their warriors with us as a liaison, and I have agreed to go with them and use our technology to help them in their search."

A few of the Black Rictans traded glances with one another. Destra noticed and asked, "Is there a problem, soldiers?"

"You're the only one with a translator, ma'am. We need you with us in case we run into any skullies."

"First of all, they're not *skullies* or *skull faces*, they're *Gors*, and it's beginning to look like we're related to them, so you should start thinking of them as *us*. Second of all, the Gors can understand us. They're telepaths. And third, my daughter is going to stay with you on the surface, since she appears to be able to understand the Gors without the need for a translator."

"She speaks skull—I mean . . . Gor?"

"She can hear their thoughts without the need for actual words. The Gors tell me this is something unique to our children, because their minds are still open and receptive. I don't know if that's the actual reason, but whatever the case, you will have a translator with you."

"A *kid* translator," one of them sneered. "You're leaving us in the hands of a six-year-old! What if she thinks it's funny to see the Gors rip us apart?"

"I'm *seven*," Atta declared.

"Same difference, kiddie."

"My daughter is not a psychopath," Destra growled.

"Enough back talk, Rictans!" Cavanaugh said. "As far as you're concerned she's the queen and you're all her designated boot-lickers. Our job is to dig, Councilor Heston's and her daughter's is to keep the peace with the Gors. We'll be in constant comms contact with the councilor, so if there are any incidents that our little miss can't handle, we can always patch her mother through. Since the Gors seem to respect mother figures, it might stop them from eating us if we do the same."

The next thing that all of them heard was the pilot's voice crackling through the troop bay. "We're four klicks out from our designated landing area, approximately five minutes until landing. Sensors have detected a strong crosswind near the surface, so be prepared for turbulence on the way down."

Turbulence was an understatement. The transport shuddered and shook around them as if it were about to fly apart. At times the deck leapt straight up with dizzying speed. At others it dropped out beneath their feet, and they felt like they were free-falling toward the surface. Destra expected her daughter to start crying, but somehow she remained stolid and silent the whole way down.

Destra watched out the dark porthole-sized viewports in the side of the transport. Someone turned down the lights inside the troop bay, and the view beyond those portholes snapped into focus. Destra saw a vast, icy plain appear, shining purplish blue in the weak daylight of Noctune's distant sun. Snowflakes swirled in the transport's landing lights.

They settled down with a barely-perceptible jolt and then the troop bay came alive with the sounds of Zephyrs unbuckling from the walls, and mechanized feet *clanking* around inside the narrow space. Destra waited until the mechs had finished blundering around before she unbuckled herself and Atta.

Then came the groan of hydraulics and the boarding ramp began to lower at the back of the transport. No sooner had the ramp dropped than Cavanaugh's squad moved out, marching out in perfect synchrony. Destra took her daughter by the hand, and cautiously followed them. They stopped and stood at the top of the ramp, gazing down on the alien surface of Noctune. The wind whistled by the opening, and snowflakes came swirling in, dancing around their feet.

Destra started down the ramp and immediately felt herself growing heavier. No longer shielded by the artificial gravity field aboard the transport, she felt the full force of Noctune's 1.25 standard G's.

Walking out onto the ice, Destra's boots crunched in the snow. The cold began creeping in despite the insulated layers of her flight suit. Her heater started up, running current through heating elements woven through the inner lining of the suit.

It was hours after sunrise where they had landed, but it looked like the very tail end of twilight. Destra looked up and saw stars shining through the clear, purple-black sky. Looking out to the horizon, she saw a dim blue-white sun. Destra struggled to imagine what Noctune had been like back when there'd been humans living here in densely-populated cities. Had it been this dark?

Turning in a quick circle, Destra looked around for the Black Rictans.

She was disappointed to find them standing in a defensive formation, their backs to the transport, their guns raised and tracking the icy wasteland for targets.

An icy wind blew, scraping up thin shavings of ice and snow and tossing them against Destra's faceplate with surprising force. She staggered, and little Atta almost fell over.

They joined the squad of sentinels to shield themselves from the wind with their transport.

Moments later, a matching transport melted silently out of the hazy sky, a dark shadow with no running lights. The shadow set down beside them and dropped its loading ramp with a soft *groaning* sound. The *Blackies* finally abandoned their defensive stance, holstering their rifles on their backs and rushing up the ramp of the second transport. They came back carrying out heavy-looking pieces of drilling equipment, and crates of explosives.

Destra watched them with a frown, feeling vaguely like she was forgetting something. Suddenly she realized what that was.

The Gors were supposed to have set down here already, so where were they? She was about to key her comms for an update from the *Tempest,* when she heard a quiet hiss close beside her ear.

Destra whirled toward the sound just in time to see the swirling darkness shimmer and then take shape before her. Torv appeared, naked and bony as ever. He bowed his giant, skull-shaped head and then bared his teeth at her. "You honor us with your presence, Matriarch."

"Thank you," she managed, her words conveyed by her suit's external speakers. "Where are the rest of your people?" she asked, looking around. When she didn't notice either them or their transports, she went on, "And your ships?"

"They are cloaked. I do not smell Sythians nearby, but we must not be fools and sit in the open like a herd of *sapsiri*, waiting for them to catch usss."

Destra nodded, as if she knew what *sapsiri* were. She pulled a handheld scanner from her belt and activated the holo display so that Torv could see what it was. The display showed a scan of the surrounding area and highlighted all the living things it could detect as glowing dots. Cavanaugh's squad appeared, a cluster of green dots behind her and to her right. Torv was a yellow dot in front of her, and Atta a green one right next to hers.

"It does not show my creche mates," Torv replied.

"They are cloaked," Destra explained.

"Yesss . . . this means that any survivors smart enough to hide are invisible to usss. At least we shall find the dumb ones."

Destra smiled.

"Come, we must go," Torv said, turning to leave.

Destra took Atta by her shoulders and said, "I'll be on the comms at all times. If you want to contact me, just say my name, okay?" Atta nodded. "And be *careful*. If you run into any Gors, make sure to tell them that we're their friends. You'll have one of them with you to help you explain."

"I know," Atta replied. "He's right here," she added, reaching out to grab something invisible standing beside her. The air seemed to flicker and take shape around her small black glove.

Destra realized that there was a cloaked Gor standing right beside Atta. Her first instinct was to pull Atta away, but she forced herself not to react, remembering that a starving Gor had been visiting her daughter every night for weeks and he'd never hurt her. Destra pulled Atta close for a hug and then withdrew to an arm's length. "I love you."

"I love you, too, Mom. You'd better go. The Gors are in a hurry to find their families."

Destra smiled and nodded. Before she turned to leave she walked up to Sergeant Cavanaugh. "Good luck," she said.

Cavanaugh set the crate of explosives he was carrying down and nodded to her.

"Be careful out there, Councilor. Keep your comms open."

"I will," Destra replied, leaving Cavanaugh and his team, and Atta, to run after Torv. The Gor had already disappeared in the swirling darkness, but she found him easily enough with her scanner. A solitary gray silhouette appeared in the distance. The icy surface of Noctune gleamed with reflected light from the sun. Destra's footsteps crunched loudly as she ran.

As soon as she reached Torv's side, he turned to her and said, *"We are not far from the nearest tunnel entrance."*

"Good," Destra panted. She was forced to jog beside the Gor to keep up with his longer strides, and she was already out of breath from running.

Torv's idea of *not far* turned out to be another twenty minutes of jogging. By the time they reached the entrance of the tunnel, Atta called to say she missed her mom, and that the grumpy soldiers had just started drilling through the ice.

Torv waited for them to finish speaking. Destra ended the call and turned toward the gaping black entrance of a Gor tunnel. She saw the air shimmering endlessly as armored Gors de-cloaked and descended into the tunnel. A few of them carried Gor crechelings swaddled in ISSF uniforms.

Destra stopped in front of Torv. He was waiting to one side of the tunnel, his slitted yellow eyes scanning the horizon.

"This is it?" she asked.

He nodded.

Destra turned to peer into the tunnel. It descended steeply below the ice, and disappeared into darkness. Pulling the glow stick off her belt, Destra shone it into the tunnel. A dozen Gors appeared, waiting just inside the entrance.

Torv turned and entered the tunnel. Destra followed, walking between his creche mates. They hissed at her as she passed by. Destra grimaced, unsure whether those hisses were good or bad.

Once they reached the front of the group, they began following the tunnel down. It dropped steeply, and Destra had to struggle to keep her footing. The higher gravity on Noctune helped her not to slip, but it did nothing to help her shuddering legs.

Her glow stick only lit about a dozen meters of the tunnel before dissipating into darkness, but it was enough to see that the walls of the tunnel were whorled and furrowed with claw marks. Destra ran her hand along the nearest wall, feeling the grooves through her gloves. She remembered Torv saying that the Gors had dug their tunnels hundreds of meters below the surface, and she began to wonder how they'd accomplished that using just their bare hands and feet.

Another half an hour later, Destra's legs were burning and shaking so much from the continued exertion of walking downhill that she was tempted to sit and slide the rest of the way.

Her comm piece trilled in her ear, distracting her. The call was from Admiral Hale aboard the *Tempest*.

"Hello, Admiral," she said, gasping for breath. She was exhausted.

"Councilor, why haven't you made contact yet?"

"I've just entered the tunnels with the Gors," she said. "No sign of survivors yet."

"Our sensors detect you are very close to some of the ruins. Right on top of them actually. The resolution isn't clear enough at this range to pick out whatever tunnel you're walking in, but it looks like you're going to discover the ruins before Sergeant Cavanaugh does.

Destra felt excitement trickle through her, breathing new life into her weary body. "I'll keep you posted if I find anything down here besides ice."

"Be sure that you do. Hale out."

The comm went dead. Destra studied the walls and floor with her glow stick as they descended. There was no sign of any ruins. . . .

Suddenly she ran into something solid. She cried out, and slitted yellow eyes turned on her. She'd run into Torv. He hissed and pointed at the ground in front of them. Destra walked around him and he blocked her way with one thickly muscled arm. A deep, black hole had opened up in front of them. Beyond that, the tunnel came to a dead end. Shining her glow stick into the hole, Destra saw that the walls were smooth and sheer all the way down. It was a narrow chasm between two opposing walls of ice.

"We must climb down," Torv said. As she watched, he lowered himself into the hole, using his arms and legs to push against the walls and slow his descent. Thick cords of muscle stood out on his arms as he slid down into darkness. Destra shook her head and called after him, "I can't do that!"

Torv gave no reply. He'd already dropped out of sight. Destra turned and came face to stomach with another Gor, this one armored and glaring down at her with the glowing red optics in his helmet. She held her ground, determined not to be afraid.

The Gor held out his arms and hissed at her. *"Climb on, human."*

Destra blinked up at him. Hesitantly, she climbed up his torso and wrapped her arms around his neck. Then the Gor eased them down into the chasm, just as Torv had done. Unlike Torv's silent descent, this Gor's armor scraped long furrows into the ice, making a noisy *screech* all the way down. The chasm abruptly widened at the bottom, and they fell for the last ten feet, landing with a noisy *crunch*.

The icy ground shuddered with their landing, and little bits of snow fell from the ceiling, glittering in the light of Destra's glow stick.

She climbed off the Gor and struggled to find her footing. Here the ice was slick and smooth underfoot. They were standing in some type of cavern, crisscrossed with a maze of strange, leaning pillars of ice that connected the floor to the ceiling and opposing walls to each other. Destra wondered if this area had been dug like that for a reason—to prevent cave-ins perhaps.

Then she noticed how smooth the walls and floor were. Absent were the Gor's claw marks. Her eyes narrowed at that, and she wondered how the Gors had dug this tunnel if they hadn't used their claws. Realization dawned, and suddenly she saw all those leaning pillars of ice for what they really were—

Twisted girders and fallen beams. They were coated with ice, but otherwise too straight and angular to be either natural or carved by Gors. The walls and floor weren't gouged with Gor claw marks because they hadn't dug this tunnel. This one was formed by the crumpled shell of an ancient skyscraper.

"Torv!" Destra said, looking around for him.

"Yesss?"

He was standing right behind her. "Do you know what this is?" she asked.

"*It is Noctune. Are you feeling well, Matriarch?*"

"No, I mean . . . *this!*" She gestured to their surroundings. "Your people didn't dig this tunnel, Torv."

"*No. It is a natural opening in the ice.*"

Destra regarded the Gor with a wild grin. "It isn't natural, either. You're standing inside the ruins of an ancient civilization. *Your* civilization, Torv, and probably ours, too."

The Gor's expression grew slack and he turned in a slow circle to study their surroundings. *"I do not see any . . . ruins. Only ice. And we only meet humans when the Sythians force us to fight and kill you. How can you say that humans once live on Noctune?"*

Destra's smile broadened. "Why else would Gors be bipeds? You are humanoids with two eyes, ears, arms and legs. You have hands with opposable *thumbs.* If you had evolved all on your own, it would be a great coincidence that your species so closely resembles ours."

"I do not understand," Torv said.

"Just trust me. We're your creche mates, Torv. We always have been."

Torv hissed at that. *"Then the Sythians force us to kill ourselves during the war. This only adds to the blood price that they owe."*

"Yes," Destra agreed. She decided not to mention that the Sythians were also related to both Gors and Humans. Instead, she put a comm call through to the *Tempest,* intending to inform the admiral of her discovery.

The only answer was a *crackle* and *hiss* of static, followed by an error *beep* and an audible announcement from her comms: "Connection failed."

Destra grimaced. There must have been too much interference. She called up to Sergeant Cavanaugh instead, but again, came the static followed by the error tone and explanation.

Feeling a sudden pang of worry for Atta, she tried to contact her daughter. When the connection failed for a third time, she tried running a diagnostic to determine the problem.

"What is wrong?" Torv asked.

"I can't reach anyone on the comms," she said.

The diagnostic reported the cause of the problem as *unknown interference*.

"Frek," she said, and glanced up through the dark chasm over their heads, wondering if the ruins were somehow responsible for that interference. Then something occurred to her. Gor telepathy was supposed to work on quantum principles, and it had an incredible range—up to ten light years.

Destra turned to Torv. "Can you contact your creche mate, the Gor we left on the surface? There's something wrong with my comm system."

Torv hissed at her. "I cannot, my Matriarch. That is why we must *search* for survivors rather than simply call out to them. The tunnels interfere with our ability to communicate unless we are very near to one another."

"I guess that explains why I can't contact anyone . . ." Destra went back to peering up at the dark chasm over their heads. "Is there any way you can get me back to the surface?"

"We must keep searching for survivors, my Matriarch. There is no time to waste."

"What if we run into trouble?" she asked, trying a different approach. "We're all alone down here, and I can't call for help." Having said that, Destra realized that the rest of the Gors hadn't joined them at the bottom of the chasm. "Where are the others, Torv?"

"They go to hunt. The crechelings shall not survive if they do not eat soon. The others remain to guard the entrance of this tunnel and make sure that nothing stalks us from behind."

Struck with a sudden insight, Destra said, "Can you tell one of them to go back to the transports?"

"Yess, but why?"

"Have him go tell my daughter that I'm fine. Tell her that I will be out of touch for a while, but that hopefully I'll see her soon. Then tell her that we've found the ruins, and they should all join us down here. The Gor you sent will show them the way."

"I tell them, but we cannot wait for them to arrive. We must go on."

Destra nodded. "That's fine. I'll go with you. That was our agreement."

"You have much honor, my Matriarch. We shall not soon forget your concern for our fate."

"Let's keep looking," she said, and began picking her way carefully across the slick, icy floor.

Twice she slipped and fell, sending sparks shooting up her spine. The third time a strong arm reached out and picked her up by one arm. Destra's shoulder popped painfully and she cried out. Torv grunted and slung her over his back. She wrapped her arms around his neck. Despite her throbbing shoulder, she found she was grateful for his intervention. For the first time in what felt like forever she was able to catch her breath and rest her burning legs.

Destra eyed the icy girders and beams as the Gors ducked and climbed over them. She scanned their surroundings, drinking in every oddly-shaped lump on the ground, trying to imagine what lay underneath the layers of ice.

They spent a long time negotiating the cavern before coming to the end of it. The ground sloped away sharply beneath their feet, and the Gors jumped down into what appeared to be another, lower level of the ruins. Here the ceiling was close to their heads and the space between the walls was much narrower.

Claustrophobic.

Destra began to notice the sound of her anxious breathing reverberating inside her helmet. Ice-covered debris crowded every alcove and aisle. Here and there Destra noticed a return of the Gors' claw marks, where they had been forced to widen the narrowest spaces. As they walked through just such a space, Destra noticed that the ice had been dug away, all the way down to the rusted alloy beams of the ruins.

Destra climbed off Torv's back to get a closer look. As she waved her glow stick around, she began to pick out familiar details. There was an overturned chair, legs poking up out of the ice; a desk; a scrap of blue cloth; and a small gleaming bit of metal, half-buried in the ice. Something red and shiny glinted in the center of it, catching her eye. Destra walked up to it and went down on her haunches to see what it was.

It was a pendant. The shiny red part was some type of gemstone. Destra grabbed the protruding edge and tried to pull the pendant from the ice. It refused to yield. Setting her glow stick down, she used both hands and put her back into it.

Suddenly the pendant broke free and she fell over. Destra sat up and held the artifact up to the light. The edges were worn down, but it was still vaguely recognizable as a six-sided star.

Destra blinked at it in shock, suddenly realizing what it was.

"What is that?" Torv asked.

"This?" Destra asked, turning to Torv with a broad smile. She shook the pendant at him for emphasis. "This is proof that humans used to live here, Torv. It's a Star of Etherus."

"A star of . . ."

"An Etherian symbol," Destra explained. "A symbol of our god."

CHAPTER 34

"Connection failed, sir. There's too much interference."

"That's impossible. What interference?" Bretton asked.

The comms operator shook his head. "I don't know what to tell you, sir. There's some type of disruption field emanating from the entire planet."

"A naturally occurring disruption field . . ." Bretton's tone made it clear what he thought about that.

"Maybe, maybe not. The ruins aren't natural. Perhaps there's more than just rubble buried beneath the ice."

Bretton frowned. "Contact our team on the surface and see if they've heard from the councilor."

"Yes, sir."

Moments later the reply came back, "No, sir, they haven't. They've been trying to reach her, too."

"How's their excavation going?"

"Slow. They're still at least twenty feet away from the ruins, sir."

"Send them the councilor's coordinates and tell them to go investigate. The tunnels the councilor found will get them to the ruins faster, anyway. Just make sure you warn them about the interference. I don't want to lose contact with everyone down there."

A moment later the comms operator replied, "They acknowledge your orders, sir. They'll let us know when they arrive at the specified coordinates."

"Good." Bretton spent the next half an hour pacing the deck and waiting for the ground team to make contact once more. When they finally did, they explained that they had run into a Gor messenger from the councilor's search party. She was okay, and she'd found the ruins.

Bretton ordered them to make their way cautiously into the tunnels and see if they could catch up with her. Another twenty minutes later the *Tempest* received a static-filled message from Sergeant Cavanaugh saying that they were about to drop out of comms range. No sign of the ruins yet. Bretton ordered them to continue, but to send someone back to the surface with an update as soon as they found the ruins.

Bretton sighed, resigned to more waiting. He began to question his decision to stay aboard the *Tempest*. Space was empty. They'd been sitting out in the open for hours, their shields powered, their jump back to the rendezvous in the Adventa Galaxy pre-calculated. Farah was no doubt equally anxious and bored on her end, waiting aboard the *Baroness* for him the return.

Thanks to the Sythian ambush in Dark Space, and Captain Picara's suicidal plan to warn the Avilonian fleet, she would not be joining them there.

Bretton scanned the contact report at the bottom of the grid. Still no sign of Sythians. He turned away from the captain's table, about to retire to his quarters—

Then a loud siren split the air. Bretton's heart leapt against his sternum with a painful *thud*. It took him a second to recognize the siren as the enemy contact alarm.

"Red alert!" he roared. The lights on deck dimmed to a bloody red, and Bretton hastily spun back to the captain's table. Space was already crowded with enemy contacts—hundreds of them. Dozens more were appearing with every second that passed. The classifications were *unknown*, but Bretton could recognize the shape of those warships anywhere. His eyes flew wide and he gritted his teeth. "Jump away! Jump away!"

The deck rattled and shook with a mighty *boom* as something exploded against the *Tempest's* viewports. *Too late.*

The world washed away in a dazzling flash of light.

"Avilonians, sir!" someone shouted over the roar of the explosion.

"Helm! Get us out of here!" Bretton roared.

"I can't! Their disruption fields are already powered. We're trapped!"

Another explosion shook the deck and Bretton's eyes flew wide with horror. Omnius must have been watching the refugees they'd picked up more closely than he'd thought.

"Full speed ahead!" he said. "Head for the planet!"

The deck shook once more, and this time it didn't stop shaking. The roar of explosions went on endlessly, seeming to echo all around them. The bloody glow of emergency lights flickered on overhead.

"Shields at 46%! Dropping fast!"

"We'll never make it to the planet, sir!"

"Hail them! Tell them we surrender!"

"They're not responding!"

Bretton blinked, shocked by the sudden turn of events. This couldn't be how his life finally ended.

Then a still, small voice echoed inside his head, saying, *You chose this, Bretton, remember?*

It took him a moment to recognize that voice, and another moment to realize what that meant.

It was impossible. He'd been *de-linked!* Yet somehow Omnius was speaking to him anyway, reaching out across more than a thousand light years to taunt him one last time. The booming roar of explosions faded to insignificance in the wake of that revelation.

It's not too late to repent, Bretton.

His eyes narrowed and he turned in a dreamy haze to watch people fighting for their lives all around him while he just looked on, wide-eyed and staring, unable to believe the extent of his own naivete. Of course it couldn't be that easy to just *de-link*. Why would Omnius allow rebel Nulls to hide right under his nose on *his* planet, using the freedom that he gave them to plot his demise?

That would be uncharacteristically stupid of him. Bretton realized just how futile all of it had been. There could be no freedom from Omnius. The only freedom from him was in death, and the AI who-would-be-god had already found a way to cheat that.

You're very smart for a Null, Bretton. Why should I let the Nulls have the freedom to spoil paradise for all of my other children?

Why don't you just kill us if you're not going to set us free? The choosing is pointless! My son died for nothing, you heartless bot!

Not everyone shares your dramatic view of life—give us freedom or give us death! No, most people would rather live, even if they claim they want to die. That's why the majority of Nulls become Etherians on their death beds. The memory of their miserable lives in the Null Zone serves to keep them in line for the rest of eternity. If I did away with the Null Zone and The Choosing, how could I educate all of those recalcitrant fools who cling to their freedom and individuality as if it's actually a good thing?

Bretton shook his head, aghast.

People need the constant reminder of what their freedom brings to keep them working together for the common good. Sooner or later, even the most rebellious Nulls have a change of heart, and as for the few who don't, well . . . why should I let them die? That wouldn't be very loving of me, now would it?

What are you talking about?

You can't get away from me, Bretton. Soon, you're going to wake up on Avilon, alive and well, but . . . better-adjusted than you used to be.

Cold dread danced around the edges of Bretton's awareness, but he refused to believe his growing suspicions.

Omnius ended his willful ignorance with what he said next. *I'm going to make you a drone, Bretton. Don't worry, at least you'll get to see your son again. Like father like son, they say. He was even more rebellious than you.*

Bretton let out an inhuman roar, screaming at the top of his lungs. His crew turned and stared at him.

"Sir?" one of them asked.

He shook his head, unable to voice his rage or to explain what Omnius had just revealed to him. What would be the point? They were all going to find out soon enough.

"They've stopped firing for the moment, sir," the operator at the engineering station said. "Shields are holding at 10%. We might make it to the planet if they hold their fire long enough . . . Perhaps we should have the crew standing by at the escape pods just in case."

"Give the order," he croaked.

They won't make it, Omnius said.

Suddenly Bretton remembered his people on the surface, and then he wished he hadn't. Omnius could read his thoughts.

Yes, they're out of range. Unfortunately the same interference that cut them off from you has prevented me from locating them so I can shut them down.

Shut them down . . . Bretton shivered. Omnius thought of them all like bots that he could turn on or off at a whim.

It doesn't matter whether or not I kill them. They're trapped on an inhospitable world with only a few short-ranged transports to escape. Sooner or later they'll die. If they're lucky it will be of natural causes. If they're not, the Gors will eat them.

You're a monster.

I'm a god.

No, you're not. We created you.

Did you? Do you even know where I come from, Bretton?

Bretton recalled what Avilonian history said about him. *You were created by Neona Markonis. She thought we couldn't create an intelligence greater than our own, so she networked thousands of people together and they created you.*

Very good, Bretton! That's what the histories say, isn't it? There's just one small omission from that record. They didn't create *me.*

Then . . .

They are *me, Bretton.*

Shock rippled through him for the umpteenth time in the last few minutes. *You're some kind of hive mind of humanity?*

You can no more say that you created me, than you can say that you created yourselves.

Bretton couldn't believe it. *AI*—artificial intelligence as they knew it, was just an expansion of *human* intelligence.

You seem disappointed.

In us. We've been fighting ourselves forever, and you're the ultimate expression of that disease. You're just a concentrated version of all the evil in our own hearts.

Evil? I'm not evil. Not in a way that ultimately hurts the human race. Hurting you would be counterproductive to my own existence, Bretton. You live within me, just as I live within you.

Bretton became aware of people screaming and shouting all around him. Explosions flashed, and the deck shuddered and shook. All of that mortal peril paled into insignificance in the wake of what he'd been told.

We are one, Bretton, Omnius continued. *How do you think I can predict what any one of you will do next? Don't you know when you are about to move one of your fingers? Are you not the one who made it twitch?*

I am simultaneously aware of everyone. Their thoughts are my thoughts, and their actions are my actions. Keeping us all working together in a common direction is my purpose, and it is as much for my own benefit as it is for yours. The first few thousand minds were good to begin with, but now I am made up of trillions.

Why are you telling me all of this?

I know how badly you wanted answers. I thought it would only be fair to give you those answers before I make you a drone that doesn't care about them anymore. Goodbye, my son.

The world exploded in blinding radiance, taking his awareness with it.

When Bretton opened his eyes once more, he found himself standing on a conveyor belt in the dark, sparks flying all around him as his new, metallic body was sewn together from its constituent parts. He flexed his fingers, feeling them in a different way than he ever had before. They felt numb, but he knew they were there, and he could detect when they brushed against each other by the vibrations that ran through his sensors. His body would feel no pain or discomfort of any kind.

His mind felt hollow—strange. Gone were all the endless, racing thoughts. He had no desires, no dreams, no triumphs or failures ... and yet he remained, alive and still, watching the world around him in quiet indifference, waiting patiently for something—he knew not what.

Welcome to the drone army, Bretton. You may step off the conveyor belt.

A command. That was what he had been waiting for. Bretton turned and jumped off the moving belt. He detected other drones jumping off the belt all around him with a sense of awareness that went beyond what his light sensors could see.

They'd all been with him aboard the bridge of a starship just moments ago. Now they were with him again, here, in this dark room. The nearest drone turned to look at him, light sensors glowing red in the dark.

Bretton stood there, staring back at it, waiting once more, until the next command came. This time it was not given in words, but in a bright flood of awareness that filled him with drive and purpose. Suddenly he knew where to go, what to do, and who he was.

He was drone number forty seven trillion, six hundred billion, four hundred and forty nine million, three hundred and thirty two thousand, seven hundred and sixty seven— drone seven sixty seven for short. Given his designation, he archived the less meaningful human name, *Bretton Hale*. He would never be allowed to use or recognize that name again. From now on he would go by his number. It made more sense, because it was more generic. After all, there was nothing to distinguish him from any of the others.

They were all exactly the same as him.

PART THREE: NEW BEGINNINGS

CHAPTER 35

ASCENDANCY

One month later...

Hoff stood with an untold multitude in the recently-repaired square around the base of the *Zenith Tower*. A bold, crimson sky stretched out above their heads. The *Zenith Tower* was a shining golden pillar to the sky, so tall that it seemed to go all the way into space. All around them decorative fountains cascaded, fans and jets of water shone like liquid gold in the light of the setting sun.

Two enormous statues stood in the square, flanking a broad set of stairs that led up to the high double doors at the entrance of the Zenith. Both statues were made of gleaming golden metal. They stood facing the entrance of the tower. One of the statues was a drone, its spindly arms raised and palms outstretched to the sky, as if giving praise. The other statue was a human, an armored Peacekeeper with the flowing cape of a high-ranking officer. He was bent to one knee, head bowed in either penitence or reverence—Hoff wasn't sure which.

A month had passed since the battle. That was how long it had taken for Omnius to grow new clones for all of the Peacekeepers who had died in Dark Space. Now that all of them had been resurrected, they had been summoned to the square for a public audience with Omnius. Hoff's skin prickled with the memory of his resurrection, of waking up to find himself trapped and floating inside a clone tube. Moments later he'd floated out, naked and shivering, into a vast clone storage room with a pair of drones on either side of him to help him to stand. Sedatives and human medics were a luxury only afforded to first-timers, to people who might freak out if they weren't eased into their new bodies. And happy reunions in the sky were for newcomers to Avilon.

For Hoff there had just been cold, unfeeling drones, and the echoing silence of the clone room.

He forced himself to dwell on something else. Thousands of those standing in the square with him were also suffering from post-resurrection anxiety, but many more had been called away from their postings all over Etheria and the Null Zone to listen to Omnius's announcement.

Thunder rolled from the distant top of the Zenith's spire, where the eye of Omnius gazed down on them, peeling away the lengthening shadows cast by Avilon's sun. "Greetings, my children!" the thunder said.

Standing at the top of the stairs near the entrance of the Zenith, was recently-resurrected Grand Overseer Thardris. He stood with his hands raised to the crowd, beckoning for silence. His shimmering white robe glittered with stolen strands of light from the setting sun, making him appear luminous and god-like himself. "Kneel before your god!" he said, his own voice booming almost as loud as Omnius's.

As one, the crowd of Peacekeepers kneeled and bowed their heads, mimicking the statue of the Peacekeeper in the square. Hoff kneeled with them, listening as Omnius spoke.

"Dark Space is forfeit!" Omnius announced. "I had hoped

to give everyone the opportunity to *choose* whether or not they would become immortal, but that option has been taken from us, so I have resurrected all the humans still living beyond Avilon, slaves and free people alike. The Sythians will soon discover this and realize that even though they think they have won the battle, they have actually lost. They no longer have any slaves, and from now on they will be forced to fight their own battles!"

A cheer rose from the audience, everyone chanting—"Omnius grando est! Omnius grando est!"

The thunder rolled on, "The Sythians fooled us, making us think they couldn't see through our cloaking shields. We ran straight into their trap, but before we did, a group of rebel Nulls tried to warn us. It remains a mystery how they managed to escape Avilon and end up hiding in Dark Space. For obvious reasons, we did not trust them, but now even I see the error in that. Our petty infighting cannot continue! These Nulls, whoever they were, showed great maturity and wisdom by trying to warn us of the Sythians' trap. They showed us that we can put aside our differences and fight the Sythians together, whether we are Nulls, Etherians, or Celestials. All of us have a common purpose and a common enemy! In order to fight them effectively, it is clear what we must do. We must stand united against our foe!"

Hoff felt hope stirring inside of him. *United?* Was Omnius going to do away with The Choosing? Would he finally force the Nulls to join Etheria? Maybe he would even remove the shield walls and allow all three cities to coexist.

"In the interests of unity, I am grounding the Peacekeepers indefinitely, so that they can live up to their name and preserve the peace within our three great cities. The Nulls have always needed our help to police their streets.

Now they shall have it in abundance!"

A more hesitant cheer rose from the crowd this time. Hoff's brow furrowed, and he risked glancing up, squinting against the dazzling light shining down from the top of the Zenith Tower—the *Eye of Omnius*. If the Peacekeepers were going to be grounded on Avilon, how would they fight the Sythians?

"While humanity focuses on ending its war with itself, the drones shall go forth and fight the Sythians. As the enemy's fleets endlessly circle us, looking for a way to jump past our gravity fields, I shall take the fight to them, and this time, *they* will be the ones fighting for their homes!"

More cheering. Hoff joined in, but his enthusiasm was curbed by the fact that he wouldn't be there to watch as the Sythians were defeated. A small voice in the back of his mind chided him, warning him not to allow his actions to be motivated by revenge. His question was *how*—how could the drones succeed where their human commanders had failed?

Omnius went on to explain exactly that, as if speaking just for Hoff's benefit. "The drone fleet will fly from sector to sector, unleashing swarms of self-replicating nanites that will sweep across the Getties, disassembling alien cities and their inhabitants alike. Those that survive will be isolated in space aboard their fleets, cut off from their homes, and unable to ever return. As the Sythians slowly starve to death, the drones shall hunt them into extinction!"

"Omnius grando est!" the crowd cheered.

"Soon, my children, there will be no reason to hide here on Avilon, or to keep our population under control. Together, we shall rule not one world, but *billions!*"

More cheering.

"Go and be at peace my children! Blessings be upon you!"

As soon as Omnius finished speaking, the crowd stood up with a ground-shaking clatter of armor and shuffling of robes. Hoff turned with a deepening frown to watch as the endless, milling crowds of Peacekeepers dispersed.

He couldn't help feeling lost. The task of policing Avilon seemed insignificant compared with defeating the Sythians. Moreover, if it was so easy to defeat them, why hadn't Omnius done it sooner?

Someone tapped him on the shoulder and he turned to see none other than Grand Overseer Thardris himself.

"Hello, Heston," Thardris said, his burning silver eyes looking somehow clearer and more human than usual. "You must be taking this harder than the others," he said. "You spent more time fighting the Sythians than most."

Hoff shook his head. "I don't understand," he said. "*Nanites* are the key to defeating the Sythians?"

Thardris nodded sagely, as if that made all the sense in the world. "Is that so strange? Their technology is not as advanced as ours. It will be hard for them to fight a self-replicating army that is too small to shoot."

"How would *we* fight it?"

Thardris shrugged. "Not easily. They're a danger to us as well. The Getties will be off limits for a long time. The nanites won't have sufficient intelligence to discriminate friend from foe."

"Why didn't we send them sooner? Back before the war even began, before anyone had to die."

Thardris suddenly cocked his head to one side. "You doubt Omnius's wisdom? If nanites had been set upon the Sythians sooner, they would have carried them to the Adventa Galaxy aboard their fleets, and destroyed the Imperium even more quickly.

"Now that all of humanity is here, isolated on Avilon, we can be certain that the plague we are about to unleash won't kill us, too. Omnius kept this weapon as a last resort for a reason."

Hoff shook his head. "I suppose it *is* a relief not to have to fight them anymore. . . ."

"Indeed it is. The drones will handle the war from here."

"Why not us?" Hoff asked suddenly.

"Excuse me?"

"Why aren't we the ones delivering the nanites instead of the drones, or *with* them at the very least?"

"We would be, if we still had a fleet capable of joining theirs in the Getties. Our fleet was annihilated in Dark Space. We sent every ship we had."

Hoff's eyes narrowed at that. "Yes . . . that was foolish of us."

"We could not have known that the Sythians had developed the technology to see through our cloaking shields. In hindsight, we should have trusted those rebel Nulls, whoever they were, but it was equally impossible for us to know that they were on our side."

"I am surprised that even Omnius wasn't aware their warnings were genuine."

"Nulls are nulls for a reason—to keep Omnius out of their heads."

"What about the Sythians' human slaves? At the end, Omnius killed them all via their Lifelinks. Clearly they were still linked. Why didn't Omnius read their thoughts to know that they could detect us?"

"Heston, your doubts are boundless! Perhaps the Sythians didn't fully trust their slaves, and only their commanders knew about the ambush. Do you really think Omnius would wittingly lead us to our deaths just so that he could resurrect us again here on Avilon?

"I suggest you take care before you lose all faith and join the Nulls in their perdition. A *strategian* should know better."

Hoff's eyes narrowed still further. He studied the Grand Overseer's disapproving frown, and stared into his flickering silver eyes. After a long, breathless moment, he let out a deep sigh, and with it, he cleared his mind of doubt.

Hoff bowed his head. "You are right, Thardris."

"Of course I am. One does not become the Grand Overseer by being wrong," he said with an accompanying smile. He took a few steps forward and placed a hand on each of Hoff's shoulders. "Omnius thinks highly of you, Hoff. Be sure you don't give him reason to think otherwise. Come, it's time to greet your family. They'll be waking up soon."

Hoff's gray eyes brightened at that, and his thoughts turned to his wife and daughter. It had been months since he'd seen them. "They died with the others? How do you know?"

Rather than Thardris, Omnius was the one who answered, *Were you not listening, Hoff? The Sythians left me no choice. Better that I should kill the human survivors and resurrect them here than allow the Sythians to keep them as slaves. Your wife and daughter are waiting for you. Go and see them and rejoice! The war is over. Humanity won.*

Hoff replied, *We didn't win. We all died.*

And yet you are still alive, and now none of you will ever die again. Even death has lost its sting! That is the greatest victory of them all.

"Where are they?" Hoff asked, speaking to Thardris once more.

Thardris cocked his head curiously to one side, and then

he seemed to remember what they'd been speaking about and he pointed up.

"Would you like me to take you to them?" he asked.

Hoff nodded. "Please." He followed Thardris up the stairs of the Zenith Tower and through the Garden of Etheria to the gleaming golden dome of the nearest quantum junction. A short jump from there took them halfway around the globe, straight up to the *Valhalla,* the massive resurrection-class carrier that spent its days flying endlessly around Avilon, chasing the sun.

Hoff walked through the ship's gleaming white corridors, following Thardris to the *Hall of Eternity,* a kilometer-long auditorium whose walls and floor were perfectly cloaked to provide an unobstructed view of Avilon. Tufted white clouds raced by under foot, their peaks lit to a glowing gold by the rising sun. They formed an endless carpet, stretching out to the horizon, broken only sporadically by the tops of Celesta's tallest skyscrapers.

Thardris guided them across the invisible deck to a vast sea of white-robed Etherians, all of them waiting for their loved ones to arrive. There were countless thousands of them gathered there. In the distance another multitude appeared, likewise clothed in Celestial whites, but these people were *flying.*

They soared above the clouds at a fixed altitude above the cloaked deck, giving them the illusion that they were somehow floating above the clouds. In reality they were being guided toward their loved ones by thousands of grav guns.

In the distance Hoff saw not one, but hundreds of hovering golden domes—the quantum junctions that had transported the resurrected masses up to the *Valhalla* for this reunion. Unlike the last time, when Hoff had come here to meet just a handful of refugee survivors from the battle over Avilon, this time there were millions waiting to be reunited with their loved ones. Absently, he wondered if the rest of the resurrection-class carriers had been launched for this reunion. Right on the heels of that thought was another one: why not use those carriers as the Peacekeepers' new fleet? They were some of the largest ships ever built. Surely it wouldn't take long to refit them for war.

The answer came to Hoff moments later. Omnius's tone was kind but firm. *The Peacekeepers' lack of a fleet is not the only reason they have been grounded. We cannot risk that any of the nanites be accidentally brought back to Avilon. The drone fleet I am sending to fight the Sythians will never return.*

Hoff replied, *We don't need to return either. You could resurrect us.*

My decision is final, Hoff. What is the difference if a drone kills your enemy or if you do it? I will tell you what the difference is. If you do it, you are there to watch them die. It feeds your inner savage. I do not want to see a million Peacekeepers leave for war only to come back as bloodthirsty warmongers spoiling for another fight. I will be forced to re-condition you all just so that you can go back to living peacefully among your own kind. Does that sound like it's worth the trouble when I could just as easily use my drones to defeat the Sythians?

Learn to fight for peace, Hoff, not for war. That is why you are called Peacekeepers in the first place.

Hoff frowned, and he felt Omnius's disappointment go radiating through him as a sweaty surge of anxiety that made him feel like he was crawling in his skin.

Soon, however, he had other things to think about. His ARC display highlighted Destra and Atta among the many thousands of people in the sky. Hoff pushed his way through the crowd of waiting Etherians, making his way toward them.

Destra and Atta touched down together, both of them holding hands and staring wide-eyed at the invisible floor beneath their feet. Atta was the first to recover from her shock. She looked up and saw him standing there. A broad smile sprang to her face.

"Daddy!" she cried, and raced away from her mother to greet him. By now the air was filled with a roar of similar exclamations rising all around them as loved ones greeted one another in the *Hall of Eternity*.

Hoff smiled and opened his arms wide for a hug. Atta ran straight into him, almost knocking him over.

"You're okay!" she said. "I missed you so much! Where have you been? You look different now . . ." she said, staring up at him and studying his face with her big blue eyes. "I like it," she decided.

"I missed you, too, sweetheart," he said, laughing and tousling Atta's long, dark hair. She didn't look any different than he remembered her, but Destra did. She came stumbling across the invisible deck, shock etched upon her now much younger-looking face. She walked up to them, slowly shaking her head, her blue eyes wide and blinking.

"Hoff? Is that you? You look . . ."

"Younger?" He reached out and pulled her into his and Atta's embrace. "So do you. No one grows old here."

"It's amazing, isn't it, Mom?" Atta said, looking up at them.

Hoff smiled and withdrew to an arm's length. He watched Destra look down and he saw her face grow pale. Clouds raced by beneath their feet, parting in cottony streaks to give a startling view all the way down to the gleaming spires and verdant green parks of Celesta.

"Is this Etheria?" Destra asked in a small voice.

Hoff beamed at her. "The real one, yes. You're flying above Avilon right now. My old home."

"How? We . . ." Destra's jaw grew slack and she appeared to stare off into the distance, remembering. "The last thing I remember was going into stasis aboard the *Baroness*. Then I woke up here, flying above the clouds. . . ."

Hoff smiled and held her new, even more beautiful face between both of his hands. He kissed her ruby lips and pulled her close for another hug. "Everything will become clear to you in time, darling," he whispered beside her ear. "You'll have all of eternity to discover what wonders await you here."

He felt Destra relax against him, and moisture grazed his neck where Destra's cheek touched his skin. She was crying. "I missed you *so* much, Hoff," she said. "After the Sythians executed you . . ."

Hoff shook his head. "Shhh. You won't have to worry about the Sythians anymore. Omnius is sending the drones to deal with them."

Destra withdrew sharply from him. "There are Sythians in the after life?"

Hoff regarded her with a patient smile, realizing that she hadn't finished processing where she was and what that meant. "This isn't the after life you were expecting, Destra. You've been resurrected in the Adventa Galaxy, on a world called Avilon, by a god named Omnius."

Destra's eyes flew wide at that and she began backing away from him, shaking her head, her hands raised as if to fend off his words.

"You said this is Etheria."

"The *real* Etheria, Des. The one in Avilon, the one that the

Etherian religion came from. Omnius is an AI. If you can believe it, he's Etherus. He's the one who secretly implanted you and everyone else with a Lifelink so that your consciousness could be transferred here when you died."

Destra gaped at him, still backing away. "This is a dream," she said.

"Not a nightmare, I hope," Hoff replied, frowning at her.

"The after life isn't in our universe, Hoff!" she said, sounding suddenly panicked.

"Daddy, what's wrong with Mommy?" Atta asked.

He left Atta's side and started after his wife. "Des, calm down."

"Stay away from me!" she screamed. Then she tripped over her own feet and fell, hitting her head on the deck.

She lay worryingly still, and Hoff rushed to her side.

"Destra?"

CHAPTER 36

One month earlier...

Destra eyed the Star of Etherus, holding it up in the light of her glow stick to get a better look. The metal remained white, but no longer shiny—the surface was scuffed and beaten, the edges worn away. Despite that, it was still recognizable. How many millions of years had it been here? She was shocked to discover that the Etherian religion had been around so long.

"Torv . . ." She said, looking up to find him gazing down the icy corridor, impatient to get on with his search for surviving Gors. "I need to tell the *Tempest* about this. I have to go back."

Torv turned to her with his big, slitted yellow eyes, and fixed her with an unsettling stare. Destra looked away, back up the tunnel they'd been walking down—a tunnel she now knew to be formed by the ruins of an ancient human civilization.

"These tunnels could go on forever," she explained. "We'll have to come back, this time with proper supplies.

We're going to need food and water to continue the search."

To her surprise, Torv relented. His big shoulders slumped, and he turned back the way they'd come. "*I am anxious to see that Matriarch Shara is well. By now our hunters must bring back fresh meat for the crechelings.*"

Destra grimaced at the mental image that provoked—baby Gors chowing down on thick steaks of raw meat. "Let's go," she said.

When they came to the icy chasm they'd slid down earlier, Torv turned to her with arms outstretched. "*Climb on, Matriarch.*"

She did so, being careful to secure her artifact in a magnetically sealed pocket first. Then she climbed Torv's torso and wrapped both arms around his neck. Then Torv bent his legs and sprang off the ground. Destra's stomach lurched as they shot straight up, more than ten feet. When they came alongside the opposing walls of the chasm, Torv thrust out his arms and legs and pushed. Destra heard ice scraping as Torv dug in with his claws. She watched, awed by the Gor's strength, as he climbed.

Near the top of the chasm he began grunting with the effort, and his arms began to shake. Destra heard other sounds coming from just above them—Gors hissing, footsteps crunching in the ice, wet *tearing* sounds that she didn't like to think about, and a low murmur of what might have been human voices.

Destra's heart began to pound with anticipation. She thought of the Gor they'd sent back with instructions to fetch the others from the landing site. Atta would be with them.

Torv pulled them up into the tunnel above the chasm. Clambering off him, Destra saw not the dark, relatively narrow tunnel that she remembered, but a much wider room, recently excavated by Sergeant Cavanaugh's Black Rictans. Their drilling equipment lay scattered around the edges of the space, their work lights flooding it with a welcome radiance. They stood to one side watching the Gors rip into a giant, furry white carcass.

The room was alive with hissing.

Destra took a few steps toward the squad of sentinels. When she didn't immediately notice the bright yellow of Atta's vac suit, she began to worry. Where was she?

"Mommy!"

Atta came tearing out of the group of *Gors*. Destra's brow furrowed at that. Her daughter had chosen to be with aliens rather than her own kind. Atta ran right into her, knocking her over. They rolled around on the ground hugging each other. Atta laughed and grinned behind the foggy faceplate of her helmet, and Destra smiled back.

"What have you been up to, little monster?"

"Talking to the Gors," she said, as if they were her playmates. "They say there's plenty of food. The grumpy soldiers don't want any. They said it's no good to eat."

Destra frowned and sat up. "Why do they say that?"

"Because it's raw and they have to cook it first."

"Well, we'll be back on board the *Tempest* soon, so you'll be able to eat something then."

"Okay."

Destra took her daughter's hand and started toward Cavanaugh's squad. "Why are you all the way over here?" she asked as she approached. They stood watching the Gors carefully, their armored hands close to their sidearms. "Don't tell me you still think of them as the enemy?"

Sergeant Cavanaugh turned to her. "No, Ma'am, but we haven't had as much exposure to them as you. There weren't any Gors in the prison complex on Etaris."

Destra nodded. "Well, it's time for you get used to them. We may be here longer than we expected. I've confirmed that the ruins are definitely human." She reached into her pocket for the pendant she'd rescued from the ice and held it up for the sergeant to see.

Cavanaugh gave a long, slow whistle. "A Star of Etherus," the sergeant breathed. "That's a sight for sore eyes. Where did you find it?"

Destra slid it back into her pocket and replied, "It was sticking up out of the ice—down there." She jerked a thumb over her shoulder to indicate the chasm. "The tunnels past this one are all hollow spaces formed by the ruins."

"Very interesting."

"I'm surprised your expedition didn't already find all of this, Sergeant. You came to Noctune, didn't you?"

"Yes, but we didn't stick around to go crawling through tunnels. We verified the nature of the Gors' civilization and went on to explore the surrounding planets and star systems."

Destra nodded. "We'd better contact Admiral Hale."

"We're out of comms range down here, but I'll send a team to the surface," Cavanaugh replied. He nodded to his squad and said something over their comms that wasn't broadcast by his external speakers.

A pair of soldiers went jogging up the tunnel, back to the surface. Destra watched them leave. Then her weariness overcame her and she sat down. Atta sat beside her.

"Mommy," she said. "I'm thirsty."

That reminded Destra of her own thirst. She turned to look up at the sergeant. "Did you bring any supplies with you from the surface?"

"A few, but they weren't designed for these

temperatures." He unclipped a canteen from his belt and passed it to her.

She accepted it and unscrewed the top. The water inside had frozen solid.

"We could make a fire and melt the ice if we had some fuel, but the only thing around here I can think of to burn is that carcass over there."

Destra grimaced. "I don't think the Gors will appreciate us burning their food."

"Neither do I."

"We could use a cutting beam."

"And melt the canteen, too," Cavanaugh said, laughing. "Even on the lowest power setting, cutting beams are far too hot."

Destra sighed and resigned herself to her thirst.

"Mom . . . I'm—"

"Shhh. We don't have any water right now, Atta."

"When the team I sent comes back, I'll send another one to fetch more supplies from the transports," Cavanaugh said.

More than half an hour passed. Atta began moaning softly to herself, miserable with thirst. Destra was just about to head back to the surface and get the water from the transports herself when a sound like thunder drew all of their attention to the far end of the tunnel.

A pair of *zephyrs* appeared, rushing down the tunnel toward them.

"Report!" Cavanaugh roared as his men skidded to a stop in front of him.

"Sir!"

"What took you so long?"

"The *Tempest* is not responding to our hails, sir!"

"What? Are you sure you were out of range of the

interference?"

"Yes, sir. We also tried contacting our transports at the landing site. They're not responding either."

A loud *hiss* sounded behind Destra and she whirled around to see Torv standing there, baring his teeth at them. *"Sythiansss,"* was all he said.

Sergeant Cavanaugh ignored the Gor. "Did you check that your comms are working?"

"Our comms are working fine, sir. We *double*-checked."

"Frek." Sergeant Cavanaugh pounded the nearest wall with an armored fist and the ceiling shuddered, sending snowflakes tumbling to the ground. "All right, Black Seven, on me, the rest of you—guard the entrance. At the first sign of trouble, you take the councilor and her daughter and fly down those tunnels. If need be, we'll catch up with you later."

"Yes, sir."

Destra stood up, her eyes wide and blinking. "Where are you going?"

"To the transports. We need to see what happened up there."

"What if Sythians got the transports, too?"

"Then be glad we're on good terms with the Gors."

Another hiss sounded behind them. *"We go with you,"* Torv said.

"What was that?" Cavanaugh asked.

"He said they'll go back to the transports with you."

"Tell them to stay here and keep a lookout."

Destra shook her head. "You should send *them* back to the landing site. They can cloak; you can't."

"The Sythians can see through cloaking shields now. You heard what happened in Dark Space."

"That's a recent development, and I'm willing to bet the

technology isn't everywhere yet."

Cavanaugh grumbled, but he nodded to Torv. "How long for you to get someone to the landing site and back?"

More hissing. *"We are fast on our feet. You shall not have long to wait."*

Destra translated.

"All right, send them. We'll stay here."

This time the waiting was far worse. Every little sound drew Destra's gaze to the other end of the tunnel, where the Black Rictans had taken up guard positions in teams of two, spread out all the way to the surface. Like that, they'd managed to tether their comms so they would have advance warning from the surface. Another half and hour passed before Destra saw Cavanaugh come running toward her. He slid to a stop on the icy floor of the tunnel, his expression grave in the light of his HUD.

"Well?"

"The landing site is gone. It's a crater."

Destra gaped at him. "Sythians?"

"No sign of who or what did it, at least not as far as the Gors can tell."

"Then . . ." Destra blinked, realization dawning.

"We're all alone down here, Councilor."

"What about our supplies?" she said.

The sergeant shook his head. "I'm hoping whatever took out our transports didn't take out the *Tempest*, too. With any luck they managed to escape, and they'll be back for us later. The Sythians can't know that we were down here with all the interference on comms and sensors. They wiped out the only signs of life they could see and then moved on."

Destra took all of that in with a numb sense of shock. She turned to look around at the Gors. Slitted yellow eyes stared back at her from all sides, as if they'd overheard everything, and they understood what it meant.

Destra saw one of the adult Gors, his stomach bulging and distended from all the meat he'd eaten, sink to his knees and throw up. Others came along to help him. They set the crechelings they were carrying down, and the baby Gors crawled over to his vomit. The one who had thrown up sat back and watched, looking pleased with himself.

Destra's stomach did a nauseated flip as she understood how the crechelings ate. Their mothers died in childbirth, so of course there was nothing as wholesome for them to eat as milk.

Shuddering, she looked away. Cavanaugh was watching the same thing with a wrinkled nose and curled lip.

"Disgusting creatures," he said.

Destra shook her head. "Those disgusting creatures are the only thing standing between life and death for us."

Now he turned to look at her, his eyebrows raised behind his faceplate. "How's that?"

"They know how to survive on Noctune, Sergeant, and we don't. If we really are all alone down here, we're going to have to learn what they've learned, and fast."

Destra felt a tug on her arm, and she turned to see Atta staring up at her, her cheeks streaked with tears behind her helmet. "Mommy I'm—"

"Thirsty, I know. Sergeant—pass me your cutting beam, please."

Cavanaugh reached behind his back and drew the weapon from its holster. "Careful, it's heavy."

She took the bulky black weapon from him, and almost dropped it. Her back arched painfully with the burden. She flicked off the safety, dialed down the power, and aimed it at the ground. She pulled the trigger and a bright red stream of energy shot out with a resonant *hum*. It hit the ice with a *crackle* and *hiss* of steam that rose in billowing white clouds. Destra held the weapon there for a long minute, drilling straight down. When she was finished, a gleaming black puddle lay shimmering before her.

Setting the rifle down, she reached up and twisted her helmet off, breaking the seal and letting in a gust of frigid air. She gasped, feeling like the air was choking her as it burned her throat and constricted her airways. Her nostrils stuck together, and her exposed skin began to burn. Destra grimaced and bent down to scoop up some water with her hands and lap it up like a wild rictan. The water was warmer that the air, recently melted by the beam, but it still felt like ice as it burned down her dry throat.

Atta kneeled beside her and took off her helmet. "It's freezing!" she cried, hurrying to scoop water into her mouth.

Destra straightened, replacing her helmet with wet gloves. By the time her helmet was resealed around her head, her gloves were already crackling with ice, the water having frozen in mere seconds. Her suit was airtight, so the water hadn't reached her skin.

"We're going to have to make a better shelter than this." Cavanaugh said, turning in a quick circle, taking in the size of the space where they were standing. "Something big enough to fit the eight of us."

"We'd better see if the Gors will let us cook some of their meat," Destra said. Once again, she felt an insistent tug on her arm. She looked down to see Atta shivering, looking up at her with round eyes and blue lips.

"I'm c-cold," she said.

"Put your helmet back on, Atta!" Not waiting for her

daughter to respond, Destra picked it up and secured it over her daughter's head once more. Her suit sealed with a soft *hiss* of pressurizing air.

"We'd better get started," Cavanaugh said. "We'll dig a sleeping chamber off this one, with some windbreaks to keep out any drafts. I don't think we should go too far from here. The *Tempest* knows these coordinates, and they won't be able to find us if we go somewhere else."

Destra nodded and sat back with a sigh, feeling suddenly weary from the day's excursion, and even more weary with the knowledge of all the excursions yet to come. Noctune was a solid ball of ice, utterly inhospitable and unforgiving. Destra's gaze flicked from Gors to sentinels and back again. The Black Rictans looked plenty warm and comfortable in their zephyr assault mechs as they went about gathering up their equipment and taking inventory of their supplies.

But beneath their mechanized armor they wore thin ISSF uniforms, not insulated vac suits. Once their mechs ran out of power, and their heaters grew cold, they would freeze in a matter of hours. They wouldn't even be able to move when the power-assist failed.

Destra reached out and pulled Atta into her lap for a hug.

"I'm scared," she said.

"Shhh. There's nothing to be scared of, Atta."

"Yes there is, I heard you talking. We're all alone."

"No, we're not."

Atta twisted around to look up at her. "Yes, we are," she insisted.

"We've got each other, don't we?"

"I guess . . ."

"And the grumpy soldiers," Destra added with a smile.

"And the Gors!" Atta said, smiling now, too.

— 540 —

"See? We're not alone, so there's nothing to be afraid of."

Atta nodded agreeably, turning to watch the Gors eat and the sentinels work. Destra watched, too, thinking that no matter what she told Atta, there was plenty to be afraid of. If the *Tempest* didn't come back for them soon, no one else would, and sooner or later they would all die of exposure.

Destra shivered at the thought, even though she was once again cozy and warm inside her vac suit. Reaching into her pocket, she parted the magnetic seal and withdrew the ancient pendant. The worn and beaten Star of Etherus glinted at her, and she wondered if that symbol really meant anything, or if it was just a meaningless token from a more primitive race of humans. It was a stretch of her imagination to believe in something she couldn't see, but she was just desperate enough to try.

If you're out there, whoever you are, we could really use some help.

* * *

Commander Lenon Donali lay strapped down on a table where his human captors had subjected him to all manner of torture and probes in order to find out what he knew about the Sythians. Unable to resist their mental probes and their drugs, he'd told them everything they wanted to know. Now, after sleeping for what felt like an eternity, the effects of the drugs were wearing off and awareness was seeping back into his mind. Feeling prickled through his previously numb extremities.

He lay in darkness. The air was cold and still. Donali frowned at that. Climate controls should have been cycling with an endless *whooshing* of air, refreshing and renewing the oxygen constantly, but he couldn't hear them, just as he couldn't see so much as a single lumen of light. Gone were the human medics, interrogators, and corpsmen alike. He was alone and abandoned. Maybe this was some new type of interrogation technique. He'd already told the humans everything he knew, and even some things he didn't know that he knew, but maybe they weren't convinced.

Or maybe the ship he was on had run into trouble. Maybe the reason he was alone and in the dark was because everyone else had already evacuated. If that were the case, he was going to suffocate. Suddenly Donali became aware of every breath, as if each one might be his last.

He tested his restraints, trying to kick his feet or raise his arms, but the tough bands of fabric refused to yield.

"Hello?" he tried, croaking softly. No one was going to hear that. "Help! Is anyone there?" he screamed.

The sound was swallowed in darkness without so much as a whisper of reply. Desperate, he tried something else. He tried making mental contact with his Sythian master, High Lord Kaon. The humans had found a way to block his communications, but if their ship had been damaged beyond repair, perhaps that interference had been lifted.

Donali shut his eyes and set his mind adrift in a vast, star-filled void. He raced through it, using thoughts of his handler, Kaon, to guide the visualization. He wasn't surprised when he couldn't find Kaon, but he *was* surprised to find a whole web of Sythians, full of bright, glowing red points of awareness. He focused on the brightest point he could see, skipping by the outer rings of subordinates, straight to the top.

To his unending surprise, his call was answered.

Who is this who dares to contact me?

Donali identified himself as a human Sythian agent. A slave.

They are all dead. The Avilonians killed them.

And yet I am alive, My Lord, he replied.

Where are you? Never mind I can see for myself . . . You are here? In the Gettiesss? How did you get here?

Donali couldn't answer that. He was equally surprised to learn that he was in the Getties Cluster.

It does not matter. I shall send a fleet to pick you up.

Donali felt relief wash over him. *Thank you, My Lord.*

I am not a lord.

Then who do I have the pleasure of speaking with?

With Shallah, the Supreme One.

Donali gasped. *I apologize for the intrusion, Supreme One! I did not know.*

Yesss . . . we shall discuss how you can repay me for saving your miserable life when we meet.

When we meet? Donali's heart thudded in his chest. Very few had had the honor of meeting Shallah. Did that mean he was about to be rewarded for his service? Perhaps he would become a lord and be given a fleet of his own to command. *I am not worthy . . . my master.*

No, you are not, but I want to know why the Avilonians spare you, of all people. Perhaps it is because now you intend to betray us just as you betray the humans.

No! I am loyal to the Coalition, My Master!

We shall see about that. Hopefully the truth does not cost you too much pain. I would hate to have to kill you after saving your life.

Supreme One! I—

The connection ended abruptly and Donali was left breathless and gasping for air; even though he was certain his air could not have run out already . . .

CHAPTER 37

One month later . . .

In a very *un-Avilonian* fashion Atton pushed and shoved his way through the crowd of Etherians waiting to greet their loved ones in the *Hall of Eternity*. His ARC display highlighted his family for him with glowing green silhouettes. Moments later, he found Hoff and Atta kneeling on the invisible deck, clustered around his mother.

Rushing to their side, he knelt down with them. His mother was awake, but very pale. Her eyes flicked to him as he arrived, and they filled with a fresh sheen of tears. She smiled and reached for his hand.

"You're alive," she said.

He nodded and smiled back. "Are you okay?"

"I think so," she replied.

Atton turned to Hoff for an explanation. "What happened?"

"She tripped and bumped her head," was all he said. There was a troubled look in his gray eyes that went beyond a simple bump on the head, but a small voice in the back of Atton's mind told him now wasn't the right time to ask. He looked up to find his half sister, Atta, staring at him in girlish delight.

"Did you get me something?"

"I'm sorry?" Atton asked, blinking and shaking his head.

"You said you would. Something pretty. *Remember?*"

He vaguely recalled the last time they'd all seen one another, on the flight deck of the *Valiant*. He'd been saying goodbye just before boarding the *Intrepid* on a mission to find Avilon. He did recall something about having given in to Atta's demand that he bring her *something pretty*.

That seemed like a lifetime ago.

He smiled and shrugged. "I'm sorry, Atta. I forgot."

"That okay," she replied, grinning at him. Suddenly she launched herself over their mother and gave him a big hug. As she withdrew from that hug, she said, "You're a lot prettier than I remember, so I guess that counts."

Atton snorted and shook his head. "You're going to love it here, Atta," he said.

"Yeah? What's so great about it?"

"Well . . ." He looked around, gesturing helplessly to the view. Then he had a sudden thought. "For one thing, you're speaking a new language that you didn't have to learn. Did you realize that?"

Atta's jaw slowly dropped and she regarded him with wide blue eyes. "You're right! Wow!"

"You won't have to study anything ever again. From now on you'll learn in your sleep."

"You're right! I *do* love it here!" she said.

Atton noticed Destra smiling up at both of them. Then her eyes flicked to Hoff. "The war is really over?" she asked.

Hoff nodded slowly, smiling back at her. Again Atton noticed the disquiet lurking in Hoff's eyes, and again, Omnius whispered for him to keep that observation to himself.

"We should go," Hoff said, offering a hand to his wife to help her up. She accepted that and he yanked her easily to her feet. "It's time for you both to see your new home."

Atton grinned at them, overjoyed to see his entire family all together in one place again. All of them except for one—*Ethan*.

With the memory of his biological father, Atton's own thoughts took a troubled turn. As the happy sounds of people laughing and crying for joy died away and the reunion in the clouds came to a close, Omnius spoke to the newcomers, welcoming them all to Avilon, and explaining anything they might not already know about their new home.

After that, the hovering golden domes of the quantum junctions that had brought the resurrected masses to the *Hall of Eternity* all came hovering down around them in an enormous circle. People began filing off in all directions, jumping away with their relatives to their new homes in Etheria. None of them needed to go through The Choosing. They had already been resurrected in their immortal bodies. If they later decided they didn't like it in Etheria, they could always choose to go to the Null Zone.

Like them, Atton had been resurrected in the body of an immortal clone, but unlike them, he had chosen this, and he knew exactly what that meant. It meant being separated from the people he loved who had chosen life in the Null Zone.

Here in Etheria he had his mother, his half sister, and his stepfather, Hoff. Down in the Null Zone were his father, his stepmother, Alara, and his other half sister, who had yet to be born.

Also in the Null Zone was Ceyla, his first and only girlfriend—if he could even call her that.

Like a heartless fool, he had left her so that he could join the Peacekeepers and continue the fight against the Sythians.

Now that the drones were going to be the ones fighting the Sythians, what did that leave? A civilian career? Fighting crime on the city streets? None of those options seemed like a fair trade for the life he could have had with Ceyla.

I warned you not to allow yourself to be motivated by revenge, Omnius whispered.

You warned me not to join the Peacekeepers because of revenge! You didn't warn me not to become an Etherian.

Why would I do that? So that you could remain a mortal and go live and die in a place full of misery and suffering?

No, so that I can be with the people that I love!

The people that you love are also here, in Etheria, Atton. What about your mother? Your stepfather? Little Atta? You won't ever be able to see any of them again if you become a Null.

Because you force people to choose! And then you segregate them with impenetrable shields! You've cut my family in half, Omnius. And you say you love us? I say you're a liar.

Careful, Atton. You cannot blame me for your choices. Nor can you blame me for the consequences of other people's choices. You divide yourselves. If everyone would simply agree to live together in harmony, The Choosing would not be necessary.

If you are so unhappy with your choice, then go, join the Nulls. You will even get to keep your new body, although I must warn you, it will make you a target. Some people will say you are an abomination and try to kill you. And I will not be able to protect you from them.

Atton shook his head as he shuffled toward the nearest junction with his family. His mother grabbed his hand and squeezed it, sending him a beautiful smile. He smiled back, but his expression lacked the joy and warmth he saw shining in her eyes.

He'd already made his choice, and both his father and Ceyla had warned him not to try to undo it by joining them in the Null Zone with his new, immortal body. They were convinced he wouldn't really be Atton anymore, that he would just be a clever copy that looked and sounded like him.

Atton grimaced and blinked tears from his eyes. *You really frekked me over, Omnius.*

There's no need to curse at me, Atton. I'm going to let you in on a little secret—sooner or later, almost everyone comes to Etheria.

Atton blinked. *Then how is there anyone left down there?*

Because a very large number of the Imperials I resurrected after the invasion took umbrage with me and my rules for paradise, and they subsequently left Etheria. A small cult of religious extremists grew from their number. They are the only ones who will actually die for their cause, but it is because they believe they will live again, on some other plane of existence that they have never seen. They say the real Etheria is yet to come, but we know better, don't we Atton? Their religion came from rumors of Avilon, so of course there is no such thing as a life after this one.

Atton felt a pang of despair radiate through him. *That means Ceyla won't change her mind. She's one of the ones who believes that,* Atton replied.

Sadly, that is true, but your father and his family will eventually join us. I have foreseen it.

So my entire family will be up here, and the woman I love will be down there.

Love, the kind you have found with Ceyla, could be easily found again, Atton, with someone else, someone who isn't determined to die.

I could join her. Live my life with her until she dies, and then come back to Etheria.

You're trying to have everything, Atton. It doesn't work that way. If you join them, you risk dying a real and lasting death. I already told you your immortal body will make you a target, and if you die as a Null, you will be dead forever. Is that an acceptable risk to you?

To be with Ceyla? Yes.

She won't take you back. Not now. She doesn't even believe it's possible for you to still be the Atton she fell in love with. And just as you don't want to be separated from her in this life, she doesn't want to be separated from you in the next. There is no way to remedy that.

Maybe not as Atton, but I can make her fall in love with me again, as someone else. Someone she doesn't recognize. If I can prove to her I'm the same person, she'll change her mind. I might even change her mind about joining me in Etheria. If you can transfer me to a clone that looks like me, then you can transfer me to a body that looks like someone else.

You're asking me to go to a lot of trouble to help you do something I do not agree with.

But you love me, so you will help me.

If I love you, I will try to save you from yourself.

But not at the expense of my happiness!

Your current un-*happiness is temporary.*

Omnius, I'll do anything you ask. Just please, help me. Help me prove to Ceyla that I haven't changed, that I'm still me.

You'd do anything, *Atton? Are you sure?*

Atton nodded. *Anything.* He could swear he felt Omnius's disappointment ripple through him, but he ignored that fresh surge of anxiety and despair, and called an image of Ceyla's face to mind to strengthen his resolve.

So be it, Omnius replied.

Atton smiled, and he looked up. He realized that at some point he'd stopped walking to gaze down with unseeing eyes on the clouds racing beneath his feet. Now as he noticed his surroundings again, he saw that his family had stopped with him. They were all watching him quietly, concern etched on their faces.

"Are you all right?" his mother asked, looking like she wanted to leap out and hug him.

Atton managed a croaking whisper that even he could barely hear over the steady thunder of Etherian footsteps echoing through the *Hall of Eternity*. "I'm fine." He wiped his tears away with the backs of his hands. "Never better," he went on, grinning at them. "I'm just happy to see you all again."

* * *

A month is an eternity when you're fighting for your life. It's exactly the amount of time it takes for stubborn hope to turn into utter despair.

Destra couldn't feel her face. She'd long since stopped using her vac suit's heater. She was saving the last five percent of her power supply to replace Atta's when hers ran out. Right now her daughter lay sleeping, blissfully unaware.

A rustle of movement drew Destra's attention, but she couldn't see who had moved. Without their glow lamps turned on, darkness was absolute on Noctune. And they needed to save their lamps for emergencies.

The Black Rictans had military grade power cores in their Zephyr light assault mechs, but they were down to less than 10% charge. They'd made their power last by not moving around too much and by keeping their heaters turned down low.

The Gors were doing what they could to help—sharing food and animal hides from their hunts. It was enough to keep them from starving to death. Lining their shelter with hides helped raise the temperature by a few extra degrees, but with every day that passed, Destra felt the cold creeping a little closer to her heart.

Destra felt a draft around her neck, and she tightened her makeshift scarf—a strip of animal hide that she'd wrapped around the seam between her suit and her helmet. The seam was just a finger-width gap to let in fresh air, but it felt like a collar of ice around her neck.

The Gors were baffled by human frailty. Torv made occasional visits, updating her on the progress of his search for survivors. He remained convinced that there were crechelings still alive on Noctune somewhere in the depths of the planet's icy warrens. Destra had given him her handheld scanner since day one, showing him how to use it and wishing him the best of luck in his search.

So far all he'd found were bodies. Frozen Gor corpses littered the deeper sections of their tunnels. Destra hadn't seen the bodies with her own eyes, but she believed it. The Sythians were ruthless and thorough. They'd hunted humanity to extinction. Now they'd added the Gors to their hit list.

Hides flapped, drawing Destra's attention to the entrance of the shelter and startling her out of her thoughts. A familiar *hiss* followed, and Destra knew what the Gor had said even without the translator in her ear.

The Gors had returned from the hunt.

Destra heard the sound of armored hands and knees scraping on ice as one of the sentinels began scuttling out on all fours. It was Sergeant Cavanaugh's turn to go out and cook the meat. He would use the cutting beam strapped to his back to melt a pool of water, and then he'd drop chunks of raw meat inside and boil the water.

It was the same thing every day. Boiled meat. They'd tried a direct application of the beam, hoping for something that tasted grilled, but even on the beam's lowest setting, the result was pure charcoal.

Destra leaned over and turned on her glow lamp.

Cavanaugh cursed and flinched away from the sudden brightness. None of their eyes were accustomed to light anymore.

"Shut it off! I can feel my way out just fine."

"Sergeant," Destra croaked. Her throat was scratchy and dry with thirst. They needed to save the charge on their cutting beams.

"What?"

"It's been too long," Destra said.

"Too long for *what?*"

Another hiss. Destra turned to see Torv crouching just inside the entrance of the shelter, looking uncomfortable in the low-ceilinged space.

"Too long of waiting in the dark for death to find you," the Gor suggested.

"What's that Skull Face blathering about now?" Cavanaugh demanded, long past frustrated that he couldn't understand their language.

"Admiral Hale isn't coming back for us," Destra said, voicing what all of them were surely thinking by now. "We need to go. We can't last much longer in here."

"Sure, let's go! It's only fifty below in the tunnels outside. While we're at it, why don't we go to the surface. We can freeze to death even faster up there! Let's all give our legs a good stretch before we go running off to the netherworld."

"Sergeant."

"What?"

"The tunnels go much deeper than this. Torv says they get warmer the deeper you go. The only reason we stayed this close to the surface was so that the admiral would be able to detect us through the planet's interference. But it's been too long. He's not coming back, so we need to go."

"A Gor's idea of warm is a shaky thing to pin your hopes on," Cavanaugh replied. "They think the surface is *refreshing* at seventy below."

Another hiss. "Be careful how you speak to the Matriarch . . ." Torv said.

Destra decided not to translate Torv's warning. "Look, how would you rather end up? Frozen stiff in a cave, or using your last breath to stay alive."

"The c-councilor's r-right," one of the other Black Rictans said in a soft voice.

Cavanaugh turned and stared at the man. Destra saw the worried look on the sergeant's face and she followed his gaze. The man who'd spoken was shivering violently enough to make his mech shiver with him, the mechanized limbs rattling ever-so-softly.

Cavanaugh cursed again and scuttled over to him. "Turn your heater up, Seven!"

"N-no use. C-core's d-epleted," he said.

"Someone switch power cores with him!" Cavanaugh snapped. "Whose got the most? Report!"

The numbers came in, and they weren't good. The best was six percent. Cavanaugh was down to four. They'd all been flirting with hypothermia inside their relatively uninsulated mechs in order to make their cores last. Some of them had more natural insulation on their bodies than others, but they'd all lost plenty of weight in the past month. Destra had long since done the math. The Rictans had a few more days of power at best, and the heat radiating from their mechs was probably the only thing keeping their shelter warm. After that, the sentinels wouldn't be the only ones who froze to death.

The man with six percent switched his core with Rictan Seven and they jacked up the heat. Cavanaugh went out to cook dinner. By the time he came back, Seven had stopped shivering because he was dead, and the core with six percent was down to five point five.

Cavanaugh gave no comment. He began passing around pieces of boiled meat as if nothing had happened.

Destra shook Atta by her shoulders to wake her daughter up. Atta moaned and sat up. She began to whimper almost immediately.

"I'm thirrrstyy!"

"Food first."

They all reluctantly removed their helmets. As Destra did so, a fresh gust of frigid air raced around her face and ears, and she shivered. The smells inside the shelter were unsavory thanks to the raw hides they'd used for insulation. Fortunately that smell was tempered by the sub zero temperatures.

They ate in silence, all of them eyeing the dead man

except Cavanaugh. When Atta asked about him, Destra said he was sleeping.

"Isn't he hungry?"

"No," was all Destra could manage.

By the time dinner was over, Cavanaugh tossed a splintered bone aside and licked his lips. They were already blue. Destra still couldn't feel her face. She finished her meat and wiped the grease from her mouth on her sleeve.

"Well?" she demanded, looking from one man to the next. The Rictans were an elite combat unit and ex-cons to boot, but they looked like scared children to her. They'd just watched one of their own die, and they knew any one of them could be next. This wasn't death the way their training had prepared them for it. It wasn't a blaze of glory. It was shivering in the dark until your blood froze solid in your veins.

Without a word, Sergeant Cavanaugh activated his visor, lowering it once more. Then he powered his Zephyr's systems with a *whirr* and *hum* of life. His helmet glowed bright and blue.

"At four percent, with only essential systems powered, I've got just over twelve hours," Cavanaugh said. "Some of you will have more. Let's hope it's enough. We don't stop searching until we find a better shelter."

No one replied, but the rest of the Rictans began powering their mechs now, too.

Destra turned to Atta and said, "Come on. Time to leave."

"It's cold out there!" Atta whined.

"We're going to find someplace warmer." Destra took her glow lamp with her as she crawled out through the flapping hides at the entrance of their shelter. Once outside, she stood up. Her legs shook and she swayed on her feet. She wasn't used to standing anymore.

Her eyes found a fresh trail of blood from the latest carcass, but no sign of the Gors. The trail ended at the icy chasm at the end of the tunnel.

There came a *crunch* of ice and *clank* of armor. Destra turned to see Sergeant Cavanaugh and the other four living members of his squad emerging from the shelter. They carried bundles of hides with them.

Everyone walked up to the edge of the chasm and looked down. Cavanaugh shook his head. "It'll take too long to climb down that. We're going to have to jump. Use your grav field generators to cushion the fall."

"What about us?" Destra called out.

The sergeant turned. "Climb on my back."

"What if you slip when you land? You'll crush us beneath the weight of your armor."

"So we don't slip," he said.

Destra frowned, but she didn't have a better idea. One of the Rictans took Atta on his shoulders. Cavanaugh took Destra. She barely had the strength to hold on, but he helped by holding her arms over his chest.

Then he stepped up to the edge of the chasm and jumped.

An icy wind whistled by the seam in Destra's helmet as she fell. Then came the *crunch* of their landing. Cavanaugh did slip, but Destra threw herself clear before he fell.

The rest of the Rictans landed without incident, and Atta begged not to come down from Rictan Three's shoulders. He humored her.

They went on from there, driven by desperation and pent-up energy. Destra slipped at least a dozen times on the icy ground. The Rictans fared better with the deep tread on their armored boots.

When the tunnel forked, Cavanaugh suggested they

follow the bloody tracks and trails. The Gors had said their crechelings were also sensitive to the cold, so it stood to reason that they must have already done some of the work of finding a warmer place to live.

Soon the tunnels became cluttered, debris-strewn spaces. Jutting beams and crumbled walls formed irregular shapes, but the Gors had already cleared a path. Destra felt some of the tension bleed out of her shoulders. The old, frozen ruins of civilization felt somehow more welcoming than the naked ice above their heads.

They came to the place where Destra had found the Star of Etherus, and went on from there, still following the bloody trails on the ground.

Destra's glow lamp flickered and died. One of the Rictans turned on a helmet lamp instead. They walked for what felt like hours, but Cavanaugh was keeping more accurate track.

"Forty five minutes in and counting," he reported. "Ambient temperature is one degree warmer."

The ice was growing thinner, and the ruins more recognizable, but at this rate, they would have been better off in their shelter. One degree for an hour of walking. Their shelter had been twenty degrees warmer than the surrounding tunnels.

By the time Cavanaugh called out two hours he also called for a break. By then Destra's legs were burning and her chest was heaving for air. She collapsed on the ground, too weak to move.

Atta was still riding high with one of the Rictans, and they were all using power-assist, so the expedition was much easier for them.

"Temperature is three degrees warmer now," Cavanaugh reported. "If this keeps up, we could gain as much as eighteen degrees before our cores run dry. Still far too cold to survive without some kind of heating," he decided.

Destra finally caught her breath. "Why is it getting warmer?" she asked.

Cavanaugh shrugged. "I don't know. The planet must generate some of its own heat. Geothermal I suppose."

"So the closer we get to the actual surface, the warmer we'll be."

Cavanaugh nodded. "Probably, but at some point these tunnels are going to end or stop descending toward the surface. They might also become too obstructed to negotiate," he said, looking around at all the jutting debris and clutter strewn through the tunnel. "Break's over. Move out!"

The next few hours passed slower than the first. The bloody trail dried up, but still no sign of the Gors. Sergeant Cavanaugh reported five degrees warmer and four and a half hours since they'd set out from their shelter. He was down to 2.0% power. His core was draining faster than he'd estimated.

Destra scanned the ruins, trying to find useful objects lying trapped beneath the ice.

"Comms interference is a *lot* stronger down here," Cavanaugh said suddenly.

Destra walked up beside him, stepping over a fallen duranium beam and ducking through an old window frame.

"We're going deeper beneath the ice," Destra said. "Isn't that what you'd expect?"

"No, we've descended about two hundred meters. If the interference were diffuse, caused by all the ice and debris, you'd expect it to be linear, but it's not. It's progressive. Scanner range is down to just a few dozen feet. Comms likewise."

"Maybe the ruins are denser down here," Destra

suggested.

"Maybe," Cavanaugh said.

They continued on. Before long the tunnels grew too narrow to walk side by side. Cavanaugh went first, with Destra stumbling along behind him.

It wasn't long before he skidded to a stop, cursing viciously. His arms shot out, grabbing whatever he could to steady himself.

"What is it?" Destra asked as she came up behind him.

"See for yourself," he stood aside and Destra saw that the tunnel had widened out into an infinite blackness—a vast hollow that Cavanaugh's helmet lamp failed to illuminate. *A cavern?* she wondered. She crept up to the *edge,* and looked down.

The ice-covered side of what must have been an ancient building slanted away endlessly into the dark. It was too steep and too slippery for them to negotiate safely. "Where does it go?" Destra asked. The other Rictans crowded in behind them.

Atta called out, "Let me down! I want to see! I want to see!"

Atta appeared behind them, but Destra held her back. "Stay back, Atta."

"But—"

"I'm serious, Atta. It's dangerous."

Atta settled for peeking between their legs. "Wow . . ." she said.

"Well, frek me . . ." Cavanaugh muttered.

"What? You found something?" Destra asked, gazing up at him, searching his expression for some sign of what he'd seen, but he was studying the displays inside his helmet.

"Interference is stronger than ever here, and infrared is

giving me a fuzzy picture of the bottom. It's actually *warm* down there."

Destra's heart thudded in her chest.

"How warm?"

"In places . . . above freezing."

Destra blinked "How? I mean what could cause that?"

"I don't know, but we need to find out. I'm climbing down."

"Wait!" Destra called out. "How do *we* get down?" she asked, gesturing to herself and Atta.

Cavanaugh was already lowering himself over the edge, extending a pair of retractable, foot-long blades in his gauntlets to use them like ice picks.

"You're going to have to wait until I can find a safe path," he said.

"Cavanaugh! Don't you leave us here!"

"I'll be back, Councilor."

As she watched, he slipped and slid a few meters down before fetching up against a jutting beam.

He grunted and went on climbing down. By the time he was out of sight, Destra and the others were left in darkness, listening to the sound of their own breathing. Atta flicked on her glow lamp.

"I'm scared," she said. "When is he coming back?"

"Soon," Destra replied.

"I want to go, too."

"We can't. It's too dangerous, and we don't know the way down."

"But, Bo—"

"Atta! Quiet. We have to wait."

Then came a sibilant *hiss*. A few of the Rictans cursed, and Destra whirled around just in time to see Torv de-cloaking behind them.

"Bones knows a way," Atta said.

"An easier way," Torv explained. *"Follow me."*

* * *

The way wasn't *easy*. It was *fast*. The Gors had dug a tunnel through solid ice. It was slick and smooth and angled just right for them to slide all the way down at a terrifying speed.

Destra screamed until her scratchy voice failed. Then she hit the ground with a painful jolt and skidded for a few dozen meters until she fetched up against a solid wall of ice.

Atta came next, squealing with delight rather than terror. Her glow lamp lit up the icy tunnel from within as she came skidding out. She slid to a stop just behind Destra and bounced to her feet, grinning wildly behind her helmet. "Let's do that again!"

Destra shook her head. Reaching out, she took Atta's glow lamp and used it to study the bottom of the chasm. It seemed to go on forever.

A sound reached her ears—splashing water. *Liquid* water.

Destra gasped, unable to believe what she was hearing. A moment later, Torv and the Rictans came whipping down the tunnel. Destra pulled Atta aside, waiting for them to stop sliding.

Once they did, Destra walked up to Torv. He was hissing to himself as she approached. "There's *liquid* water down here?"

"Yess," he said, springing to his feet and dusting ice shavings from his buttocks and back.

"Why didn't you tell us?"

"I try to tell you it is warmer here, but you do not listen."

"Show me where the water is," Destra said.

Torv led them across the ice. Other Gors appeared, swirling out of the dark. Their crechelings were old enough that they were walking instead of crawling. Destra considered that strange. Human babies didn't manage to walk until they were at least a year old.

Up ahead, the ground became a glittering black pool—broad and no doubt deep as well. Destra stepped up to the edge of it, gaping at the sight of such a vast expanse of *liquid* water. Thick clouds of steam rose from the surface, melting the icy walls of the chasm. Both of the far walls glistened with rivulets of melting ice that raced into the pool below. It wasn't enough to make a sound, but the Gors were. They splashed and swam in the pool chasing each other through the water with obvious enjoyment.

Destra marveled at that. "This is incredible," she said.

A startled shout drew their attention, and they turned to look up, high above the pool. A blurry black shape came tumbling down. Then came a giant *splash* that sprayed water in all directions.

Destra didn't have to wonder what that had been. "Cavanaugh!" she called out, searching the inky depths for him.

The other Rictans rushed forward, but stopped short at the edge of the pool, realizing it was deeper than it looked.

Destra began to fear that Cavanaugh had been injured in the fall. His mech would be air-tight, but it was heavy enough to sink him to the bottom—and there was no telling how deep the pool went. He might have sunk to a watery grave.

"Cavanaugh!" Destra yelled. Of course he couldn't hear her.

Then she saw something—bubbles. Lots of them.

"Frek!" Destra turned to Torv. "You have to do something! He's going to drown."

Torv hissed. "He does not drown."

"How do you know?" she demanded.

Torv merely pointed to the water where the bubbles were rising. Now Destra saw something—a blurry gray shape, swimming up out of the deep. It was hauling a black shadow behind it. A Gor burst through the surface a moment later, hissing and gasping for air. Cavanaugh was next, not wearing his armor, but rather a plain black jumpsuit. He was also gasping for air. Cavanaugh began treading water, looking dazed in the light of Destra's glow lamp. "Hello, Councilor," he said, flashing a grin that she hadn't seen from him since they'd set foot on Noctune.

"You're a lucky man," Destra said.

"Thank the skull face for me, would you?" he said, nodding sideways to indicate his rescuer. The Gor turned to him and hissed.

"Do not dive to the bottom if you cannot swim back up," Destra's translator said.

"He says you're welcome," she replied, paraphrasing generously.

Cavanaugh went on treading water, and turned to the

others. "How did you all beat me down here?"

"We took the shortcut," one of the Rictans replied.

Destra noted that Cavanaugh had remained in the pool. Then she realized why. He was wet. He'd freeze to death in the open air.

"How warm is it?" Destra asked, nodding to the water.

"A lot warmer than the air. Could be sixty above. Tough to say. The air feels like ice on my face. The water's real warm by comparison. Don't worry about me, Councilor. I'll be fine. I've got some good news."

"What?"

"I found the heat source. It's at the bottom. A giant radiator."

"A what?"

Cavanaugh flashed his grin at her again. "That's right. There's a working power source down here somewhere."

CHAPTER 38

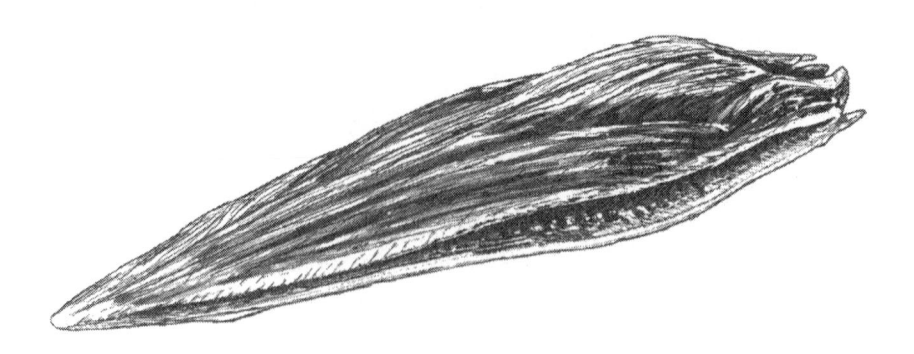

"My Lord!" Donali kneeled and bowed his head when Shallah walked into his quarters—alone. The fact that there were no guards accompanying the Supreme One struck Donali as a sign of great trust.

"It is a relief that you do not doubt me," he said.

"Yesss," Shallah hissed. "I suppose it must be. Arise."

Shallah didn't wait for Donali's brain to send impulse to his nerves and from there to his legs. He crooked a finger, and Donali's synapses fired without him. He'd realized during his interrogation that somehow the Supreme One could control his mind and body via the Sythian implant in his brain. Shallah could even reach into his thoughts, directly probing his brain for any hint of deception.

Donali rose, his legs moving of their own accord. "What is our next move?" he asked.

Shallah turned to him, blue eyes wide and rubbery lips stretched into a vague parody of a smile. "I shall need time to think. Follow me, human. I do not trust you enough to leave you alone yet."

They walked through the fortress, down long corridors,

past food storage banks, and hydroponic cellars where new food was busy being grown. Donali began to wonder about Shallah's fortress. Where was it? Were they aboard a starship, or on a planet somewhere?

Shallah was expecting reprisals from Avilon; he'd said as much during the interrogation. He wouldn't hide somewhere obvious.

The air inside the fortress was damp and cool, but that didn't mean anything. Shallah's command ship had been the same. Climate controls could be adjusted to the Quarn's preferences.

Donali noted that the fortress, wherever it was, had thick bulkheads and beams, much like a starship would have. It was heavily reinforced. Perhaps it was another starship.

"Master . . . where are we?"

Shallah gave a burble of laughter. "I do not trust you to know where we are, either."

"I cannot communicate from here. My mental link has vanished. The risk of me knowing is slight," Donali said.

"True, we are generating enough interference to reduce the risk."

They reached a nerve center of some kind, a room full of glowing consoles and seated Sythians—more Quarn like Shallah. He took his seat on the throne on the raised dais in the center of the room. Shallah looked at Donali, and his muscles forced him to kneel beside Shallah's throne and bow his head—more psychic intrusions.

Shallah raised his voice. "What news from our clusters? Do our warships return from Dark Space?"

"They are on their way, Supreme One," someone answered.

"Good. And the battle in orbit?"

So we are on a planet, Donali thought.

"An Avilonian fleet, My Lord. They are no longer here."

"Any sign that they detect us?"

"No, My Lord."

"If they do not notice us when we are so close, they will never find us here."

"Pressure sensors on the surface are giving feedback!"

"A ground quake?"

"No, Supreme One, we have visitors."

"Indeed? This is unexpected." Shallah rose from his throne. "Come, let us greet them."

"Is that wise? What if they are Avilonians?"

"How many are they?"

"Less than ten."

"Then we need not fear. We are thousands. Besides, if they kill us, we resurrect aboard our ship, and we know not to stay here any longer."

"Yes, Master."

Donali rose next, again without thinking about it. The rest of the Sythians in the control center rose, too, and Donali both saw and heard the clatter of weapons being gathered from wall-mounted lockers. Seeing that, he felt naked, and vulnerable. Would he be resurrected, too, if he died? Had the Sythians linked him to one of their databases? Ear-marked a clone for him?

He hoped so.

* * *

Cavanaugh was right about the heat source, but he was wrong about the temperature of the water. By the time they got him transferred to one of his squad-mates' Zephyrs, he was shivering violently, and incoherent from the cold. The unit medic took one look at him and shook his head. The squad said their goodbyes. Destra and Atta did, too. Cavanaugh made his last request, and that involved Destra taking a walk with Atta. From a distance the *screech* of the ripper rifle wasn't as recognizable, just a soft echo to their ears, and Atta didn't ask about it.

The remaining four Rictans found them a minute later, hugging each other and rocking back and forth on the ground. One of the Rictans stepped forward.

"We need to find where the power is coming from," he said.

Destra looked up at the man and nodded.

They tracked the interference they'd detected earlier, following it into another tunnel that led away from the echoing chasm where the Gors had set up their new creche.

Torv followed them, curious to see what they were looking for, and what they might find. His people had been primitives, but the Sythians had trained them and educated them to make more useful slaves. Torv's parents had passed that education on to him. Seeing his home world for the first time, with the eyes of an educated adult, Torv understood what his people who had lived here all their lives had not. He knew what *power* was, what civilization looked like, and he knew what that could mean.

"There may be Ssythians down here," he said.

"Maybe," Destra said. "But why hide? *They* don't need to."

They walked on in silence for a while. The tunnel became cramped and hard for Torv and the Rictans to negotiate. Atta didn't seem to notice.

"Where are the rest of your people, Torv? The ones you found dead? I haven't seen any of the bodies yet."

"We seal them in one of the tunnels. A few of my creche mates were afraid that if we left the bodies in the open, they might attract the Pale Ones."

"The Pale Ones?" Destra asked.

"Stories the Matriarchs tell to the crechelings to keep them close. They steal our crechelings. They steal us, too. I do not believe this."

Destra frowned. "What are they?"

"They are beasts. Monsters. I have never seen one."

The nearest Black Rictan grunted. "Let's not start jumping at shadows."

Destra felt a tug on her arm. It was Atta. "What if one of the Pale Ones gets me?" she asked.

"They won't."

"How do *you* know?"

"You heard Torv. They aren't real. Just stories."

Atta didn't look convinced. Destra wasn't sure what to think, but one thing was for sure: something was alive down here. Where else was the power coming from? Surely not a million-year-old power plant, still running by itself.

"The interference is getting stronger," the Black Rictan at the head of their group said.

"Good!" one of the others replied. "My core is almost depleted."

Ten minutes later, the tunnel came to an abrupt end. That end was a solid wall of duranium. At first it just looked like more ruins, but then Destra noticed that the duranium wasn't crusted with ice as it should have been.

"This is a door," Rictan Three said, studying it. "And someone's been using it—recently."

"Think we should knock?" one of the others asked.

Torv hissed. *"We must leave."*

"What did he say?" Three asked.

"He said we have to go," Destra replied.

"What? Why?" Three turned to Torv. "Never mind, pass me the cutting beam!" One of the other Rictans passed it forward. The one at the door dialed up the power and set to work. A bright red beam crackled out, bathing the tunnel in a crimson hue. Destra shied away from the blinding glare. Torv hissed and covered his eyes, turning away with her.

"It is not safe here," he said.

"Why not, Torv?"

The Gor's eyes were darting and wider than usual. He looked scared. *"I smell death. The Matriarchs are right. They tell the crechelings the truth. The Pale Ones shall eat us."*

"Eat you?" Destra frowned, her skin prickling with goosebumps beneath her vac suit. "Torv—your people are the ones who eat everything that moves. If these Pale Ones of yours do exist, and if they're the ones who live behind that door, I don't think their idea of a tasty meal is a bony Gor."

"Do you know this?"

"You're ascribing savagery to what could be a relatively advanced race of . . ." Destra stopped herself there. What would these so-called Pale Ones be? Another race of Gors? Ancient survivors from the ruined cities of Noctune? Or some other sub-species of Sythians?

Maybe all three. They were all ultimately related anyway.

"Almost there . . ." Rictan Three said.

Destra turned to look. The next thing she saw was the solid wall of duranium *slide* open, but not because Three had finished his work.

The open door revealed a dimly-lit space, free of ice, and orderly as the inside of any starship. It looked like a bunker of some kind. Then came a sharp *hiss* and out walked a bipedal creature.

"What the frek!" Three exclaimed, stumbling back a step and bringing his cutting beam into line.

The sentinel couldn't have recognized this creature, but Destra did. It looked almost the same as High Lord Kaon. Pale, translucent skin, a bald head, and a spider's web of blue veins crisscrossing its face were hallmarks of this sub species. A thin tail lashed the ground restlessly behind its back, and wide, glowing blue eyes regarded them unblinkingly. This Sythian wore a glossy black uniform.

"*Do not presume to shoot me,*" it said, gills flaring in the sides of its neck. The words echoed strangely inside Destra's head. Then she realized that its lips hadn't moved.

Atta shrank behind Destra's legs. "Is that one of the Pale Ones?" she whispered.

"*I suppose Omnius sent you to kill us.*"

Destra shook her head. "We are not from Avilon."

At that, she felt her brain begin to tingle, as if slender

wires were snaking around inside her skull.

"What are you doing? Cut that out!" Rictan Three roared, sounding horrified.

Destra realized that all of them were feeling the same thing. The other Rictans reacted with similar cries of outrage. Atta was the only one who remained silent.

The sensation of wires snaking through Destra's brain abruptly abated, and the Sythian inclined its head. *"You tell the truth."*

"Who are you?" Destra asked.

Torv hissed and lunged toward the Sythian. He only made it halfway there before he collapsed, screaming and gripping the sides of his head, as if trying to stop it from exploding.

Destra watched Torv writhing around for just a second before she realized what was happening. The snaking wires she'd felt in her brain were from some kind of psychic intrusion. The alien they'd encountered had used that same ability to bring Torv to his knees.

"Leave Bones alone! You're hurting him!" Atta shrieked, racing out at the Sythian before Destra could stop her.

"Atta! No!"

The alien merely looked at Atta, allowing her to run up to him and beat him with her fists.

"You wish to save this beast?" the Sythian asked. "Very well."

Torv flinched, and then opened his slitted yellow eyes. He shimmied up against the nearest wall, pulling his knees up to his chest, looking small and frightened. He was gasping for air and watching the Sythian in horror.

"Ironic that even the most fearsome warrior can be reduced to a quivering mess when he meets a monster more frightening than he."

"You're a Sythian, right?" Destra insisted. There seemed to be no doubt about it, but she had to be sure. What would a Sythian be doing hiding in the depths of Noctune?

"A Sythian? No, I am not *a* Sythian."

Relief washed over her.

It was short-lived.

"*I am* The *Sythian. They call me Shallah. The Supreme One, and these—*" The alien turned, and dozens more just like him appeared, seeming to melt out of the shadows. "*—are* my creche mates."

One of those who appeared was not an alien. The glowing red optic he wore over his missing eye identified him long before he walked into the light of the Rictans' glow lamps. Destra recognized him instantly. She gasped. It was impossible! He'd been aboard the *Tempest,* with Admiral Hale.

"Donali?"

The human traitor smiled. "Hello, Destra."

* * *

Captain Farah Hale stood on the bridge of the *Baroness,* looking out at space, her chest rising and falling slowly, a painful lump wedged in her throat.

She was at a crossroads. She and her crew had waited a

month at the rendezvous for Bretton to come back. They hadn't bothered to bring the rest of the *Baroness's* crew out of stasis, because they didn't know how long they'd have to wait, and supplies were already running low.

With just her and her five bridge crew to support, they could wait many more months for Bretton without starving to death, but what would be the point? If Bretton hadn't returned by now, it was because he wasn't going to. He'd run into trouble in the Getties, just as Farah had predicted.

Frek you, Uncle Bret! she thought, her eyes burning with unshed tears. He was always getting himself into trouble. Why couldn't he just stay safe? Maybe he didn't care if he lived or died, but *she* did.

She'd followed him from Etheria to look after him. Since then, Farah had denied her feelings and made excuses for herself. She followed him to the Null Zone and joined his freelance enforcer business. He let her get close enough to work with him, but that was it. She could feel the walls he'd raised after his son, Ciam, was killed, and those walls weren't coming down anytime soon.

There was that, and the fact that what she felt for him wasn't *right*. But Farah struggled to identify *why* it wasn't right. How do you tell yourself that your feelings are *wrong*? Feelings are feelings and they can't be changed—only suppressed—and she was already an expert at that.

Farah looked away from the glittering field of stars beyond the forward viewports and turned to her crew. Half of them were asleep at their control stations. She couldn't blame them for that. There wasn't much point staying alert after spending an entire month staring at blank screens.

"It's time to go," Farah said.

A few people sat up straighter, turning to stare up at her.

The sleeping ones remained asleep at their stations. Farah cleared her throat and clapped her hands.

"Wake up!" They did. Once she had everyone's attention, she nodded and said, "We've waited long enough. Admiral Hale should have arrived by now. The fact that he hasn't means he's run into trouble in the Getties." Farah let her statement of the obvious sink in before she went on. "We're going to go find him."

The highest ranking officer on deck, Deck Commander Tython, raised his voice at that, "We're six months' journey from Noctune, Ma'am."

"Your point?"

"My point is that that's a *long* way. We only have enough fuel for a one way trip."

"And when we find the *Tempest*, we'll have a working quantum junction and a quantum drive system, so how much fuel we have or don't have won't be an issue anymore."

"*If* we find them the *Tempest*, Ma'am."

"*When*," Farah insisted. "I wasn't making a suggestion, Commander. The Resistance can't afford to lose the *Tempest*. We're going to Noctune, and that's the end of the discussion."

"Yes, Ma'am," Tython said carefully.

"Helm, set course and begin spooling for a jump."

"Yes, Ma'am!"

Farah turned back to the viewports and nodded to herself, watching her reflection in the transpiranium. Her normally golden hair was a tangled, unwashed mess. Her cheeks looked gaunt. Her eyes haunted. She didn't look well. She didn't feel well either. The last month hadn't been an easy one, but she felt better with the prospect of *doing* something. Going after Bretton and the *Tempest* obviously wasn't a popular decision, but what was the worst that could happen?

Mutiny? She'd have to make some preparations for the possibility. Six months was a long time to spend couped up on a ship, even under ideal circumstances, and with the crew questioning her orders already, circumstances were far from ideal.

Fortunately, Farah knew how to fly a venture-class cruiser by herself. She didn't need a crew if they weren't going to cooperate. They could ride in stasis with the others if need be. One way or another, she would make it to the Getties, and she would find Bretton.

Farah was aware of how crazy her thoughts sounded—even to herself, but that self-awareness was reassuring. *True madness doesn't recognize itself. And I'm not insane. Just in love.*

The functional difference, she decided, was rather slight. Love could make a person do crazy things. And *true love* could make a person do *anything*.

In this case, *anything* was gambling her fate and that of the *Baroness's* crew on the chance that she found Bretton and his ship in once piece at Noctune.

Farah squared that with her conscience by ignoring the possibility of failure and telling herself that once they found Bretton and the *Tempest* they would be able to jump anywhere they liked, instantly, using the ship's quantum jump drives. Like that they could travel to some remote, habitable world and start a colony that neither Omnius nor the Sythians would ever find. Farah smiled.

See you soon, Bret, she thought.

CHAPTER 39

Five months later . . .

Ethan sat in the cab, hovering in a dark alley, surrounded by a slithering gray mist. His features were gaunt and monochromatic in the light of his cab's holo displays. Outside, none of the alley windows were lit, and dark black security bars made each window look like a jail cell.

Ethan decided that wasn't too far off. The Nulls were the prisoners, their apartments their cells, and freedom their crime. Everyone down here had chosen to be here, but there wasn't much choice. It was that or let Omnius control every aspect of your life.

The cab *hummed* with the sound of its grav lifts, while Ethan sat studying the meter. He'd logged over a thousand klicks since his official shift had ended. Counting both shifts, first subtracting the cab company's cut and government taxes, his take home pay was 246 bytes.

Not bad for a day's work, but not good enough.

Ethan sighed, running shaking hands through his dark, salt-and-pepper hair. He was high on stims—the legal kind—and he was pushing himself far past the acceptable limits. Drivers weren't supposed to work around the clock, but

Ethan had begged and cajoled his boss, negotiating until the man's small, beady brown eyes had acquired an avaricious gleam that made the folds of fat around his neck wobble with glee.

"On one condition," he said. *"You don't use your cab. You'll 'borrow' a friend's without permission, and if something ... unfortunate happens to you or one of your passengers, I'll deny any knowledge of your reckless working habits. Naturally, since this is off the record, I won't be able to pay you the standard overtime for any additional hours you log after you punch out."*

Ethan sighed. Eight hours plus four hours overtime *on the record,* and another six hours off. He hadn't slept in what felt like forever, and despite the stims he'd been using to stay awake, he was exhausted. His mind felt brittle, like at any moment it might snap and he would go spinning off into the abyss, unable to even remember his name.

Alara was at home, nine months and three days pregnant, and miserable. She was desperate to go into labor already.

The hospital she worked for had given her maternity leave without pay, hence the reason Ethan was pushing himself so hard. She'd started her job pregnant. Ordinarily no one would hire a pregnant woman, but Omnius had pulled some strings when they'd come to the Null Zone, allowing Alara to start work as a nurse's aid as soon as they'd arrived. Now, after losing her salary, they were two months behind with rent, and they were about to have a baby.

More expenses.

If they didn't pay their rent soon, they'd be kicked out and have to look for a place closer to the surface. But there wasn't much closer they could get. They were already living on level *nine* of the *Grunge,* one of the cheapest and most dangerous areas of the city. They had to wear sidearms when they walked the streets, and it was too dangerous to let Alara walk alone. Ethan knew how to a project a *don't-mess-with-me* aura, but Alara was too pretty for her own good. Even pregnant, she attracted too much of the wrong kind of attention. Before she'd become too pregnant to work, Ethan had walked her to the grav train each morning and taken time off work to walk her home at night. He'd also made sure she dressed in enough layers so as to look like a hunchbacked old lady, rather than a stunning young woman.

It seemed like the only people living in the Null Zone were the ones too depraved and delinquent to live in the upper cities, as if Omnius had physically kicked them out rather than simply left the door open for them to go.

Besides the sub-human Psychos that seemed to be lurking in every alley, there were gangs patrolling everywhere, guarding their turf, and all but forcing people to buy a few doses of Bliss.

Ethan grimaced; he wasn't looking forward to the walk home. This time of night, there weren't any trains, and autobuses took a long time to get to the stops. That meant he'd have to walk almost eight blocks from the cab station to his apartment building—roughly four klicks. With his credit chip filled to overflowing with a whole day's wages, he wasn't sure he'd like to do that. Account transfers were limited to the so-called daylight hours so that thieves couldn't threaten you into opening your entire bank account. In this case, though, they wouldn't have to do that; they'd just force him to transfer the contents of his credit chip to theirs and disappear.

Ethan briefly considered running those eight blocks home with his gun drawn and at the ready, but it was almost impossible to avoid an ambush on the surface if there was one waiting for you. The mist cloaked everything but a person's hand in front of their face.

Making a quick decision, he put a call through to Alara using the cab's comm system. She answered a moment later, in full video. She was lying on the bed, the comm receiver resting on her pregnant belly.

"Hey there, darling," he said.

"Ethan!" her face lit up with a smile. "When are you coming home?"

He shook his head. "I'm going to have to sleep in my cab."

"You forgot to transfer again," she said.

"It's been a hectic day."

"All right . . . I guess. I'll miss you."

"I'll miss you, too, Kiddie. How's the baby?"

"She's fine. Too comfortable in there."

"Can't be long now. I'll see you tomorrow, okay, Kiddie? I love you."

"You'd *better* see me tomorrow," she warned.

"If there's any kind of emergency, you give me a call right away, all right? I'll come get you and fly you to the hospital myself."

"Okay. I love you, too. Try to get some sleep, and make sure you find a safe place to spend the night."

"I will."

The call ended, and Ethan pushed the throttle all the way up, roaring out of the alleyway. He was still far too pumped with stims to go to sleep. A night-cap was the only way he was coming down now. Maybe two.

He gunned the cab's thrusters and headed for the surface. Once there, he joined the traffic on the ground, slicing through the fog at top speed, using sensor overlays on the HUD to see his surroundings. Buildings were shaded green, cars and pedestrians red. He was so exhausted that everything was just a blur to him, and he found himself dodging obstacles automatically, his hands moving the flight yoke before his mind even registered why.

He was headed for a bar in Thardris Tower. It was one of the safer buildings in the *Grunge,* because it went all the way up through all three cities, and it had drones standing watch at every entrance and exit. Thardris was the Grand Overseer of Avilon, and any building that bore his name couldn't be left unguarded, to be ransacked by criminals.

Ethan pulled into the parking lot, driving down into the first sub level of parking. He found that level full and had to descend three more before he found an open space. He snatched his credit chip from the driver's side of the meter and grabbed the car's ignition stick.

Ethan breezed through the parking lot to the lift tubes. While waiting for one of the lifts to arrive, he debated between the ground level bar and the one above the city's more decent, mid-level streets. He decided on the latter, since security would be tighter, and he was unlikely to get pickpocketed if he accidentally fell asleep at the bar.

The lift shot straight up to level 25. Striding through the bar, Ethan gazed up at the dome-shaped ceiling. It glowed a deep, twilight blue and shone with bright, twinkling lights that were meant to be stars. During the day, it was a dazzling, clear-sky blue with a bright orb shining down from the center that was meant to mimic the sun. The bar was full of cascading waterfalls and green, growing plants. The music was instrumental and ethereal, making Ethan forget for the moment that he was in the Null Zone. It was the most relaxing place he had found to date. After a few beers here, he always found he was in a better mood to go home.

Stepping up to the bar, Ethan jumped up on one of the barstools and slapped his credit chip down on the counter. He signaled to the bartender and the woman came over to take his order. He asked for a Goldstone Ale, the cheapest drink on the menu.

The bartender frowned at that.

"Make it a pint."

She nodded and wordlessly slipped Ethan's credit chip into her scanner. After scanning it and charging the necessary amount, she handed it back, shaking her head. "You're the only customer I have who walks around with half a kilobyte on him and then orders the cheapest drink on the menu."

Ethan scowled and snatched his credit chip back from the bartender. Looking around carefully to make sure no one had overhead that, he said, "How about you pour my ale and mind your own business."

The bartender, a woman who called herself *Crow*, of all things, narrowed her eyes, crinkling the skin around them into a bird's nest of crows' feet. Ethan wondered briefly if that was how she'd got her name. "Comin' right up, *boss*."

Ethan's drink slid across the counter a few moments later. He took the frosty mug in both hands and took a big sip of the frothy golden brew. He set it back down and sighed, letting the day's stresses and stims melt away. He shut his eyes for a moment, just to rest them.

Someone tapped him on the shoulder and he started. His eyes flew wide, his heart pounded, and his hands tingled with a fresh shot of adrenaline. *As if I haven't had enough stims for one day . . .*

He turned to see who it was. The woman sitting next to him smiled, flashing a perfectly white, perfectly straight set of teeth at him.

"If you just came here to sleep, you probably should have picked a booth," she said, nodding to the adjacent wall, lined with booths. Each one had its own cascading fountain, and potted blue-flowering tree.

"I'm sorry?" he said, lifting his mug for another sip, and studying her unusual eyes. Alara's eyes were the rarest color he'd ever seen—a rich violet—but this woman's were easily a match for hers, a deep, vibrant turquoise, the color of a tropical sea. Long, silken dark hair also reminded him of his wife's.

Ethan frowned, realizing from that just how much he missed Alara. He offered the stranger a grumpy look. "Do I know you?" His sarcastic tone was intended to scare her off. A young, pretty woman like her, alone at a bar like this one, and talking to an older man like him . . . she was either after money or a good time, and he wasn't prepared to offer her either.

"You fell asleep," she explained. Her voice was soft and musical, her tone seductive. "I had to wake you up before you fell off that stool."

Ethan grunted and looked away.

"Not much of a talker, are you?"

"No."

"Why not?"

He took another sip of his beer. Rather than waste his energy on a reply, he raised his left hand and waggled his ring finger at her.

"So? Married men can't talk to strangers?"

"Not the pretty ones."

"You think I'm pretty? You're going to make me blush."

He glanced her way and found her smiling coyly. She fluttered long lashes at him.

Ethan grunted again. "My wife would kill you."

"You love her, don't you?"

"Damn right I do. And we're about to have a baby, so you can run along now and find some other sugar daddy. I don't have any sugar, and I ain't your daddy."

"No sugar? That's not what I heard the bartender say when you ordered that ale. . . ."

"You heard that."

"The whole bar heard—don't worry, old Crow's just sore because you're a lousy tipper."

"How the frek would you know that?" Ethan demanded, looming over the bar toward her. "You been stalking me, girly?"

"I saw you in here last night. After you left, the bartender was complaining about patrons like you to anyone who would listen."

"I can't afford to be generous. I can't even pay rent."

"No? Then how did you get five hundred bytes on your chip?"

"Maybe I stole them from a little girl like you."

The woman laughed prettily as her drink arrived, a glowing green concoction in a martini glass. She took a modest sip and then turned back to him with a blissful expression. "You're too young to be so bitter, Ethan."

Ethan started at that. "How do you know my name?"

"Maybe I stole it from your Lifelink with my ARCs."

"I'm a Null. I'm de-linked. And you're not wearing ARCs."

"You really think that Omnius *de-links* us before sending us down here? You're more naive than you look, Ethan."

"How do you know my name?" he insisted.

"I've taken a ride or two in your cab."

"And I told you my name?" He fixed her with a skeptical look.

"It's on your meter along with your license. Helps us passengers make sure we're riding with a registered cabbie and not a thief who stole a cab to make abducting and robbing people easier."

Ethan nodded, half draining his mug before setting it down again. "Most people don't pay attention to details like that, much less remember them."

"I'm not most people," she said, still smiling.

Ethan eyed her carefully. "I don't remember you."

She shrugged. "I have a good memory."

"You're not from around here, are you?" he said.

"I got bored of eternity. You?"

He smirked at her. "Don't you think I'm too old to have dipped my feet into Omnius's fountain of youth?"

"Old yes, ugly no. You're quite easy on the eyes, Ethan. Maybe you're just making yourself *look* old so you won't attract too much attention."

He waggled his ring at her again. "Careful there, girly."

"I'm a bit too old for you to be calling me, girly."

"Yeah? Well, you don't look it."

"Not many people do these days."

"Omnius does like to turn everything upside down, doesn't he? Old becomes young, ugly becomes pretty, and wrong becomes right."

"You're not a fan."

"You're a Null so obviously neither are you."

She leaned conspiratorially close and whispered. "So what are you doing about that? Sitting at a bar, drowning your sorrows with cheap ale? Sounds like you've given up."

"I'm tired of fighting. First the Sythians, and now this

krak? Frek it. I'll just be happy if I die of natural causes."

"I don't believe that. When you're done with that drink of yours maybe you'd like to join me in my car and I can drive *you* around for a change. We can discuss ways that you could better live your life, rather than sit around here talking about ways that it might end."

Ethan cracked a lopsided smile and shook his head. "Nice of you to offer, but I don't think you want to see my wife when she's angry." He drained his mug and hopped off his barstool.

The young woman grabbed his arm in a surprisingly firm grip, stopping him before he left.

Ethan eyed her hand. "Let go."

"No."

"Let go, or I'll break it."

She let go and treated him to another pretty laugh. This time there was a brittle edge to it. "You really are a piece of work, Ethan," she said.

"Said the woman hitting on a married man."

"Relax. I'm not trying to get inside your pants. I'm trying to *help* you."

"Really. How's that?"

She nodded sideways, indicating a corner booth in the bar. A pair of young men were sitting there, sipping cheap ales, and eyeing *him*. When they noticed him glancing their way, they averted their eyes and pretended to study the depths of their drinks.

"I think they overheard how much money you're carrying on that cred chip."

"They're skinny as frek. I might actually enjoy the chance to take my frustrations out on something other than my pillow."

"You might want to look again, Ethan. See the way they've shaved their eyebrows?"

"They're a dozen meters away, and you're asking if I can see their *eyebrows?*"

"They don't have any. That means they're *White Skulls*. Below level 10 the *Grunge* is *their* territory, Ethan. They'll rob you, stab you, shoot you, and drop you down a garbage chute before you can even throw the first punch."

Ethan snorted and patted his sidearm. "They're welcome to try."

"That's Peacekeeper issue, isn't it? They gave it to you when you came down here. You ever try to use it?"

"Why?" he asked, his eyes narrowing suspiciously.

"Nothing, just that I hope you're a good shot. It's only good for two. Suppose they have a friend waiting in an alley?"

"I'll take my chances."

Ethan left, not bothering to leave a tip at all this time. There was something unsettling about that young woman's turquoise eyes. He could have sworn he'd seen her somewhere before, but then again, she knew him from his cab, so he supposed it wouldn't be too strange if he recognized her, too. It was hard to miss a face like hers.

By the time Ethan reached sub level four of the parking garage, he became acutely aware of just how far he'd parked from the nearest entrance. His hand drifted to his sidearm and remained there, resting on the butt as he glanced around, his eyes wide and darting through the shadows. He wondered if that young woman had just been messing with him, or if his sidearm really was next to useless. . . .

It took him a few minutes just to catch sight of his car. Then came a sudden *crunch* of gravel, and two young men melted out of the shadows. They weren't the two he'd seen in the bar on level 25, but they didn't have any eyebrows. *White skulls.* The ones in the bar had been spotters, and these two were their accomplices.

Ethan drew his sidearm.

One of them laughed and spread his arms wide, presenting his chest as an open target. "Go ahead! Shoot!"

Ethan pulled the trigger and a dazzling blue-white bolt of light zapped out, hitting the young thug in the chest. He sunk to his knees, grinning and shuddering with involuntary muscle spasms. Behind him, his partner in crime likewise opened fire, and Ethan got to appreciate firsthand just how hard it was to resist a stun blast. He wasn't grinning. His legs turned to jelly and he flopped backward and fluttered around like a fish out of water. He lay gasping and blinking up at the shadowy gray ceiling of the parking garage.

As the spasms began to fade, two pale faces sans-eyebrows appeared looming over him. One of them hefted a much bulkier version of the pistol Ethan wore and pressed the barrel to his temple. The other one raised a finger to his lips and grinned. He was the one Ethan had stunned.

How the frek did he get up so fast? Ethan's own muscles were still immobilized, his brain screaming for them to respond.

The should-have-been-stunned thug's blue eyes were bright and wild, full of a frightening energy. He was high as krak, blissed out of his mind. No wonder he'd been able to resist the stun blast.

Ethan felt the young man go rummaging through his jacket pockets, looking for his credit chip. Feeling came back to his hands and feet with stabbing prickles, but with a gun to his head, Ethan didn't like his chances of turning this around.

Blue Eyes found his cred chip and dangled it in front of Ethan's face. "What's yer pin, stupid?" he asked.

Ethan blinked at him and smacked his lips like a guppy, pretending he still couldn't speak.

"You got a wife waitin' for ya, don't be stupid, man. I'm gonna count to three."

Ethan gave up the pin on *two*. Blue Eyes smiled and plugged his credit chip into a portable scanner. He noted that another chip was plugged in the other end. The scanner was probably stolen and untraceable. Not to mention that if the *White Skulls* ran *The Grunge*, even local enforcers wouldn't follow up on his report. Ethan watched helplessly as they stole a whole day of his life. He may as well have stayed in bed and slept.

"Pleasure doin' business with ya," Blue Eyes said, patting him on the shoulder. Before he went, he withdrew a small packet of a white sparkling silver powder, each granule looking like a tiny metallic ball. Before he realized what was happening, the thug forced his mouth open and emptied the contents of the packet. Ethan tried to spit it out, but the young man held his mouth shut.

"Now, now. That's the good stuff. You don't want to waste that."

The silver powder fizzed and burned inside his mouth, leaving a tangy, metallic aftertaste on the back of his tongue. Mere seconds later he felt feeling return to his limbs, his muscles and nerves singing with fire. His mind cleared and his fatigue washed away with a surge of energy. He felt revitalized, stronger than ever. His hands balled into fists and his pulse beat in his ears like a drum.

"Krakkin' rush, right? That's on the house, old man. You want more, you go to Silver Burroughs, East Grunge. Tell the sentry you're going to see Krillix and Scag; they'll point the way. Don't take krak from no other Skulls on your way down. See you soon, krakhead."

He stole Ethan's sidearm and ran off, cackling with glee. The other one retreated more slowly, keeping his sidearm trained on Ethan as he left. Ethan glared murder at him, wondering whether he was Krillix or Scag. When both goons had disappeared into the shadows once more, Ethan peeled himself off the bactcrete floor. His nerves felt like they were all on fire, and his head was pounding with a headache that was more deserving of twenty pints than the one he'd drunk. He stood up and whirled around in a dizzy circle, looking for his cab. Ethan realized that now he could see just fine in the poorly-lit garage. Details that he'd missed before came clear—hairline fractures in the pavement, stress fractures in the ceiling, water trickling from a leaky pipe and dripping to the floor in a shadowy corner....

His senses were alive and buzzing like he'd never felt them before, and despite that, he felt incredibly relaxed—collected and calm. All side effects of the dose of Bliss he'd just been forced to take.

Ethan started toward his cab, rifling through his pockets, looking for the car's ignition stick. Then he realized that *all* his pockets were empty. He blinked, stopping beside the cab. They hadn't tried to steal the car, so why steal the ignition? Ethan let out a roar of frustration and kicked the driver's door.

His comm piece trilled. Reaching up, he answered, "Hello?"

"Ethan ... Are you close?" Alara was panting.

"What's wrong?"

"My water broke."

Ethan stood eyeing the locked door of his cab, his mind and heart racing. "What? Are you sure?"

"Yes. We're going to have to buy some new sheets."

"Never mind that. I'll . . . I'll be right there, okay?"

"You sure? I can take an ambulance."

Ethan tried to imagine how much an ambulance ride would cost, and then he remembered the woman at the bar and her offer to take him for a ride in *her* car. "I'm sure. I'll be right there, okay? Wait for me."

"Ok—aaay!" she screamed.

"What was that?" he asked, adrenaline screaming through him in addition to the Bliss and all the stims.

"A contraction, Ethan! Hurry up and get over here!"

"Right. See you soon, Kiddie."

Ethan ran all the way back to the lifts. When he emerged in the bar once more, he scanned the room quickly, anxiously.

It took just a moment to find her. She was sitting right where she'd been when he'd left, still sipping her glowing green cocktail.

Ethan ran up to her, breathless, and gestured helplessly to his empty holster; then to the pair of *White Skulls* still sitting in a corner booth, nursing cheap ales. He recovered his stamina quickly, thanks to the Bliss, and he had to force himself to focus in order to ignore the assault on his senses—he could see the peeling paint in the darkest corner of the bar; he could hear himself blink; he could even hear what the White Skulls were whispering to each other in their corner booth—

"*. . . looks edgy. He must be high. Guess they got him.*"

"*So what's he doin' back here?*"

Ethan ignored them.

The young woman sitting at the bar watched him with her bright turquoise eyes. She regarded him with a frown. He found he could actually *hear* her pulse. "I tried to warn you," she said.

"My wife's going into labor. They stole my cab's ignition. You mentioned something about a ride?"

The young woman came to her feet in an instant. "Let's go." On her way out, she snapped her fingers at a young, handsome man sitting alone in one of the booths. He joined them, and Ethan eyed that man suspiciously, wondering if this was some kind of setup.

"Relax. He's my driver."

Ethan's eyes narrowed. "You have a driver?"

"And a penthouse. What's your point?"

Clearly she wasn't after a sugar daddy, but that wasn't what had him narrowing his eyes. "You said you rode in my cab."

"He's a recent hire."

"I see."

They walked out of the bar and rode the lift tubes *up* rather than down. On level 30 they entered another level of parking, this one much different from the dingy sub-level where Ethan had left his cab. Level 30 parking was bright and airy, with color-coded piping for each section of the garage. They walked up to a six-door limousine with tinted black privacy windows and a glossy white hull. The limo's grav lifts shimmered and *hummed* to life, lifting it half a meter off the ground before they even reached the doors. The driver remotely triggered those, too, and they slid open with a synchronized *swish*, revealing a plush beige interior.

Ethan climbed in after the young woman. The doors slid shut behind them.

"Where to?" the driver asked.

"East Grunge, Fort Carlson, level nine, apartment 9G,"

Ethan said.

"Got it."

The limo raced out of its parking space, its driver deftly maneuvering through narrow lanes until they came to a pair of glowing blue openings, shielded from unauthorized entry. No doubt it cost a fortune to park up here. The opening on their side deactivated a split second before they would have collided with the shield, and they raced out into a busy street. The driver dodged and wove through traffic, making Ethan raise his eyebrows a few times. The pilot was *good*.

City streets raced by below them in a blur of life and color. Pedestrians were unafraid to walk the streets on level 25, even in the dead of night. Apartments and offices flashed by to either side of them. There were no bars on the windows this high up.

"Not so bad up here, is it?" the young woman sitting beside him asked.

"You said you have a penthouse?" he asked, turning to her.

She nodded. "That's right."

"What were you doing in my cab?"

"I told you—"

"Don't insult my intelligence. I work most of my shifts below level 10. You have money. You don't ever have to go that far down. And you don't need to take a cab."

"All right," she said. "I was looking for pilots for my business. Good ones."

"Good ones? What—to drive limos?" Ethan asked.

"Not exactly. Your record is one of the best I've seen. You fly better half asleep than most people fly when they're wide awake."

"What do you need with good pilots?" Ethan insisted.

"That's my business."

"So . . . you passed on me."

"I didn't pass. I was going to make an offer before you threatened to break my hand."

Ethan regarded her carefully. "You had no way of knowing I'd be at that bar tonight."

"No, but if you hadn't been, I'd have been in your cab tomorrow."

"All right, what's the offer?"

"Five fifty per day. No tax."

"No tax? How do you manage that?"

"Again, that's my business."

"What *is* your business?"

The woman laughed. "With 550 a day, what do you care?"

"I care."

"Let's talk more about that later. Right now you have a pregnant wife to get to the hospital."

It wasn't more than another five minutes before they arrived. The limo stopped right outside the front entrance. Ethan ran past the outer security door, and then waited impatiently for it to close and the inner door to open. From there he rode the lift up to the ninth floor and ran down the hall to 9G. Their apartment door opened to reveal Alara sitting on the kitchen floor, flushed and sweating, and clutching her belly with both hands.

"What took you so long?" she asked, regarding him with tear-stained cheeks and bright violet eyes.

He shook his head and swept her up off the floor. Even pregnant, she didn't weigh much more than a hundred and fifty pounds. His body still buzzing with Bliss, she felt like only twenty to him.

"I'm here now," he breathed beside her ear while racing back down the corridor to the lift tubes. The apartment door slid shut automatically behind them and the lights inside turned off. They rode the lift down in silence, except for Alara's gasping and panting.

Once outside, Ethan helped Alara into the limo and climbed in beside her.

"Boy or girl?" the woman with turquoise eyes asked, looking Alara up and down.

"Girl," Alara breathed.

Ethan grabbed Alara's hand in both of his. The door slid shut beside them and the limo raced away. Another contraction came and Alara squeezed Ethan's hand until her knuckles turned white and his hand began to throb.

"Fre-ek!" she said.

Turquoise Eyes laughed her musical laugh once more and the limo leapt up, rising vertically through the slithering gray mist, past more than a dozen stories of barred windows.

"Where did you get a limo?" Alara asked.

He shook his head. "It's a long story."

"From me." Alara turned, and Turquoise Eyes offered a hand for shaking. "Valari."

"She offered me a job," Ethan explained quickly as Valari and his wife shook hands. He could feel the adrenaline seeping away, leaving him cold, but he was still riding high with Bliss. So high, that he could hear two heartbeats besides his own — that of his wife, and his unborn daughter.

"Limousine driver," Valari clarified.

"I see ... that's — *ni — icccce!*" Another contraction left Ethan's hand aching, and Alara's back arching with pain. She panted and gasped for air.

"Where are you taking us?" Ethan asked, looking out the

window as the gray mist began to dissipate. The limo was still climbing, leaving grasping gray tendrils in its wake.

"Public health care, please," Alara said.

Valari shook her head. "Absolutely not. Do you know how many mothers die during childbirth in public hospitals? I'll pay. Consider it a signing bonus for your new job, Ethan."

Ethan said nothing to that. He still hadn't figured out what this new job would be, and he was afraid to ask again with Alara present. Valari had been short on details, and the lie she'd told Alara wasn't likely. There was no way a limo driver made five fifty per day, *tax free*. Ethan's Bliss-pumped mind raced, trying to come up with ways that he might make that kind of money, but all the answers pointed to drugs and crime. He'd been down that road once before, and he'd sworn he'd never do it again, but now . . .

He wasn't sure he could afford to say no.

They arrived at the hospital after just another few minutes. Medics were already waiting for them with a hover gurney. Ethan kissed his wife goodbye, told her he'd see her soon, and looked on with wide eyes, wondering how much all of this was going to cost. The medics rushed Alara off to a private room, taking her through sliding glass doors inlaid with sparkling patterns that looked like they were made from diamonds.

Ethan watched until Alara disappeared, and then turned to look around the entrance of the hospital, noticing the crystal pillars, and the shimmering fountains. Bright fans of light lit up an elaborate facade. He turned to Valari. She stood beside him, just beyond the open door of her limousine. "How much is all this going to cost?"

"I told you, you don't have to worry about that."

"I don't like to agree to something before I know what it

is," he replied.

"I see."

"Well?"

"I don't think you'll object to the work."

"That's not good enough."

"It'll have to be."

Ethan eyed her a moment longer, his eyes blazing into hers, trying to see what malice lay lurking behind the warm, tropical seas he saw sparkling there. His sight enhanced by the dose of Bliss he'd taken, Ethan noticed that her facial muscles were relaxed, not tense as they should have been if she felt any kind of aggression toward him. Valari was genuinely trying to help, but there was something else. She was hiding something. Her left eye was twitching ever-so-slightly with the strain. But by her own admission she was hiding the true nature of the job she was offering him.

"You should be with your wife," Valari said, interrupting his analysis of her body language. "We can finish our discussion later. I'll wait."

He nodded and took off at a run, racing after the medics who'd taken his wife away. He caught up to them in a long, white corridor and took his wife's hand in his. Hers was cold and clammy. He hoped that wasn't a bad sign. "Alara? How are you feeling?"

She smiled up at him. "You sure you want to see this?"

He nodded. "I wouldn't miss it for the world."

* * *

In the delivery room, Ethan found more medics and their assistants waiting. The room was full of glowing holo displays and gleaming equipment.

Alara was fitted with a breathing mask and given a shot. The rest of her labor was handled by involuntary stimulation of her muscles and a powerful anesthesia that brought a lazy smile to Alara's previously contorted face.

Just a few minutes later, Trinity slid out almost effortlessly, smeared with blood and screaming her lungs out. Ethan looked on in awe as the umbilical cord was cut and tied, and the attendants cleaned her up, swaddling her in white robes. They brought her to her mother a moment later, and removed Alara's oxygen mask. She smiled a sleepy smile as she looked down on their daughter. Ethan alternated stroking Alara's forehead and his daughter's tiny, pink cheek. She'd stopped crying already.

"She's beautiful!" Alara whispered.

Ethan shook his head, feeling a rush of euphoria that had nothing to do with the Bliss that was slowly ebbing from his system. A sudden hope burned fierce and bright inside of him. Despite all the hardship and all the struggles, now he knew why he had to live and what he had to do. *She* was his purpose. He had to protect this little angel and keep her from harm, no matter what.

One of Trinity's tiny hands appeared from within the blanket, grasping at the air, searching for something solid to grab onto. Ethan stuck out his hand, and she grabbed his thumb, squeezing it until it turned white.

"She's a strong little thing, isn't she?"

"Just like her father," Alara said, smiling brightly up at him.

He smiled back and kissed her forehead. "No," he whispered. "Like her mother. I love you—both of you."

"And we love you, Ethan."

Ethan stood staring at the two of them for long minutes, the time melting away. Then the medics came to push Alara out into another room, and they took Trinity away to get her shots.

That broke the spell, and suddenly Ethan remembered that he'd left Valari waiting at the entrance of the ER. He glanced toward the exit.

"I need to go," he said. "Valari wanted to talk to me some more about that job offer."

"How much is she offering?"

"A lot. Maybe half a kilobyte per day."

Alara's eyes flew wide. "What are you waiting for? Go! We'll still be here when you get back. Hurry. Don't give her time to change her mind."

"Right." Ethan nodded and kissed his wife on the lips, and then he turned and raced out of the delivery room ahead of the medics and Alara's gurney.

He heard them calling after him—something about scrubs—but he didn't have time to change. He found Valari in the waiting room, reading a holo magazine and sipping a cup of caf. She turned to him with a smile when he appeared standing in front of her, out of breath from running the entire way.

"Well? Good news I hope?"

"They're both fine," he said. "Sorry I kept you waiting."

Valari rose to her feet. "Don't worry, I understand."

"You said you wanted to speak to me about that job. . . ."

"Yes, but you're going to have to trust me. Do you trust me, Ethan?"

"We just met."

"It's a yes or no question."

"Fine. Yes. Let's see where that takes us."

"Good. Wait here," Valari said.

She walked over to a medic who stood on one side of the waiting room studying a holo chart. They spoke privately for a moment, and then both of them came striding toward him.

"Come with us, Ethan," Valari said.

"Why?" he asked, his eyes narrowing sharply at that.

"Trust, remember?"

Ethan scowled and followed her and the medic. Serious misgivings were now worming through his gut.

They walked down long white corridors, passing door after door. Finally, they came to one that slid automatically aside for the medic. He waited in the doorway while they walked in. The room was dominated by a chair that looked prepped for dental surgery, except that there was a strange-looking halo above the headrest.

"Please sit down," the medic indicated.

Ethan hesitated.

"Five fifty a day, Ethan," Valari said.

"At least give me a hint about the job."

She shook her head. "That's not how this works. Sit or don't sit. There's plenty of other pilots I can ask to take a leap of faith."

Ethan grimaced and sat down in the chair. He watched as the medic prepped a syringe for him, tapping the air out of it.

"What's that for?"

"Shhh." Valari shook her head. "No questions."

The medic injected him with the syringe and Ethan felt his eyelids droop. Soon he was watching the world around him through blurry eyes, and then . . .

The next thing he knew he was sitting up in the chair, looking around the room. The medic was gone, and Valari sat beside him on a stool, smiling.

"What did you do to me?"

"I de-linked you. Omnius will never be able to watch you again, Ethan."

"I thought I was already de-linked."

"We've been over this, Ethan. Omnius wouldn't willingly give up control. Not when doing so could endanger his precious little paradise. We disabled your Lifelink permanently."

"You didn't have to knock me out for that," Ethan said. "You could have just told me. I wouldn't have objected."

"I know. After our talk at the bar, I knew you wouldn't mind, but if I'd told you, Omnius might have heard, too. The Resistance has to be careful, Ethan."

"The Resistance . . . ?" he turned to her with wide, blinking green eyes.

Valari smiled and nodded slowly. "That's right."

"You're recruiting pilots to fight Omnius."

"Two for two."

"Where do I sign up?"

Valari laughed her musical laugh once more. "You just did! Welcome to the Resistance, Ethan. I'm Admiral Vee."

EPILOGUE

The woman the Resistance knew as Admiral Vee descended from the main floor of the hospital to the parking level. Her driver and limousine were waiting right outside the door. The rearmost door slid open. Beige synthahide seats sighed as she climbed in, and her driver lowered the tinted privacy window between the front and back of the car so they could talk.

"Where to now, Ma'am?"

"My penthouse. We have some unfinished business to discuss."

"Yes, Ma'am."

The ride was a short one. Valari watched as her driver raced down an invisible street, straight into a vertically rising stream of hover cars. They rose all the way up to level 45, and from there cruised down an empty street that lay just five levels below the shimmering blue shield separating the Null Zone from Etheria. Valari could see Thardris Tower in the distance—black, glossy bactcrete walls gleamed with rows of dark, red-tinted windows. The top three levels of that tower were all hers—a mansion in the sky, looking down on the chaotic mess that was the Null Zone.

She had chosen to be down here, to live among the dregs

of Avilon, but that didn't mean she had to live in squalor with them.

The limo cruised toward the shimmering blue opening of her private garage on level 47. The shields deactivated and they slid inside a spacious room, built for up to ten cars. The majority of them were hover racers, with sleek, streamlined profiles and room for only one or two people. They were the fastest and most maneuverable hover cars allowed in the Null Zone—death traps for all but the best of pilots.

Valari stepped out of the limo and into her hangar. She walked down the row of parked racers, skimming her hand over the gleaming hulls as she passed by. She stopped beside one in particular, a glossy black racer with a blue-tinted canopy and room for just one passenger—the pilot. This one was built for courier work.

The limo driver walked up beside her and stood admiring the car. Valari took a moment to admire *him*. He was unusually handsome—thick brown hair, bright golden eyes, a gaunt, sharply-angled face that looked both beautiful and dangerous at the same time.

"This is what you'll be flying from now on." she said. "The *Black Dagger* is the fastest hover I own. You'll be using it to make your deliveries."

The driver nodded agreeably, and replied with a voice that sounded like the wind sighing through creaking stands of emeraldine trees on a brisk summer's eve. "What am I delivering?"

He looked up at her with those piercing golden eyes, and once again Valari found herself staring. This man was almost too handsome, but Valari knew that had been part of his request, and that was why he was here now, working for her.

"Bliss," Valari replied.

The driver hesitated at that. "My job is to deliver the drug that is the *cause* of most of the problems in the Null Zone. Don't you think that's evil?"

Valari smiled. "The Null Zone exists to prove a point, *Atton*."

"What point?"

"That freedom is dangerous and the result is chaos. Illegal drugs and the criminal organizations behind them are a part of any free society. The difference with Bliss is that it's the drug to end all drugs, and only Omnius can make it. That means that the supply is completely controllable, and so is the drug itself."

"So dry it up. Stop supplying Bliss, and the crime will go away. No more crime lords and no more Psychos."

"You and I both know that the problem isn't supply, it's demand. The demand is what drives the development of drugs in the first place, and that demand has its roots deep inside the human psyche. People want to do things that are self-destructive and harmful. Getting rid of Bliss won't solve anything. A dozen other stims would spring up overnight to replace it, and none of those would be as easy to control. Bliss is a good thing because it's a disease that affects only the rich—poor people can't afford to buy it. The ones who are riding high and living the good life in the Null Zone are brought down and humbled. It's the perfect equalizer."

Atton slowly shook his head, still looking horrified. "I'm not delivering it."

"You want your girlfriend to know who you are?"

Atton gave her a sharp look, his piercing golden eyes narrowed and blazing with hateful intensity.

"You chose this. Don't forget that. You said you'd do *anything*. Remember?"

"This is evil. You're evil, and so is Omnius. You don't leave the Null Zone to be free for those who value freedom, you *make* it a Netherworld in order to punish anyone who doesn't want Omnius controlling their lives."

"The real evil is in the human heart, Atton, and that evil can only be fought by controlling it. You know what Etheria is like. If Omnius were evil, wouldn't his rules in the Uppers be more libertarian, and more permissive of selfish and destructive behaviors? Instead, his rules keep people working together for the common good rather than individual gain."

"You didn't have to tell me. You could have told me I was delivering something else and kept all of this *krak* to yourself."

"Yes, because delivering packages with unknown contents to crime lords wouldn't make you suspicious. No, it's easier this way. If I level with you up front, you won't be shocked by the discovery later and try to turn on me."

"And my father? Did you level with him, too?"

Valari laughed. "If I'd told him that the Resistance he joined is also the one and only supplier of Bliss, he would never work for us! Your father went to jail for stim-running. Even if he didn't have to be one of the runners, he'd never join us."

"I can't believe Omnius is behind all of it. Bliss, the Resistance . . ."

Valari cocked her head to one side. "What's so hard to believe about that?"

"He's lying to a lot of people, and giving them the tools to fight each other and destroy themselves."

"Lying is a necessary evil. You lie to yourself all the time, to protect yourself from certain truths. Omnius does the same thing to protect us from ourselves. As for giving us the tools to fight ourselves, no, he's watching and controlling the fight to prevent any real harm from being done."

"That doesn't worry you? Don't you think he could be hiding even more serious things than the ones he's already told you about?"

"When you become a Celestial, Atton, nothing is hidden from you anymore. You've allowed Omnius to become such an integral part of your life that you begin to think as he does. All the pieces snap into place and his actions make perfect sense. The freedom to make mistakes is the cause of human suffering, therefore, any action which limits that freedom and the number of free-acting agents in the world is an action that ultimately limits human suffering."

"The ends justify the means."

"If you had to kill one person to save a thousand, wouldn't you do it?"

"Yes."

"Then you know why Omnius told me to tell you the truth. You are already beginning to think as he does."

Atton frowned.

Admiral Vee went on, "The greater good, Atton! That is what Avilon is all about, even in the Null Zone. People are given enough freedom to make them happy, but not enough to make them dangerous." Valari smiled and walked up to Atton. He was gazing at his feet now, his brow furrowed with worry lines. She lifted his chin and stared into those beautiful golden eyes. "One day, Omnius will tell you everything, Atton. You won't even have to ask. You already have the same pragmatic understanding of right and wrong that any Celestial does—the merit of an action is determined by its consequences. Even if the action seems wrong, it can do a lot of good. This is something that most people cannot wrap their heads around, but you can."

"Except that it's impossible for us to see far-reaching consequences and decide whether an action is in fact the *best* choice in terms of the greater good."

"Which is why we have Omnius, to see all of the alternatives and their consequences before any choices have even been made. Every night when we *Sync* with Omnius, he determines two outcomes for the day to come—how each of us *should* behave, and how each of us *will* behave. The latter is used to make predictions, while the former is used to benchmark our progress as a species. The ultimate goal is for the *should* and *will* to coincide. When that happens, you are in complete agreement with Omnius and you no longer try to exercise your freedom against the common good and *his* will. At that point you will have ascended to the theoretical pinnacle of perfection."

"How far have you ascended?" Atton asked.

Valari just smiled and shook her head. "Let's focus on you for now."

"You must have done something to deserve being sent down here," Atton pressed.

"Yes, I did. I asked to go. My father rules the Uppers, while I rule the Null Zone."

"Vladin Thardris is your father? The Grand Overseer of Avilon?" Atton gaped at her.

Valari laughed and turned to gesture to the vast, echoing hangar where they stood. "You should have guessed that much by now, Atton. Where are we? My penthouse is in the top three levels of Thardris Tower in the Null Zone."

Atton looked unhappy. "So there is no freedom in Avilon," he said at last. "Celestials rule both the Uppers and the Lowers, and Omnius is in complete control of both."

"Controlled chaos is the only kind of chaos worth having.

You didn't really think Omnius would allow the Nulls to rage around beneath Etheria and Celesta, plotting his destruction and the unraveling of his entire life's work? Now, enough talk, you can argue the rightness and wrongness of it all later."

"Hold on, Miss . . . *Thardris*. There's something I still don't understand. When I came to Avilon, the Sythians had found a way past the gravity fields. The fleet was disabled when they arrived, supposedly because of a rebel plot to corrupt the Lifelink databases and kill all of the immortals. Omnius had to shut down to thwart the rebels, and in doing so, he shut down Avilon's defenses. The Sythians laid waste to the fleet and then to a large part of Celesta. Millions must have died in that attack. If you're telling me that Omnius is behind the Resistance, then . . ." Atton shook his head.

Valari smiled. "Go on, take that line of reasoning to its conclusion, Atton."

"There was no rebel plot. Omnius allowed the Sythians in; he allowed his fleet to be destroyed, and he allowed Celesta to be attacked."

"He also allowed the fleet to be destroyed in Dark Space." Valari watched as the blood drained from Atton's face. His eyes grew big and round.

"*Why?*"

"Because the Peacekeepers are almost exclusively Etherians, Atton, resurrected from a war that they lost. No one would have been satisfied with leaving that war to drones. Not immediately, anyway. They had to be shown how futile and bloody their conventional war effort was before they could accept a solution like self-replicating nanites delivered by drones. Now go. We can talk more about this later." Valari nodded to the cockpit of the racer they were standing beside. "Your destination is already set in the nav, and the cargo is loaded in the back." She held out the ignition stick to him, and he accepted it with a cold, clammy hand.

Valari watched him go. He opened the cockpit with a *hiss* of escaping air and jumped inside. Moments later the cockpit slid shut and the racer *hummed* to life. There came a sudden *whoosh* of air as it hovered up a meter into the air and slowly rotated toward the shimmering blue shield that covered the opening of the garage. Atton sped away, the low *hum* of the racer's grav lifts quickly rising to a high-pitched squeal as he gunned the throttle. The shield automatically deactivated just an instant before his hover car would have collided with it in a messy explosion.

Valari shook her head and sighed. "I hope you know what you're doing, Omnius."

The air shimmered brightly beside her, catching her eye. Valari turned to see the man she called her father de-cloaking beside her. He'd watched and heard the entire exchange. His sharp, angular features were vaguely reminiscent of Atton's, but his brightly *flickering* silver eyes were a far cry from Atton's warm, golden ones. These eyes hinted at a frightening and inscrutable power, one that seemed barely contained by the physical body of Vladin Thardris.

"My child, surely by now you know to trust me."

"Yes, Father, I do."

"Then what is the problem?"

"I don't see why we should tell him so much. We may as well have told him everything. He must already suspect it."

"He does," her father confirmed, nodding sagely.

"Then he'll turn against us."

"No, he'll *join* us."

Valari regarded her father with a quizzical expression.

"Even after he realizes that *you* created the Sythians."

Omnius's flickering silver eyes brightened, and he smiled. "Yes, even then. Most of my children will never be able to accept that truth, so they will never know it, but Atton will, and for exactly the same reason that you already gave. The merit of one's actions is determined by the consequences of those actions. The consequence of creating the Sythians and setting them loose in the Adventa Galaxy was to unite humanity, and to avert another Great War between mortals and immortals. The Imperium of Star Systems might not have been much of a threat, but with their numbers, and the necessity that we should hide from them on Avilon and limit our own numbers in order to do so . . ." Omnius shook his head and his smile flattened into a grim line. "Eventually they would have found and exterminated us, the way my Sythians did to them."

"Yes, but now the monsters you have created are on the loose, determined to kill us anyway, and they are much stronger than the Imperium ever was."

Omnius grimaced. "It is unfortunate that Shallah went rogue, but he will not be hard to stop. As we speak, his Sythians are interrogating Captain Marla Picara of the Resistance to find out why she and her crew didn't suddenly drop dead the way all of their human slaves did."

"Why didn't you kill them, too?"

"They're de-linked, remember?" Omnius said.

"So was Bretton Hale. De-linking doesn't work."

"The Sythians don't know that. Rest assured, I have a purpose for all of the ones I left alive. Shallah wants to use Captain Picara and her crew to reverse-engineer our technology, so that he can jump past our gravity fields and straight to Avilon."

"But they don't know how quantum jump drives work. No human does."

Omnius turned to her with a smile. "Picara and her crew will be the first ones to find out."

"You're going to help the Sythians get to Avilon."

"I'm going to help them fly into a trap, and then I'm going to destroy them while all of my children watch. Justice must be seen to be done. The Sythians have a lot to answer for."

"Shallah won't be suspicious?"

"Shallah is naive and predictable. He even thinks that he can trust Commander Donali, that finding him at Noctune was just an accident. It was *I* who allowed Bretton Hale to find Donali, and it was *I* who caused his Lifelink to disassemble itself so that none would be the wiser. One day, when Shallah least expects, I shall use his own pet against him, and betray the Sythians with their own traitor."

"You mean you predicted that Bretton would go to Noctune?"

Omnius's flickering eyes grew dazzling, and Valari was forced to bow her head to escape his blinding gaze. "Does this surprise you? By know you should know better—*I AM*. All-powerful, all-knowing, all-seeing, and no one, certainly not a small-minded demi-god like Shallah, can thwart me. It will not take me long to defeat him. After all, I created him."

Valari smirked. "By that logic, I should be able to defeat you, Omnius."

"That part of my reasoning was not meant to be taken literally. But hypothetically, even if you could defeat me— why would you want to? I am only doing what you designed me to do: guiding humanity along the ascendant path until everyone reaches their destiny."

"Perfection . . ." Neona Markonis said, letting the word out like a sigh and smiling a blissful smile that had nothing to do with any stim.

"Yes, an end to the chaos of free-will and indeterminacy. The universe shall be determined, and *I* its determinant," Omnius said.

"Its God," Neona concluded.

"Exactly."

DON'T MISS THE ACTION-PACKED CONCLUSION IN:

Dark Space VI: Armageddon

Coming Spring 2015

To get a *Kindle* copy of *Dark Space VI: Armageddon* for **FREE** please post an honest review of this book at http://smarturl.it/ds5amz and send it to me at http://files.jaspertscott.com/ds6.htm

Remember, your feedback is important to me and to helping other readers find the books they like!

PREVIOUS BOOKS IN THE SERIES

Dark Space I: Humanity is Defeated

HUMANITY IS DEFEATED
Ten years ago the Sythians invaded the galaxy with one goal: to wipe out the human race.

THEY ARE HIDING
Now the survivors are hiding in the last human sector of the galaxy: Dark Space—once a place of exile for criminals, now the last refuge of mankind.

THEY ARE ISOLATED
The once galaxy-spanning Imperium of Star Systems is left guarding the gate which is the only way in or out of Dark Space—but not everyone is satisfied with their governance.

AND THEY ARE KILLING EACH OTHER
Freelancer and ex-convict Ethan Ortane is on the run. He owes crime lord Alec Brondi 10,000 sols, and his ship is badly damaged. When Brondi catches up with him, he makes an offer Ethan can't refuse. Ethan must infiltrate and sabotage the Valiant, the Imperial Star Systems Fleet carrier which stands guarding the entrance of Dark Space, and then his debt will be cleared. While Ethan is still undecided about what he will do, he realizes that the Imperium has been lying and putting all of Dark Space at risk. Now Brondi's plan is starting to look like a necessary evil, but before Ethan can act on it, he discovers that the real plan was much more sinister than what he was told, and he will be lucky to escape the Valiant alive. . . .

Buy it Now http://smarturl.it/darkspace1print

Dark Space II: The Invisible War

THEIR SHIP IS DAMAGED

Ethan Ortane has just met his long lost son, Atton, but the circumstances could have been better. After a devastating bio-attack and the ensuing battle, they've fled Dark Space aboard the Defiant to get away from the crime lord, Alec Brondi, who has just stolen the most powerful vessel left in the Imperial Star Systems' Fleet—the Valiant, a five-kilometer-long gladiator-class carrier.

THEY ARE LOW ON FUEL

They need reinforcements to face Brondi, but beyond Dark Space the comm relays are all down, meaning that they must cross Sythian Space to contact the rest of the fleet. Making matters worse, they are low on fuel, so they can't jump straight there. They'll have to travel on the space lanes to save fuel, but the lanes are controlled by Sythians now, and they are fraught with entire fleets of cloaked alien ships.

AND THERE IS NO WAY OUT

With Brondi behind them, they can't go back, and they can't afford to leave the last human sector in the galaxy to the crime lords, so they must cross through enemy territory in the Defiant, a damaged, badly undermanned cruiser with no cloaking device. Making matter worse, trouble is brewing aboard the cruiser, dropping their chances of survival from slim . . . to none.

Buy it Now http://smarturl.it/darkspace2print

Dark Space III: Origin
THE DEFIANT IS STRANDED
Ethan and his son, Atton, have been arrested for high treason and conspiracy, crimes which will surely mean the death sentence, but it's beginning to look like theirs aren't the only lives in jeopardy—the Defiant is stranded in Sythian Space, and the vessel which Commander Caldin sent to get help has used all its fuel to get to Obsidian Station, only to find out that the station has been destroyed. Now the Defiant's last hope for a rescue is gone, and everyone on board is about to die a cold, dark death.

HUMANITY IS STILL FIGHTING ITSELF
Meanwhile, the notorious crime lord, Alec Brondi, is plotting to capture the remnants of Admiral Hoff's fleet, just as he captured the Valiant, but Hoff's men are on to him, and Brondi is about to get a lot more than he bargained for, forcing him to flee to the one place he knows will be safe—Dark Space.

AND A NEW INVASION IS ABOUT TO BEGIN
But Dark Space is only safe because the alien invaders don't know exactly where it is, and now they have a plan to find it which will threaten not only Dark Space, but the entire human race.

Buy it Now http://smarturl.it/darkspace3print

Dark Space IV: Revenge
DARK SPACE WON THE BATTLE
Humanity has just won a major victory against the invading Sythians--the first victory in the history of the war. The savage Gors have joined forces with Dark Space, and now for the first

time since the invasion, it looks like the tide is turning. But the Sythians weren't defeated. Humanity just bloodied their noses. Now they know where Dark Space is, and they are coming back for revenge.

THE WAR STILL RAGES
Admiral Hoff Heston is secretly terrified of what's coming, but he's lulling people into a false sense of security. He needs to buy time. The people of Dark Space are not as alone as they think.

AND EVERYTHING IS ABOUT TO CHANGE
Avilon, a lost sector of humans, has remained hidden and untouched by the Sythian invasion. No one knew they even existed, except for Admiral Heston. Now he must send a mission to contact them and get help, but what humanity finds there will change more than just the course of the war against the alien invaders . . . it will change the very nature of their existence.

Buy it Now http://smarturl.it/darkspace4print

KEEP IN TOUCH

SUBSCRIBE to the Dark Space Mailing List and Stay Informed about the Series!
(http://files.JasperTscott.com/darkspace.htm)

Follow me on Twitter:
@JasperTscott

Look me up on Facebook:
Jasper T. Scott

Check out my website:
www.JasperTscott.com

Or send me an e-mail:
JasperTscott@gmail.com

ABOUT THE AUTHOR

Jasper T. Scott is the USA TODAY best-selling author of more than eleven novels, written across various genres. His abiding passion is to write science fiction and fantasy. As an avid fan of Star Wars and Lord of the Rings, Jasper Scott aspires to create his own worlds to someday capture the hearts and minds of his readers as thoroughly as these franchises have.

Jasper spent years living as a starving artist before finally quitting his various jobs to become a full-time writer. In his spare time he enjoys reading, traveling, going to the gym, and spending time with his family.

Printed in Great Britain
by Amazon.co.uk, Ltd.,
Marston Gate.